FALLING NIGHT

LEE LARSEN

For Jessica. Without her unwavering support, this story would still be trapped inside my mind.

PROLOGUE

Nathan jumped to his feet as a loud scream shattered the night's calm. He had been sleeping heavily and at first wasn't sure if he merely imagined the scream or dreamt it. His wife was still asleep on the bed beside him, her long blond hair flowing onto the pillow behind her. The dim moonlight coming through the curtains told him dawn had yet to arrive, and both hands of the dark oak clock on the wall were just past the three.

"Dadda!" he heard another scream and recognized the voice of his four-year-old son Leuken. He ran into the bedroom across the hallway. His son was a sound sleeper, so something must be wrong.

Leuken was sitting up in his bed with tears running down his cheeks. His thermal blanket lay thrown on the floor beside him, and his dark hair was soaked with sweat. He was breathing heavily while holding his brown Teddy bear tightly against his chest with both arms. Relief began to sweep across his face as he saw Nathan enter the room. His next words were forced out in a panic. "Dadda, the bad man is coming! We have to go now!"

"What are you talking about son? Everything is ok. You were just having a bad…"

"No Dadda!" Leuken interrupted "We have to go! I saw the bad man come in my window, he is gonna hurt me and baby Benjy, please Dadda, can we go?"

"What bad man are you talking about Leuken?"

"He is more big than you dadda, and he has a red beard and a scary mean face."

Upon hearing that, the hair on the back of Nathan's neck began to stand up. "Sara wake up!" He quickly shouted to his wife in the other room. Sara appeared at the doorway with a concerned expression on her face.

"What is it honey?"

"We have to leave now." He replied. "A tainted one is on its way here."

"Okay, let me throw some food in the cooler for the kids, and I'll get ready real…"

"There's no time!" He cut in, unable to keep the urgency out of his voice as he felt the ring on his middle finger begin to heat up. He held the hand up with the ring on it. "Grab Ben quick and get him in the car." Her eyes noticed the ring and the implications behind it, and she disappeared down the hall without a word. If the ring was already heating up that meant the tainted one was less than a mile away, which left him with very little time to get his family to safety.

Nathan set Leuken down on the ground. "Okay son, I need you to put your shoes on quick, and go to the car." He said as he ran back into the master bedroom and threw open the closet doors. Two large brown duffel bags sat on the wood floor, but he grabbed another thin bag first and threw it over his shoulder before grabbing the two larger bags.

It had been a little over a year, but Nathan could never forget the man with the red beard. He had been through too much in his short life to believe in chance, and if his son thought that one of the tainted ones was coming, he was not about to risk it. If the tainted one was newly made and alone, he should be able to handle it, but he doubted that was the case. The only way to assure his family's safety would be if they left before any tainted ones arrived.

When he opened the door to the garage Sara was just putting Leuken in the back seat. She was still wearing her blue flannel pajamas and pink slippers, and appeared to be doing her very best to keep panic out of her voice as she said "Leuken I need you to hold your brother's hand because we might have to drive fast okay?"

"Okay mommy. Let's go. I'm scared. I don't wanna be here when the bad man comes." Nathan threw both duffel bags in the trunk and slammed it shut. He slid the warm ring from his finger and pulled a small silver handled dagger from the thin bag and handed them to Sara.

"Remember, if you need to use it you must keep the dagger hidden until the last possible instant. It is your only chance." She raised her eyebrows quizzically as she noticed the ring being held out to her also. "Just in case we get separated, no matter what happens you keep going until you get to Isaac's house, if I am not there by dawn then leave without me. I will meet you at our spot in one week." She started to shake her head and a tear slipped down her right cheek. "This is the only way to make sure the kids are safe. You should drive in case I have to jump out." He said before she could protest as he handed her the keys to the car.

Sara took the keys and ran around the car as Nathan opened the garage door from inside. It was times like this that he was glad he had married such a strong woman. He knew it was hard being married to someone from the bloodline. In their six years together, they had already moved five times, but Sara never complained about anything.

Quickly glancing out the garage he noticed the moon slipping under the tree line to his right. The thick forest in front of him lay just on the other side of the main road, which his long driveway connected to. Scattered clouds covered most of the sky, and without his enhanced vision he would have seen very little in the dim light.

About fifty feet away to his left he saw movement. What at first looked like a large man was walking quickly towards him from the direction of the road. It was the same tainted one he had encountered a year before. The creature stood half a head taller than Nathan with unkempt dark red hair and a long beard hanging from its pale face. Its broad shoulders and muscular frame were covered by a black tunic and Nathan had no doubt that if he could see the back of the creature's neck the mark would be there.

"Nathaniel." The creature said in a deep resonating voice as Nathan's eyes met his. "You are a hard one to find."

"What do you want?" Nathan asked, already knowing the answer, but trying to think of how to escape with his family. He knew that this creature was likely not alone, as tainted ones usually hunted in pairs. The year before he and Isaac had killed this one's companion, and seen this creature arrive in town the next day, searching for its fallen friend. Perhaps it had not yet found a new partner, but he doubted it. He heard his wife start the car behind him.

"I am here to return a favor." The creature growled. "You killed someone who actually meant something to me, and I cannot allow such actions to go unpunished. After I am finished with you, rest assured that your pretty wife and child will share your fate."

"SARA GO!" Nathan shouted, and his wife slammed on the gas. The tires spun for a split second before the car raced past Nathan out of the garage. Nathan started moving as the car passed him. He saw the tainted one un-sling a large battle axe from its back and charge to intercept the car. The creature was fast, but Nathan was a little faster. As the creature was about to smash the axe through his wife's door Nathan jumped at it and knocked it backwards, tumbling over it as he reached for the creature's axe. They tumbled a few times and Nathan kicked off of the creature's chest as they rolled, landing on his feet with the axe, a few paces away from the creature. It was lying face down on the ground beside him.

Nathan jumped away from the creature's reach and threw the axe as hard as he could to the south, hoping that it was the only weapon it possessed. The axe would be worthless against a tainted one anyway. It landed in the trees a couple hundred feet away as his wife was turning onto the main road. Then he saw the other creature. It looked like an average man with pale skin and dark hair and emerged from the tree line at a dead sprint for the car.

While the first creature ran after his thrown weapon, Nathan ran after his wife. The dark-haired creature had just landed on the trunk of the car and smashed in the back window with its bare fist, as Nathan caught up to the vehicle. He jumped, grabbing the creature by the neck and waist as his wife hit the brakes, throwing both of them over the top of the car.

This time the creature landed on top of Nathan and kicked him on the right side of his body. Nathan felt his ribs break as he kicked the creature's legs out from under it and jumped to his feet. His wife drove around them continuing down the highway as he pulled his sword from the bag on his back, unsheathing it. The blade was glowing white with heat, and as the creature jumped to its feet its eyes widened in surprise. It must have realized that the blade was forged from the same metal as the stone in Nathan's ring, for it jumped backwards as Nathan slashed at its body. It screamed as

Nathan's blade sliced across its left shoulder, but it had moved enough to keep its arm from being severed.

The creature turned to run as Nathan cut its left calf from behind, dropping it instantly as its leg was sliced off just above the ankle. He could smell the pungent odor of burned flesh, and it screamed even louder as it rose up onto its hands and knees. Nathan drove his sword through the center of the creature's back. The screaming quickly stopped as it let out a final breath, and Nathan would have been relieved, but he heard a noise behind him and turned.

As he turned, he felt a sharp pain in his left leg and fell to the ground. He tried to jump back up but fell again as he realized his left leg had been severed at the knee. The bearded creature was standing over him with its axe raised. Nathan slashed at its hands as the creature swung the axe down at an angle towards him. His sword hit the creature's right hand, but it wasn't enough to stop the axe from cutting through Nathan's right arm and into his ribs. With his hand still attached his sword fell to the ground as the creature screamed in agony, looking at its right hand which was now missing the two end fingers.

The creature snarled as it again raised its axe and swung. In that instant time seemed to slow. He knew that the axe was falling towards him, and that he was powerless to stop it. Desperation consumed him, for he realized that he had just taken his last breath. With every ounce of his strength, he wanted to fight back, but couldn't. Then something strange happened. Calmness suddenly flooded through his body, as he felt faint light surrounding him. The only thing he saw were the faces of his wife and two little boys. Memories of the last few years of his life flashed before him: His beautiful wife in her wedding dress, smiling as they walked out of the church with their arms entwined; The happiness on her face as she held their son Leuken in her arms for the first time; Leuken riding his tricycle on the driveway and smiling proudly up at him; His baby Benjamin giggling while taking his first steps.

Nathan felt assured that he had bought his family enough time to escape, and that Isaac would keep them safe. He knew that he was a dead man but could not think of a better way to die than protecting them. Contentment spread across his face as the creature's axe tore through his neck. His family would survive.

CHAPTER I

"What did you think of the movie?" My father asked as he glanced back at my four-year-old brother from the driver seat.

"I liked it. It was funny." My brother replied as he looked over at me and smiled. I smiled back at him. It was hard not to smile at Alex when he flashed those dimples. "Did you like it, Izzie?"

"I didn't like it." I answered still smiling. "I loved it!"

"Did you love it this much?" he said spreading both arms as wide as he could.

"No. I loved it this much." I stretched out my arms, and then with my right hand I tickled him under his ribs. He giggled. Sometimes he pretended not to be ticklish, but he wasn't fooling anyone.

"No..." He laughed harder as I began tickling him with both hands. "No tickles..."

"Don't get him too riled up." My mom chided from the front seat. "It's already half an hour past his bedtime." She turned and smiled at both of us, her blue eyes shining from the glow of the streetlights. It was amazing how beautiful she looked, especially since she had just had her fortieth birthday a week ago. If only I could look half as good as her, I would be happy. But no… I had to be cursed with dark hair like my father and green eyes instead of blue.

"Oh mom, can't I stay up just a little longer? After all I am four now." He said matter of fact-like.

"Nine O'clock is already plenty late for a four-year-old." She pulled her long blond hair behind her head and into a ponytail using a black band. As she turned to look at us again, I got a sinking feeling in my stomach. Bright headlights appeared off to my right.

In a flash of light, I heard a loud crash and saw my mother disappear as the front end of a pickup truck smashed into us. My world spun into oblivion.

"NO!" I shouted as I sat up in my bed. It took a moment to realize that I had only been dreaming. I would have felt relief, except this had been a frequent nightmare ever since the accident. Memories are supposed to fade, but every time I have the dream it feels just as real as the day Mom died.

I wiped the tears from my cheeks as the door creaked open. Alex poked his head into the room. "Izzie… are you okay?" He asked with a concerned look on his face.

"I'm fine, Alex, just had a bad dream." I scooted out of my bed and stood. He approached without saying a word and threw his arms around me. His head barely came to my waist as he looked up at me. "Sorry for waking you up."

"That's okay Izzie. It's light outside anyway, and I'm hungry." He let go of me and rubbed his stomach repeatedly, making a puppy dog face. Alex knew I was a sucker for his begging and had learned how to get what he wanted. I smiled at him and noticed sun light starting to creep through the blinds. The dim light cast a shadow on the white closet door from my dark oak dresser.

Alex wanted eggs, so I made some toast to go with it. After eating, I set aside a plate for my father and got ready for school. Alex only protested a little about brushing his teeth, and his fine blond hair took a few seconds to comb. He had picked out a blue shirt and khaki shorts to wear for school later.

I just finished grabbing my schoolbooks when I heard the car pulling into the driveway. As I walked down the stairs toward the front door, my father opened it and walked in. The door was a heavy rosewood and creaked a little whenever it opened and closed. Counting on my father to fix it was hopeless, since I had already been asking him to do it for months.

Wearing his brown jacket over his tan uniform, my father looked more like a lumberjack or construction worker than he did a security guard working graveyard. It didn't help that his uniform was tight around his chest, and one of the buttons looked like it was going to pop. He was a rather large man, with a mostly muscular build. His forearms were almost as wide as my thighs, but I had chicken legs, so that wasn't saying much.

"Good morning Liz." He said as he looked at me with dark circles under his eyes. "How did you sleep?"

A few days ago, Alex had mentioned the nightmares to him at the dinner table, and now he asked me about it almost every morning. It was bad enough having the dreams. The last thing I wanted to do was talk about them. This morning he seemed only halfway concerned and looked like he was ready to collapse from exhaustion.

"Good." I lied. "There's breakfast on the table for you, and Alex is ready for school. He just needs to brush his teeth."

I opened the door to leave and heard him mumble, "Thanks for breakfast" as the door closed behind me.

My father was trying. I had to give him credit for that. The first few months after mom's death he had broke down. At the young age of sixteen the last thing I would have wanted was to lose my mom and then have my father sink into a depression at the same time. Not to mention having to care for my four-year-old brother. It had taken me finally getting so frustrated that I screamed at him and smashed all of the liquor bottles in the house before my father finally changed. I told him that he needed to man up and start being the father that Alex and I needed. It probably drove the point home when I said: "Look at you. Mom would be disgusted by what you have become." Since that day, he never drank around us again, and he started talking to us more. Alex seemed to appreciate it.

The next week we had moved to Harrisburg, Oregon. I had never heard of the town before my father said that we were buying a house there. He had picked up a job doing night security at the town museum. The pay wasn't great, but he had done twenty years with the Portland Police Department, so between his pension and his job we got by all right, at least financially. There were only a few thousand people in the town, but having a big city like Eugene only half an hour away made conditions more tolerable. We had been living here over a year now, and my eighteenth birthday was just a few months away.

I stepped up into my Tahoe and started the engine. After the minivan was totaled in the accident, my father had bought me a white Chevy Tahoe. It was already a couple years old, but looked new enough. "You need something that will keep you safe" he had said when he first surprised me with the keys the day after we finished moving. I did feel a little safer being so high off the ground, even if I had to slide the seat almost all the way forward just to reach the pedals. I was only five feet, four inches tall.

Alex was waving out the window at me, so I returned the favor. As I pulled out of the half circle driveway onto the street I glanced back at the house. It was one of the nicer houses in town, and could almost have passed for a log cabin, except that it was massive. Easily twice the size of our last house, the contrast of the dark brown window frames against the light cedar actually looked nice. Well... in a lumberjack sort of way. My father had said that while nothing good could ever come from losing mom, he was glad she at least had life insurance. It had allowed him to pay cash for the house and keep money in the bank. Having a river a stone's throw from our back porch was a bonus too.

Harrisburg was a pretty little town. If moving here had been under different circumstances I might have actually liked it. Most of the houses in the town had wood siding and dark gray shingles for roofing, and they were more spread out than houses in Portland had been.

Five minutes and three stop signs later I was pulling into the parking lot at school. Harrisburg High school had a whopping two hundred and eighty students, and the brick school was painted white. Purple and gold stripes along the bottom of each building signified the school colors. I found a parking space at the edge of the parking lot and started walking. A few of the cars in the lot were newer than mine, but most were older. It seemed like some of the kids in town were well to do, but most were just average.

I wasn't sure if I was beginning to hate the school less, or just used to being miserable, but I was glad to get out of the house. Mornings after the nightmare were always the worst, and it was especially difficult to be around Alex, who had the same hair and eyes as Mom. I loved my little brother, yet sometimes looking at him just brought back the pain. It had been over a year, but the sadness hadn't faded much.

I made my way towards my first class, where Nikki was waiting impatiently for me. "Liz!" she almost shouted in her usual loud voice. She was wearing a blue blouse that buttoned up the top half and white jeans that almost looked too tight. Her brown seashell earrings matched her dark brown hair and eyes, and her usual smile spread across her lips as she held her arms out. It was Monday, so of course she would have to fill me in on her weekend. "Hey girl, how was your weekend?" She gave me a quick hug.

"Good. I..."

"That's good. My weekend was totally lame." She interjected as she pulled away. Clearly she had something she wanted to say, and was only being polite in asking about my weekend.

Nikki was a good friend. The only good one I had managed to make since moving here. She was predictable and open, which I liked; Even if she was a little too prissy at times. My first day at school she had made it her personal goal to see that I felt welcome here. Once she knew my story, we had quickly become best friends. It probably helped that she had recently lost her mom as well. She had run off to Europe with another man and called Nikki a few days later to say goodbye. Her dad had a new wife now, but Nikki didn't care for her much. Most of the other girls at school were jealous of Nikki because she looked like a Latina Barbie, which left me as her only girlfriend and confidant.

Nikki went on to tell me about her "lame" weekend down in Laguna Beach, California. Her dad had rented a penthouse at some fancy hotel, and she had spent most of her time shopping. The rest of her time had been spent eating at fancy restaurants and tanning on the beach. Like she needed a tan. My skin looked white in comparison to hers.

"So, you would think that when you pay like a hundred and fifty dollars for a steak, it would at least taste good. It totally tasted like the cow was still alive. I guess maybe if you are a stuck-up fancy waiter than medium well means bloody raw." She finished talking about her last meal in Laguna Beach with a disgusted look on her face, and I laughed. We walked into our physics class and sat down.

Physics was boring as usual. We were on our way to second period government when someone grabbed Nikki from behind. It was Greg Dunn, captain of the football team and Nikki's boyfriend. She turned, and he picked her up and spun her around while they kissed. The kiss was a little too long, and by the time he set her down his face had flushed a little. He was a good enough looking guy, even if he was a jock. His brown hair had a tint of red in it, but his muscular jaw and blue eyes made up for that. Nikki said that she liked red heads anyway so more power to her. He was a head taller than her and probably weighed more than twice what she did.

"Did you miss me?" She asked making googly eyes at him.

"Only more than anything." He replied and stared at her for an uncomfortably long amount of time.

"Okay guys, unless you are gonna get a room, we have government class in about two minutes." They reluctantly broke eye contact.

"Hey Liz. I see you are your chippery self as usual." He smiled at me and started walking with his arm around Nikki. "Did you guys see the new kids? I think they are brothers. The older one looks like he would fit nicely on the team. Too bad the season is already almost over."

"All you ever think about is football." Nikki teased "ME GREG. GREG LIKE FOOTBALL. GREG THROW FOOTBALL FAR." She tried to imitate his voice, and we both laughed.

"It's not all I think about." He pulled her up to him and they kissed again.

"Okay seriously. You guys need to get a room. Haven't you heard of too much PDA? Well, that is you guys... every day." I pretended to be disgusted, but in truth I was so used to them that it really didn't bother me anymore. Well... Usually it didn't anyway.

We walked into Mr. Melvin's class and sat down in the back row. Greg sat in front of Nikki on the end because there were only two seats left by each other. Two dozen desks lined the room, but there were only fifteen kids in our class. "Wake me up when he's done talking." Greg told Nikki as he leaned back in his chair.

The tardy bell sounded and then the classroom door opened. I glanced over to see who was late and had to do a double take. I knew most of the kids in school, and all of the seniors, so it took me by surprise when a stranger walked into the class. He was tall with dark brown wavy hair and blue eyes.

"Alright class," Mr. Melvin began in his nasally voice while peering over his brown glasses "This is Luke Bennett. Today is his first day at Harrisburg High so everyone be sure to say hello after class." He turned to the newcomer and added "You can take any open seat Mr. Bennett."

Luke quickly scanned the room, and I could see what Greg meant about him being a good addition to the football team. He wasn't the biggest guy I had ever seen, but he had broad shoulders and his black sweater was rolled up to his elbows, revealing well defined forearms. I noticed that his eyes had stopped on me, and widened quickly in surprise when they took me in. Remembering that I was staring, I quickly looked away as I felt my cheeks flush. I glanced back and noticed that he was still staring at me. By the expression on his face, he seemed to be in a trance, with his full lips parted just a little. He suddenly seemed to notice me looking at him too and started for the open seat at the back of the room two over from me. I caught him stealing glances at me as he walked. Judging by his expression it almost seemed like he knew me.

I looked at Nikki, and she was smiling at me. She raised her eyebrows and nodded towards him, then started writing on a piece of paper. I glanced over at where Luke had just sat and caught him staring at me again. He still had a strange expression on his face but looked away quickly when our eyes met. Was he really staring at me? I looked down to make sure I didn't have something stuck to my clothes. Why was he staring at me? I was absolutely positive I had never seen him before because there is no way I would have forgotten that face. It wasn't fair for someone to look so good.

Nikki slipped me a piece of paper as Mr. Melvin began speaking. He was saying something about the thirteenth amendment. I read the paper.

PRETTY BOY WAS TOTALLY CHECKING YOU OUT.

So, it hadn't been my imagination. I wrote back to her.

DO I HAVE SOMETHING ON MY FACE? I THOUGHT I HAD JUST IMAGINED IT.

She passed the note back to me.

NO, YOU LOOK GOOD. AND OBVIOUSLY HE THINKS SO TOO. I THINK SOMEONE NEEDS TO WORK HER MAGIC.

MAYBE IF HE WORKS OUT THEN YOU CAN STOP BEING JEALOUS OF ME AND GREG.

I'M NOT JEALOUS OF YOU TWO. I AM PERFECTLY CONTENT BEING SINGLE. AND BESIDES, WE DON'T KNOW ANYTHING ABOUT THIS GUY. HE MIGHT BE CRAZY.

She looked up at me and laughed before writing back.

MAYBE CRAZY FOR YOU... BUT EVEN IF HE IS WHO CARES? HE IS GORGEOUS. I'LL GIVE YOU TILL FRIDAY TO DO YOUR THING. IF YOU HAVEN'T BY THEN I AM TOTALLY SETTING YOU TWO UP.

I smiled at her and shook my head. The last thing I needed was Nikki trying to set me up. A relationship was not what I was looking for right now. I doubted that Nikki would understand though. She had probably only gone a few days in her entire life without a boyfriend. Before the accident I'd had my fair share too, but everything was different now.

PLEASE DON'T. HOW ABOUT I WILL TALK TO HIM AND SEE IF HE IS EVEN NORMAL? THEN WE CAN GO FROM THERE, BUT YOU ARE NOT SETTING ME UP WITH ANYBODY OKAY? I CAN TAKE CARE OF MYSELF.

JUDGING BY THE WAY YOU WERE CHECKING HIM OUT, I THINK YOU'LL THANK ME FOR IT LATER... HE'S LOOKING AT YOU AGAIN.

I looked over at him without thinking and caught his eyes for a second. Someone must have turned the heat up in the classroom because I suddenly felt warm. He looked away and I turned back towards Nikki. She was smiling at me and shaking her head.

"Miss Calata, would you like to share something with the rest of the class?" Mr. Melvin was staring at Nikki disapprovingly.

"No Mr. Melvin. Sorry I just remembered a funny joke. I would share it but it's a little… inappropriate." She said in a teasing voice. A few of the kids in the class laughed.

"Okay then please keep it to yourself. As I was saying, three fifths of the state legislature has to…" he kept on lecturing for the rest of the class, but I didn't hear a word he said. I couldn't stop thinking about the new boy in class, Luke Bennett. Maybe I looked like someone he used to know. Or maybe… could it be that he did find me attractive? My heart beat a little faster at the thought. What was I thinking about? I didn't even know this kid. I gave up on passing any more notes to Nikki for fear of drawing attention to myself.

The bell rang and I followed Nikki and Greg out of the classroom. Greg had just whispered something in Nikki's ear. "Don't worry Greg." She said. "You are still the only one for me baby. I was actually thinking that we should set Liz up with him. He was totally checking her out in class, and she really needs a boyfriend bad." She noticed me walking behind her and turned "No offense Liz, but you do need a man. It's time you start moving on with your life." She shrugged and fell back into pace next to me. The last thing I needed was someone telling me to move on with life, but Nikki meant well, so I just bit my tongue. She must have noticed my frustration.

"Don't get all mad at me Liz." Nikki stopped and grabbed me by the shoulders. "You know I love you girl, but I just want you to be happy." She looked me straight in the eyes. Anyone else would have made me feel uncomfortable, but Nikki and I were close. "I tell you what. I'll back off and give you time to make sure this boy is not crazy, but if he is normal, then I like think you should… befriend him. That's all." She smiled as she finished speaking. People were starting to look at us weird for blocking the hallway, so we turned and started walking again.

"Well, I will give him a chance, but I'm not looking for anything serious right now. Okay?"

"Okay Liz. I'll see you at lunch." She started to turn down a side hallway with Greg.

I kept going straight. Nikki had tried setting me up in the past. At least three of Greg's friends had asked me on dates in my first few months here, but after making up poor excuses to turn them all down, everyone got the hint. No boys had even tried talking to me since then besides Greg, and he didn't really count anyway.

Third period was boring as usual, but at least it went by fast. Mrs. Thomas had me grade all of the quizzes from her first two algebra classes, and then I worked on homework until the bell rang. Being a student aid was better than playing an instrument or taking Spanish, which were my only other options for an elective class. Another drawback to living in a small town. Mrs. Thomas usually didn't have a lot of work for me, which left time to get most of my homework done before I even got home.

I made my way to the cafeteria, and after buying a deli turkey sandwich I sat at my usual table by myself. Nikki was customarily late for lunch, so I was used to it. About halfway through my sandwich I noticed Luke walk by my table and sit at another one just a few tables away. I thought I could see him looking at me out of the corner of my eyes, but I didn't want him to catch me looking at him again. A couple minutes went by, and I had just finished half my sandwich when I saw movement to my right.

A blond-haired boy wearing a blue sweater and dark blue jeans was walking up to me. He smiled as he got close and sat across the table from me. His light blue eyes seemed to light up with his face as he looked at me.

"What did the cauliflower say to the celery?" He asked with a smirk on his face. He didn't look a day older than fifteen, but he was pretty tall. Something about his personality just seemed… happy, so I humored him.

"I'm guessing you're about to tell me." I smiled back at him. He sort of reminded me of Alex.

"Are you stalking me?" he finished the joke and gave a small laugh. I laughed too. "By the way, my name is Benjamin Bennett." He held his hand out to me.

I took his hand and while shaking said "And I am Elizabeth Scott." Did he say Bennett? Just then I noticed some of the similarities. This must be Luke's brother.

"What a pleasure to make your acquaintance." He said in a proper tone "You see, today is my first day here, and I don't know anyone, so I figured I would start by introducing myself to the prettiest girl I saw."

"Well then you're either blind or you didn't look around much, but thanks anyway for the compliment." I smiled again and released his grip. He chuckled.

"I'm just being honest Elizabeth. It's one of my many faults."

"Oh, please. Call me Liz. Do you go by Ben or Benjamin?"

"Most people call me Ben, but you can call me whatever you want." His flirting seemed too over the top to be serious, so I just smiled and shook my head. "Okay, so on a more serious note, what do people do around here for fun? I love all the scenic trees, hills, and the river and all, but I don't see a lot of kids out and about."

"Well…" I thought about it for a minute. "Most people here in town either hang out by the river or drive into Eugene for fun I suppose. Some of them go hiking or mountain biking in the hills too."

"So did you grow up here in Harrisburg?" Ben inquired.

"No. I grew up in Portland. We only moved here about a year ago. What about you? Where are you from?"

"Most recently Colorado, but we move around quite a bit. My mom doesn't like to stay in one place too long. She gets too stir crazy." Ben glanced over at his brother Luke, who I noticed was intent on our conversation. If I didn't know better, I would say that he could hear us, but there was no way we were talking loud enough for that. "That's my brother Luke over there." He added pointing and waving. Luke gave a quick wave back at us and I waved too. He almost seemed annoyed by his little brother talking to me.

Just then Nikki came walking up to us. "So, I like totally hate third period." She said in an exasperated tone. "Mr. Wirtz kept me five minutes after because he said that he needed to talk to me about the topic for my research paper. And I swear the whole time he just kept staring at me. Not only is he way weird and creepy, but he has that retarded German accent, so I can barely understand anything he says. If my dad hadn't promised to buy me a new Mercedes for getting straight A's I would definitely ditch his class on a daily basis." She seemed to notice Benjamin for the first time and looked at me, expecting an introduction.

"Hey Nikki, this is Benjamin Bennett. Ben this is Nikki." I gestured with my right hand as I spoke. Ben was already smiling at Nikki the same way he had smiled at me.

"So now I have met both of the two most beautiful girls in town. I guess there's no need to make friends with anyone else." He smirked.

"Except maybe Nikki's boyfriend." Greg appeared from behind and startled me. His voice sounded a little upset and was louder than usual. He walked around to Nikki, giving Benjamin a look that said "back off" as he put his arm around her. "Hi, I'm Greg Dunn."

Ben had not seemed startled at all by Greg sneaking up behind us "It's nice to meet you, Greg. I am Benjamin Bennett, but most people just call me Ben." He held his hand out to Greg, who took it reluctantly. "I was just commenting on how these two are the best-looking girls I've seen since moving here. You are a lucky man." Greg just stared at Ben as they stopped shaking and there was an awkward silence for a couple seconds. "So, I hear you have one heck of an arm, and that you can take a hit too. It's too bad there are only a couple weeks left till the State championships; I would love to play for you." Greg seemed to calm down a little as the topic switched to football, and the tension in the air vanished.

"Yeah, I'm okay. Our school isn't very good though, so it doesn't really matter. Did you play for your school back where you came from?" Greg and Nikki both sat down as everyone seemed more relaxed.

"We came from Colorado, and yes. I played wide receiver and safety. We almost won state last year when my brother played, but this year we weren't that great." Benjamin glanced over at Luke, who wasn't looking at us but appeared to be trying to listen. He seemed to be frowning. I couldn't imagine that he could hear a word we were saying from so far away. "Well, I probably better get back to my lunch. It was nice to meet you all." Ben turned to me. "Especially you Miss Scott." He grabbed my hand with his and gently kissed the top of it, then turned around and walked back to where his brother was sitting.

I just sat there for a second, taken back a little by his farewell. He sure seemed like a character. If only he weren't so young, I would say I could be attracted to him. Even though he was a little over the top, something about him seemed somehow… sincere. Ben was definitely good friend material.

"Well, he seems like a nice kid." Greg stated after a few seconds had passed. I was surprised that he had gone from being his normal jealous self to calm so quickly. Usually he didn't lighten up so easily.

"Yeah," I said, "Almost too nice."

"Well, I think that he and his brother are both totally hot." Nikki stated as I glanced over at Luke and Ben again. They both seemed to grin when she said that. Could they possibly hear us? There was no way.

Greg gave Nikki a disapproving look and she quickly added "Not as hot as you baby." While touching his cheek. "But I'm just looking out for Liz, since you are all mine."

"Okay." I interrupted "You guys are doing it again. We are in a cafeteria, remember?"

"Don't you think they look hot Liz?" Nikki put me on the spot.

"Well of course I do but… when you are not looking for a relationship that's kind of irrelevant. Don't you think?" I tried to sound uninterested, but it probably wasn't very convincing since I inadvertently glanced over at Luke again as I said this.

Nikki gave me a knowing smile. "Okay Liz, sure. Whatever you say." We finished eating in silence, and the bell rang. I made my way towards Literature class alone. Third and Fourth periods were always the worst because Nikki had her other classes. She took advanced government and physics classes, but for some reason either wasn't very good at English or just hated the subject, because it was the only regular class that she was in. It wasn't that I minded being alone in some classes, it was just nice to have her around.

I think that maybe deep down a part of me missed the large group of friends I had been accustomed to in Portland. There were a lot of things that I missed from before the accident, but I knew I could do nothing to change the past, so I tried not to dwell on it. I wasn't always successful though.

Taking my seat in Mr. Sassenburg's class, I began to remove the books from my backpack. Sassenburg's class was actually somewhat interesting at times. He was a well-built man from somewhere back east. I think Pennsylvania or Connecticut. Rumor had it that he used to be a body builder and a thespian. Neither one would have surprised me. He sometimes dressed up and started quoting Shakespeare or other plays, and he seemed to have a genuine love for literature. I also liked to read, so the class wasn't too bad.

Just before the bell rang, I saw Luke enter the classroom. There were only a couple of open seats, and one of them was next to me in the second row. He glanced around the room, and then headed for the other seat across the room from me. I might have been overanalyzing it, but he seemed to be avoiding looking at me. It must have been my imagination. Maybe he just hadn't seen me.

As he was about to sit down Mr. Sassenburg spoke. "Ah Mr. Bennett… It is a pleasure to have you with us. If you don't mind, we actually have prearranged seating in this classroom. I feel it better assists the students with focusing on the task at hand. You will be assigned to sit here, adjacent to Ms. Scott." He gestured towards the empty seat next to me. "We frequently engage in cooperative projects, and she is currently the only person without a partner. She is one of my brightest students, and I don't doubt you will make a good companion." Luke glanced at me, then hesitantly made his way across the room and sat down beside me.

Mr. Sassenburg went on to talk about our next chapter, which included Hamlet. Normally I would be paying attention to him, but it was hard not to think about the boy next to me. Luke Bennett looked even better from this close. His jaw seemed a little stronger, and his lips softer. I tried only looking at him out of the corner of my eye but had a feeling he knew I was watching him. He never looked at me though. I noticed him glance around the room away from me a couple times, but he never even looked in my direction. It almost seemed deliberate.

Time crawled by a fraction of a second at a time, and it became increasingly clear that Luke was ignoring my existence. What had changed? Less than an hour ago he couldn't keep his eyes off of me, and now I seemed to have been discarded. I sat… confused for quite some time and eventually resolved that I would introduce myself to him at the end of class.

Mr. Sassenburg finished his closing remarks just as the bell rang, and I turned to introduce myself. Luke had also turned to stand and made his way nonchalantly out of the classroom. I sat with my mouth half open. Calling after him would have been too awkward.

Embarrassed, I made my way toward the parking lot. Nikki was probably sucking face with Greg before his football practice, so I would have to wait until tomorrow to talk to her about Luke. Or perhaps I would just call her later. My dad had said that my cell phone was only to be used for emergencies, but I knew he rarely used any of our shared minutes anyway. As I approached my car, I saw Ben sitting behind the wheel of a silver H2 Hummer that was pulling out of a parking spot near mine. Luke was in the passenger seat, but only Ben waved as they drove slowly past me. The hummer looked almost brand new.

I drove to Alex's elementary school, listening to the classic rock station out of Eugene as I went. There were only two local radio stations; one was a news radio station that played mostly classical music between announcements, and the other was an oldies station that rarely had a live DJ. At least most of the radio stations from

Eugene came through pretty clear; otherwise, I would be limited to CDs.

After waiting in the car for about fifteen minutes, Alex finally appeared tapping on the passenger door. I reached over and opened the door for him. "How was school?" I asked absentmindedly.

"Well Mrs. Schneider was our substitute teacher again, so of course it was boring." He made a sour face and continued on about some projects that they had done and mentioned something about another kid being mean to one of his friends. My mind went back to Luke, and how he had seemed to purposely ignore me the second half of the day. "Don't you think so Liz?" Alex finished, and I realized that I had not been paying attention.

"Oh yeah, absolutely." I replied, pretending to have heard what he had said. He nodded while scratching the side of his head. His blonde hair was all disheveled in the back. The ride home was short, and I was not surprised to find my father still sleeping when we arrived.

I helped Alex with his homework, and then started on dinner. Barbeque chicken and leftover mashed potatoes from the night before were all I felt like making. My father must have smelled the chicken because sure enough he appeared in the kitchen doorway as I was taking it out of the oven.

"Good morning, Liz." He said sounding only half awake. His dark hair seemed to be getting more gray in it every day, especially around his temples. "You didn't have to make dinner, but thanks. It sure smells tasty." He offered a little smile, and I nodded.

"You're welcome dad. Sorry it's nothing fancy." He didn't like it when I called him Father, so I gave him a sympathetic "dad" from time to time. I didn't bother correcting his morning comment, even though it was clearly almost sunset. "Alexander Scott!" I shouted up the stairs to Alex, who was playing in his room. "Dinner's ready! You better come down now or it will all be gone!"

I heard his footsteps pounding across the hallway and down the stairs, and he popped into the kitchen a moment later. "Don't eat all my food Liz." He sounded out of breath. His chubby cheeks were a little flushed from running. "I'm hungry."

"You're always hungry." I smiled while setting his plate in front of him as he hopped up into his chair. I then sat across from him, to the left of where my father was sitting at the head of the table.

"Hey Alex, how was school?" My father asked while taking a bite of chicken. Alex went on at length, telling him about school and Mrs. Schneider, but again my mind was pre-occupied. After dinner my dad offered to wash up, and I wasn't complaining. I spent an hour doing homework, and then watched some TV with Alex before tucking him into bed. Calling Nikki got me her voicemail, but I didn't bother to leave a message. I would have to tell her about Luke tomorrow.

By the time I laid down in bed it was just before ten o'clock. After an eternity of laying there without sleep coming, I looked at the clock again and the small hand was almost to the twelve. For some reason I couldn't stop thinking about Luke and the mixed signals he was sending me. Why could he not keep his eyes off of me all morning, and then after lunch he avoided me like I had the Bubonic Plague? It didn't make any sense. Maybe Ben had said something about me that turned him off during lunch. Except… that didn't make sense because Ben seemed to like me well enough, and he even waved after school. Luke had not though.

I couldn't stop thinking about the way he had looked at me. His expression had been surprised and yet strangely… familiar, as if we had known each other for a very long time. It took me quite some time to relax with so many thoughts racing through my head, but eventually sleep came.

****

"What do you… want from me?" The blonde-haired man asked with labored breath.

Jareth was holding him by the throat against the cracked wall of the kitchen. His head was on the same level as Jareth's, even though his feet dangled a foot off the ground. The man's right arm was missing just above where his elbow should have been, and dark blood stained the sleeve of his once white button up shirt. He didn't look a day older than twenty, but Jareth had said that these "bloodline" people usually looked younger than they were.

Jeremy was standing next to Jareth, holding the man's remaining arm. It wasn't where he wanted to be, standing next to this grisly creature of a man, but the silver-colored bracelet on Jeremy's wrist left him without a choice. Jareth had told him to hold the man's arm, so that is what he did. The man attempted to break free of Jeremy's grip every few seconds but was always unsuccessful. Apparently not even members of the bloodline were stronger than the Auserwalt. That was the title Jareth claimed belonged to those who had been transformed as they had been.

Looking around, Jeremy wasn't surprised by the ruined state of the house around them. Shattered glass and broken pieces of drywall littered the floor. Several of the walls had human size holes in the drywall, and in some places even the framing was broken. The skirmish between this man and Jareth couldn't have lasted more than a minute, but it had been quite a violent encounter. The man's speed had been impressive at first, and it wasn't until Jareth hacked off one of his arms with that gargantuan axe that the man had finally begun to slow down.

"I have what I want." Jareth's deep voice finally replied to the man's question. "What I don't understand is why you didn't try to run?"

The man's eyes were angry, but underneath that defiance Jeremy could sense fear welling up in him. His premonition was confirmed as the man's struggling ceased and he glanced down in defeat, shoulders slumping.

"What are you?" the man's struggling whisper was barely audible with Jareth's hand still clenched around his throat.

Instead of answering Jareth began to laugh. It was a deep, sinister chuckle, causing even the hair on Jeremy's neck to stand up. The blonde man's eyes widened as Jareth's grip on his throat tightened even more. His wide-eyed expression lasted only a few seconds, and then his eyelids slid shut as his body went limp.

"Let go boy." Jareth barked at Jeremy as the man's body slid to the floor. No sooner had the body come to rest on the tile floor than Jareth raised his axe and brought it down towards the man's neck. Jeremy looked away as he heard the weapon crunch through the man and into the floor.

"Search every inch of the house. If you find anyone else…" Jareth turned to Jeremy and grinned, his face dripping on one side with splattered blood. "Kill them."

Jeremy turned quickly to check the rest of the house. He wasn't sure if his prompt obedience to that last command came more from the bracelet on his arm that Jareth used to control him, or the fear and disgust he felt when looking at his master's bloody face. There were so many things about Jareth that were unsettling. Never before had Jeremy seen someone so heartless and cruel.

CHAPTER II

I felt a light tug on my arm and opened my eyes. "Wake up sleepy head." Alex was smiling down at me and giggled when he saw me wake up. "Izzie, I'm hungry." He rubbed his hand over his stomach in circles, making a puppy dog face just like he did every time he wanted food.

"You're always hungry." I teased. Part of me didn't want to get out of bed, since I had actually slept well for once, but I knew Alex wouldn't leave me alone until he had food in his stomach. I sat up begrudgingly. "You know that sort of loses its effect when you do it every day?" I mumbled sliding out of bed. The cool hardwood floor felt good on my bare feet.

He just smiled at me "I know… but it gets me food." I went into the bathroom to get ready. The clock above my bathroom door read six thirty-four.

"Oh shoot, I must have missed my alarm. I'll be down in a minute Alex, why don't you get dressed." He disappeared around the corner, and I heard his thudding footsteps as he ran towards his room. I brushed my hair out quickly and pulled it into a ponytail. Two minutes later I was throwing on a baby blue blouse and dark blue jeans. *I hope Luke likes blue.* I thought to myself. Although the way he had ignored me in fourth period made me think that it wouldn't matter what color I wore. I heard the front door creek open as I was coming down the stairs with my backpack.

My father seemed a little less tired than he had yesterday as he started taking his brown work boots off by the front door. "Hey Liz, running a little late?" he sounded concerned.

"Yeah, I slept in." I hurried past him into the kitchen and grabbed a bagel out of the bag on the counter. "Would you mind making something for you and Alex? I didn't have time to." Grabbing a knife from the drawer, I cut the bagel in half and got some cream cheese out of the black refrigerator.

"Sure." He walked by me slowly and opened the fridge, pausing to look inside. "Uh… what should I make Alex?" He actually sounded like he had no idea what to make, which made me realize that the last time he had made breakfast was probably a few months ago when I was sick. It was just something that I always took care of, and most mornings we were already done eating before he got home from work. I was in too much of a hurry to feel sorry for him though. He would have to fend for himself. After all, he was supposed to be the parent.

"Whatever you want, he's not picky." I put my bagel on a paper towel and headed for the front door. "I'll see you after school. Sorry about breakfast." Alex was just coming down the stairs with a confused look on his face as I opened the door. "Alex, I have to go so tell Dad what you want for breakfast okay? I'll see you later." I closed the door behind me and hurried to my Tahoe, taking a bite of bagel as I walked.

When I pulled into the parking lot at school it was six fifty-five, so I hurried to my first class. I noticed that the Bennett's hummer was parked next to the spot I had been in yesterday. Probably just a coincidence. I finished my last bite of bagel just in time to throw the paper towel in the trash as I entered the front courtyard. Nikki was standing in front of Physics again, and I was glad that it was the second classroom from the front of the school. She looked concerned as I approached.

"So, I like, totally got here extra early so we could talk, since I saw I missed your call, and you show up one minute before class starts?" She was standing with her hands on her hips and her hair curled falling halfway down her back. Of course, her large hoop earrings and hair band perfectly matched her brown sweater, and she was almost bouncing with impatience.

"I'll explain in class." I said giving her a rushed hug. We walked into class, and the bell rang as we sat at our table near the back of the room. The room was laid out with three two person tables in each row, and four rows. Each table was black with a small lab station in the middle. "Sorry I slept in." I whispered once we were both situated.

"That's okay. I didn't notice that I had missed your call until about eleven last night, so I didn't want to call you back so late. What's up?" Mr. Anderson began his lecture, and we both looked forward as we whispered so as not to draw attention.

"Well, other than Luke being assigned to sit next to me in fourth period and treating me like I had some kind of disease for the rest of the day… nothing." I tried to keep the frustration out of my voice.

"What?" She glanced at me with one eyebrow raised. "That's great that he's sitting next to you in class, but what do you mean? How was he treating you?"

"Well, when he first walked in, he looked at everyone in the class but me. Then, even though there was an open seat right next to me in front of him, he tried to sit on the other side of the room."

"But I thought you said…"

"He only sat by me because Mr. Sassenburg told him he had to." I could tell where she was going and didn't feel like waiting for her to finish so I cut her off. "And then… when Mr. Sassenburg told him that he had to sit by me, he looked annoyed. The whole class he just looked straight forward or away from me. You would have thought I was medusa or something. It was so blatant."

"Whoa Liz, he did what? Are you sure you aren't mistaken? Maybe he just got shy or something. There is no way any guy could not want to look at you." She put an emphasis on the word you.

"Yeah… right…" Nikki was always too generous with her compliments. "That's what I thought at first too, that he was just shy. But then at the end of class I turned to speak to him, and he just got up and walked out of the room. And, to top it all off, I saw him and Ben leaving the parking lot after school, so I waved… but he didn't wave back."

"Are you sure he saw you? Did you make eye contact?" she turned and faced me. By the expression on her face, she seemed more worried than I even felt.

"Well, his brother Ben was driving and waved at me first, and I looked Luke straight in the eye. I'm sure." My voice dropped a little as I finished the account, and I realized something. I cared about this way more than I logically should have. So, what if this boy looked like heaven? I didn't know him from a can of paint, and for all I knew he could be some sort of psychopath. It didn't feel good knowing I was acting like a teenage schoolgirl with my emotions. Just because I was one is no excuse.

"Hmmm…" Nikki seemed to be contemplating something. "Well with a face like yours there is no way this guy could not find you attractive… which means it must be one of two things. Either he just gets really nervous around girls, or…he's crazy." She spoke with such finality. "Or maybe…" She paused again. "That's it. I know what it is."

"What?" She had my full attention.

"He's gay." The way she said it she might has well have been saying the sky was blue. I hadn't even thought of that. Maybe she was right.

"You think maybe…?" I trailed off, thinking about the implications.

"Well just think about it. He was staring at you, obviously because you are so beautiful, but not for the same reason most other guys check you out." I gave her an incredulous look. *Yeah right*. I thought to myself. "He sees you as like… competition, and once he realized how flawless you are, he got upset and doesn't want to look at you." She seemed satisfied with her assessment.

"I don't know." I replied thoughtfully. "Nothing about him seems gay."

"Oh please. Girl, not all gay guys are the same. And besides, I'm not saying he is. I am only saying that it is a possibility. He is either shy, crazy, or gay. That's all." She turned and faced back towards the front of the classroom. "And for your sake, I hope he's just shy." Her hand patted my knee as she finished.

Mr. Anderson started handing out a quiz. After taking it we sat in silence for the rest of class while everyone else finished. The more I thought about the possibility of Luke being gay, the less it made sense, and the same was true of the shy theory. Nothing about him seemed crazy either, that was for sure. Which meant that there was something else going on. I just couldn't put my finger on it. The bell ringing brought me back to reality, and I followed Nikki out of class.

We made our way to second period, but this time Greg was waiting in the hallway. He and Nikki embraced as usual, and a few seconds later he nodded at me. "Hey Liz."

"Hi Greg." I answered back.

"So baby, Liz and I were talking, and I wanted to get your take on something." Nikki turned to look at Greg as she spoke. "Do you think the new guy is gay?"

"Which one? The young kid or the older brother?" He had a confused look on his face.

"The older brother."

He paused thoughtfully for a moment. "I doubt it. Not with the way he was checking Liz out during lunch yesterday."

"He wasn't checking me out" I began, but Nikki cut in.

"I'm not saying for sure he is gay, but like… maybe he sees her as competition."

"Competition to what?" Greg asked incredulously. "There are only two gay kids in the whole school, and they are with each other. I can guarantee you that with the way he was looking at Liz yesterday… he wasn't thinking about competition. Besides, Liz is the hottest girl in school." Nikki raised her eyebrows at him and folded her arms. "Besides you of course baby. It's only natural he would be checking her out."

"Yeah… I guess you're right." She turned to look at me again. "He must just be shy." She finished reassuringly.

"I suppose." I replied, but I didn't believe it. The way he had intentionally not looked at me made me think there was something more, but I wasn't sure what. We made our way into second period, where Luke was waiting for us.

He sat in the same seat as yesterday, but today he was wearing a dark blue polo shirt, again with the sleeves pulled up halfway to his elbows. His dark hair had a messy styled look to it, and his piercing blue eyes glanced up at us as we walked in. He looked away, but I could have sworn that his eyes lingered on me for a little first. We took our same seats as usual, and the bell rang a few seconds later.

Maybe he wasn't mad at me after all. I glanced over at him, and he was looking forward, but seemed to be extremely alert. It was almost as if he was constantly looking out the corners of his eyes. His demeanor reminded me of a Lion: resting in the field, but very aware of his surroundings. For the first time I noticed that he had a small scar on the back side of his neck. It was barely visible, and I only caught it because of the slight contrast between the pale scar and his lightly tanned skin. It was a small circle, about the size of a dime. *I wonder where that could have come from.* I thought to myself.

Mr. Melvin started class with a pop quiz, so Nikki and I didn't chance passing any notes. What was with the quizzes today? It was a good thing I had taken the time to study the night before. Government had always been an easy class for me, but maybe I had been a little too distracted while studying, because I had to guess on a few of the questions. We traded quizzes to grade them, and I handed mine to the blonde boy sitting to my right. I think his name was Mike. He was one of the shy… intellectual types, to put it kindly, so he didn't talk much.

Glancing over the rims of his large brown glasses, he smiled at me. "Piece of cake huh?" He sounded like he had something in his throat, but that was just his normal voice.

"Yeah, it wasn't too bad." I replied, grabbing the quiz from his outstretched hand.

He pulled a red marker out of his SpongeBob SquarePants backpack and held onto it. I could still remember the first time I had noticed the backpack and pointed it out to Nikki. We had started tearing up because we were laughing so hard. Mike's girlfriend also had a matching backpack so it must be a couple's thing. Why it was SpongeBob of all things? I couldn't tell you, but honestly, I didn't want to know. It's like my father always said: "There's a shoe for every foot."

"I doubt I'll need this for you." He added, taking off the cap of his marker.

Mr. Melvin went through the answers to the quiz, and I realized that I might have missed one. Mike confirmed this when I saw him placing a large red checkmark on my quiz with his marker. If I didn't know better, I would say he had a slight grin and looked satisfied as he did so. Well… I think it was the first time I had missed a question on one of his quizzes, but did nerd boy really have to grin like that?

I gave him a dirty look as he handed the quiz back. "Looks like you missed one for once. That's okay. Nobody's perfect." He sounded like he was trying to be reassuring, but with the large "-1" he had marked on the top of the quiz, I was just annoyed.

Lunch was uneventful. Nikki and I sat by ourselves and ate. Greg sat with his friends because they had all been teasing him about being whipped. Luke and Ben sat at the same table again. Ben waved at me when I first sat down, but neither one of them tried talking to us. I did catch Luke staring at me one time, but he immediately looked away when I noticed.

He beat me to fourth period, and was already sitting down with his books out when I walked in. Again, the entire class crept by without him so much as glancing in my direction. Mr. Sassenburg introduced our semester projects, which would consist of individual monologues from a literature selection of our choice. By "our choice" he really meant we could pick one of the thirty plays and novels that he had selected as approvable. As the end of class approached, I was getting frustrated with being ignored by Luke, and by the time the bell rang I was upset. Why was he pretending I didn't exist?

Luke almost jumped to his feet and started for the door. I was just starting to stand when Mr. Sassenburg said loudly "Mr. Bennett, Ms. Scott, can I have a word with you?" Luke stopped dead in his tracks and turned towards Mr. Sassenburg, who was sitting at his desk. Leaning back on his chair with his metallic pen pressed against his lips, he looked every inch the college professor.

"The reason I wished to address you" he began as we both approached "is to supplicate your cooperation with a matter that has been weighing heavily on my mind." I was growing accustomed to the strange way he always spoke. "You see I feel that reservations and personal comfort zones would be best defeated if I presented an example for the semester project to inspire confidence and exuberance among the other students. To this end, I would like to formally request support from your persons." He leaned forward in his chair and looked us both in the eye, lowering his voice. "Could you two go a week ahead of everyone else? I'll give you ten extra credit points if you do."

I glanced at Luke whose eyes were fixed on Mr. Sassenburg. "Of course." He answered in a surprisingly normal voice.

"Sure." I echoed.

"Great." He smiled at us and looked genuinely excited. "I simply wish to instill excitement in the other children, and I have faith that you two will be absolutely exemplary. Just make sure you get in a lot of practice together. Feedback is crucial to the success of such thespian endeavors."

"Okay, we will." Luke replied, and we both turned to leave. As we walked out the door, I tapped him on the shoulder.

"By the way, I'm Elizabeth Scott. I've met your little brother Ben, but never introduced myself." I smiled at him and held out my hand. He took it and shook with a surprisingly strong grip. His hands were unexpectedly warm.

"I'm Luke Bennett." He said hesitantly. "It's nice to meet you." He smiled back. I was amazed by how white his teeth were. His whole face seemed to light up as he smiled, and our eyes lingered on each other for a long second. He gently let go of my hand. "Well, I better not keep my brother waiting. I'll see you tomorrow."

"Yeah" I tried to keep the excitement out of my voice. "I'll see you tomorrow." He turned and started walking for the parking lot, and I followed after him. His stride was long. By the time I reached the parking lot he was already getting to his hummer. Ben was standing in front of it with the hood up, looking at the engine. Another sophomore, whose name I couldn't remember, had just pulled his car up next to theirs. I noticed black jumper cables in Ben's hands.

He was attaching the cables as I walked by, and I overheard Luke telling him "We'll drive down to Eugene and pick one up." I assumed he was talking about a new battery.

I got into my Tahoe and started the engine just as the clouds decided to release some of their moisture. A few drops turned into a light drizzle as I pulled past Luke and Ben on my way out of the parking lot. The other dark-haired kid helping them was getting back in his car as I went by. I pulled out of the parking lot and thought that I saw Luke looking after me in my side view mirror. *He must just be shy*. I thought to myself as I started to accelerate down the street. I still felt a little dazed from our short conversation, and I couldn't wait to call Nikki.

I reached for my cell phone in excitement, and then felt a panic rush over me as I caught sight of something in front of my car. An older looking tan Cadillac had swerved onto the road in front of me. I slammed on the brakes, and my tires screeched as the Tahoe came to a stop just a few feet from the Cadillac. It was parked diagonally with the passenger door directly in front of my hood.

I was about to honk my horn when I noticed the passenger door open. A scream involuntarily left my throat. Stepping out of the car was a tall man wearing all black with a ski mask. I noticed him holding a black handgun in his right hand. He pointed it directly at me while shouting, but I was so flustered I couldn't even register what he was saying.

"Out of the car!" he shouted again as he walked around the front of my car towards my door. Not wanting to get shot, I opened the door and started to step out, grabbing my purse with my right hand as I exited. The man grabbed my neck as I was stepping down and shoved me to the ground. "I said out woman!" the man spat as I hit the ground. I barely got my hands out in time to keep my face from slamming into the pavement.

Rolling onto my back, I was surprised to see that the man hadn't entered my Tahoe. I had assumed I was just getting car jacked. Instead, he was standing over me with the gun pointed down at my head. His dark hands were shaking slightly as they gripped the gun, and his brown eyes looked angry as they squinted at me. What had I ever done to this guy?

"Give me the purse!" He yelled, and I remembered that I was still clutching my purse. I quickly raised it towards him with my outstretched hand, unable to take my eyes off of the barrel. I was staring down the end of it into a black hole. He reached for the purse with his free hand, and unexpectedly something blurred in front of me.

All of the sudden Luke was there. He ripped the gun from the man's hand with lightning speed, and I heard something crunch as he did so. It almost sounded like bone breaking, but it happened too fast to be certain. The man's eyes widened in pain and surprise as he screamed. His scream was cut short as Luke grabbed his other arm and threw him. It looked anything but natural as the man's body flipped through the air over Luke's head and landed on its side about fifteen feet away. Luke turned to look at me, and his eyes changed from hard ice to worry as they rested on me.

"Are you okay Liz?" He asked as he extended a hand to help me up. I had never been much of a romantic person, but at that moment he was every inch my knight in shining armor.

"Yeah." I replied as I took his hand, and he helped me to my feet. "But how did you…" I began to ask but was interrupted by a loud bang. The left side of Luke's head suddenly exploded red with blood as he fell to the ground. I screamed. The loud bang had come from the driver of the Cadillac, who was now standing about ten feet away with a gun pointed at me. His skin was lighter than his accomplice, and his hand looked steady as he pointed the gun at me. He wore the same black clothing and ski mask as the other man had. His expression was unnaturally calm, yet evil, as he looked at me.

"What a waste." He said sighing as his finger moved back towards the trigger. "You are a pretty little thing. It's a shame I made too much noise killing your friend."

I knew he was about to shoot me but was too terrorized to move. When the man mentioned Luke a flood of sadness hit me. *Oh no! I've killed him!* I screamed inside my head. Glancing down at Luke's body, I was astounded to find it wasn't there. Where could he possibly have…? My thought was still forming when suddenly I saw another blur moving around the back side of my Tahoe.

Luke appeared next to the man, ripping the gun from his hand as he kicked the front of the man's kneecap. With a loud crunch the man's knee seemed to snap backwards and he fell to the ground screaming in agony. Luke manipulated the gun he had taken, and it came apart into three separate pieces. He jammed the barrel of the gun into the hood of the Cadillac, placing the other two pieces in his pocket.

Reaching down Luke picked up the now whimpering man who was holding his left leg with both hands. For a split second I worried that he would kill the man, for I could see the disgust mixed with ferocious anger in Luke's eyes. Instead, he walked around the Cadillac to the open driver's door and set the man in the car. The man was whimpering in pain but said nothing. Luke then blurred over to the first attacker, who was trying to stand up. This one's right wrist was clearly broken, and he seemed unable to put any weight on his right leg. Each time he started to stand up he fell back to the ground. Half of his face was scraped from the road, and he held up a hand defensively as Luke approached him. Luke picked him up as well, carrying him in his arms back to the Cadillac as the now pathetic attacker pleaded for his life. Luke set him in the open passenger seat. Reaching into the car, he ripped off their ski masks. Underneath, they both had shaved heads. They couldn't have been more than twenty-five years old.

By this point I was standing with my mouth open, thoroughly confused. My mind was telling me not to believe what my eyes were seeing, but I knew it could not be my imagination. It was too vivid not to be real.

"You're lucky I didn't kill both of you!" Luke snarled at the two men in the car. I noticed that his fists were both clenched at his side, and his hands were shaking. Despite his voice quieting as he continued, the unmasked anger remained. "Consider this a second chance at life. If I ever see either of you in Harrisburg again, I will kill you. Do you understand?"

The two men nodded, and Luke closed the passenger door. The Cadillac reversed and spun to face the other way. Tires screeched as it sped off towards the freeway. The smell of freshly burnt rubber mixed with rain filled my nostrils, but I was too shocked to pay attention to such details.

Turning to Luke, I could see the anger fading from him. His blue eyes looked nervous as they met mine, but he didn't look dazed at all. "Are you okay?" I asked. There was no hiding the concern from my voice, as I eyed the blood on his head.

"Yeah, I'm fine." He said, wiping the blood from his temple with one hand. As he wiped, I noticed that the skin underneath the wet blood looked normal and intact. I could have sworn it had been blown open just a few seconds before. Luke quickly glanced around, so I did too. We were across the street, a hundred feet from the edge of the school. It was easily three hundred yards away from where Luke and Ben had both been just seconds before I was attacked. Where had Luke come from? There was no logical way that he could have gotten there as quickly as he did. And he had moved so fast. It was unreal. My mind was still in shock as I looked back at him.

He was staring at me with a worried expression. "Elizabeth, I need you to do me a favor. Can I trust you?" His tone was pleading. I nodded, not sure what to say. "You can't tell anyone about this, okay?"

"But" I began, completely confused and overwhelmed by what had just happened.

"I will explain later." He interrupted. "Just promise me you won't tell anyone what happened okay? If anyone asks, you tripped walking in the parking lot and scraped your elbow." He pointed to my right elbow, which I suddenly noticed had a bloody scrape on it. It stung a little too, but I had been too distracted to realize. His voice was urgent, and he seemed afraid. But of what? The whole thing didn't make any sense.

"Okay." Was all I could manage to say, but there were a thousand things spinning through my head. I heard a car approaching from behind and turned. Ben was pulling up next to us in their Hummer, and he threw open the passenger door. Luke quickly stepped up into the hummer and turned towards me with the door still open.

"Thank you." Our eyes locked for a second and his looked terrified. I thought I heard his voice inside my head: *"Please. Don't tell anyone."* It must have been my mind playing tricks on me. He closed the door and Ben drove off quickly, leaving me standing confused, and soaking wet in the middle of the street. The rain started to pour down as I walked slowly back to my Tahoe. I noticed the skid marks from my tires were about twenty feet long and ended where my car had come to a rest.

I stepped back up into my Tahoe and looked around. There was no sign of anyone, which seemed strange considering the loud gunshot. Perhaps with the rain people had mistaken the noise for thunder. A car appeared in my rear-view mirror, approaching slowly, so I put my car back in drive and pushed on the gas pedal.

My heart was still racing, and my hands had just stopped shaking as I pulled up to Alex's school. I was surprised to see other parents still waiting. Looking at the clock, I noticed that only fifteen minutes had passed since walking out of Sassenburg's class. Fifteen minutes that had sent me into a state of adrenaline overload and disbelief.

Could I have imagined the voice inside my head as Luke looked at me that last time? It had seemed calm and reassuring, yet distinctly foreign at the same time. Why had Luke seemed so afraid? After what he had just been through, there is no way he could see me as a threat. Maybe he was worried I would tell other people about him. But what would I tell them? I had a crush on the new kid, and he was some kind of superhero or something? That would go over well. Then I could be even more of an outcast at school.

I heard a bell chime inside the school and a couple minutes later Alex was walking from the front of the school towards me. Reaching over as he approached, I pulled open his door from the inside. The rain had slowed to a light sprinkle. He climbed in and set his backpack on the floor before clicking on his seatbelt. "How was school?" I asked, trying to sound normal.

"It was okay." He turned to look at me with his probing blue eyes. "What happened to you Izzie? You're all wet." His forehead crinkled with curiosity.

"Well, it was pouring when my school got out, so I got drenched walking to my car." I lied.

"Oh." He sounded satisfied. "It's not pouring now Izzie, it's just raining a little bit." We drove home, and I was so consumed with what had just happened that I didn't even think to say a word to him. Even though I didn't know why, I had promised Luke not to say anything about what happened, and I intended to keep my word.

Once we were home, I helped Alex with his homework, thinking that if I stayed busy it would help to calm my nerves. Alex must have noticed that I was distracted because as we finished up his last math problem, he looked up at me. "Izzie, are you sure you're okay?" He sounded concerned.

"Yeah, of course. I just have a lot on my mind." This didn't seem to satisfy his young curiosity.

"What's on your mind Izzie?" I let out a deep breath as I tried to think of something that would end the probing.

"Well… I'm just stressed out because I have a big English project coming up and it is going to take up a lot of time."

"Oh… well don't worry Izzie. I'll help you with your project. You'll be just fine." He smiled reassuringly at me and flashed his dimples.

I couldn't help but smile. "Really? Well then, I don't know what I was stressing about. If you help me then I am sure everything will be just perfect." I touched his cheek as I finished talking and his smile broadened. Obviously, he hadn't caught my sarcasm.

"Do you know what's on my mind Izzie?" He inquired, getting an innocent look on his face.

"Let me guess… food."

"Yep." He smiled again.

"Okay, how about you put all your homework away and watch some cartoons while I make something?"

"Sounds good to me." He answered as I stood and made my way into the kitchen. My father came down while I was finishing up with dinner, and we ate in near silence. Alex and my father spoke briefly, and he asked me about my day, but that was all.

My father offered to wash up again, so I went into the living room to work on my homework. My elbow stung when it touched my notebook, and I remembered the scrape. Pulling my sleeve up, I examined the wound. The abrasion went through the skin but was only about an inch in diameter. The blood was already dry, so I decided to go upstairs and wash it off.

After cleaning out the scrape I applied some antibiotic ointment. It felt cold as I rubbed it on, but I hardly noticed. My mind kept going back to the incident from earlier. Thinking more about it was making me feel restless, so I decided to do something I had not done in a long while. Grabbing the dusty box from the closet in my room, I pulled out my black and white Asic's running shoes. I noticed that they were still in near perfect condition. As far as I could remember, I had only used them a couple times before the accident.

I changed into my workout clothes and put the shoes on. When Mom was still around, I had been a pretty decent soccer player, and I loved to run. It wasn't that there was anything fun or glamorous about running, but something about the changing scenery, and the feel of the ground moving under your feet was just relaxing to me.

As a young child my mom had mentioned to me several times how she'd always wanted to play soccer in high school, but never actually did it. After playing in a junior league when I was nine, I had become hooked. At first, I had hated all the running and only loved the game, but over time the necessary evil became easier, and I grew to like it.

My dad was in the front yard, trimming some of the bushes with large black metal shears. He stopped when he saw me in my workout clothes. "Are you feeling okay Liz?"

"Yeah of course. Just felt like going for a run, I'll be back in a few, okay?" My father eyed me with obvious concern before his expression eventually relaxed.

"Okay. Just don't go too far, the sun's almost down and I don't want you running alone after dark. It's too dangerous."

I started with a slow jog, making sure that all my muscles were working properly. After a minute I picked up the pace. Everything seemed to be fine, except I could tell my cardio needed improvement after not running for so long. Before the accident I had played soccer three seasons out of the year and done personal defense training with a private tutor once a week for the previous five years. My father had insisted that "A pretty girl like you needs to be able to defend herself." Since the accident though, I hadn't done anything even remotely close to exercise.

Making my way down the street, I ran past a lot of large houses. The greenery was quite lush near the river and most of the homes had long driveways. I neared the end of my street and noticed that the last house on the right had a silver hummer parked in the open garage. That house had been vacant since we had moved here, and I only knew of one person who had a silver hummer. I ran right in front of the house to get a closer look and slowed to a jog. The house was offset a little way from the street, and I saw Benjamin Bennett appear in the doorway from the house that led into the garage. I quickly looked away and kept running, speeding up a little in case he hadn't seen me yet.

So, Luke Bennett lived at the end of my street. I hoped that Ben hadn't seen me. The last thing I wanted was to look like I was spying on them after what had happened earlier today. Judging by the way Ben had come racing up in the hummer right after the incident; he must have seen what happened. I couldn't help but wonder if he was different too.

About a mile into my run, I noticed that my muscles were starting to tire. The sun had also just finished ducking behind the mountain, so I turned and headed back home. When I ran back by the Bennett's house the garage was closed. There were lights on inside the house, but you couldn't see anything through the closed plantation shutters on the windows.

By the time I walked in the front door it was completely dark. Alex asked where I had been, and after explaining to him why anyone would "want to run if they didn't have to" I took a quick shower. After finishing my homework Alex wanted to do a puzzle before bed, so I helped him with it. He fell right asleep after my father tucked him in, and I went to my room to try and do the same. *Try* being the key word.

I had gone for a run to clear my head of Luke Bennett and what had transpired today. Instead, I had stumbled on his house and thought about him the entire night. *Who is he*? I wondered to myself. Had my eyes been playing tricks on me? I went over the scenario again in my head: The fear as I noticed the Cadillac appear in front of me too late. The large man with the gun throwing me to the ground. The crunching sound his body made when Luke hit him and sent him flying through the air. The gunshot wound on Luke's head that seemed to be there one second, then gone the next. The unexplainable fear he seemed to have as he pled with me not to divulge what occurred. The voice in my head that seemed to have been coming from him.

None of it made any logical sense, but I knew I wasn't dreaming. Hours passed before my eyes finally gave up on staying open, and I slipped into sleep.

***

Luke sat for a long time, staring up at the faint stars as he swung gently on the wooden rocker bench on his back porch. He couldn't stop thinking about the look on Elizabeth's face as she had looked at him after the incident earlier in the street. Her stunning green eyes, perfectly framed by those long dark eyelashes, had seemed worried for him as she looked into his. He had grown accustomed to the startled and usually panicked looks that people gave him when they saw him do something a normal human being should not be able to do, but even after she had seen the wound vanish from his head, she had not looked afraid. *Elizabeth Scott,* he thought to himself, *the girl from my dreams.*

He had first met her the day before. Knowing that he had openly stared at her for some time should have bothered him, but he had been in shock from seeing her in person for the first time. For the last few months, she had been in his dreams every night, but he hadn't known if she was even real until that moment. He at first thought that the dreams were random. Over time however, as they kept on re-occurring with the same dark-haired girl, he realized that they must be foretellings. That was the name his mother had given his dreams. The ones in which he saw the future.

The dreams had been almost the same every time and had always come with distinct impressions. The setting had changed back and forth from time to time, between a forest village and a desert town, but Elizabeth Scott had been a constant. Of course, he hadn't known her name until yesterday, but he had memorized her face. Her dark hair that curled slightly flowing down over her shoulders, those piercing deep green eyes that he couldn't look away from, and perfect lips that always seemed to be half smiling when he saw her in the dreams. In real life she was just as beautiful but didn't always wear the half smile on her lips. Throughout all the dreams she had never spoken, but he always felt drawn to her. He always felt the strong impression that he needed to find her. That he needed to keep her safe, and that by so doing she would save him.

How she would save him he didn't know. The only real threats to him or his family were the tainted ones, who had been hunting the surviving members of the bloodline for centuries. The same tainted ones who had killed his father Nathan when he was only four. They were also responsible for the deaths of tens of thousands of innocent people over the years. Only the bloodline could challenge them, and so the tainted ones hunted Luke's kind, to keep the bloodline from growing strong enough to fight them. But Luke could not understand how an ordinary girl, even if she was beautiful, could save him.

For months he was unable to figure out why he had been dreaming of her or who she was. He had mused that perhaps she was also from the bloodline, but the birthmark had been missing from her neck, and he had seen no scar indicating that it had been removed. That possibility being ruled out, he had no idea why the light wanted him to keep her safe. "The light" is what his mom and Isaac used to refer to the unknown powers that be; the powers that had given the bloodline their abilities in the first place; Abilities that had repeatedly saved his life, and the lives of countless others.

He hadn't known what to say to her, and so at school had tried to avoid her. At least until he could figure out a little more about this girl that had consumed his sleep for the last few months. One thing was strange. After meeting her the day before, he had not dreamt about her at all last night. The dreams had stopped, which only confirmed that he had found the right girl. While he didn't know why he had to protect her, or how she could save him, he did know one thing. He was going to keep Elizabeth Scott safe.

CHAPTER III

I woke early, feeling refreshed. Despite falling asleep late the night before, my slumber had been free of dreams, and I actually felt excited to get out of bed. Getting dressed, I chose a yellow polo shirt with a blue thermal underneath and dark blue jeans. For some reason I had never really been a fan of faded jeans. I liked to wear mine new looking. It seemed strange to me that people would pay more money for jeans that were faded or had holes.

After finishing getting ready, I checked the mirror, making sure that nothing looked out of place. Luke had worn a blue sweater the day before, so he must not hate the color. Besides, it had always been my favorite, so as long as he didn't hate it, I would still wear it.

I had already finished making breakfast when I heard Alex's footsteps coming down the stairs. He must have smelled the French toast, because when he came into the kitchen, he already had a smile on his face. We talked a little over breakfast, and then I helped him get ready for the day. I was already walking out the door when my father pulled into the driveway.

He drove a newer Dodge Charger, charcoal in color. Using some of the leftover money from the Life Insurance, he had purchased it in Eugene a few months after we moved to Harrisburg. I liked the car because it was a lot faster than the Tahoe. He had let me drive it once, when he first bought it, and even then, he only let me go around the block once with him in the passenger seat. I had asked him a couple of times after that to drive it again, but the answer was always no. "It's not safe enough for you." He said. It's funny how hypocritical adults can be at times. It wasn't "safe" enough for me, but he could drive it as much as he pleased, and it was somehow safe for him? I guess if you are an old person then that kind of logic makes sense.

After telling him there were French toasts waiting for him in the kitchen, I said farewell and made my way to school. I was about five minutes earlier than normal, and there was still fifteen minutes left before first period started. The parking lot was nearly empty, but I parked next to where Luke and Ben had been the day before.

Making my way to first period, I was surprised that Nikki wasn't waiting in front of the classroom. I guess being an extra five minutes earlier at school made a huge difference. I waited… and waited. Students started to trickle in more through the front corridor. When Nikki finally appeared, there were only a couple minutes left before class.

"Okay, so I think I totally jinxed myself." She began dramatically. "I never should have made fun of you for being late because I like, slept right through my alarm this morning." Her purple headband had black lines that tied in her earrings, which were silver with large black stones in them. A black blouse with a ribbon around the middle and tight black jeans finished off her outfit. Thinking back, I couldn't remember a time when Nikki hadn't matched perfectly.

We made our way into class, and I told Nikki about how Luke and I had been assigned as partners for our Literature project. "Well, that is totally awesome." had been her enthusiastic response. I made sure not to mention anything about the incident. While I liked and trusted Nikki, I also knew that she liked to talk. Besides, I had given my word to Luke.

Physics went by slowly, with Mr. Anderson lecturing the entire time. When the bell finally rang, I was relieved. Greg met us in front of government as usual, and after he and Nikki were done displaying too much public affection… again… we went into class. Expecting to see Luke sitting in his same seat, I was instantly disappointed when he wasn't there. We took our seats and Nikki turned towards me.

"Looks like pretty boy is sick." She pouted a little as she spoke. "Or maybe he's just playing hookie. Either way, I guess you won't have anyone to stare at during lunch today."

I just shook my head slowly back at her. Was it that obvious? I thought that I only glanced at him from time to time. Maybe I was staring. I made a mental note not to stare at him too obviously in the future. After seeing what I had the day before, I doubted that Luke was sick.

The bell sounded, and I was surprised when the door opened with the last chime. Luke Bennett walked into the room and took his seat. He looked over at me as he sat, and our eyes locked. Wearing a dark gray sweater and blue jeans made his eyes look especially blue. I felt like I should look away but didn't want to. So, I didn't. A few seconds went by, and his face looked calm as he looked at me. I couldn't help but smile. His lips curved up on the edges when I smiled, and I had to look away. My heart was pounding in my chest. I felt exhilarated.

What was I thinking? I don't really know anything about this guy. But something about the way he looked at me made me feel so… alive. I glanced back over at him and saw that he was still looking at me, but he quickly looked away. I couldn't help smiling again. Had he really just been staring at me? I turned excitedly towards Nikki, but she was whispering back and forth with Greg, not paying attention to anything else.

So, Luke was acting less shy, and he definitely wasn't gay. The one question to which I still had no clue was… exactly what was he? Well, I guess I had a thousand questions spinning through my head, but that one seemed to be the most pressing. He must be human… right? The blood coming from his temple had been real enough. But the wound had vanished too quickly. Mr. Melvin continued speaking for the rest of the period, but I didn't hear a word he said. There were too many things on my mind. As the end of class neared, I realized that I had to do something. I needed to know what had happened yesterday, and there was only one person who could tell me that, so I made up my mind. At lunch I would ask Luke what had happened the day before.

After the bell rang, I made my way to third period, parting with Greg and Nikki on the way. I was grateful when Mrs. Thomas had a plethora of quizzes for me to grade. It made the hour go by much faster and gave me something to keep my mind off of Luke. I was surprised when the bell came and made my way towards the cafeteria.

After grabbing my usual turkey sandwich from the deli counter, I made my way to my normal table. Ben waved at me from a couple tables over, but there was still no sign of Luke. He appeared a minute later carrying a couple platefuls of food. As he sat down, he pushed one of the plates over to Ben. Ben said something, and they both laughed. I realized that I was staring and looked away.

Nikki came walking up a few seconds later, holding a couple of protein bars. "So, I totally don't like these things, but when I got on the scale this morning, I weighed like a hundred and twenty pounds. Can you believe that? A hundred and twenty? I'm normally one fifteen!" She sounded incredulous and looked panicked. "So, I guess it's time for another lame diet." She looked apprehensively at her protein bar as she opened it, taking a seat across from me.

"Don't be ridiculous Nikki, you look great." I tried to sound reassuring, but it was only halfhearted. Nikki would go through these types of breakdowns every few weeks. She weighed herself religiously, and whenever there was any fluctuation at all in her scale, she would freak out. This was always followed by a few days of eating nothing but protein shakes or protein bars, accompanied by regularly complaining about how hungry she was. The funny thing about her ridiculousness was that I never noticed any difference in her physique. She always looked perfect, with nothing out of order. Maybe it was because she fretted so much over her appearance.

"Thanks Liz. But I really just wish that I could look good without trying. You know… like you do." She took a bite of her protein bar as she finished.

"Yeah… right." I couldn't understand why she was always saying things like that. Nothing about me seemed especially ugly, but I always just felt… plain. Not being a big fan of most make-up, I usually just wore mascara. I never took the time to look all put together like Nikki did.

Nikki and I talked for a few minutes, and then Greg appeared carrying two plates of food. I knew that his would both be for himself. "Hey Liz." He nodded at me as he took a seat next to Nikki. "Ok baby, I know you are going through another freak out phase about your weight, but I need you to help me out with some of these fries." He pushed one of his plates closer to her, and she eyed it longingly.

Greg and Nikki chatted idly as they ate, and I finished my sandwich in silence. Glancing at Luke from time to time, I thought about what to say, but couldn't think of how to begin. What would I say to him? *So... are you a superhero, or some kind of radioactive freak?* What do you say to someone who has superhuman abilities? I finished my food, but still didn't know how to start the conversation.

Finally working up the courage, I decided to just wing it and stood up. Nikki looked at me quizzically, raising her eyebrows. I hardly noticed her though. As I walked the thirty or so feet to Luke and Ben's table, I noticed that they were both looking at me. I stopped in front of their table, realizing that I still hadn't decided what to say. A couple of long seconds went by, and then Ben and Luke simultaneously said "Hi." They weren't quite in unison, but it was pretty close.

"We need to talk." I managed, looking directly at Luke.

"Okay" he replied calmly, but he looked a little nervous "does it have to be now? Or can we talk after fourth period?" He leaned forward and pressed his hands together as he spoke.

"Sure... after fourth period." I paused for a moment, feeling awkward. Why didn't he want to talk now? "I guess I'll see you later then." I turned and walked back towards my table, feeling their eyes boring holes through the back of my head. *I guess I'll see you later then?* What an idiot. Why couldn't I seem to talk straight around this guy? He made me feel like such a juvenile. I noticed some of the girls at another table eyeing me. Did they look jealous? Or maybe it was just annoyed. Either way they didn't seem happy to see me talking to Luke.

I recognized one of the girls. Theresa was her name. I only remembered because Greg mentioned that she had dated half of the football team. She was a pretty girl with light brown hair that went almost to her shoulders, but I thought she wore way too much makeup. The other girls at the table were all juniors. Some of them were vaguely familiar. They must have been the same girls I always saw following her around in the hallways like she was some kind of celebrity. Most of the girls who followed her were either anorexic looking, or overweight. It seemed like she treated the overweight girls more like servants than friends, but they just took it. I couldn't understand why. Maybe they thought she would help them get a boyfriend or something since she had a new one every other week.

I got back to my table and Greg and Nikki were both staring at me. "So…" Nikki began as I took my seat "that was unexpected."

"I thought you were shy Liz?" Greg looked sideways at me, and I wasn't sure if he meant it as a question or a statement.

"No. I'm not shy… I just don't care to talk to most people is all." I hoped that my voice didn't give away the fact that I had just made a complete fool of myself.

"Obviously Luke is not most people then eh?" Nikki teased with a smile. "Well, I think that was totally awesome how you just walked right up to him. How did it go? You weren't over there for very long."

"Well… it could have gone worse… I suppose. He said that he wanted to talk after school. Probably just doesn't want his little brother around when we get acquainted." I remembered that they were both completely oblivious to the robbery, so I threw in the last part to make the whole situation seem less awkward.

Nikki smiled again "Well you go girl. I'm sure he'll be putty in your hands." She put Greg's last french fry in her mouth as she finished.

"Whatever you say Nikki. I'm just looking to be friends though. That's all." It felt like a lie the second the statement left my lips. That was all I wanted right? Sure, I had feelings for him, but I wasn't looking for anything more… Was I? I glanced over at him again without thinking and saw that he was smiling. Ben leaned towards him saying something.

Suddenly I noticed Theresa and another skinny dark-haired girl walking towards his table. They both sat down across from Luke and started talking. *What is that tramp doing talking to him?* I thought to myself. They stayed there talking for a few minutes, with Luke and Ben laughing every so often. Ben and Theresa seemed to be doing most of the talking, but she was only looking at Luke. I felt a strange urge to walk over there and punch Theresa in the face. That probably wouldn't go well though. I noticed her touching her hair and twirling it around one of her fingers as she spoke.

"Look at that hoochy." I was surprised to hear Nikki say suddenly. "He hasn't been here a week and already she's got her sights set on him. Some girls have no class." She shook her head as she finished speaking and looked at me. "Don't worry Liz, even if he does have a thing for airheads, it's not like she's competition for you."

I sat in silence, trying not to be too obvious as I watched them out of the corner of my eye. Theresa and the other girl continued talking to them until the bell finally rang. I was relieved when they stood, and Theresa had to walk the opposite direction from Luke to go to her next class.

When I took my seat in fourth period there was no sign of Luke. He seemed to be developing a talent for either being in class early or showing up as the bell rang. It was no surprise this time when he walked through the door as the bell sounded. At least some things about him were beginning to be more predictable. If only I had answers to all of my questions.

He sat down and nodded at me, so I nodded back. Mr. Sassenburg lectured for the entire hour, except for the few times that he called on students to read. My anxiety was slowly building throughout the class, and when the bell tone came, I was excited to talk to Luke. He stood quickly and walked out of the classroom. Where was he going? I followed him out slowly, thinking that he had forgotten about his agreement to speak to me. Once I stepped outside though, I saw him standing against the wall waiting for me.

As I approached him, he turned towards the parking lot and started walking, so I fell along beside him. "Sassenburg is a real character huh?" he said after a few seconds.

"Oh yeah. He loves using big words and acting dramatic whenever he quotes anything." I replied. "I think he was in theatre or something in high school and college."

"Well, that explains his behavior. At least it makes the class go by faster."

"Yeah." I paused for a moment "So I saw you've met Theresa." I tried to sound as nonchalant as possible, hoping he didn't hear the disdain I had for her in my voice.

"Theresa?" He glanced at me with an inquisitive look.

"The girl you were talking to at lunch."

"Oh." He dragged the word out, realizing who I was talking about. "She was the overly forward, annoying one with the shorter hair?"

I laughed without thinking. "Yeah, that's Theresa."

"Sorry, I kind of tuned her out after the first few seconds. She talked about herself a lot and looked a little too… promiscuous? Maybe overly flirtatious would be a kinder way of putting it." He turned and grinned at me as he finished speaking.

"Well, you must be a good judge of people, because she definitely gets around." I was surprised by how relieved I felt that he didn't like her. He didn't seem like the shallow type at all, so I suppose I shouldn't have been surprised. Theresa was a little over the top after all.

We walked in silence again for a second while I thought of what to say next. I wasn't big for small talk, so I decided to get to the point. "Just so you know, your secret is safe with me. I didn't tell anyone."

"What are you talking about?" Luke's puzzled look was so convincing. I thought for a split second that perhaps I had only dreamt about what happened. No… I knew what I had seen, and I wasn't about to pretend that I hadn't.

"I think you know." He looked at me again confused, but this time was less convincing. So, he wasn't a very good liar. "I'll give you a hint. It has to do with you saving me from those robbers yesterday."

I could tell that I had his full attention now, but a group of students were approaching, so I waited for them to pass before continuing. "How about this Luke, I will tell you what I know, and then you can tell me what is going on?"

"Okay… I will do my best." He answered hesitantly.

"I know that somehow you covered a couple hundred yards in a matter of seconds. I know that you threw that big guy around like he was a rag doll. I know that you were shot in the head. By the way… I am sorry about that." I paused and turned to look him in the eye. His eyes were thoughtful as they watched me, and his head was nodding slightly as I spoke. I continued "I know that your head was bleeding one second, then fine the next. And I know that there is a lot more to you than just being a normal teenager who moved here from Colorado."

He stopped walking as I finished and turned to look directly at me. His eyes were locked on my face, and he seemed to be struggling with something in his head. A few seconds went by. He still hadn't spoken. I was starting to feel a little uncomfortable.

"Okay listen." I decided to break the awkward silence "I can tell that you don't want anyone else to know about you, and I can think of a million reasons why that might be. That being said… I would totally understand if you didn't want to tell me whatever it is you are hiding." He seemed to relax a little as I said this. "But" I added "you did tell me that you would explain."

"Well, you see…" he looked hesitant again as he spoke, like he was looking for somewhere to run, but instead was forced to talk to me. "It's not that I don't want to explain, it's just that I really can't tell you certain things. So, for now all I can tell you is this. I saw the Cadillac cut in front of you on the street, and the one man get out with a gun. It looked like he was going to shoot you, so I had to help out. Luckily the two of them never saw me coming." The look on his face told me he was hoping I wouldn't ask any more questions.

"All right Luke." I had an idea come to me. "First off, I want to say thank you for saving me." He still looked nervous as I spoke. "Secondly, I can understand that you don't know me that well, so how about I make you a deal?"

"I'm listening." He replied slowly, looking at me suspiciously.

"I know that you don't know me very well, so why don't we fix that first. Then, once you get to know me, you can decide when you feel comfortable telling me more. Even though I know you can trust me, there is no way for you to know that yet. So, for now I will leave the subject alone until you feel more comfortable. Does that sound fair?"

A look of relief swept across his face as I finished speaking. "That sounds more than fair." His expression changed a little and he smiled at me. "Thank you for understanding."

Understanding? Was he kidding? I was more confused than I had ever been, but I could tell he didn't want to tell me anything more, so I would respect that. "I don't understand." I managed to say calmly. "But I don't need to understand to be your friend." I smiled back at him.

A long moment passed with us looking at each other. I was starting to drown in his eyes because I was so content just staring at him, but then he surprised me. "Are you real?" he mumbled quietly. I was taken aback and didn't know what to say. I felt my heart pounding again and a strange warm feeling came over me.

"Yes. Of course." The surprised look he got when I answered made me realize that he must not have meant to say that out loud. He looked away suddenly and started walking again. Were his cheeks reddening a little? I followed him, but it was suddenly awkward, so I thought of something to change the subject. "So, about this project for Sassenburg's class, have you decided what piece you wanted to use for your monologue?"

"No, not yet. I was thinking I would figure that out though. If he wants us to go in two weeks, we should probably get started. Have you decided yet?" He looked grateful for the change of subject.

We talked about the project until we reached the parking lot where Ben was waiting by their hummer. Luke seemed completely normal as we talked. Walking on his left side I was able to look at the scar on his neck more closely. The edge of the scar was so perfectly circular it looked surgical. I would have to ask him about it later, but I felt I had done enough interrogating for one day.

Ben looked at Luke as we approached, and I noticed Luke shake his head slightly. After nodding, Ben turned towards me and smiled broadly. "Elizabeth Scott. As always, it's a pleasure to see you again." He bowed his head slightly as he spoke.

"Likewise, how was class?"

"It was painfully boring as usual, thank you for asking." Something about his over-the-top enthusiasm seemed somehow... genuine. Every time I talked to him, he sounded completely sincere, which was strange because he was so exaggeratingly complimentary when he spoke. No one could really be that nice all of the time... could they? I decided that there was definitely something different about Ben too, even if I couldn't quite put my finger on it. For now, they would just have to remain mysterious.

"Speaking of class Ben, you are a sophomore, right?" I asked.

"Yes, I am. Why?" he stood up taller as he spoke, and almost sounded a little bit defensive.

"Well, I was just wondering why you don't go to fifth or sixth period?"

"That's because I am in the work study program. I assist my mother with her consulting business, so I get two elective credits for that."

"Oh..." I had forgotten about the work study program at our high school. "I thought that you had to be a junior or senior to be in that?"

"No. You just have to be at least fifteen is all." His tone became more sarcastic as he continued. "And as much as I just absolutely love every minute of every single one of my boring classes, I would much rather make some extra cash helping my mom out."

An older looking jeep drove by, and I noticed that about half of the cars were already missing from the parking lot. I glanced at my watch and realized that it had already been fifteen minutes since class got out. I had better get Alex. "Well, it was good talking to you two." I said looking first at Ben, then Luke. "I have to go pick up my little brother from school, so I guess I will see you tomorrow."

"Oh, you have a little brother. How old is he?" Luke asked curiously.

"He's five. He is in kindergarten, so he gets out a few hours before the rest of the kids." I quickly explained, starting to turn towards my car. I was only parked a few spaces down from them in the same row.

"All right, we'll see you tomorrow." Luke said almost at the same time as Ben chimed in.

"See ya Liz." Ben smiled again, and I made my way to my car. As I was pulling out of the parking lot, I could see them both still standing next to their hummer, looking at me. I waved as I drove by. They both waved back. I sighed, driving away, relieved that I seemed to be getting along well with both of them. Ben had been cordial from the time we met, but I had been a little concerned over Luke with him acting so strange those first couple days.

I was not excited about the fact that I didn't know anything more about Luke then I had the day before. He really hadn't told me anything about himself, except that he was not very open with his deepest secrets. Would I be any different though if I had some kind of powers? I would probably be scared to death of telling anyone, for fear I would end up being some kind of lab rat for the government or something.

What a strange situation I found myself in. I had never believed in anything mystical or paranormal. Just like my father, who was a pessimistic realist, I only believed things that I could understand logically, and yet I found myself facing a situation that could not be explained by logic. Or at least if it could be, I had yet to discover that explanation. So for now I would stick to my plan, I would befriend Luke and hope to eventually learn his secret. What other choice did I have? I would not chase him away. That much I was sure of. Because if he left now I would spend the rest of my life confused and unsatisfied, wondering who he really was.

I had just come to a stop in front of Alex's school when he appeared. We chatted a little on the way home, and I did my best to listen to everything he said. To say I was distracted though would have been an understatement.

After dinner I decided to go running. "Just make sure you're back by dark." My father had called out to me as the front door closed behind me. My legs felt sore, and a couple hundred yards into my run they were already burning. When I ran by Luke's house, I was disappointed to see the garage and all of the blinds on the windows closed. I only went another half mile past their house, then I decided to turn around and head back home. Again, there was no sign of life by Luke's house, and by the time I finished the last stretch back to my house my legs felt like they were on fire. It didn't help that the last couple hundred feet were uphill. I had almost forgotten how awful running is when you are out of shape.

For some reason I was annoyed that I hadn't been able to see anyone at Luke's house. Maybe his family had gone into the city or something for dinner. Had I only gone for a run because I was hoping to see Luke? I thought long on that question as I was stretching. The day before I had realized how out of shape I was, so I decided to tell myself that I was only running to get back into shape. Luke Bennett had nothing to do with it. Did he?

The next day at school I met Nikki in front of Physics and told her about my conversation with Luke the day before. Of course, I left out most of the conversation, but she didn't know that. She laughed when I told her about Theresa.

"He really called her promiscuous?" Nikki exclaimed. "I didn't think anyone used those kinds of words, at least not in conversation. Maybe like… if you're writing an essay or something. Now that is totally hilarious. I like him already." She was grinning and sounded excited for me.

Luke was already seated when we walked into Mr. Melvin's class. He waved at me and smiled when our eyes met, so I smiled back. He was wearing a black polo shirt with blue stripes, and his eyes looked extra blue today. I suppose they always did though.

Lunch finally came, and I was surprised when Ben approached me as I sat at my usual table. He grinned as he got closer. "You don't care if we join you guys today do you?" he asked.

"Of course not, have a seat." Ben turned and motioned for Luke to join him before sitting. Luke stood and started making his way over to our table.

"Okay so I have another one for you." Ben sounded excited, but I had no idea what he was talking about.

"Okay?" I replied hesitantly, hoping he would explain.

"Why is there a gate around cemeteries?" He smiled in anticipation.

"I don't know."

"Because people are dying to get in." He smacked the table with his hand as he finished, and I couldn't help but laugh. Laughing just came easier when he was around. Even if the jokes were a little corny, the way he got so into them made it entertaining.

Luke reached us as I finished laughing and he sat down next to Ben. "Hey Elizabeth." I liked the sound of my name coming from his lips and smiled involuntarily.

"Hi Luke." Our eyes locked again. "You know, you really can call me Liz?" I felt my cheeks warm a little and hoped that I wasn't blushing. What was it about this guy that made me feel so... different? I couldn't remember ever feeling like this around anyone before, and I didn't even know anything about him.

"Oh okay. Do you have a preference though?"

"Not really, most people call me Liz, but you can call me whatever you want." I emphasized the 'you' slightly. He nodded, and we all ate in silence for a couple minutes until Nikki and Greg showed up.

"I see we have company." Nikki smiled enthusiastically as she sat down next to me. Her dark hair was pulled back into a ponytail, and she was wearing large black square earrings with a black V-neck sweater. Greg took a seat on the other side of her. "It's so nice to see you again Ben, but I don't believe I've met you yet" she turned towards Luke "It is Luke, right?"

"Yeah, Luke Bennett" he held his hand out to her and she shook it lightly. "And you are?" he paused expectantly waiting for her to answer.

"I am Nicole Calata, Liz's best friend. But everyone who's anyone just calls me Nikki." She smiled at him, then turned and put her arm around Greg. "And this is my boyfriend, Greg Dunn. He is like, the football guy at our school. But I mainly like him for other reasons." She smiled mischievously at him as she finished.

Greg smiled back at Nikki, then turned and looked at Luke. "I'm actually the quarterback, but to a woman I guess that's the same thing as 'the football guy'. He grinned sideways at Nikki. "So, Ben said that you two both played football where you came from?"

"Yeah." Luke responded. "But I wasn't very good; Ben was the superstar before we had to move. He started as a sophomore at safety and wide receiver, which is impressive considering we came from a big school." He nodded towards Ben as he spoke.

"Nice. Here in Harrisburg, you just have to have a pulse and we'll start you. Our team only has twenty-two players, and two of them only play kicker. Another four of our players are so small and slow that we can't really give them much playing time without losing. Sometimes if we are up by more than twenty or so our coach will put them in the game though."

"Wow. Only twenty-two players? I think our freshman team had thirty kids on it, and our varsity had over forty. A lot of them were special teams or second string, but we had a pretty solid team. Luke likes to exaggerate though when he talks about my football skills." Ben elbowed Luke in the ribs lightly, and they both grinned.

"Well Ben, I'm not sure what you've got going on, but I talked to coach yesterday, and he said that you only have to be at practice five days before you are eligible to play so… if you wanted to practice with us you could probably play by Regionals next weekend. I am sure we could use you somewhere on the team if you're half as good as your brother says." Ben's blue eyes lit up as Greg said this and he glanced at Luke questioningly. Luke nodded his head slightly.

"Really?" Ben said after Luke nodded. "In Colorado you had to play in at least two regular season games in order to be eligible for the postseason. I had assumed it would be the same here. What time is practice?"

"Well, some of the seniors meet just before fifth period starts to go over video and work on some plays, but officially it starts fifteen minutes after school lets out." Greg looked Ben over for a second. "I think we should have some pads that will fit you."

"That would be awesome." Ben sounded genuinely excited. Then his face got a little more somber. "I'll have to check with my mom first though, just to make sure she's cool with it."

"Sounds good man. As long as you make practice by Monday you would be eligible to play next Friday for Regionals." Greg was nodding his head slightly as he spoke. He turned to Luke. "What about you man? You down for some football too?"

"I would, but I'm not very good. Ben got all of the talent in the family. Thanks anyway though." Luke was a pretty good liar I had to admit. Judging by how fast he had run to save me, I had no doubt he would be good at football, but he actually sounded sincere as he talked. Considering his abilities, maybe he was simply afraid of attracting attention.

"All right man" Greg shrugged his shoulders "But if you change your mind just let me know. Like I said, it doesn't take much talent to make our team."

"Okay guys" Nikki jumped into the conversation "Are we seriously going to talk about football all day? Cause that is like, totally boring. Let's not forget there are two ladies here who don't give a crap about football."

"Sorry baby. Just had to handle some man business, that's all." Greg looked at her sheepishly and shrugged.

While I didn't care much for football, I was curious to see how Ben would play if he did end up on the football team. Would he be as fast as Luke? Maybe he didn't have the same abilities as his older brother, so he wasn't worried about drawing attention to himself. It did seem strange that he had looked to Luke before answering Greg about playing football. If I didn't know better I would say he seemed to be looking for permission.

"So, I think you guys should all come to the bonfire on Saturday." Nikki turned to look at Luke and Ben as she broke the short silence.

"What bonfire?" Ben asked.

"It's a tradition that we have a bonfire on the Saturday after every football game." Greg explained. "We all meet at the park by the river and hang out. Some people barbeque, and there's always music and games."

"It's not just for football people though." Nikki added. "Everyone from the High School is invited, so you guys should totally come." She turned to look at me. "Liz, are you coming?"

"I don't know…" I began. Nikki had invited me to go to the bonfire with them every week since I had moved here, but I wasn't a big fan. The one time I had gone a couple months before had been boring. Nikki and Greg had spent half of the time making out, and as much as I just loved being a third wheel, it wasn't exactly my idea of fun.

"Well, if Liz is going then I'll be there." Ben said suddenly, grinning at me.

"Yeah, me too." added Luke with a smile.

Nikki smirked at me and tapped me with her elbow. "So, what do you say Liz? Are you coming?"

"Well, I don't want Ben and Luke to miss out on the fun so… sure, I'll come." The thought of spending more time with Luke was more than enough to persuade me, but I didn't want to sound too desperate.

Ben and Greg started talking about football again, and I tuned the conversation out while I finished eating my sandwich. Luke said a word or two here and there but didn't seem super interested in what they were discussing either. I did catch him looking at me a few times though in between bites, which didn't bother me at all. The bell rang and Luke walked with Ben away from where our next class was. He made it to class about a minute after me though, so he must not have walked too far with his brother.

Most of Mr. Sassenburg's class was spent reading from our text and writing a short essay. Shakespeare wasn't my favorite, but I had to admit that the man knew how to make some interesting dramas. Luke and I didn't speak at all, but then again no one ever really talked in Sassenburg's class.

After fourth period ended, I was surprised when Luke waited for me again in front of the classroom. "So, I've noticed that no one ever says a word in his class unless they are talking to him. Why is that?" He asked as I stepped up beside him.

We started walking as I answered. "Well, the kid who sits behind you, Jack, was made an example of on the first day of class this year, and ever since then no one has even thought about speaking out of turn.

"So, what happened with Jack? He's the kid with the long shaggy red hair, right?"

"Yeah, well the first day Mr. Sassenburg was going over the syllabus, and Jack was talking to a couple of the other kids. Mr. Sassenburg gave him the look, but Jack decided that he wanted to press the issue, so he kept carrying on and laughing while Mr. Sassenburg was talking. Mr. Sassenburg politely stated that no one else was to talk while he was talking, but Jack still ignored him. Then Mr. Sassenburg suddenly stopped talking and set his book down. He took off the jacket he was wearing and was clenching one of his fists. You know how he's got huge muscles and all from body building or whatever, so he's clenching his fists, and his veins look like they are gonna pop out of his arms." I clenched my fists as I talked to simulate what he had been doing. Luke seemed enthralled by what I was saying so I continued.

"Then he walks over to where Jack is and he puts one of his big hands on Jack's shoulder and leans over next to him. I didn't hear exactly what he said to him, but I did hear Jack say something smart and then Sassenburg started squeezing his shoulder and he raised his voice to a loud whisper and said 'Listen you little punk, I just moved schools and I have no problem moving again. If you think for one second that I won't pick you up by your neck and throw you out of my classroom you've got another thing coming. No one, not even a spoiled brat like you will get in the way of my teaching. Are we clear?' Jack looked like he was about to wet himself, and everyone else in the class was dead silent until the bell rang. Ever since then no one has really tried to talk much. Sometimes someone will say something, but when he gives them the look everyone quiets down and pays attention. It's actually quite impressive."

"Nice. I guess he is actually as into his teaching as he sounds like he is then. You don't see a whole lot of that from most teachers these days." I nodded as he spoke. "Although I did come from a large school, maybe things are just different in a small town like Harrisburg huh?" He turned and looked at me.

"Yeah, I think so. I have certainly never had a teacher like him. When I went to school in Portland half of the teachers looked like they were high on something most of the time, and few of them seemed to actually care about what they were teaching."

Luke looked forward again. It would have been silent were it not for the crunch of the leaves under our feet as we made our way toward the parking lot. The sky was overcast with broken clouds, typical for Harrisburg, and a light breeze kept me from being too warm in my brown thermal sweatshirt. Luke seemed thoughtful as we walked so, I didn't say anything. Finally, as we were nearing his hummer, he spoke again.

"So, this bonfire thing on Saturday, you said you are going right?" He glanced quickly at me but then kept looking forward. If I didn't know better, I would say he seemed a little nervous.

"Yeah, I said I would, didn't I? Just because you and Ben pressured me into it doesn't mean that I won't show up." I pointed my finger at him and then myself as I spoke. "I am a girl of my word."

"Well, I was wondering if… well if you didn't already have a ride or something if maybe… I could pick you up. I mean… Ben and I… we could pick you up. Unless you already had plans or were going to drive yourself?" He looked at me again as he finished. I could tell he was definitely nervous. Something about it just made him that much more adorable, and I smiled without thinking.

"No of course." I spouted. "I mean… no, I don't have plans otherwise, and of course I would love it if you and Ben wanted to pick me up." Obviously, Luke wasn't the only one who couldn't talk straight.

"Really?" The excitement on his face looked too real to be exaggerated.

"Really." I assured him.

"I mean… cool. Well what time should I pick you up at then?"

"Well, the Bonfire starts at six, but as Nikki would say, for the sake of being fashionably late, why don't you pick me up at six fifteen. Is that good for you?"

"Absolutely, that's perfect." I noticed that we had stopped walking a short distance from his hummer where Ben was waiting. "Well, I have to help my mom with some things in the city tomorrow for her work so… I guess I will see you Saturday."

"Oh, you won't be at school tomorrow?" I don't know why I felt suddenly disappointed. It was just one day.

"No, my mom needs my help, so I'm going to have to miss a day of school." It seemed like there was something else he wasn't telling me, but I didn't press the issue.

"That doesn't sound like fun. Well, I guess Saturday it is then." I would have to ask him later about exactly what kind of consulting his mom did that required his and Ben's help. After waving at him I turned towards my car, which was again only two spots down from his. Ben waved at me, so I waved back.

"Hello Liz" He said jovially as I walked past him, "And goodbye Liz."

"See ya later Ben." I smiled back at him. Reaching the door of my Tahoe, I saw Luke say something to Ben and he shouted "Awesome!" in response. Then he noticed me looking and looked down. I started my car and drove past them out of the parking lot.

The smile still hadn't left my lips when Alex got into the Tahoe a few minutes later at his school.

"What are you so happy for Izzie?" He had asked after putting on his seatbelt. His red Lightning McQueen shirt looked like it had something brown spilled on the front of it.

"Oh, nothing Alex, just had a good day at school." I wiped the smile off my face so that he wouldn't ask any more questions. "How was your day?" He went on at length to tell me about every little thing that they had done in class, including how the teacher had made them all s'mores. That he had spilled a little on himself explained the stain on his shirt. Hopefully it would come off in the wash. He looked so cute in that shirt. I had bought it for him on his fifth birthday a few weeks before. He had been obsessed with cars since he was a baby, and the movie Cars was his favorite. Alex had just finished talking when we pulled into the driveway at home.

The rest of the day seemed to crawl by. I helped Alex with his homework, and then did mine. Making dinner only took twenty minutes, and that's even with making the chicken casserole my father loved. That got me a big "Thanks Liz" from him, but the whole time we were eating it I only had Luke on my mind. Without realizing it I had stuffed myself at dinner, so going for a run was out of the question. Instead, I put on a movie and watched it with my father and Alex. By the time I crawled into bed it was only nine thirty, but it felt like Saturday was still ages away.

At least an hour went by before I finally fell asleep, and when dreams came, Luke was in them.

CHAPTER IV

I woke with a smile on my lips, until I realized that I had only been dreaming. The night I had dreamt about with Luke had seemed so real, his warm embrace so tangible. We had met at the bonfire and gone walking through the park hand in hand. I had been at first surprised when he suddenly wrapped his arms around me and leaned slowly towards me, but my surprise had quickly changed to excitement when our lips were about to touch. Then I woke up.

My disappointment with reality was intensified when I remembered that Luke had said he would not be at school today. Begrudgingly, I got dressed for the day. Selecting a brown long sleeve shirt and jeans, I didn't bother spending a lot of time with my hair.

Alex was excited when he came downstairs and smelled the fresh made pancakes with chocolate chips that I had cooked for him. "You're the best Izzie." He said while giving me a long hug. "You know I love chocolate… and pancakes." I met my dad at the front door as I was leaving and told him that his breakfast was on the table.

"Thanks Liz." was his quick reply as he picked up Alex to say good morning. I closed the door behind me on the way out and looked around.

The sky was dark and menacing, with clouds covering half of the sky to the west. They swirled ominously towards Harrisburg as I walked towards my Tahoe. The wind was almost nonexistent, and I thought it strange that it could be so calm with a storm like that just a couple miles away.

I eyed the clouds in my rear-view mirror as I drove to school. They seemed to be swirling faster as they got closer, and I thought about how glad I was that I hadn't washed my car the day before. The thought had crossed my mind, but I had decided against it in case it sprinkled later. Today it looked like we would be getting more than some scattered drizzle.

I parked next to the Bennett's hummer, excited at the prospect that perhaps Luke had decided to show up for school after all. Once the bell rang for second period without any sign of him, I realized that it must have been Ben who drove the Hummer to school. My premonition was confirmed when Ben approached me at Lunch.

"Liz Scott it is such a pleasure to see you again." He smiled as he took a seat across from me. He was wearing a baby blue sweater with khaki pants and it really brought the color in his eyes out. They were almost identical to his sweater, and something about them just seemed... warm.

"No Ben, the pleasure is mine." I replied with a smile.

"You are too kind." He sat down and un-wrapped his sandwich. Then his eyes looked behind me at something. "That rain is really coming down. Does it usually pour like this here in Harrisburg?"

I turned to see what he was looking at and noticed the rain falling hard in the courtyard outside the window. On my way to the cafeteria, I had smelled rain in the air, but at the time it hadn't started pouring yet. Now it looked like the clouds were trying to dump all their moisture at once. Fat drops created thousands of little splashes as they pelted the already soaked courtyard. A couple of younger students came running in out of the rain, and they both looked drenched.

"No, not usually. It does rain quite a bit, but storms like this with the darker clouds and heavy rain only happen a few times a year. Usually, it's the lighter gray clouds that come with a constant drizzle. Like the ones that we had on Tuesday." He nodded as I spoke. "What about where you came from, does it rain like this in Colorado?"

He pointed towards the window with his free hand as he spoke. "Not like this. We got a decent amount of rainfall, but it never came down in torrents like that. In the winters we got a lot of snow though."

"Huh. We hardly ever get snow here, usually just cold rain. It probably doesn't help that it hardly ever gets below forty during the day. Even during the coldest parts of winter, it only snows a little at night."

"Well, I guess I'll just have to get used to missing the snow then." He said with a grin. His smile reminded me of Luke. They both had the same full lips and perfectly straight teeth.

"So, Luke had to help your mom today with her work?" I asked casually.

"Yeah. She needed his help with one of her projects." He answered after he finished chewing.

I noticed that he didn't look at me as he spoke, and I thought that was strange. A minute or so went by in silence while we both ate, but he didn't say anything else about Luke or his mother, so I decided not to ask any more questions. I didn't want Ben telling his brother that I had been inquiring about him.

Nikki showed up a few minutes later, complaining about how Greg was sitting with the other football players since it was a game day today. She and Ben chatted a little bit for the rest of lunch, and I added in a few words here and there.

When the bell rang, I had to run to keep myself from getting soaked as I passed through the courtyard. Even still my hair was damp by the time I arrived at Sassenburg's class. Sitting through his lectures seemed more boring without Luke there, which was strange because his class used to be the most interesting.

I found my mind wandering as I thought about Luke. What was he doing to help his mom? What kind of work could she possibly do that required Ben and Luke's help? The ways that both of them were secretive about it made me wonder if perhaps she worked for the government in some capacity. I remembered that one of my father's friends from Portland had worked for the government, and he had always been tight lipped about exactly what it was that he did for them.

Suddenly a thought came to me. I had not even considered the possibility that perhaps Luke was himself some kind of government experiment. Maybe that was how Luke got his abilities and why it was that he said he could not tell me anything more about the incident. Here I was thinking that he was being secretive because he didn't want to become some kind of lab rat, when in actuality it may have been because he already was one.

The idea intrigued me, and I didn't even notice my mind wandering. I thought of Luke, lying on a gurney with all kinds of machines and tubes hooked up to his body. He was in a white room with a glass wall on one side for observation. A government scientist was standing over him with a clipboard while a couple others, all of whom wore white body suits, poked him with needles and drew blood samples from him. I cringed as I thought about the pain it must cause him.

"Ms. Scott, can you read the next passage please?" Mr. Sassenburg's voice brought me back to reality, and I realized that I had only been daydreaming. He was staring at me with one eyebrow raised. I realized that he must have said my name more than once.

"Yes, of course." I quickly found my place in the text and began reading. For the rest of class I tried not to think about Luke too much, but my newest epiphany had my mind racing with possibilities. I wonder if Ben could be part of some experiment too. It didn't seem too likely. So far, I hadn't really seen him do anything spectacular, and he was at school today while Luke was not. If there were some experiments going on, wouldn't they bring them both in at once? Or perhaps they would study them one at a time.

The bell rang, and I walked to my car. Puddles of water still dotted the parking lot, and I tried not to step in them as I walked. I also noticed that the clouds in the sky had moved on to the eastern horizon, and the sky above was clear blue. Ben's hummer was already gone from the space it had been parked in that morning.

After picking up Alex from school I decided that I would go for a run before dinner. The night before I hadn't had the chance. One of my old coaches had once said that it's not good to take more than one day off at a time when you're trying to get back in shape. Plus, I wanted to get out and run to clear my head. There was still so much about Luke Bennett that simply didn't make sense.

The leaves were all soaked, so they didn't crunch under my feet as they had the last time I ran. My legs were definitely less sore as well, and I welcomed both changes. As I neared the end of the street, I slowed a little to look at Luke's house as I passed. The garage door was again closed, with no signs of anyone being home.

I turned around after about a mile and made my way back home. There was too much water on the street to completely avoid it, but I did stay clear of the deeper puddles. Running with wet socks was not my idea of fun.

Most of the run I spent thinking about my new hypothesis. Could Luke be a test subject for some government experiment? The theory seemed to be getting more probable as I thought about it. He being the result of some kind of genetic mutation or government super drug might explain a lot. Like why his skin seemed so perfect, and his eyes so blue. More importantly it would clarify the cause of his superhuman speed and ability to heal. Perhaps the scar on his neck was from one of their operations on him.

When I got back home my father was awake and sitting in the front room with Alex. His dark hair was matted on one side and disheveled on the other. He looked like he had just crawled out of bed. Wearing a black tank top and black gym shorts, I guessed he would be working out before dinner.

"Hey, did you have a good run?" He looked up from the newspaper he was holding as he spoke.

"Yeah, it was still wet outside from all the rain, so I just did a couple miles." I answered as I slipped off my running shoes and made my way towards the stairs.

"Hey Liz." His voice stopped me, and I took a step back so I could see him around the wall by the stairs. "I'm glad you locked the door behind you when you left, and Alex told me you talked to him about getting me if he needed anything, but would you mind waking me up next time before you go?" He must have seen the frustration on my face, because then he added "I just would feel better if I was awake while you're gone, that's all."

"Sure Dad. I just wanted to let you sleep, but next time I will wake you up first." It's not like anything was going to happen to

Alex, but I knew that my father was paranoid, and arguing with him never seemed to do any good.

"Thanks Liz." He went back to reading the paper, so I took the opportunity to ascend the stairs. After a quick shower I decided to get my homework out of the way for the weekend. I still needed to decide on a topic for the big project in Sassenburg's class, but I decided to wait. Leaving that unfinished would be another thing I could talk to Luke about tomorrow night.

When I finished my homework the clock on the wall in my room said 5:15. I spent the better part of the next 24 hours trying to keep myself extremely busy, but even still the time seemed to creep by. I ran first thing in the morning on Saturday and spent the rest of the day playing with Alex and watching TV. Of course, eating was Alex's favorite thing to do, so I made him breakfast and lunch.

I was sitting at the dinner table with my father and Alex when I noticed that the time on the oven clock was five thirty. Realizing that I still hadn't mentioned anything about going to the bonfire at the park, I thought about how I would pose the question to my dad. No sooner had I decided what I was going to say than my father suddenly spoke.

"So, I was thinking I would take you guys to get Ice Cream tonight after dinner." He looked first at Alex, whose head perked up and he smiled. "What do you say Liz? Does Ice Cream sound good?" He turned to look at me, and I decided I had better ask the question now.

"Well actually dad… I was going to ask if you cared if I went to the bonfire tonight at the park. Nikki invited me to go, so I was going to meet up with her and a couple other friends there. Would that be okay?" I tried to make it sound casual. Something told me he would say no if I mentioned that the boy of my dreams, who I had a crush on, was picking me up.

"Oh really? No, I think that would be great Liz. You should go and hang out with your friends. No pretty teenage girl should be sitting at home with her family on a Saturday night. What time are you leaving?" He sounded genuinely excited for me, which was a surprise. I suppose I rarely did anything with friends since we had moved, so maybe he had been worried about me or something.

"Well, my friends are going to pick me up at like six fifteen, but I am not sure what time it goes until. The last time I went to a bonfire I left after a couple hours, but I think they usually last until at least ten or eleven o'clock."

"Okay, just try to be home by eleven then, I don't want to have to wait up too long for you." He turned to look at Alex again. "What do you say buddy, how about you and me hit the town tonight? We can get Ice Cream and maybe go to one of those toy shops down in Eugene."

"I do love Ice Cream dad," Alex replied excitedly. "And toys are okay too."

After finishing my food, I spent a few minutes getting ready to go. I picked out a dark blue long sleeve shirt and dark blue jeans. Parting my hair in the middle, I decided to curl the ends a little after I brushed it down. Next, I put on my favorite silver earrings, which consisted of three small stars that dangled from each ear.

Stars had been my favorite since I was a little girl. I could still remember when my mom had taken me to get my ears pierced at the mall for my fifth birthday. For the longest time I had wanted star earrings like one of the pairs that she had, so she had bought me a pair. They were just little studs shaped like stars, but I had spent so long looking at myself in the mirror as I admired the new earrings. The proud look on my mom's face as she had smiled down at me was one of the first memories I still had of her.

Thinking about her made the dull ache in my chest come back momentarily. Oh, how I missed her. If only she were here now. I could talk to her about Luke, and she would know what to do. She always had the answers to every problem. Whether it was getting impossible stains out of my clothes, calming Alex down when he was throwing a fit, or helping me deal with the most complicated teenage drama, she was there. And she masterfully resolved every situation.

Glancing at the clock on the wall, I realized that it was already six o' five. I decided I had better get downstairs so that my father wouldn't answer the door and interrogate Luke and Ben when they showed up. Giving myself one more look-over, I started downstairs. Nothing about my appearance was glamorous, but it would have to do. I had long since accepted the fact that I would never be beautiful like my mother and being plain usually didn't bother me. But tonight was different… I really wanted to look good for Luke.

As I came to the bottom of the stairs, I saw that my dad had put on a brown button up shirt and jeans. He was standing next to Alex, who was sitting on the couch putting his shoes on. Both of them looked up as I walked towards the front door.

"Hey, you sure look nice Liz." My father said raising an eyebrow. "If any of those guys at the park try to mess with you just let me know. I have no problem breaking some fingers for ya if I have to." He popped his knuckles loudly as he finished.

"Don't worry dad, I can handle myself. Remember, you put me in those self defense classes for like five years? Besides I will be with my friends the whole time, and they are all good people." I reached the front door and turned to wave. "See you later tonight."

"Bye Liz." Alex said waving back.

"Don't have too much fun." My father added.

I closed the door behind me and heard a car approaching from down the street. Turning, I noticed that it was Luke's hummer, and surprisingly he was driving. Ben was sitting in the passenger's seat for once. I crossed the driveway towards the street, and they flipped a U-turn and pulled in front of the house. The silver paint on the hummer was shiny and looked like it had just been washed. Ben and Luke both got out and waved.

"Hey Liz." Luke said first with a smile.

"Elizabeth Bennett. You look like you are ready to escape." Ben grinned as he spoke. "You weren't waiting outside for long, were you?"

"Oh no. I had just walked outside when I saw you guys pulling up. How's it going?" I redirected my eyes from Ben to Luke as I spoke.

"Good." Luke answered as he walked around the front of the hummer. He went to reach for the passenger door handle, but Ben beat him to it and opened the door, motioning to me.

"Why thank you." I smiled at Ben quickly and then lingered for a moment, smiling at Luke. Why did I find it so hard to look away when his eyes caught me like that?

He was wearing a white and blue tee shirt with a dark blue hooded sweatshirt unzipped in the front. Combined with his light blue jeans, he was stunning. I had never seen anyone make casual look so good before. It took some willpower and a couple seconds, but I finally pulled my eyes away as I stepped up into the hummer.

"You're quite welcome." Ben said as he gently closed my door.

The interior of the hummer was dark brown leather, and there was a disc changer and navigation system in the middle of the dash. Luke walked back around the front of the car as Ben jumped in the back seat and closed his door. Just as Luke was stepping into the car I glanced back at my house and saw my father emerging, followed by Alex.

At first my father just glanced at us, but then he did a long second look a moment later. He squinted a little, and then started walking quickly towards us. Luke must have seen him, because he had just closed his door, but he reopened it as my father approached. He came around the front of the car again as my dad stopped a few feet away. I rolled down my window, hoping that he wouldn't interrogate them and embarrass me. The door behind me opened and Ben stepped out too.

"You must be Mr. Scott." Luke began and stretched out his hand as he approached my father. "I am Luke Bennett, and this is my brother Ben." He gestured at Ben with his free hand as he spoke. "It is a pleasure to meet you sir and thank you for allowing us to drive Liz to the bonfire."

"Well to be honest she didn't mention anything about you guys picking her up." He said as he firmly shook Luke's hand. His New York accent was more pronounced than usual. The way he eyed me didn't seem too happy either. Luke and Ben both glanced at me confused.

"Sorry dad. I thought that I mentioned it when I said that I was going with friends." I tried to sound forgetful, but don't think I pulled it off very well.

Ben decided to step in. "Well sir we just moved into town, so Liz said that she would show us how to get to the park."

My dad folded his arms across his chest and gave me the 'You're going to get a lecture for this later' look.

"Well, where are you guys from?" he managed to say civilly, even though I could tell he was upset.

"Colorado" Luke Replied. "We're from the Grand Junction area, just north of the city." He pulled out a small note card and handed it to my father.

My father examined the business size card, which looked like it had handwriting on it, then looked quizzically at Luke. "What's this?" he asked.

"Well sir my mom said that it wouldn't be proper to drive a lady somewhere without giving her parents some contact info, so that is my cell phone number and address. We just live up the street."

My father stood still for a second looking at Luke, then looked back at the card. His face seemed to visibly relax. "Okay Luke. At least your mother taught you some decent manners. Make sure my daughter is home by eleven o' clock, and if anything happens to her, I'll hold you personally responsible. Is that clear?" He pointed a finger at Luke as he finished speaking.

"Yes sir. I'll bring her back safe. You have my word." He held his hand out again and my father shook it briefly.

"Call me if you need anything Liz." My father looked at me one more time, then nodded and turned back towards where Alex was waiting by the car. He tucked the card into his pocket as he walked away.

I have to admit I was quite impressed by how Luke handled my father. Having anticipated a ten-to-fifteen-minute interrogation, the conversation had been relatively short. The more I learned about Luke Bennett the higher he ascended on my pedestal. He turned and smiled at me, then walked back around the car and got in.

"So, I take it your dad didn't know that we were picking you up?" Ben said from the back as we started driving down the street.

"Yeah… sorry about that guys. I was hoping to leave without him noticing who picked me up." I felt embarrassed, and it came through a little bit in my tone. "He's a retired cop, and as you can see, he is a little bit… overprotective… and that's putting it mildly."

"Yeah, but can you really blame him, Liz?" Ben continued. "If my daughter looked like you, I would be protective too."

I shook my head slightly and looked out the window. What do you say to something like that? Knowing that he was just being himself made it easier to shrug off his comments. I couldn't help but smile slightly. It was nice to be complimented, even if it was only Ben being generous.

"Where was your dad a cop at?" Luke asked.

"Portland Police, he did twenty-one years there before retiring. Most of that time was spent as a detective though, so he has seen a lot of shady stuff and has a hard time trusting anyone. I wouldn't be surprised if he wrote down your license plate too as we were driving away. Sometimes his paranoia can be embarrassing."

"Judging by his accent I would have guessed New York. But that's cool that he was a detective. I think police are way too unappreciated. They deal with the most despicable and heartless criminals, putting their life on the line every day, and most people don't even like them. At least until they get into trouble that is." He paused for a moment and then glanced at me. "I do have to say that I agree with Ben. Having a daughter like you would make any dad protective."

"I guess. He never really talked about work much. The accent is from New York though. He grew up in Long Island and didn't move out to Oregon until he became a cop." I was again unsure how to respond to the compliment.

It was quiet but for the sound of the engine as we drove unhurriedly down the street. We turned left onto another road, and then left again on the road that led to the park. Riverfront road was the name of the street that the park was on. About a mile up the road we came to the park.

Even though the drive to the park was almost two miles, my house was only half a mile south of the edge of the park, just down the river a way. The street I lived on dead ended into the small, gated community that nestled up to the south end of the park.

A russet stone sign about four feet high and ten feet long had "Riverfront Park" etched in dark brown letters across the front of it. I turned back and smirked at Ben as we turned into the park.

"So, you needed me to show you how to get here huh?" I teased.

"Well, I didn't want to tell your dad that we were mainly just picking you up because you are drop dead gorgeous and we enjoy your company, so I made something up." He smiled back at me, and I just shook my head again, looking around.

The park was quite beautiful. Grass and trees took up most of the space, with a long narrow parking lot stretching half the length of it. The trees were mostly evergreens with some firs and pines scattered about as well. Several large fields filled the space between the parking lot and the rest of the park's attractions. A sand volleyball court occupied the center of the park near the river, with tennis and basketball courts just beyond that. Just ahead of the volleyball court was another sandy area with half a dozen brick fire pits scattered about. The edge of the river was about thirty feet from the closest fire pit, but a line in the dirt stretched another ten feet closer to the pit on an uphill slope. That line was where the river frequently rose to after heavy rainfall.

Almost half of the parking spaces were filled up. They were mostly the ones near where the bonfires were, so we drove down and pulled into a space in front of the basketball courts. I noticed that there were a couple of small fires already burning, and one large one in the center of the sand area had flames rising about five feet off the ground. That larger fire would be where the football team and their friends would be.

"Here we are." Luke said as he put the car in park and glanced over at me. "We weren't supposed to bring anything were we?"

"No" Ben chimed in from the back seat. "At practice yesterday coach said that all of the football and cheerleading parents provide the food."

"Oh, Okay." Luke opened his door and walked quickly around the front of the hummer. At first, I thought that something was wrong, but then he grabbed the handle to my door and held it open for me. "Ms. Scott." He said as he extended his left arm to me with a smile. I gladly took it smiling back at him.

"Why thank you." I managed, taken back by his chivalry. Having doors opened for me wasn't something that I was accustomed to.

I stepped down, holding his forearm and noticed Ben standing right next to him. Ben was looking at Luke strangely, and if I hadn't known better, I would say that he looked a little jealous. It couldn't be over me, could it? Luke started to lower his arm and I realized that I was still holding on to it and reluctantly let go.

That must have been why Luke had almost run around the car. He had wanted to beat Ben to the door. A week ago, I had never had anyone try and open doors for me, except maybe my father sometimes, and now there were two boys fighting over the opportunity. It felt kind of nice.

We walked slowly towards where the large bonfire was in the middle of the park, with Ben and Luke walking on either side of me. The leaves on the sidewalk crunched beneath our feet as we walked. I wanted to say something to Luke, but nothing came to mind.

"So how was the football game yesterday, Ben?" I asked after a few seconds of silence.

"Good. We won twenty-one to seventeen, but Dustin, the star wide receiver, fell on his arm weird and broke his wrist in the last quarter." He grabbed his wrist as he spoke. "They only have one other decent wide receiver, so coach said he will probably start me at that position also next week. Without Dustin it might be a tough game, he made two of our three touchdowns last night.”

“Well, that’s too bad for Dustin, but at least you should be able to play more now.” I smiled excitedly at him.

“Yeah, hopefully I can fill his shoes okay.” He shrugged.

“I’m sure you will. After all, you are a Bennett.” Ben eyed Luke suspiciously after I said that, and when I turned to look at him Luke was raising an eyebrow at me. It was awkwardly quiet after that, and I just walked with my head tilted down a little. Had I said something wrong? I was grateful when a scream from off to our left broke the silence.

“Liz!” I recognized Nikki’s voice even before I turned and saw her. She was walking from the parking lot with Greg, who was carrying a large cooler. She sped up as they got closer and threw her arms around me. “Oh, I am so glad you actually came.” She said squeezing me.

I let go of her and stepped back. “Of course, I came. I said I would, didn’t I?”

“Well yeah but… I’m just so glad you made it.” She looked at Luke and Ben, as if noticing them for the first time. “Hi guys.” Then she leaned in towards me and added in a softer yet sinister voice. “I see why you came.”

Nikki’s whisper was louder than most people’s normal voice, and I felt my cheeks flush a little involuntarily. Did she have to talk like that in front of them? I looked down again, hoping they wouldn’t see me blush. Blushing was the one genetic trait I had inherited from my mom. Of all the things she could have passed on to me it had to be the cursed blushing.

Greg fell in beside us, and we made our way over to the large Bonfire. I recognized most of the kids that were there, though I couldn’t remember all their names. It was one of the drawbacks to only having one real friend in the school. Ben waved to a couple people, then turned towards me and touched my lower back lightly.

"If you'll excuse me, Liz." He said before walking over to a couple of other boys who were sitting on the opposite side of the fire. I recognized one of them as the same dark-haired kid who had helped jump their car earlier in the week. The other two didn't look familiar.

The configuration around the campfire was interesting. There were three circular rows of chairs set up. The innermost row was all white folding chairs, most of which were occupied, and the second row also had the same white chairs. Comprised of an assortment of different colored camping chairs, the third circle of chairs was filled with people. The smell of barbeque permeated the air, and I instinctively searched for where the cooking was taking place. At the next bonfire over were half a dozen parents, as well as two large portable grills. That's where another man, who looked like an older version of Greg, was grilling some hamburgers.

"If you guys are hungry my dad makes some mean burgers." Greg said to us as he made his way to the inside row of chairs and sat down.

Nikki sat down next to him and pointed to three other chairs that were open next to her. They must have been saving those for Ben, Luke and I.

"Thanks, but I already ate." I said to Greg, then looked at Luke. "What about you, are you hungry?"

"I actually ate too." He responded. "Which is unfortunate because those hamburgers smell good."

"Well next time you guys come to a bonfire come hungry, because these burgers are incredible." Greg replied.

I sat down next to Nikki, and Luke took a seat next to me. The sun had just disappeared behind the mountains, and the glow of the fire off of his eyes was breathtaking. He sat there staring at the fire for a long minute. Nikki was saying something to Greg, but I really wasn't paying attention. Luke looked over at me, and I realized that I must have been staring so I looked away hurriedly. When I glanced back a second later, he was still looking at me, and I felt my heart speed up. I decided to say something before he thought I was some kind of creep with the way I was staring at him.

"So how was work with your mom yesterday?" I tried to sound casual.

"It was good." He replied. "How was school?"

"Honestly, it was pretty boring. You certainly didn't miss out on much."

"What about Sassenburg's class? Did he do any monologues or speeches?" He asked with a grin.

"No, mostly he just had us read. It was more Shakespeare." I paused for a moment before continuing. "So, I'm curious, exactly what do you do to help your mom with her work?"

"Well yesterday, I mostly just carried things for her, but depending on the job she's on she has me do all sorts of things." His response sounded calculated, so I decided not to question him anymore about his mom or the kind of work she did. Obviously, he didn't want to talk about it, so I would respect that. The last thing I wanted to do was come across as nosy or prying.

We chatted a little more, and Nikki and Greg turned to talk to us also. After a minute Luke asked Greg about the football game from yesterday, and that sent Greg into a ten-minute explanation about the game. He explained Dustin's injury again in detail, and how they were up twenty-one to seven until Dustin got hurt. Then the other team's receivers had made a few good catches and almost tied up the game, but they had to settle for a field goal. Greg also talked about how glad he was that Ben was joining the team because they would need him now that Dustin was injured. After that I tuned Greg out and told Nikki how I was in love with her jacket. It was brown with a silver fur collar and silver buttons on the front.

"Oh, I know. Isn't it great? My dad bought it for me at like some fancy store in the mall in Eugene." She looked down at her jacket as she spoke, stroking one of the large silver buttons. Then she glanced over at Greg, who had moved his chair in front of hers so that he could converse with Luke more easily. "You would think Greg would get sick of football with how much he talks about it. I love him and all, but I think if I hear about last night's game in play-by-play detail one more time, I might strangle him."

"Yeah, I wouldn't blame you. This is only my second time hearing the story, and I'm already bored."

Just then the man who had been barbequing earlier, who must be Greg's dad, came walking up carrying a large box. "Anyone up for some football?" He shouted jovially.

Nikki rolled her eyes, and Greg jumped to his feet. He looked excited and took a step towards his dad, then stopped. Turning to Nikki, he made a pleading face. "Baby, do you care if I go play for a few minutes?"

"Go ahead; I know you'd like totally hold it against me if I said no." She folded her arms across her chest as she spoke. Clearly, she didn't like the idea, but being the male that he was he just kissed her on the forehead then turned and ran off with a dozen or so others. I didn't doubt that she would be giving him a piece of her mind later.

Nikki turned towards Luke. "What about you pretty boy, you going to play with the rest of the jocks?"

"No" he replied. "I gave up playing football a while ago." He turned to look at where Greg and the others were gathering around the box.

Greg's father dumped the contents onto the grass near the edge of the sandbox. It looked like red and blue mesh jerseys and white belts with red and blue flags attached to them. So, they must be playing flag football. It was a large open field, and the only grass in the park that had good lighting thanks to two tall poles with large flood lights on both ends.

"Well…" Nikki said, rising from her chair "I suppose I had better go cheer for my man." She took a couple steps and then spun around to face us and poked a finger at us. "You two be good now." She said with a mischievous grin. Then she walked over to the edge of the field and sat down on the curb next to the grass.

Luke looked at me with an eyebrow raised, and I just shook my head. "Don't mind her. She's a good friend, but she can be crazy sometimes." I said, hoping that he wouldn't hold her awkward statements against me. It wasn't like I was telling Nikki to say those sorts of things. She was just being… Nikki.

I noticed that Ben and his three comrades had joined the group of kids who were going to play. He looked excited as he slid a blue jersey over his shirt. I looked over at Luke again, who seemed to be looking longingly at those gathering.

"Are you sure you don't want to play Luke. I really won't mind." As the words left my lips, I realized that I really meant them. While I wanted Luke all to myself, he could pretty much do anything, and I would forgive him; especially if it was just playing football with the rest of the guys.

"Yeah, I'm sure. My football playing days are behind me." He turned to look at me, and I just stared into his eyes. The fire seemed extra warm suddenly. "Besides, I'd much rather just hang out with you. You promised that we could get to know each other, and I plan on taking you up on that offer." He smiled and seemed to be thinking about something. "Do you want to go for a walk?"

"Sure." I replied, a little bit surprised. I hadn't expected him to say that, but the idea was exciting.

"Just so we can talk. You know… away from…all this." He nodded his head at the rest of the crowd that was now gathering on the edge of the grass to watch the boys play.

"There's a path that goes down by the river." I said pointing to the water's edge. "It's actually the same path that goes along the back side of our houses. If you want to go that way."

"That sounds good to me." He said standing.

I stood too, and we walked slowly across the sand to the path near the river. The path was packed gravel, and it curved along the edge of the park about 20 feet up the slope from the river's edge. Halfway between the path and the water was the line that signified where the water rose to after it rained. Several different green plants had randomly sprouted along the riverbank. Luke stopped when we got to the trail and looked down at me.

"Which way did you want to go?" He asked looking up and down the river.

"Let's go that way." I said, pointing down the river towards where our houses were. "You know, I've seen this trail from my back yard, but I've never actually walked down it."

We both started walking down the path, and it was silent except for the crunch of the gravel under our feet. The moon overhead was almost full. It was a good thing because as we neared the edge of the park the lights began to fade. With the moonlight casting a shine on the top of the water, you could see the water flowing slowly. The Willamette River was about fifty feet wide where it passed through town.

"So, tell me Elizabeth Scott. How does a beautiful girl like you from the big city end up in a small town like Harrisburg?" I was glad that Luke spoke, because I was at a loss for what to say to him.

"Well, my dad bought a house here after he retired from the Police Department, so we moved down."

"And your mom was cool with moving to a small town?"

"Well…" The little ache in my chest came back. "I think that was actually part of the reason why my dad wanted a change. You see, my mom died in a car accident just before we moved here."

"Oh no. I'm so sorry. I didn't know…"

"It's okay. It's been a little over a year now. I should probably be over it by now, but I still think about her a lot."

"I can only imagine how difficult that must be for you. If something happened to my mom, I'm not sure I would ever get over it."

"Yeah. It is tough sometimes. Most days I do just fine, but then sometimes something will happen that reminds me of her and… I really just miss her." Tears rolled slowly down my cheeks, and I turned away, embarrassed. Luke put his hand gently on my shoulder.

"It's okay Liz. I'm sorry for bringing it up."

"No. It's not your fault." I said wiping the tears off my face while trying to control my faltering voice. "You didn't know, and it has been a long time. It's just… I really haven't talked to anyone about it since it happened. Other than Alex, but a five-year-old isn't much help when you are dealing with something like losing your mom. Even then I was mostly just trying to comfort him. And my dad never really wanted to talk about it so… I just held it all in I guess." Another tear crept down my cheek as I spoke. I wiped it away too.

"I am so sorry Liz." Luke said softly. His hand still rested on my shoulder, and I was grateful for his soothing touch.

"No, I'm sorry. You don't even know me, and here I am crying in front of you. I swear I'm not normally like this. I don't know what's wrong with me." I turned to look at him, fearing that he would be annoyed.

The look on his face was one of pure compassion. "Liz don't apologize. Sometimes it helps to talk about things. And I would only think that there was something wrong with you if you didn't show emotion over something so tragic." He grabbed my other shoulder with his other hand as he spoke, and his blue eyes looked so concerned, so caring.

In that moment, as I looked at him something inside me seemed to snap. The dam that had been keeping back my emotions suddenly burst. Involuntarily I leaned into him and buried my head on his shoulder, sobbing uncontrollably. He put his arms around me gently, and as embarrassed as I should have felt, I didn't. With his arms encircling me I felt… secure. A minute went by with me crying on his shoulder, and when I finally pulled away, I instantly regretted it. His embrace was so warm, his scent so wonderful. Like a mixture of fresh Tide and… something else even more pleasant. I could have breathed him in for hours and been content.

"I'm so sorry." I managed to say, wiping my snot and tears on my sleeve. Silently I hoped he wasn't disgusted by it. "I don't know what came over me. This is so embarrassing."

I finally came back to reality and realized what I had just done. Mustering the courage, I looked up at him. He still had one hand stretched out on my shoulder and was looking down at me with… sympathy. Not only did he seem genuinely concerned for me, but he also didn't look the least bit annoyed or bothered.

"There is nothing to apologize for. I am here for you. Just because you don't know me very well doesn't mean I don't care about you."

"Are you real?" I thought out loud, copying his statement from earlier in the week.

He smiled when I said that, and I suddenly realized how close our faces were, and how close our lips were. They couldn't have been more than eighteen inches apart, and I unexpectedly felt something pulling me towards him. I started to lean in a little, feeling goose bumps on my skin as I closed half the distance between us. Never before in my life had I felt so powerless to my own emotions. It took all my willpower not to throw my arms around him and pull his lips to mine. My mind was racing at the thought. Luke started to lean closer, until he was only a couple inches away. My heart nearly leapt from my chest it was beating so hard. Then Luke suddenly turned his head to the side and stepped back, letting go of my shoulder.

In an instant I went from soaring through the clouds, to lying in the gutter. To say I felt rejected would be an understatement. I must have done something wrong. Was I being too forward? I'm such a fool. What was I thinking? I jumped from hey let's get to know each other, to crying on his shoulder, to trying to kiss him. He must think I was some kind of drama queen or something. I glanced around, hoping to find a rock big enough to hide behind.

Surprisingly, Luke looked back over at me and grinned shaking his head. "Elizabeth Scott you really are amazing you know." He said it more like a statement than a question, so I didn't try to respond. "What do you say we keep walking? I'll try my best not to put my foot in my mouth any more tonight."

Maybe it wasn't me that had made him stop. He obviously felt something too, or he wouldn't have leaned closer, but what was it? Another question I would have to bite my tongue on.

We walked for a few more minutes. I told him about my father, and then Alex. He laughed when I told him about Alex's obsession with food. "It sounds like he and Ben would get along just fine. My brother could just eat all day and never get sick of it."

"So, what about you?" I asked. "You haven't told me anything about yourself."

He glanced at me and shrugged. "Well, what do you want to know?"

"Oh, I don't know. What's your family like? What do you like to do for fun? What's your favorite color? You know… tell me about Luke Bennett."

He paused for a moment, looking away before answering. "Okay well… my favorite color is Green."

"What?" I interrupted. "But you are always wearing blue?"

"Well, I like to wear blue because my mom says that color looks best on me, but green is definitely my favorite. What about you?"

"Definitely blue for me." I replied.

So, I had been wrong all along. For the first time in my life, I was actually excited about my green eyes. I had always been more preferential to blue, but if Luke liked green that was fine with me.

"And for fun, well let's see…" He paused and let his breath out slowly. "I used to love playing football, but that's not an option anymore so… I think basketball is fun too, but I probably like swimming and hiking more than that. Reading can be fun on occasion, but only if it's a good book."

"Why isn't football an option anymore?" I asked.

"Again, that's something that I can't really get into."

"So, then it must be because you don't want anyone else seeing what you can do." I decided to push just a little bit.

His silent lack of objection confirmed my suspicion. I decided I had better change the subject before it seemed like I was prying again.

"So, you like swimming and hiking too huh? Have you ever been to Fern Ridge Lake?"

"No, I haven't. Is it nearby?" he replied.

"Yeah, the lake is about a half hour from here towards Eugene. It's beautiful there; especially if you don't mind that the water is usually freezing. My dad has dragged me and Alex with him there a few times when he went fishing. I'm not a huge fan of fishing, but the lake is really pretty." I glanced over at him and saw that he was listening intently.

"I'll have to check it out. Maybe we could go there sometime, and you could show me all the good spots." He grinned at me as he finished.

"I would like that." I said smiling.

Without realizing it we had walked quite a way from the park. I noticed the back of my house a few houses up on the left. The back fence was at least a foot over my head, but I recognized the two large pine trees that were on either end of our back yard.

"Well, we probably better start heading back. It's a little after nine, and I want to make sure we get you back on time." Luke said glancing down at his watch; he must have read my mind.

"That's probably a good idea." We turned and started walking back towards the park. "So, you still haven't told me anything about your family. Is it just you, Ben and your mom?"

"Yeah, for now anyway." I gave him a puzzled look. "I have a sister too, but she is going to college at the University of Oregon down in Eugene. She lives on campus but drives up on the weekends sometimes."

"Oh, that's nice. How much older than you is she?"

"Just under two years, she turns twenty a week after my eighteenth birthday."

"And when is that?"

"My birthday? It's actually New Year's Day, so it's kind of easy to remember."

"Really? That's cool. I've never met anyone with a New Years birthday before."

He nodded. "Yeah, my mom said that I was supposed to come January 27th, but then her water broke a couple hours before midnight on New Year's Eve. I was actually delivered right at midnight. Or at least within a couple seconds anyway."

"That is awesome." He hadn't said anything about his father, so I figured I'd ask. "Are your parents divorced then?"

"No, my dad died when I was very little. It was just after my fourth birthday." He looked straight ahead as he spoke.

"Oh no…" I put my hand to my mouth and stopped for a second. "I am so sorry, I just assumed…"

He turned back towards me. "It's okay. It was a long time ago, so it's not really that emotional for me anymore." I started walking again and fell back in beside him as he spoke. "To be perfectly honest I can barely even remember him. My mom has one picture of him, but I only have a couple of memories with him in them."

It was quiet for a while except for our footsteps. I wasn't sure exactly what to say, so I just said nothing. We arrived back at the park, and I could see people running on the field with the lights on it. So, they were still playing, that was good. Finding Nikki on the sidelines wasn't too hard, and the game ended right when we reached her.

After talking for a few more minutes Luke decided he had better get me home, so he and Ben walked me back to the hummer. My phone said ten forty-one as we pulled up in front of my house. Luke opened my door for me and offered his hand to help me down, which I eagerly accepted. We had just started walking up the walkway to the front door when the door opened, revealing my father. Any hopes I'd had about a nice farewell went out the window.

"Hey Liz. Did you have fun?" His eyes looked tired as he stood leaning against the doorframe.

"Yeah, actually I did." I said cheerfully, then turned and gave Luke a little smile.

"Thanks for bringing her back on time. I didn't wanna have to come looking for ya." My father said as he looked calmly at Luke.

"No thank you Mr. Scott, for allowing her to accompany us for the evening." Luke politely replied. Then he turned towards me. "Well, I just wanted to make sure you got to your door safely. Thanks for coming with us; it was a lot of fun. I guess I'll see you on Monday?" He said extending his hand.

"Thanks for picking me up." I ignored his hand and gave him a hug. "And thanks for being so understanding." I whispered as he gently hugged back. My father cleared his throat loudly, and I realized that Luke had already let go of me. I reluctantly let go and started towards my front door.

"Have a good night, Elizabeth." Luke voice came from behind me. "And you too Mr. Scott."

"Thanks, you too." I said turning to wave.

"You too kid." My dad echoed.

I walked past my dad into the house, and he closed the door behind me.

"You know Liz, I have to admit. Even though I don't really like boys picking you up, cause I don't trust any of them, that Luke actually seems like a nice kid. He even knows how to talk to people proper. I like that."

"Yeah, he really is nice." I said thoughtfully. "He's not like most other boys." The second part I hadn't meant to say out loud.

"Okay Liz, well I'm wiped so I'm gonna go to bed. Sleep good sweetheart." He walked by me towards the stairs.

"You too dad."

A few minutes later I was lying in my bed, thinking about how much I liked the sound of it when Luke called me Elizabeth. I normally didn't like the sound of my full name but coming from his lips it just sounded better. Everything sounded better when he said it though. I replayed the night's events in my mind, smiling when I thought about how nice it was when he held me. There were still so many things that I wasn't sure about, but I knew one thing for certain. I was falling head over heels for Luke, and it didn't bother me one bit.

CHAPTER V

A small bird was hoping around on the front lawn. Most of its feathers were a light silvery color, but its wing tips and the top of its head were almost black. It looked peaceful as it jumped about on the grass, poking its head down into the blades as if it was eating or pecking at something. Perhaps there were seeds or bugs in the lawn.

I had been staring at it through the kitchen window for the last few minutes, while slowly sipping my orange juice. It was fresh squeezed, or at least that's what the Tropicana people claimed. Either way it tasted exquisite, and I felt like I was starting to get a sore throat. My mom had always made us drink orange juice when she thought we were getting sick. There had been quite a few concocted illnesses when I was younger, just to get my mom to run to the store and buy more juice when we ran out.

I noticed one of the neighbor's cats creeping up from the other side of a pine tree towards where the bird was at. Whenever the bird would stop eating to look up, the cat froze. It was quite an ugly feline, with mangy brown fur and tan splotches on its back. Eventually working its way closer to the bird, the cat was now only a few feet away. I leaned forward and slapped the window to try and warn the little creature, but I was too late. The cat pounced as the bird fluttered its wings, and it never made it off the ground. With its victim lodged in its mouth, the cat ran back towards the neighbors' yard. That poor bird never saw the cat coming and hadn't stood a chance. Seeing it taken like that was kind of depressing. I had always been more of a dog person, so my dislike of felines was reaffirmed.

"Izzie, can I have some more pancakes?" Alex asked from behind me.

"You've already had five Alex." I said turning to look where he was seated at the kitchen table. My father was sitting next to him, reading the Sunday paper. "Why don't you drink your orange juice first and then see if you are even still hungry."

Alex made a pouty face at me and eyed his orange juice with dislike. "No Izzie. I don't want my orange juice. You gave me too much, and I'm too full to drink it all." The glass was only half full, and he hadn't even touched it yet.

"Well, if you're too full for orange juice then you don't need any more pancakes."

"Okay Izzie. Can I just have some more syrup instead?" His face went from pouty to a wide-eyed innocent expression.

I laughed in spite of myself. Alex's love of everything sweet and unhealthy was comical. "No Alex, you've had plenty of syrup too."

"Aw shucks. Can't blame me for tryin." He shrugged, and then carried his plate over to the sink.

My father was reading the newspaper so intently that he seemed completely oblivious to our conversation. I finished the last of my orange juice and started to wash the dishes.

"Liz." My father said calmly without looking up from the paper. "I'll wash up, why don't you go relax for a little bit."

"Okay." I replied, thinking that I really didn't mind washing, but I also didn't feel like arguing.

Most of the rest of the day was spent just lounging around the house. Alex wanted me to watch a movie with him, and then we played some games. After lunch my father took his usual Sunday afternoon nap. He always said it was so that he could be rested for his night shift since his week started Sunday nights, but during football season he usually only slept for a couple of hours so that he wouldn't miss any of his football games. I never understood why he was such an Eagles fan when he was from New York, but that was the one thing that he and my mom always had in common. They both loved Philadelphia football for some reason.

He had only been asleep for a little over an hour when I started getting stir crazy, so I decided I would go for another run when he woke up. All I could think about was Luke, and I needed to do something else to keep my mind occupied.

An hour later I was on the front porch stretching lightly before my run. The weather had cooled a bit since the day before, and the wind felt like it was starting to pick up. The breeze felt good, but it made me shiver slightly. I had on my green long-sleeve athletic shirt and black addidas running pants. I knew once I started running my body would heat up.

Starting at a slow pace, I started running down my street towards Luke's house. My legs were a little stiff, and my throat still felt scratchy, but other than that I felt good. Red and orange leaves swirled with the wind around me and crunched underneath my feet as I ran.

My mind kept going back to the walk with Luke by the riverside the night before. I could still remember the excitement I had felt when we had almost kissed, and the sting of disappointment when he had pulled back at the last second. Feeling like the rest of the walk had gone just fine, I was uncertain what it was that had made him stop.

An older looking gray van with no windows on the sides and dark tint drove by me slowly. It was one of the cargo looking passenger vans that my dad always called a "creeper van". I had asked him several times why he called them that, but he had always just said "Don't worry about it sweetheart, it's just cop lingo."

As I approached the Bennett's house, I noticed a black truck pulling into Ben and Luke's driveway. I was still a couple houses down, but the passenger looked female. Slowing to an easy jog, I saw the female exit the passenger side of the truck as another older male got out of the driver seat. The man looked about forty, with blondish hair that was starting to gray, while the female had light olive skin and looked part Asian. The most striking thing about her was her beauty. If Nikki was a Latin Princess, this girl could have passed for an Asian one. Except that she looked half white too. Jet black hair flowed down nearly the whole length of her back, and she reminded me of a super model. She was wearing all black and was tall and thin with perfect skin. No sooner had she exited the car then I heard her shout.

"Luke!" She held her arms out wide. It was then that I noticed Luke, almost running from the open garage towards her.

He grabbed her in a big hug and swung around in a full circle while lifting her up off the ground. I saw the widest smile on her face as they spun, and my jealousy exploded into rage when I saw her kiss him on the cheek as he set her down.

Suddenly I fell forward onto the ground and realized that I had tripped over a small trash bag that was sitting on the sidewalk near the middle of their house. I grunted, catching myself with both hands before my body hit the ground. As I got back up, I saw Luke and the new girl looking over at me. A flood of embarrassment added to my anger, and I quickly ran away from them. It must look strange to them that I was almost sprinting, but I was too upset to care. A couple hundred yards down the street I started to tire, so I slowed substantially.

Tears began to roll down my cheeks, but I fought back the sadness for a minute with anger. What a fool I had been. Everything made sense now. The reason that Luke hadn't wanted to kiss me was because he already had a girlfriend. That dirty scoundrel. The night before, and all of the looks and flirting must have been some kind of game to him. A sick and twisted game. And like the fool that I was, I had fallen for every minute of it. What had I been thinking? As if any gorgeous new kid at our school would legitimately be interested in me, Elizabeth Scott.

While I did my best to fuel my anger, it quickly turned to depression. A sick feeling began to worm its way into my stomach. I felt too sad to cry. Too sad to let myself even care. I probably ran at least another mile in that gloomy trance, until the little logic that was left in me told me I should turn around. The sun had just set and already the light was beginning to fade from the sky on the eastern horizon.

The same gray van from before drove slowly by me, but I hardly noticed it in my current state. A thousand things were racing through my head. Oh, but that girl had been so beautiful… and so tall. It just wasn't fair. I finally had something in my life to be excited about, for the first time since mom had died, and now my dreams had been crushed. Like a tornado, that hussy had swooped in and taken my man. Or even worse, he had been hers all along.

I was pulled from my depressed musings when I suddenly had the sinking feeling that I was being watched. Looking ahead more attentively, I noticed the same old van parked on the side of the road less than a hundred feet in front of me. I glanced around, taking in my surroundings. The dirt path I was running on next to the road had a lot of trees and bushes. There was not another soul in sight, and the next houses were the ones at the end of my street, still a couple hundred yards ahead.

Without any time to make a real plan, I decided I would just speed up and run quickly past the van. Just then a man with scraggly long brown hair and a short beard jumped onto the path in front of me. He didn't say anything, but the desperate look on his face spoke volumes. While I didn't have time to stop, I did have time to process that this man meant me harm. He spread his arms to grab me, and I tried to sidestep around him.

His arms caught me by the shoulders, and he pulled me sideways. My momentum was still going forward, however, so this resulted in me falling to the ground, face down. The man hadn't fallen with me, but he quickly jumped on top of me as I turned over, grabbing both of my arms so I couldn't move. I screamed as loud as I could, and he covered my mouth with one hand. With one arm free, I pushed up on his face and pushed off the ground with my hips, trying to knock him off of me using one of the escape techniques that I had learned in my self-defense classes, but he was too strong, and I was too small.

He grunted, then grabbed my hair and smashed my head backwards onto the ground, shouting "Just hold still and it won't hurt!" I felt dizzy for a second, and then noticed that he was tugging me by my arms towards his van. I flailed around and fought him as hard as I could, but he must have been at least twice my size. I could smell his rotten stench: a mixture of alcohol, soiled clothes and putrid body odor. Had I not been fighting for my life I would have hurled.

I felt a sharp pain on the back of my head and realized that we had reached the side of the van, where the sliding side door was open. My head must have struck the bottom of the open door.

"Don't fight it!" the man snarled as he stepped around and over the top of me. As he grabbed my waist with one hand and hoisted me off the ground, I grabbed his hair with my hand. Finding one of his eye sockets with my other hand, I pushed as hard as I could on his eye with my thumb and he screamed. Dropping me back to the ground, I saw him reach in his waistband and pull something out. He pointed it at me, and I saw that it was a large black knife.

"You stupid little whore!" He spat, punching me in my abdomen. I turned and rolled out of his reach but tripped as I tried to get up and run, suddenly feeling a sharp and intense pain in my upper stomach. I heard my attacker step towards me again and I turned to face him, gasping at the burning pain the movement caused. He must have stabbed me with the knife when I thought he'd only punched me.

The man took another step towards me and started to raise the knife, this time holding it over his head. "Look at what you made me do." He said as he paused for a second. His hand holding the knife was visibly shaking, and I could see the blade was covered in dark blood. My blood. He seemed to be considering if he was going to finish me off or not. Suddenly his jaw tightened, and he got a committed expression on his face as he lunged at me again. I closed my eyes, thinking my time was up, and put my arms up in a pathetic attempt to shield myself. Surprisingly, the man screamed shortly, and then I heard a thump, like someone had hit a tree with a baseball bat or something. I opened my eyes confused.

The evil man who less than a second before had been about to kill me, was now laying with his face hanging over his chest, unconscious against a tree trunk about ten feet away. Standing over him was Luke Bennett; wearing the same blue polo shirt and jeans that I had seen him in just minutes before in front of his house.

Luke bent over quickly and put two of his fingers on the man's neck, then grunted and turned towards me. He jumped and landed right in front of me. Squatting down, he looked me in the eyes. In that instant I forgot about how much I had wanted to strangle him, and instead just wanted to wrap my arms around him.

"Are you okay Elizabeth?" he asked tenderly, then looked at my stomach and gently reached towards it. I looked down and realized that my green shirt had a large brown stain on the front of it. Without thinking I touched it and my hand came away wet with blood.

I wasn't sure if it was seeing the blood, or touching it, but suddenly I felt lightheaded, so I leaned all the way back and lay flat on the dirt. Luke ripped the bottom part of my shirt, then took his off and wiped at my stomach. Lifting my head just enough to see my exposed stomach, I saw Luke wipe away blood from a long hole just below my rib cage. It gushed back out as quickly as he wiped it. He then pushed the shirt tight against me and the pain sharpened, causing me to gasp.

"I'm sorry Liz, but I need to keep pressure on the wound until the paramedics get here. Just lie still." His face looked worried as he spoke. My vision was starting to get hazy around the edges and I could feel my body starting to go into shock.

"Oh no Luke, where did he stab her?" I was surprised to hear Ben's voice and opened my eyes to see him standing over me next to Luke. It took too much effort to keep my eyes open, so I let them close again.

"It went through the stomach, but he must have cut a major artery because she is losing blood way too fast." He sounded panicked.

It was so cold, and I could feel my whole body shaking. Trying to open my eyes didn't help either because I couldn't see. I could tell that I was dying but was powerless to stop it.

"Do we have time for an ambulance?" Ben's voice sounded stressed.

"No… There's not enough time, she wouldn't make it to the hospital. Run and get a change of clothes from Jazmine and a couple towels. Go now!" Luke's voice got louder as he snapped orders at Ben.

I suddenly felt a warm sensation in my stomach, before drifting out of consciousness. *I will never know the real Luke Bennett.* I thought sadly as my life slipped away.

At first, I thought I was dreaming. I felt something soft underneath me, and someone was holding one of my hands. Slowly opening my eyes, I took in my new surroundings. Luke was sitting next to me holding my hand, and it looked like we were in the back of an ambulance or something. At my feet the doors were open revealing the street I had just been on. Luke let go of my hand when he noticed my eyes open, but I quickly grabbed his again as he was pulling it away.

"Hey there." He said calmly, squeezing my hand gently. His warm touch felt so good, so reassuring. He smiled down at me, and a smile spread across my lips.

"Hi" I managed to say drowsily.

Hearing my own voice brought me to the realization that I wasn't dreaming. More importantly I realized that I wasn't dead. My first instinct would have been to think that perhaps the whole incident had been a dream, but that wouldn't explain why I was laying on a gurney in the back of an ambulance. I felt down on my stomach to where I had been stabbed, but the skin looked fine, except for a small scar where the wound had been.

"Liz, I hate to ask you this after what you have just been through, but I need another favor." He wore the same worried expression he'd had the week before, after the other incident.

"Okay, I'm listening." I replied hesitantly.

"I need you to tell everyone about what happened but leave out that you were actually stabbed. Say he pulled the knife on you but missed. When he tried to stab you again someone you have never seen before came out of nowhere and hit that creep in the back of the head with a baseball bat. He was driving an older looking gray pick-up truck, but you don't remember very much about him because you fainted after he hit the guy with the bat. Can you remember that?"

"Sure… but only under one condition."

"What's that?" He asked.

"I need you to promise that when this whole ordeal is over, you tell me exactly what happened and answer some of my questions."

"I'm not sure if I can promise that." He said after a long pause.

"Well then I'm not sure if I can remember the story you just told me." I wasn't about to commit to anything without getting some kind of answers. While I had no intention of betraying his secret, I was hoping he wouldn't call my bluff.

Sitting up on the gurney, I noticed that my black pants were rolled up at the bottom and had a Nike symbol on them. The green athletic shirt I had worn running had also been replaced with a black athletic shirt. *These aren't my clothes*, I thought. I suddenly remembered the girl who had kissed Luke, and I pulled my hand away from his. He looked at me confused after I yanked my hand away, but I didn't care.

Thinking about her brought back the anger I had felt before the whole incident occurred. Maybe he had saved my life, but that didn't excuse that he had played me. To top it all off he had put his little hussy's clothes on me. Luke must have sensed my frustration, but he looked at me all innocent like.

"Liz, I didn't change your clothes, Jazmine did. And you have my word Ben and I both faced away while she did. Okay?"

He thought that I was worried about him seeing me almost naked? I honestly hadn't even thought about that. The nerve of him to try and act innocent, and to continue toying with my emotions. He must have known that I had seen them hugging and kissing. My blood started to boil, and I clenched my fists, thinking about how bad I wanted to punch him in the face.

"So that's her name huh, Jazmine?" my words came out as ice. "And when were you planning on telling me about her?" I couldn't even look at him I was so upset. Feeling my eyes starting to water, I looked away, trying to fight back the tears.

"Liz." He started to say, placing his hand on my shoulder.

I jerked back from him, and he laughed. He actually laughed. *Oh the nerve!* So, he thought this whole thing was funny did he?

"Liz, I did tell you about her. She's my sister."

I froze. That didn't make any sense at all. After a long moment had passed, I managed to speak. "But she doesn't... even look like you and... I saw her kiss you..."

"Yeah, she doesn't look like me because my mom adopted her when I was six. And she kissed me on the cheek, that's how family greets each other where she came from." He explained patiently.

A wave of relief rolled over me as I realized just how mistaken I had been. It actually made perfect sense. She had only kissed him on the cheek after all. My relief quickly morphed into embarrassment as I realized how I had just behaved. I looked at him and smiled sheepishly.

"So, she's not your girlfriend?" I realized it was a stupid question as the words left my mouth.

"Liz, that's gross." He made a sour face.

"So, you don't have a girlfriend?"

"No."

I couldn't keep myself from smiling. To say I was elated would be an understatement. Luke smiled too and chuckled lightly.

"What?" I asked, wondering what prompted his laughing.

"Oh nothing… it's just… you really thought that she was my girlfriend?" He asked with a smirk.

"Yeah. Well in my defense she doesn't look like your sister, and she is really pretty."

"Jazmine? Well, I guess she looks okay, but she's not nearly as pretty as some other girls." He looked at me as he finished, and my stomach fluttered. He smiled again and added "You know Liz, if I didn't know better, I would say you almost sounded jealous." He leaned a little closer as he spoke and lowered his voice.

"Well… maybe I was." I looked down as I spoke. There was no point in lying about it. I hadn't done a very good job of concealing my emotions.

He reached forward and lifted my chin with two fingers, meeting my eyes with his. My heart sped up.

"Liz, I can promise you have no reason to be jealous of anyone. There is only one girl I care about, and I'm looking at her right now."

His face was so close I couldn't resist the urge to kiss him… so I didn't. Without thinking I leaned in slowly, and his lips met mine. It wasn't a long kiss, but it felt so good that when he started to pull away, I grabbed his head with both hands and pulled him back for more. After a few seconds he started to pull away again, this time gently prying my hands from where I was touching the side and back of his head.

"Liz." He said gently. I felt dizzy as he pulled away, and didn't want him to, so I reached for him again.

"Liz, your dad is coming." He said more urgently, and mention of my father brought me back to reality.

No sooner had I pulled away then I heard my father's voice from outside the ambulance.

"Where is she?" he asked loudly from outside.

I heard another female's voice that I didn't recognize, but I couldn't understand what she said. Then my father appeared at the foot of my gurney, peering in from the road where he was standing. He looked me over quickly, shot a disapproving glance at Luke, and then looked back at me.

"Hey Liz, are you okay?"

"Yeah, I'm fine dad. How did you know I was here?"

"Tyler called me as soon as he got here."

Tyler King was the name of the town's Sheriff. My father and he went bowling every other weekend down in Eugene. Occasionally he would come by our house to watch football games as well. He was a lot nicer than most of my father's other cop friends in Portland had been. Maybe that was because he worked in a small town.

I scooted to the edge of the gurney, and my father reached towards my hair, pulling out a few blades of grass. The realization that I probably looked like I had been dragged through the mud hit me. *Oh no, I don't want Luke to see me like this*. My breath probably stunk too, and I could feel all the dried sweat from running. Luke hadn't seemed to mind, but I found myself badly wanting a shower and some fresh clothes. My father was staring at me, and his jaw looked tight. I realized for the first time that he looked angry. Extremely angry.

"Liz" he said between gritted teeth "Did he hurt you?"

"No dad, not really. Luckily that man showed up when he did. Otherwise, I think I would probably be dead right now. Where did he go? Is he still here?"

"Is who still here?" Sheriff King's voice came from the side of the ambulance as he stepped into view next to my father. He was about my father's age, with a shaved head that looked like it would probably only grow hair on the sides if he tried. I also saw Alex poke his head in between the two of them and look at me.

"Hi Izzie." He said with a smile. I waved at him before answering the sheriff.

"The man with the gray pickup truck. He's the one who hit that psychopath with the bat when he was about to stab me. Where is he at? I want to thank him for saving my life."

The sheriff stared at me for a second, and then glanced at my father. My father turned towards Luke.

"What are you doing here?" he asked sharply.

"He's the one who found them here and called 9-1-1." The sheriff answered before Luke had a chance to speak. "He was headed to the store to pick up some things. That's when he found Liz lying there on the ground, and the suspect knocked out about ten feet away."

My father seemed to relax a little and put his hand on Luke's shoulder. "Thanks for your help kid; I guess I owe you one."

"No sir, you don't owe me anything, I'm just glad I was in the right place at the right time. It was nothing but pure dumb luck that I found her here."

"Okay, well we need to interview her now son, so can you wait outside for us?" the sheriff asked.

"Sure thing." Luke said as he stepped around me and went out the side door of the ambulance.

For the next ten minutes the sheriff and my father tag teamed me with questions about what had happened. They wanted every little detail, from what I was thinking while being attacked, to every word the psycho had said. My father also asked a lot of questions about the man with the baseball bat. It was easy to say I didn't remember a lot about him, since he didn't really exist anyway.

When the interrogation was finally over, I asked the Sheriff where the man who had attacked me was.

"Oh him? Well, whoever hit him with the bat did a good job, because his neck was actually broken. He was also bleeding from one of his eyes. Unfortunately, he is going to live, but he will never be hurting anyone ever again. He was actually wanted for murdering three people down in Texas, so as soon as he gets out of the hospital, he'll be on a plane back there. The nice thing about Texas is that they still have the death penalty. After killing three teenage girls, he'll definitely get it too."

He had already killed three other girls. So, I really would be dead right now if it wasn't for Luke showing up when he had. I would have to ask him exactly how the murderer had broken his neck. If only I hadn't closed my eyes when I thought he was going to finish me off. Although I must admit, of all the reasons for closing my eyes, being stabbed in the stomach and almost dying was at least a decent excuse. A part of me regretted that I wouldn't be able to give Luke the praise he deserved for saving me, but something told me that would be the last thing he wanted anyway.

As I stepped out of the ambulance, I saw Alex sitting on the curb next to Luke. The two of them were talking, and Alex laughed as Luke pointed down the road. Seeing Luke make my brother laugh struck a chord with me, and I found myself somehow more impressed by him. As if it was even possible to be more impressed. How could anyone be so perfect?

"Okay Alex, it's time to go. Why don't you go and get in the car buddy." My father said.

"Okay Dad." He replied, and then added to Luke. "I have to go now, but hopefully I will see you later."

"I hope so too Alex. It was nice to meet you." Luke replied with a cheerful smile. Alex stood up and started walking towards the car, which was parked in front of the ambulance.

"Thanks again kid." My father waved at Luke before turning to walk back to the car.

At first, I waved, then started to turn away from him. But after all that Luke had just done for me, simply waving goodbye felt wrong. I walked quickly back to him and threw my arms around him.

"By the way, thank you." I whispered in his ear.

"For what?"

"For saving me… again."

"You are so welcome Elizabeth Scott. Although… for the record… I have no idea what you are talking about."

I squeezed him tightly, not wanting to let go, but then I heard my father clear his throat. Reluctantly, I let go and took a step back. After flashing him one more smile, I turned and walked back to my father. I really think I could have been content just looking at Luke all day. Although holding him was even more appealing, and kissing was… well…I couldn't remember ever feeling more alive than when our lips had touched.

My dad got in the car, and I sat down in the passenger seat. Alex was already buckled in the back seat. He smiled at me as I glanced back at him.

"Izzie, I'm so glad you are safe." He sounded much older than his five years when he said that. I couldn't help but smile.

"Me too Alex."

We drove back to the house in silence, which was nice because it gave me some time to process what had just transpired.

Once we were home, Alex started bombarding me with questions. Fearing he was too young to know exactly what had happened, I left out all the details and just said that a bad man had tried to hurt me. Eventually he must have realized that I had told him everything he was going to get, because then he left me alone.

No sooner had Alex left then I headed straight for the shower. As I was undressing, I noticed that my underwear had dark blood stains on them, which re-assured me once again that I hadn't been dreaming. So at least I hadn't been completely naked. There must have been quite a bit of blood for it to soak that low. When I finished showering my stomach growled, and I realized that I was famished.

Alex got excited when he saw me making dinner, which was typical for him. About an hour and three plates full of Spaghetti and Meatballs later, I felt satisfied. Looking back, I don't think that I had ever been so hungry before. Maybe hunger was a side effect of whatever Luke had done to fix me.

After dinner I felt exhausted, so I went up to my bed and just laid on top of the sheets. The next thing I knew it was the middle of the night. I was cold, so I tucked myself under the blanket and sheets, then fell back asleep.

The next morning, I felt well rested as I pulled into the parking lot at school. I was also surprised when I parked next to the Bennett's Hummer, to see Luke leaning against the driver's door.

"Good morning Liz." He said cheerfully as I stepped out of my Tahoe. I walked around the back of it so that I could see him without my car blocking the view.

"Hey Luke. Sorry I had to leave in kind of a hurry yesterday; my dad was pretty upset about what happened to me, so I didn't want to give him anything else to be angry about."

"No worries, I completely understood. How are you feeling?" he turned, and we started walking towards the building as we talked.

"Honestly, I feel great. But it was strange yesterday after I got home."

"What do you mean?"

"Well for some reason after I took a shower, I had the most ravenous appetite. Then after dinner I was so exhausted that I went right to sleep. Which for me is an anomaly. I can usually never fall asleep before ten or eleven, and it was only seven when I laid down. Is that some kind of side effect of whatever you did to heal me?"

"Well, I don't think we should talk about this at school, there are too many ears around, but how about we meet up after school, and I will explain everything?"

"Really? That would be nice." I replied, trying not to sound too excited.

The thought of having him explain anything to me was exciting. Hopefully it would be a better explanation than he had given me after the first incident. Even though it had only been six days, it seemed like ages ago that he had saved me from those robbers. Perhaps it was because of all that I had been through the day before.

I remembered that I had to pick up Alex from school. How would I be able to watch him and talk to Luke at the same time? Well, either way I decided I should probably bring it up.

"Hey Luke, there is one little problem."

"What's that?" He turned to eye me curiously.

"Well, I have to pick up my little brother from school after fourth period. And then I have to watch him until my dad wakes up. He usually sleeps till at least four, because he's always tired from working graveyard shift."

"That's not a problem." I was surprised to hear him say. "Would you care if I just went with you to pick him up? We can talk at your place. Unless you think that would be too awkward?"

I quickly thought about all of the different possible scenarios and decided that it wouldn't be too difficult to go outside and talk while Alex did his homework or watched TV. My dad couldn't get mad about me having a friend over. If anything, he would probably be glad that I was hanging out with boys at home rather than somewhere else where he couldn't keep tabs on us.

"I think it would be fine, as long as you don't mind him tagging along. We could still talk in private of course, once we got to my house."

"Okay, I'll see you later then." He said with a smile.

"Sounds good." I said smiling back at him.

He turned to walk away, and I suddenly noticed Nikki standing just twenty feet away in front of our first period class. She must have been watching us walking the entire time because she was staring at me with a knowing smile. I was grateful that she at least waited until I reached her before talking.

"I knew it!" She practically shouted she was so excited. "I knew there was something going on with you two after you like, took that long walk on Saturday. And now he's like walking you to class." She smiled broadly and gave me a quick hug. "You guys are like, totally going out, aren't you?"

"What?" I couldn't help but smile, but I tried to look innocent. "I don't know what you're talking about. We are just friends. That's all."

"That's all? Yeah, right Liz. If you two are just friends, then Greg and I don't even like each other."

She put her hands on her hips and looked at me with disbelief. "Oh, I get it, let me guess. You like, don't want to tell anyone, because you don't want people to know about you yet. Is that it?"

"No Nikki, we really are just friends. But I do hope that eventually it will lead to more than that." I smiled again involuntarily as I finished. To be honest I really didn't know exactly what we were, but I could hardly explain the complexity of mine and Luke's relationship.

"Well by the looks of things, I think you are totally headed in the right direction."

The day seemed to drag by, and even though I got to see Luke in Second period, we weren't able to talk at all. Just knowing that I would be able to learn more about the mystery of Luke Bennett kept my mind racing all day. It took quite a bit of effort to think about anything but him. Lunch came, and it was nice to talk to Luke and Ben, but with everyone else around it just wasn't the same. I longed to be alone with him again. He did walk me to Sassenburg's class, which as expected was especially long today. When the bell finally rang I was ecstatic.

Luke again waited for me outside the door. Today he was wearing a blue and white striped polo shirt and blue jeans. I was surprised that he wasn't wearing a jacket, because I was a little cold even with mine on. Maybe the cold didn't bother him either.

"Aren't you cold?" I asked as we walked towards the parking lot.

"No, not really. It's actually kind of nice out today. Perhaps a little on the cool side, but I don't get cold very easy." His tone was casual as he spoke. "In Colorado it was freezing, so this isn't bad at all."

"Oh yeah. I guess compared to all the snow this must be nice."

"Yes, it is. There are a lot of really nice things about Harrisburg though." He smiled as he spoke and looked me in the eyes.

"Like what?" I asked, hoping to be on his list.

"The people." He replied. "Especially certain ones." Looking at me as he finished, I realized that I was blushing.

I looked down at my feet, not sure how to respond. It felt good thinking that I was a part of those "certain ones", but I didn't want to put my foot in my mouth, so I didn't say anything. The last thing I wanted was to come across as arrogant or presumptuous.

We reached my Tahoe and I had to move Alex's booster seat to the back so that he could sit down. The drive to Alex's school was quiet, but it wasn't awkward. For some reason when I was with Luke, even if we weren't talking, I just felt... happy. It didn't help that I was so anxious to talk to him about yesterday that I couldn't think of much else to say.

When we pulled in front of Alex's school, I looked at my clock and noticed that there was still four minutes left until his bell would be ringing.

"So, do you like music?" I asked, trying to fill the silence. The quietness didn't bother me, but I wasn't sure if he felt the same way.

He chuckled softly. "Yeah, just because I am a little different doesn't mean I'm not normal."

"Oh of course. Sorry, I meant to say: what kind of music do you like?"

"Honestly, I like everything. Well... everything except some rap. I'm not really a big fan of death metal either."

"Death metal?" I asked confused.

"You know, Heavy Metal but even more extreme? That's what some of the kids at my last school in Colorado called it. Usually, you can't understand the words because the singers are just screaming incoherently the entire time."

"Oh okay. I have heard heavy metal, just never death metal. It sounds pretty lame though."

"Lame is putting it kindly."

I turned on my radio, which was still on the local mixed music station. *Every Breath You Take* by the Police was on, so I quickly changed the station. Even though I wasn't a huge eighties fan, there were some songs that I loved, and that was definitely one of them. Just in case he didn't like it though, I decided to play it safe.

"Why'd you change it? I love that song." Luke unexpectedly said.

"Really?" I asked him as I changed the dial back.

"Absolutely, it's a classic. Why... you don't like it?"

"No actually I do. It's one of my favorites. I just assumed that you might not like it, so I figured I'd change it just in case."

"Don't be silly. Like I said, I like everything." He smiled again, and I just stared at him for a long moment.

With the music playing in the background, I couldn't help but think about how much I was falling for the boy sitting next to me. Looking in his eyes I felt trapped, but in a good way. Like I knew I should look away, even if only for courtesy's sake, but I didn't care.

Since Luke had come to town, I had been robbed, and I had been stabbed. Yet for some reason I felt safer with him than I had ever felt before in my life. Something deep down inside told me that there was something dangerous about him, but every other fiber of my being wanted to be close to him so badly that I didn't care. I was hopeful that before the sun set today, I would know the truth about him, but I knew in my heart that no matter what he told me it wouldn't change my feelings for him.

As the song ended, I realized that I was still staring at Luke. He was looking out the window and appeared deep in thought. His face also looked... nervous. Hopefully he didn't think I was crazy for staring. It didn't seem to bother him, but then again maybe he hadn't noticed. I looked away and heard the bell chiming.

A minute later Alex was walking up to the Tahoe. He looked surprised when he saw Luke sitting in the front passenger seat, but as he opened the back door, I saw a smile spread across his lips.

"Izzie what is Luke doing in my seat?" He asked still smiling.

"Luke was going to come over and play with us for a little while, is that okay?" I asked enthusiastically. To be honest I was surprised that he could even remember Luke's name.

"That's a silly question Izzie. Of course, Luke can come play." His tone was very matter of fact.

"Sorry for taking your seat Alex." Luke said in a concerned tone.

"It's okay Luke. You can sit there, just don't let anyone else take it okay?" Alex replied.

"Okay Alex, you got it buddy." Luke turned to look at Alex as he finished speaking with a smile.

"I didn't know you two were such good friends." I said casually after a moment of silence had passed.

"Oh yeah, Alex and I got to hang out yesterday while you were talking to your father and the Sherriff."

I vaguely remembered seeing them talking, but I was surprised to see Alex behave so amiably towards Luke. He was usually very shy and reserved with people until he got to know them.

Luke asked Alex about how his day went, and Alex excitedly talked about every detail. By the time we pulled into the driveway I was ready for Alex to stop talking, but Luke didn't seem the least bit annoyed by the endless chatter.

Once we went inside, I got out a lunchable for Alex, and then told him that Luke and I needed to talk alone outside for a minute.

"Why Izzie?" had been his curious response.

"We have a boring English project to work on, and we don't want you to be bored, so how about you can watch cartoons first? We will do your homework later. Does that sound good?" I held my breath, hoping he would like the arrangement.

"Really? I get to watch cartoons first?" He smiled at me then turned to Luke, who was sitting across the kitchen table from us. "Luke, you can come over anytime you want."

We both laughed, then made our way out the rear sliding glass door. The back yard had a large patch of grass in the middle, with a tall pine tree on either end of it. The side walls had mostly square cut green hedges, with a few rose bushes interspersed, and the rear wall had an assortment of flowers and plants lining most of it. The only exception was the solid iron gate that led to the river, there were not plants in front of that. A large chain and several padlocks held the gate closed. Overall, the yard was beautiful, and the landscaper who came once a week kept it looking that way. It would have made my mother happy, having such a beautiful back yard. She had always loved gardening, and everything related to nature. Thinking of her made me remember why I rarely spent any time back here, but I had needed somewhere that I could talk to Luke in peace and quiet without interruption.

We took a seat on the oak bench, which sat just a few feet from the sliding glass door. It wasn't a long bench, and our knees were almost touching as we sat. Of course, I didn't mind at all. I looked at him in anticipation, but he was looking off again. Now I could tell he definitely looked nervous.

I thought about telling him that he didn't have to tell me anything, because I felt bad for him. After all that I had been through though, I deserved some kind of explanation, so I just bit my tongue. A couple minutes went by with us sitting in silence, and then finally he turned to look at me. He let out a long breath as his expression changed, and he looked determined.

"I really don't know exactly where to start, because I have never told anyone what I am about to tell you, so… I suppose I should start with the disclaimer." His voice sounded calm, but his eyes gave away his uneasiness. "Elizabeth Scott, once I tell you what I am about to tell you, you cannot speak of it to anyone else, is that understood?"

"Yes." I replied, nodding my head.

"If you talk to anyone outside my family, then we will be forced to move, and you will never see or hear from us ever again."

The finality in what he said was unnerving. The mere suggestion of never seeing Luke again brought a sinking feeling to my stomach. I couldn't bear the thought. Surely, he must know that he could trust me.

"You have my word, Luke. I won't tell anyone unless you say it's okay. I promise." I hoped he could sense the sincerity of my vow. "I don't want you to leave."

"Okay, that's good enough for me. For some reason I can't even understand myself, I know I can trust you. Otherwise, we wouldn't be having this conversation. Anyways, with that being said, I really don't know where else to start, so I suppose I will start by telling you exactly who and what I am." He paused for a moment and looked me directly in the eyes.

"My real name is Leuken Bennett, and I am from The Bloodline."

CHAPTER VI

I sat confused, looking into Luke's eyes. So, his real name was Leuken, and he was from the bloodline? Should I have known what that was? I actually liked the sound of Leuken, but I couldn't understand why he said his name was Luke. Then again, a lot of people use nicknames or shortened versions of their own name, so nothing about that was especially strange. Luke hadn't spoken for a few seconds, so I decided I had better ask him as many questions as I could before he changed his mind about sharing his secrets with me.

"Okay…so… what is the bloodline?"

"This is going to sound crazy, so please hear me out before you think I am some kind of weirdo, okay?"

"I would never think that of you but go on. I'm listening."

"I'll start with the reader's digest version, and then if you have any questions, I can fill in later."

"Sounds good." I replied.

"The bloodline is a group of people with special abilities that are passed down from generation to generation. My father was from the bloodline, as was his father before him. Ben and I are both from the bloodline, and so is Jazmine."

"But I thought that Jazmine was adopted." I interjected.

"She was, but only because both of her parents were killed by the Verdorben." He answered patiently.

"The Ver- what?" I asked confused.

"The Verdorben, or the tainted ones, as most people call them, and when I say most people, I mean most of the few people who even know they exist."

"What are they?"

"They are demons. For the most part anyway. All of them were once human, but once the mark of the Verdorben takes someone, there is little humanity left in them. That is why we call them the tainted ones. They are pure evil, and most of them dedicate their time to hunting down those few of us members of the bloodline who are still alive."

"They hunt you?" I asked as an unsettling feeling came over me.

"Well… let me explain. The tainted ones were first created over a thousand years ago. They are virtually immortal and can only be killed by very difficult means. Members of the bloodline are the only people who possess the means to kill one of the Verdorben. It is because of this that most of them dedicate their entire lives towards hunting down and killing every last member of the bloodline. They are why my family and I live such secretive lives. We are forced to move every few years so that they never find us. It is the only way to stay safe. The last time that they found us was when they killed my father. His name was Nathaniel Bennett. He died fighting off two of them so that my mother could escape with Ben and I."

"Oh no that is terrible." I said. My head was spinning. This was quite a bit of information to process, and none of it had been expected.

"Since then, we have not crossed paths with any of them, but it is only a matter of time. They have many abilities, and if anyone they came across knew who and what we were, things could get ugly real fast."

"Sorry to interrupt you, but didn't you say that you guys are capable of killing them since you are members of the bloodline? Why not just let them find you and kill them first?"

"Well, you see, that's part of the problem. You can never truly kill a tainted one, because when they die their evil powers transfer to someone else. It also doesn't help that you never know how many Verdorben you will have to face. There are twelve of them total, but some of them hunt in packs. A couple of them usually hunt solo, but they haven't been seen in decades. The main group has six tainted ones, and then there are four others who hunt in pairs. One of those pairs is the two who killed my father thirteen years ago." He paused for a moment. His blue eyes looked thoughtful as they studied me. Maybe he was expecting some kind of reaction from me, but I was too intrigued by his story to think about anything else.

"Isaac says that the six other tainted ones don't associate with the main group, but we don't know that for sure. So, to answer your question, the reason we don't kill them is because we don't think we can. Even if we could kill a couple of them, they would only jump into a new body, and then the others might know where we were. Even with all four of us fighting together, the odds of us taking on six tainted ones at a time are not good. Even a one-on-one matchup is dangerous. We would prefer to only fight them if we outnumber them. At least two to one is ideal."

"Are they stronger than you are?" I asked curiously.

"Yes. Well… physically they are. But only by a little bit, and we are slightly faster than they are. Only for short periods of time though." He noticed my confused look. "Well let me explain. Their skin is virtually impenetrable except for terralium. Our skin is much stronger than a normal person, but still vulnerable as you saw when I was shot."

"Sorry about that." I interrupted.

"Don't be, it barely even hurt, and to be fair, I did know what I was getting into." He smirked at me. "Anyways, getting back to the tainted ones. We are strong, but they are a little stronger. They are fast, but we are even faster. The problem with speed though lies in the fact that they have more endurance than we do. For example, the fastest I have ever run is about fifty-five miles per hour. They can probably only run about forty-five miles an hour, but they don't get tired. I could only hold that speed for a little over a minute, but they could hold their speed for much longer. Other than that, we are pretty evenly matched."

Did he really say fifty-five miles an hour? I thought to myself. He had seemed to appear out of nowhere when he had come to my rescue. Remembering the incident brought back to my mind some of the questions I had wanted to ask him.

"So… going back to the robbery, remember how you were shot in the head, then looked fine a few seconds later?"

"Yeah." He replied.

"How did that happen?"

"That is another one of our abilities. Our bodies heal extraordinarily fast. The bullet ricocheted off my skull and only did skin damage, so it healed in just a few seconds. Our bones are much stronger than a normal person."

"Then what about me?" I added, putting one hand over the scar on my stomach. "I know that I was dying, so how did you save me?"

"That is something else we can do. We can push our healing abilities into others, but it is much more tiring when we do, and we have to be touching the person. I was hoping that I wouldn't have to heal you because I didn't want to reveal myself, but you would have died if I had waited for an ambulance, and I could never let that happen." His eyes reflected genuine concern as he spoke.

So, he had healed me. I figured as much, but it was nice to know for sure. The more he told me though, the more questions I came up with.

"So, what really happened yesterday then?" I asked

"Honestly, I was helping Jazmine unload some things from her truck when I heard you scream. From inside my house, I barely heard the scream, and I didn't know if it was you or not. I did remember seeing you run by however, so I just ran towards where I had last seen you go. I was already halfway to you when I heard more screaming, and I had a sinking feeling that it was you. That was confirmed when I got closer and saw you laying on the ground with that monster standing over you." He gritted his teeth as he spoke. "At first, I thought I wasn't going to get to you in time, but luckily, he saw me and lifted the knife at me just before I hit him. Unfortunately, he lived, but at least he won't be able to hurt anyone else ever again."

It should have bothered me that Luke so casually spoke about my attacker's life, but after what he had tried to do to me, it didn't. Some people just don't deserve to live. Not when they are as dangerous as that wretched man was. Allowing a murderer like that to live would just put everyone else's lives at risk. I hoped he would get the death penalty back in Texas.

"So... how did I end up in Jazmine's clothes?" I inquired.

"Well... when I could tell that you weren't going to make it without our intervention, I told Ben to go get some towels and clothes for you. I knew once I healed you it would be difficult to explain why you were covered in blood but didn't have a scratch on your body. Ben came back with Jazmine and she had us turn around while she undressed you, cleaned you up, and then put her clothes on you. Then I called 9-1-1 and thought up the story I was going to tell the Sheriff when he arrived.”

“So, Ben and Jazmine were already gone when the Sheriff arrived?”

“Oh yeah. It’s easier to make up a story when only one person has to remember details as opposed to three.” He answered.

“Well thank you… again… for saving my life.” I glanced sideways at him and smiled.

“You are welcome Elizabeth.” He said smiling back.

There was something about hearing my name from his lips that just felt good. I smiled wider without thinking and shook my head ever so slightly.

“What?” He asked.

“Oh nothing, it’s just… I have always hated my full name.” He opened his mouth, probably to apologize, but I continued before he had the chance to speak. “But for some reason when you say it, it doesn’t bother me. To be honest, I kind of like it.”

With him sitting so close, I could breathe him in. It was the same pleasant aroma I remembered from the other night when we had embraced. When I had made a fool of myself crying on his shoulder. He was looking me in the eyes again, and I thought about how easy it would be to just lean over and kiss him. I remembered that I still had a lot of questions though, so I refrained. But it wasn’t easy.

“To be perfectly honest Liz, you shouldn’t be thanking me for saving you. It is because of me that you were put in danger in the first place. I should be begging for your forgiveness for placing you in harm’s way.”

What in the world are you talking about? I thought to myself. What I said was: “What do you mean?”

“I’m not positive, but I would be willing to bet that the only reason you were in danger in the first place is because we moved to town.” He looked down at his feet as he spoke.

"What are you talking about?" I asked exasperated.

"I am talking about the curse of the bloodline." He said looking up to meet my eyes again. "Even though we have many abilities, they do come with a curse."

"What curse?" I raised an eyebrow at him, still without a clue what he was talking about.

"It's difficult to explain, but I will do my best. You see, whenever we move somewhere, or even just when we are traveling, we seem to attract… evil. For reasons unknown to any of us, the worst people seem to find themselves in close proximity to us. For example, before we lived in Colorado, we lived in a small town called Logandale, which is in southern Nevada. Before we moved there, the town had virtually no problems. There had never been any homicides, and all other crimes were virtually nonexistent because they were so rare. After we had lived there for about one year, there had been four murders. Four! And that's with Jazmine and I stopping half a dozen other attempts.

For some reason we attract the vilest criminals and end up having to use our abilities to save people quite frequently. Isaac has said that he thinks it is the lights way of putting us where we will be able to do the most good, but I am not sure how I feel about that." He paused, looking down at his feet. "All I know is that I am glad I was able to hear you scream and get to you in time, because I wouldn't have been able to live with myself if I knew that I was responsible for your death."

Luke seemed to have a talent for saying all of the right things. As if my heart wasn't already wrapped around his little finger. I wasn't sure what to think about this curse he was talking about though. The murderer who had attacked me had simply seemed to be a random act of violence. Was it possible that Luke's curse had something to do with the whole situation? Even if it had, it didn't change the way I felt about him. He had still saved my life.

With all of the information he had shared in the last few minutes I felt like my head was going to explode, or that I was going to wake up. Everything sounded like something that would take place in a dream, but I knew that I wasn't sleeping. More questions came to mind, and I decided I might as well keep firing away.

"Does Ben have the same abilities that you do?" I asked curiously.

"Yes. Well… for the most part anyway. You see every member of the bloodline has certain abilities that are standard. One of those abilities is that we are able to emanate certain feelings to people around us. It's kind of difficult to explain, but just as we can push our healing abilities to others, we can also push other emotions. For Ben, he is gifted with the ability to soothe and help people to be calm and at ease. Everyone from the bloodline could learn to do it, but not everyone has equal abilities.

Let me give you an example. If I were surrounded by ten people who all wanted to attack me, I would have to focus very hard just to calm one of them down a little bit, but Ben could calm all ten of them using half the effort. Does that make sense?" I nodded and he continued. "But everyone from the bloodline is gifted in certain abilities, some more so than others."

"What about you? What are your abilities?" I inquired.

"Well Isaac calls me a dreamer." He said, looking away thoughtfully.

"Why is that?"

"Because sometimes I am able to see the future in my dreams." He said casually.

"You what? You mean you can actually see the future? That is amazing." I said incredulously.

"It's not quite what you think. I can't see the future at will, and it is only occasionally that I have the foretelling dreams. You see, my dreams usually only come when we are in some kind of danger, or when there is something important that the light wants me to do."

"The light?" I was again confused.

"That's just what Isaac calls it. The light is what we use to describe the unknown force that we draw our powers from. No one knows exactly what it is, but it affects all members of the bloodline. Sometimes we can feel it influencing us, and it is a wide held belief that the light originally gave us our abilities to fight the demons."

"You keep saying the name Isaac, who is he?"

"He is my uncle. Well, there isn't any blood relation, but he helped to raise and mentor my brother and I. Ever since my father died he has been like a father to both of us, and to Jazmine as well. Our story is that he is our uncle, even though he is way too old to be that.

He was the one who trained my father as well. Everything that we know about the bloodline and the Verdorben is thanks to him." He spoke of Isaac with an almost reverent tone.

"Have you ever seen one of the Verdorben?" I asked.

"In person… no. At least not since I was a small child, and I can barely remember that incident. There was one time a few months ago that I drove by one on the freeway, but I couldn't be sure if I saw its face or not."

"What do you mean?"

He held his left hand up and for the first time I noticed what looked like a small silver ring on his middle finger. At first it just looked like a medium sized band with a line on it, but as I looked closer, I could see that the line was actually a series of small symbols. They were etched into the metal. Each small round symbol touched the one next to it, creating the false impression that it was just a black line. He turned the hand over, and I noticed a tiny dark stone set in the ring on the inside part of his finger.

"Do you see this ring?" He asked, and I nodded. "I am not sure what the frame of the ring is made from, except that it is virtually indestructible, but I do know what that small stone is."

"What is it?"

"That small stone is terralium. It heats whenever one of the Verdorben is nearby. It can sense them up to about a mile, but it gets progressively hotter the closer the creatures come. It will literally burn your hand if you get within fifty feet of one. This is how I knew I passed one on the freeway." He said pointing to the ring. "Because the ring burned my skin as I drove by."

I noticed the scar on his neck again and reached out to touch it gently with my hand. "What is that from?" I asked.

"Oh, you mean the scar?" He touched it briefly with his fingers as he spoke. "That was where the mark of the bloodline was, before I had it removed. It makes it much easier to avoid being tracked down without it."

"What does the mark look like?"

"It is a red mark that looks almost like a tattoo, but much more vivid. The symbol is that of a sun. It actually doesn't appear until after the snap. So, once it does it is somewhat difficult to explain away. Even though tattoos are becoming much more popular nowadays, you don't exactly see a ton of sixteen-year-olds with their neck all tatted up."

"That makes sense." I said smiling. Something he had said had confused me, but it took me a second to realize what it was. "You said the mark appears after the snap. What is the snap?" I asked.

"The snap is just a term we used to describe the process one goes through when they become a full-fledged member of the bloodline."

"What do you mean?" I hoped I didn't sound annoying.

"Let me explain how the bloodline works. In order to become one of the bloodline, you have to be a direct blood descendant of another member. That being said, not all descendants will become one of the bloodline. Less than half of all bloodline offspring actually become one of us. Meaning actually receiving all of the talents and abilities that we have. Most of them live out their lives as normal human beings. The fact that Ben and I both snapped is remarkable in and of itself.

Now when I say snapped, I am referring to the moment in time when we get all of our abilities. This is also when we obtain the mark of the bloodline. The reason we call it snapping is because it usually occurs during a traumatic event or at a moment when the person transforming has reached an impossible situation. Usually this occurs between the ages of sixteen and seventeen, but not always."

"So, when did you snap?"

"For me, it actually happened when I was only fourteen years old. About a year before we moved to Logandale, we were living in Detroit. Isaac and Jazmine had gone to the store just down the street. I was at home with my mother and Ben when two men broke into our house. One of them held a gun to Ben's head while the other tied me and Ben up with duct tape. After they tied us up, they duct taped my mom's mouth, and then told her to take off her clothes.

At the exact instant when I realized what their intentions were with my mother, I lost it. I tried breaking the duct tape that held me to the chair I was in but couldn't. My mother at first told them no, but when one of them cocked the gun that was pointed at Benjamin's head, she started to unbutton her blouse. I knew I had to do something, and that's when it happened. Suddenly feeling a surge of anger, I snapped. Tearing through the bindings with ease, I ripped the gun from one burglar's hands before he even had a chance to pull the trigger. I then grabbed him by the head and slammed him into the tile floor. By then the other suspect had pulled a knife. He swung at me, but I easily blocked it and unintentionally broke his arm in the process. I then punched him in the face and broke a few more bones, knocking him unconscious. When Isaac returned, he took the two crooks and dumped them in the middle of the street a block away. Needless to say, after that incident, we ended up moving the very next day.”

“Wow. So, you started being a hero at just fourteen? And here I was thinking you were new at this.”
I said smiling.

“I’m no hero Liz. Just cursed is all.” He looked down at the ground again. “Or blessed as my mom likes to call it. I suppose it’s all a matter of prospective. Anyhow, you asked about the scar so now you know. The scar is from removing the mark to avoid attention.”

Just picturing Luke with a big sun tattoo on the side of his neck was interesting, and I could see how it would have drawn people’s attention. It was quiet for a minute as I tried to think of what to ask him next. I was annoyed by the fact that there was so much on my mind that I couldn’t remember any of the other questions I had wanted to ask him. Finally, something else came to me.

“You said that you have to move every couple of years or so right? How long are you planning on staying in Harrisburg for?” As much as I didn’t want to think about him leaving, I might as well know so that it didn’t come as a surprise later.

“Well…that depends. Originally the plan was just to stay here until the end of next summer, but depending on how things go, I would like to stay longer than that if possible. There is, however, always the possibility that we could have to leave at a moment’s notice. For instance, if one of the Verdorben came here looking for us, or… if you told anyone about us.”

"Well, you definitely don't have to worry about me. I am a girl of my word, and even if I wasn't I still wouldn't tell anyone. The last thing I want right now is for you to go away." I looked at him again with concern, hoping that he wouldn't sense how desperately I meant my last sentence.

For a long second he just looked at me, and I felt my heart hastening. He started to lean towards me, and I braced myself for what I hoped would be another kiss. Just before our lips touched, he pulled away quickly. The still familiar feeling of rejection stabbed at me as I started breathing again, but just then I heard a tapping on the sliding glass door.

Looking up I saw Alex with his face pressed against the glass. He was tapping on the door with both hands as he watched us. Luke was facing away from the door, so there is no way he could have seen Alex.

"Sorry Liz. It's not that I don't want to. I just heard him coming." He said as he let out a deep breath.

"You must have exceptional hearing." I said as I stood up. "Let me go see what the little twerp wants."

I walked over to the door and Alex stepped back from the glass as I approached. Pushing the door open, I gave Alex a disapproving look.

"What are you doing Alex? I thought you were going to watch a show?" I asked impatiently.

"Sorry Izzie I just got bored and wanted to see what you guys were doing." He said looking down with a lonely expression.

"Alex, we are just talking about boring stuff for school. I promise you are not missing out on anything interesting." I lied.

"Okay Izzie, but can you come back in soon? I want to play with Luke." He pleaded.

"Sure Alex, just give us a few more minutes."

"We can go back in now Liz if you want." Luke said from behind me.

I hadn't heard him move, but he was suddenly standing only a couple feet away. So, he was not only fast, but quiet as well. If I wasn't already infatuated with him it might have been a little unnerving. As it was, I was just startled a little bit. I had wanted to keep talking to him, so I gave him a look.

"Well, we still needed to talk about our English project for Sassenburg's class." I said deliberately, hoping he would catch on that I wasn't done questioning him.

"We can finish that later." He said.

Trust me Liz, I promise you will have all the time you want to interrogate me later.

I froze instantly as I heard his voice in my head, but his mouth hadn't moved. That second sentence had definitely come from him, but he hadn't spoken. Suddenly remembering the last time I had heard his voice in my head, I looked at him suspiciously and grinned.

"I knew it!" I said excitedly.

"Knew what?" He asked feigning innocence.

"I knew I hadn't imagined that last week. You can" I stopped suddenly as I remembered Alex was still standing just inside the open door.

I turned to look at him. He was staring at me confused. "What are you talking about Izzie?" He asked with a furrowed brow.

"Oh, nothing Alex." I turned and shook my head at Luke as I walked back inside. "Why don't we come inside and hang out."

"Okay. Thanks Izzie, you're the best." He smiled up at me. "Can you make me more food please? I'm very hungry still."

"It sounds like you're always hungry Alex." Luke said playfully as he slid the door shut behind him.

"Oh, I am Luke. Food is my favorite." Alex replied smiling.

"Did you want anything to eat?" I asked Luke.

"No thanks." He replied.

"Just give me a minute. I'll be right back." I made my way into the kitchen.

Without paying attention to what I was doing, I made Alex a peanut butter and jelly sandwich. My mind was still focused on everything that I had just learned about Luke. Or should I call him Leuken? I liked the sound of both, so I made a mental note to ask him later which one he preferred. Unexpectedly a thought came to me out of nowhere. If Luke could put thoughts into my head, could he also hear my thoughts? I blushed thinking about the possibility that he knew everything I had thought about him. That was something I would need to find out immediately. If I needed to control even my thoughts around him, I wanted to know.

I came back into the room with Alex's sandwich on a plate. He and Luke were sitting next to each other on the couch and Luke was holding a book in front of both of them while Alex struggled to read it. I set Alex's plate on the end table next to him, and then sat down next to Luke.

Watching him patiently listen to Alex read brought a smile to my lips. Alex's shyness seemed to be nonexistent when Luke was around. It made me happy to see them both getting along so well. Now I just had to hope that Luke and my father could get along fine also. At least so far my father hadn't threatened Luke as he had one of my old boyfriends.

Okay, well the kid hadn't exactly been my boyfriend, but we had been on a couple of dates. His name had been Peter Johnson, and I could still remember the one time my dad had told him off. It was a few weeks after my sixteenth birthday, and we had just been to dinner and to see a movie. After the movie I thought the kid was going to take me home, but instead he had taken me to a park in downtown Portland. I had been upset and begged him to leave, but instead he had tried to make out with me in the car. Of course, I was mad about him not taking me home on time, since my father had given me an eleven o'clock curfew, so I had refused to kiss him. After a while he gave up and drove me home, but by then it was almost eleven thirty. Peter had walked me to the door, probably hoping for at least one kiss, but instead he had found my father waiting for him.

"Obviously you have a problem with respect kid." My father had said to him with a heavier than normal New York accent. "If you ever want to hang out with my daughter again, I'll be coming with you. And if I find out you went anywhere with her without my knowledge, I'll fold you like a wallet." He had then slammed the door in the kids face. Not surprisingly, Peter had never talked to me again.

Unlike Peter however, I desperately wanted my father to like Luke. I would need to be sure to give Luke some pointers on things not to say around him. Although, I had to admit, Luke had handled himself extremely well around my father so far. Suddenly conscious that Luke might be reading my mind, I decided I had better ask him soon.

I waited for him to finish listening to Alex, who seemed to be reading better for Luke than he normally did for me. He was probably just trying to impress him. Luke sat patiently with him and offered praise whenever Alex pronounced a difficult word. Watching him with Alex brought him even higher on my pedestal.

No sooner had Luke set the book down then I stood and held out my hand to help him off the couch. He took my hand curiously, and I pulled him up and walked towards the kitchen, still holding his hand. I liked having an excuse to do so.

"Where are you going Izzie?" Alex asked from the couch.

"I'm just giving Luke a tour of the house. I'll be right back." I said over my shoulder as we walked.

Making our way into the kitchen, we stopped in front of the front window furthest from the other room. This should be out of Alex's earshot. I reluctantly let go of his hand and turned to face him. With our faces only a couple of feet apart, I had to look up to meet his eyes.

"Okay, there is something I need to know, and you have to promise not to lie about it." I said quickly, keeping my voice down.

"Elizabeth, I would never lie to you. What is it?" His blue eyes looked incredibly sincere as he spoke. I would have believed anything at that moment.

"I know you can somehow talk to me inside my head, because you have done it twice now. What I don't know, and need to know is: Can you also hear my thoughts?"

"No." He answered without hesitation. "But I can usually tell how you are feeling." He added.

"What do you mean?" I asked.

"It's difficult to explain, but I'll try. Another one of our abilities is that we can feel other people's moods. Whenever someone is upset or angry, they give off a certain… spirit or aura if you will. If someone is extremely happy or excited they also exude that. The same can be said for every emotion. People who are uncertain or confused also have a unique aura about them. Does that make any sense?"

"So, what you are saying is… you can tell how I am feeling, but not what I am thinking?"

"Exactly. We can also tell a lot about a person's character."

"What does that mean?" I asked confused.

"Well, everyone gives off a general aura or feeling, depending on the kind of person that they are. Most people are fairly neutral, or slightly on the good side. Some people, like young children especially, are very good and almost brighten up a room. We can actually feel their goodness. Others, like that creep who attacked you, radiate almost pure darkness." He answered.

"What impression do I give you?" I asked curiously.

"Do you really want to know?" He teased smiling.

"I wouldn't ask if I didn't." I smiled back.

"Okay, I'll tell you." He paused briefly and put his hands on my shoulders. "You, Elizabeth Scott, are an incredibly good person, even though you try to hide it." I raised an eyebrow in disbelief, and he took a small step closer. Of course, he was just being nice. "I really mean it. Even before I talked to you, I could feel that about you. So, I know it's not just because of the feelings that I have for you either." He almost whispered as he finished.

I could feel my heart racing and the proximity to him was exhilarating. It took all of my will not to lean in and kiss him, but I was glad I didn't, because not two seconds passed before I saw Alex appear in the doorway.

"Izzie, are you gonna show him the rest of the house or what?" His high-pitched little voice said impatiently. "I love the kitchen too but come on Izzie. You are so slow."

I had the thought of throwing something at him to make him go away for a few minutes but decided against it. Luke seemed to like him, so I didn't want to come across as the mean older sister.

Luke chuckled and turned towards Alex. "Alex you sure are a funny kid." He said.

"I know." Alex replied bluntly.

For the next few minutes, I kept up the pretense of giving Luke a tour of my house. We of course skipped my father's room where he was sleeping, and my room as well. I had been in such a hurry this morning that I hadn't even bothered to make the bed, so I was too embarrassed to let him see it like that.

When we sat back down on the couch in the front room Alex wanted to watch a movie, so I put in Toy Story for him. I sat next to Luke on the couch, but we didn't talk much. As much as I was hoping he would reach for my hand at some point, he didn't. About half an hour into the movie, Luke looked at his watch. Glancing at the clock on the wall, I noticed that it was almost four o'clock. I hadn't even realized how much time had passed. That always seemed to happen when I was with Luke.

"Did you have somewhere you needed to be?" I asked him.

"Yeah, I was supposed to go with my uncle to get some things down in Eugene at about four. I should probably get going." He stood slowly and turned to Alex. "Thanks for letting me come over and hang out with you Alex. I had a lot of fun."

"Anytime Luke. I'll see ya later." Alex replied as he kept staring at the television.

Luke opened the front door, and I stepped outside with him, closing the door behind me. The light breeze felt chilly against my face.

"How are you planning on getting home?" I asked, remembering that I had driven him earlier.

"Ben is coming to pick me up. He should be here any minute." He said looking down at his watch again. "Thanks for letting me come by Liz; I had a lot of fun." He looked a little bit nervous as he looked up at me.

"No, thank you for coming." I replied. He stepped in to hug me, so I put my arms around him. "And thank you for trusting me Leuken." I added softly with my face against his chest. His warmth was a pleasant contrast to the cool air.

Raising my head to look up at him, I realized again how tall he was. Or should I say how short I was. Hopefully he didn't mind. There was nothing I could do about it, so it shouldn't bother me, but sometimes I hated being short. He looked down at me and smiled, as if he knew something I did not.

"What?" I asked curiously. "Do you not like being called Leuken?"

"No, it's not that. I like it when you say my name." He was still smiling.

"Then what is it?" I asked impatiently.

"I just love it when you are so happy."

I remembered what he had said about knowing other people's feelings. *Oh well* I thought to myself. He did make me happy, and I honestly didn't care if he knew it. With our faces so close I was hoping for more than a hug, but then I heard a car approaching down the road. He kissed my forehead tenderly, and then pulled away. I barely resisted the urge not to let go of him. Turning to see who was coming, I saw Ben pulling up in their Hummer. I waved at him as he came to a stop in front of the house.

"I'll see you tomorrow?" Luke asked as he walked backwards towards the Hummer, keeping his eyes on me.

"Sounds good. Have a good night." I replied, unable to think of anything clever to say.

"You too Elizabeth." He smiled, then turned and walked to the hummer, getting in the passenger door. A moment later I still felt giddy as I watched him drive away. Like I was waking up from a good dream. Except that I hadn't been dreaming. Leuken Bennett was real. And he trusted me. If I didn't know better, I would even say he liked me. Those three things combined left me feeling happier than I had been since my mother passed away.

If only she could be here now. She would have absolutely adored Leuken. I realized that for the first time when I thought about her, I didn't feel the aching pain that always came with such thoughts. The longing to have her back was still there, and I definitely still missed her, but the pain was gone. Perhaps Leuken had healed more than just my knife wound.

I went back inside the house and was surprised to see Alex looking out the front window. He hurriedly ran back over to the couch when he saw me coming inside.

"Hey you little spy." I teased, walking over to stand by him. "So… what do you think about Luke?"

"I like him Izzie. Is he gonna come play again later?"

"Hopefully." I replied.

Not even a minute had passed when I heard my father walking down the stairs. He walked into the room yawning. Wearing a black tank top and black shorts, he must have been about to do his normal workout routine.

"Hey Liz, hey Alex. How are you guys doing?" He asked, looking at us suspiciously.

"Good." I said with hesitation.

"I saw that kid Luke getting into his car a minute ago, what did he stop by for?" he asked.

"Oh, we have to work on a project for our Literature class, and I figured after what happened yesterday you would rather we did it over here than at his place. Is that okay?" I put on my best innocent face.

"Sure Liz, that's fine. He seems like a nice enough kid."

"Yeah, he's all right." I tried to sound disinterested. "He might have to come over some more though this week because we have to study and practice together."

"That's fine Liz." He grinned at me, and I got the impression he knew about my feelings for Luke. If he didn't bring it up though, I wasn't about to.

I decided that now would be a good time to escape before the conversation got any more awkward, so I excused myself and went upstairs. An hour later I was still looking at my untouched homework, thinking about Luke. While nothing he had told me made any logical or rational sense, I unequivocally believed every word of it. That being said, I was more anxious than ever to see him again. Some of the mystery surrounding him was now gone, yet to me he seemed more mystical than ever. The rational part of me said that he was dangerous, but I didn't care. Leuken Bennett had captured my heart. And I liked being his prisoner.

CHAPTER VII

"You did say that Alex likes airplanes almost as much as food didn't you?" Luke asked from the passenger seat of my Tahoe.

We were sitting in front of Harrisburg Elementary School, waiting for Alex to get out. This morning when I had seen Luke again waiting for me in the parking lot at school, the first thing he had asked was if we could hang out again after school. I of course didn't object, so after another painfully long day at school, we were finally alone together.

"Yes, he does. Why?" I replied.

"Well, I was hoping that maybe we could drive down to the Eugene airport and watch the airplanes for a little bit with him. Yesterday he seemed kind of bored, so I thought it might be fun. What do you think?" he glanced sideways at me as he finished, probably trying to gauge my reaction.

"I actually think that would be a lot of fun. I'm sure Alex would love it."

"Okay good. I know a really good burger joint right by the airport. We could eat there while we watch the planes."

"I'm not really hungry, but you know Alex will be, so that sounds like a good idea to me." Lunch had only been a little over an hour before, and my turkey sandwich had been more than enough for me.

"Well, they also have amazing Chocolate Shakes. Why don't you leave your Tahoe at my house, and I'll drive."

I agreed and less than a minute later Alex was helping himself into the car. Alex was of course excited to see Luke again, and he flashed a big grin at him before buckling on his seatbelt.

"Hey Luke. Are you gonna come over and play with us again?" He asked excitedly.

"Actually, I'm not going to be coming over today Alex." Luke replied. Alex's smile quickly faded. "But we are all going to go for a little drive together, how does that sound buddy?"

"Really? Where are we going?" Alex's face lit up again.

"We can't tell you that, it's a surprise." He replied.

"Izzie, can you tell me where we are going?" Alex turned to face me.

"Not yet Alex. You'll see when we get there okay? I promise you will like it though."

"Will there be food there? I am so hungry."

"Yes Alex, we will make sure you get some food." We came to a stop sign, and I quickly turned and gave Alex a smile.

He of course smiled back since I had mentioned food. Luke pulled out his cell phone, and it looked like he was texting someone. A minute later I was pulling in front of Luke's house as his Hummer was backing out of the garage. Putting my car in park, I noticed that Ben was driving the hummer.

"Thanks Ben." Luke said as we exited the car. Ben was just getting out of the hummer, and he threw the keys to Luke.

"No problem." Ben replied.

He sounded a little frustrated, and it reminded me of his behavior at lunch today. Other than his standard cheerful greeting, he had been awfully quiet. If I didn't know better, I would say that something was bothering him tremendously. An idea came to me.

"Hey Ben, do you want to come down to Eugene with us?" I asked.

His countenance seemed to improve a little as he looked at me with a grin. "Absolutely Liz. That sounds like a lot of fun." He said, shooting a smug look at Luke.

I hadn't even thought to ask Luke if he would care, but I couldn't imagine why he would. Luke was pulling Alex's booster seat out of the back.

"Wow!" Alex said as he walked towards the Hummer. "That is a cool jeep. What's it called Izzie?" His big blue eyes looked up at me, full of curiosity.

"It's called a hummer." I answered.

"Well, I like it Izzie. Are we going to drive in it?"

"We sure are." I replied enthusiastically.

A few minutes later we were driving down the highway towards Eugene. The airport was in the northwest part of the city, so it should only take about fifteen minutes to get there. I was sitting in the front passenger seat, with Ben behind me and Alex next to him. Luke was driving. We crossed over the bridge that connected Harrisburg to Junction City, and I noticed that some clouds were forming on the western horizon in front of us. Judging by their dark color, I thought it a safe bet to say it would be raining later.

Luke and I didn't say much while we drove. Ben was busy talking to Alex in the back seat and I watched the scenery as we passed by. Between Junction City and northern Eugene, the landscape was fairly empty. Industrial complexes faded away behind us, and there were clear fields of grass for a couple miles on either side of the highway. Had it not been for the road signs and advertising billboards every few hundred feet, it could have passed for cattle grazing land in the Midwest. A minute later more industrial buildings appeared in the distance ahead. Soon after that the city of Eugene came into view.

We came to a stop light about a mile from the airport but didn't wait more than a few seconds before it turned green. As we neared the airport, I saw a small strip mall ahead on the right. It was directly across the street from the observation parking lot at the airport. There was a large hamburger shaped sign in front of the businesses that read "Fred's Frost Top". I guessed that must be the burger joint that Luke had mentioned. Sure enough, we pulled into the parking lot in front of Fred's a few seconds later.

Luke came around and opened my door for me, and Ben held Alex's door while he climbed out of the back seat. The smell of barbecue emanated from the building, and my stomach growled softly. A chocolate shake was actually starting to sound appealing.

"Mmmm… it smells good out here. Is this where we are eating Izzie?" Alex asked sniffing loudly.

"It sure is. And we are going to watch the airplanes taking off and landing. Won't that be fun?"

"Oh yes it will." He said back to me, before turning to Ben and Luke. "Thanks for bringing us here you guys. I like driving in your hummer."

"You're welcome, buddy." Luke replied.

"Anytime Alex." Ben added simultaneously.

Luke held the door for us as we entered the restaurant. The inside of the place was set up like a fifties joint. Half a dozen tables with glass tops over white tablecloths lined the walls by the window. The tables had wooden benches on either side, and the smell of grilling meat was even stronger inside. Other than an older couple sitting at the table furthest from the entrance, there were no other customers. A blonde girl who couldn't have been much older than me was standing at the order counter. While she looked attractive, I thought her makeup was excessive. She smiled at Luke in an overly friendly fashion as we approached the counter.

"Hi, what can I get for you?" She said eyeing Luke.

"I'm not exactly sure; can you give us just a minute?" Luke asked.

"That's fine. I'll be here when you're ready for me." Her tone was outrageously flirtatious, and I felt a stab of jealousy. She stared at Luke like he was a piece of meat.

"What did you want Liz? Their burgers are incredible, and so are their shakes." Luke said stepping a little closer to me as he looked up at the menu board above the register.

My jealousy subsided slightly when he put a hand gently on my back. The blonde girl definitely noticed the move, because she looked at me distastefully. I couldn't help but smile.

"I'm not sure, but Alex probably wants a cheeseburger and French fries. What are you going to have?" I asked.

"I don't know either. I'm not that hungry, but I love their food. Maybe do you want to split a burger and get a chocolate shake?"

"Yeah, that sounds good." I replied.

Luke ordered for all four of us. I offered to pay for mine and Alex's, but he refused to take the money. We sat two tables over from the elderly couple and waited for our food to come. The entire wall facing south was glass, so it provided an unobstructed view of the runways. A large airliner was taking off. Alex stared excitedly as it lifted into the sky.

The food came relatively quickly, and Luke hadn't been exaggerating. It was spectacular. The meat wasn't cooked quite as well as I preferred, but it tasted so exquisite I didn't mind the miniscule amount of pink in the center. My chocolate shake was also tasty, but rich, so I gave it to Alex after drinking about half. He of course loved it too.

"What are those Izzie?" Alex asked pointing across the street after he finished his food.

He was pointing at the binoculars that were affixed to poles at the observation parking lot of the airport. A few cars were parked in the small lot, but only one older man was using any of the binoculars. Another family with four kids was standing not far from them, just watching the planes take off.

"Those are binoculars." I answered. "Do you want to go and look out them when we are done eating?"

"What do they do?"

"They let you see things that are far away as if they were up close." He looked at me confused, so I added "They make things look bigger, so you can see them better."

"Oh. Okay Izzie. Can I look at them after we eat?" He asked excitedly.

"Of course."

We finished eating, then went outside to the crosswalk and waited for the walking signal on the corner to turn green. Alex held my hand, and halfway across the crosswalk he reached out and grabbed Luke's as well. Once we reached the other side Alex let go of my hand and started to run ahead, tugging Luke along with him. Ben fell in beside me as we walked slowly after them.

"So how is football going Ben?" I asked. While I wanted to know what had been bothering him earlier, I thought it best to start with casual conversation.

"It's going really good actually. I should be able to play on Friday. Coach is going to have me fill in for Dustin at wide receiver and safety, so hopefully I can play okay." He looked ahead at Luke and Alex as he spoke.

They had just reached one of the poles with Binoculars on it and Alex was putting his eyes up to it while Luke squatted down beside him. Luke had one hand on Alex shoulder, while he pointed at an airplane with the other. Seeing those two playing together made me happy.

Bringing my attention back to Ben, I noticed that he looked frustrated again. It was difficult to tell if he was angry or not, but his somber mood was uncharacteristic for him. He hadn't even told any corny jokes since last Friday.

"It's hard on you sometimes, isn't it?" I asked suddenly, surprising myself. I hadn't meant to say that out loud.

"What?" He shot me a contorted look.

"Having to move so often." I said, realizing that I wasn't sure if Luke had told Ben that I knew about their secret.

"Yeah, it is." He paused for a moment. "But you just do what you have to do to stay alive."

Judging by his statement, I gathered that he must know I was aware of their situation, but I didn't know how to reply to his comment. So, I decided to hold my tongue, and instead I just looked at him. Other than his blonde hair and green eyes, his face looked almost exactly like Luke's. Had he been a couple of years older, and Luke not in the picture, I could have even seen myself being attracted to him. As things were though, he was just Ben. And I was crazy about Luke. Ben seemed more like a younger brother than anything else, and I loved his normally cheerful personality.

"Do you ever want things that you know you can never have Liz?" Ben asked. I was surprised by the change of subject.

"Yes" I answered thoughtfully. "I wish that I could see my mom again. Or even better have her back in my life." Again, I noticed that the pain was now distant as I spoke of her. "What about you?"

He looked at me and paused before answering, as if he was wrestling with some difficult decision. After a long moment he finally spoke.

"I wish I could remember my father sometimes." He said as his shoulders slumped. "My mom always tells me how much he loved us, and what a great dad he was… but I can't remember him at all."

"I'm so sorry Ben." I said softly. "How old were you when he passed away?"

"You mean when he was murdered by those creatures?" There was no masking the anger as he turned to look at me. "Sorry Liz, it's not fair to take it out on you. It's not you I'm upset with." He seemed to calm slightly as he finished.

"That's okay Ben. I can understand the anger you must feel. The man responsible for my mom's death died in the accident too, but I still hate him. If he hadn't been too drunk to remember his seatbelt, he probably would have survived. If so, I probably would want to kill him. I think being upset is justified given your situation."

"I wasn't talking about that." Ben replied. "I will kill the tainted one who is responsible for my father's death some day. But he is not the one I was thinking about."

"Then who is it?" I asked confused.

"It's not important." He mumbled bitterly. "Being jealous is stupid anyway."

"Who are you jealous of?"

Had it not been for the look he shot at Luke, I would have been utterly lost. All of the sudden it made sense. He was jealous of Luke. Why I couldn't say, but I recognized that look. It was the same one my father had given people when they hit on mom, back when she was still alive.

"Oh… I see." I said. He turned to look at me, and I knew my hunch was correct. "Why would you be jealous of Luke? You are just as good looking as he is, and probably just as talented. You are also better at making everyone else around you happy." He raised an eyebrow at me when I said that. "Well, normally you are anyway."

"Liz, it's not who he is." He explained. "It's who he has."

I again looked at him, dumbfounded. He was eyeing me differently, and something about the glint in his eyes was… familiar. It reminded me of the way Luke looked at me sometimes. Times like when we were about to kiss. And then it hit me. I felt dense for not seeing it sooner. So, Ben had a crush on me… and I was absolutely in love with his older brother. Awkward doesn't begin to describe the feeling that came over me. What was I supposed to say to that?

Thinking about what he said, I realized something else. Ben was talking as if Luke and I were already a thing, but I still wasn't sure what we were. The only time we had even kissed had been right after a near death experience, and while the very thought of belonging to Luke excited me; there was no way Ben could know the way I felt. Technically we were still just friends.

"Ben, I don't know what you mean. I don't think that Luke *has* anyone."

"Come on Liz, I might be naive but I'm not stupid. It's obvious that you two are completely smitten with each other. It's not a matter of *if* you two will end up together, so much as when."

"You think he's smitten?" I asked getting sidetracked.

"Oh please. He won't stop talking about you. Everything he says is Liz this and Liz that." He made funny imitating faces as he spoke. "I would probably think he was crazy for being so whipped... If I didn't feel the same way about you." He looked away again as he finished.

Again feeling awkward, I couldn't find the right words. It was quiet for what seemed like an eternity but was in actuality probably only a few seconds. I could see Alex standing next to the binoculars now and Luke was taking a turn looking through them.

"Sorry for making things awkward Liz. I knew I shouldn't have said anything." He was shaking his head slightly. "You know what the hardest part about all this is? Even though I get jealous of him sometimes, he really is a good guy, and I do love him. And if anyone alive deserved you, and they don't. … But if they did… it would probably be him."

I wasn't quite sure what was crazier. All of the unwarranted praise, or the fact that he was openly telling me all of this. It's not like I was anything special.

"I don't know what you're talking about Ben. I'm just me, plain old Elizabeth Scott."

"You really don't get how amazing you are, do you?" he looked me straight in the eyes.

"Ben I'm not" I objected.

"Elizabeth listen." He interrupted before I could finish. "I know that I put you in an awkward situation and I am sorry. I do love your humility, but I think that you should know just how much people care about you. The mere fact that Luke was willing to risk everything and choose you for the telling speaks volumes. Someday, if things work out, you'll understand just how significant him telling you our secret was. In the meantime, just trust me when I say that my brother really likes you a lot.

"Now to change the subject. While it feels relieving having that all out in the open, I need to make a deal with you."

"What's that?" I replied.

"How about I will never again mention that I have a crush on you, and I will do my best not to be jealous of Luke or ever make things awkward again, if you will promise not to tell Luke about my feelings for you?" He smiled sheepishly at me, holding out his hand. I saw a glint of the old Ben.

"You've got yourself a deal." I reached out and shook his hand.

"Thanks Liz." He smiled and seemed genuinely relieved.

"Thanks for what?" I responded sarcastically. He just grinned. After a moment I added "Whatever happens Ben, just don't ever stop being you."

Luke and Alex started walking back towards us. The timing couldn't have been better, because the wind started to pick up and I was freezing in my light jacket. I could smell the moisture in the air. The dark clouds approaching confirmed my premonition that it was about to rain. Faint lines stretched from the clouds to the ground, and I knew that they were rainfall. The nearest cloud was less than a mile away now.

We walked quickly back to the car. Alex excitedly told me about how cool the binoculars were, in between saying how cold he was. My fingers were feeling numb, and I wished that I had brought gloves and a thicker jacket. With Luke walking next to me, holding his hand became more appealing than ever, as I thought of the warmth my fingers could receive.

Once we were all seated in the hummer with the doors closed it felt nice. Without the wind blowing on me I was still cold, but it was a stable cold as opposed to feeling like I was freezing to death. By the time we pulled back onto the highway the heat was blowing warm in the car. I made sure that one of my vents was facing towards Alex who was shivering in the back, then put my hands in front of the other vent. At first the air stung because my fingers had been so cold, but after a minute the sting went away, and it felt good.

Rain started pelting our windows five minutes into our drive home, and it didn't stop. The wind also picked up even more, and I could feel the car being jerked to the right by gusts. It was difficult to see more than a hundred feet or so in front of us through the heavy downpour. I became increasingly grateful that I wasn't driving.

When we got back to Luke's house I thanked him for lunch, and for the good time. It was still pouring, so I gave him a quick hug in the car, said bye to Ben, and then ran to my car holding Alex's booster seat.

I was also excited when I got home to discover my father was still sleeping. Had he woken up to find us both missing, it wouldn't have surprised me to find him waiting in the doorway with a lecture. As it was Alex still ended up telling him where we had gone. I was again surprised when all he said was: "As long as you had your cell phone on you, that's fine Liz. Just don't go across state lines without telling me, okay?"

The next couple of days went by too quickly. Luke came over again after school, and we actually spent a good deal of time working on our upcoming Literature project. After a couple more almost kisses that were interrupted by Alex, we decided against any more attempts at my house. It was remarkable how well we got along. He actually got my frequently sarcastic humor, and he even sounded genuine when he laughed. Alex seemed to love him more every day, and I found myself following suit. Just in a different way.

Every second that we spent together I felt… complete. When he left it was like a part of me had been cut out, but I didn't let it bother me too much. I knew I would be seeing him again soon enough. He gave me his cell phone number Wednesday before he left, and we talked until midnight. Thursday night we talked again until I fell asleep on the phone. I could remember seeing one seventeen on the clock but wasn't sure how long after that I had managed to stay awake. Friday morning, I was worried he would be mad about my falling asleep, but he admitted to feeling the same way because he had fallen asleep as well.

At lunch on Friday, we had decided to go watch the football game together. Nikki had been excited that she would have someone to sit with besides Greg's parents for once. And so it was that I found myself pulling in front of Luke's house on Friday night.

He was waiting outside by the road and opened the passenger door as I came to a stop. Wearing a blue thermal under his unzipped leather jacket and his hair styled perfectly messy, he looked like he had jumped right out of a GQ magazine and into my Tahoe.

"Hey Elizabeth. You look incredible." He said as he sat down and pulled the door shut.

"Thanks." I replied as I managed to peel my eyes off of him and back onto the road. "You look nice too."

"So, are you excited to go and watch some football?" He asked overenthusiastically.

"Well, I would be lying if I said I was excited about the football." I answered. "But... I am excited about watching it with you."

"Well, it has been almost four hours since I saw you last." He said grinning.

"Is that all?" I smiled back at him.

A few minutes later we were pulling up to Harrisburg High School. All of the parking spaces were taken, so we parked in front of the school. There were already a few dozen cars lining both sides of the street. Luke ran around to open my door, and I could hear the announcer's voice on the loudspeaker coming from the football field.

We saw Luke and Ben's hummer parked in the front row closest to the field. Ben had needed it for the game, which is why I picked Luke up. For some reason he had seemed bothered by asking me to drive, but Jazmine had needed her car to do something in town, and Luke said that Isaac never let anyone use his truck. Isaac always needed a vehicle in case things went bad.

As we were walking through the dark parking lot my mind wandered to the creatures Luke had mentioned. The Verdorben. It was such a strange sounding word. I glanced at the ring on his finger and remembered about how he said that the metal in it could kill those things.

"Terralium" I said to myself quietly. "That is the stuff you said can kill those Verdorben things, right? So how does it work? Is it like kryptonite where it just has to be close to them?"

He chuckled lightly. "No Liz, it's not like kryptonite. It will burn them if it touches them, and it is the only known metal that will actually pierce their skins, but it only hurts them if they touch it. It doesn't weaken them at all just based on proximity. I sure wish it did though."

"Then how can you kill them with it if it is so small. I mean, that stone is tiny." I said eyeing his ring skeptically.

"This ring isn't what we use to fight the tainted ones. It only alerts us when they are close." He said calmly, then reached in the back of his waistband and pulled out a long knife.

It looked like a knife at first anyway, but I suppose dagger would be a more fitting title. The blade was just over a foot long and looked the same color and texture as the dark stone in his ring. Its handle was much smaller, six inches at most, and looked to be pure silver. The hilt of the dagger was also made of the same silver metal, and it had a small black line going across it.

"This is what we use." He said, holding the dagger towards me.

I grabbed it from him and looked at it closely. The blade seemed sharp on both sides and especially at the tip. As I examined the hilt, I noticed that the black line was actually hundreds of small symbols, similar to the ones that were on Luke's ring. They were barely visible in the dim light we had stopped under in front of the football field.

"What do these symbols mean?" I traced the hilt of the dagger with my fingers.

"To be honest I am not entirely sure." He looked down at the dagger. "They are not written in any known language. The symbols were on the weapons when they were first given to the bloodline at the beginning of the tenth century. Isaac claims that at any given time there is one member of the bloodline who is capable of reading them. Unfortunately, we don't know who or where that person is. My people don't exactly like to be found either, so the chances of getting these translated are slim to none."

"That's too bad." I said as I handed the dagger back to him.

He tucked it back into his waistband, and I was surprised by how well he concealed it. He must have had some kind of special pocket or case to hold it sewn into his clothes. Otherwise, it would stand out whenever he sat down. I would never have known it was there if he hadn't showed it to me.

Once we made it inside, I was searching for Nikki, but the bleachers were packed. After a minute of looking, I had given up on finding her when Luke tapped my shoulder.

"There she is." He said pointing to the front row on the far side of the bleachers. How he could pick her out of the crowd from a couple hundred feet away I couldn't say.

"You've got good vision." I turned to tell him once I finally recognized her, when we were halfway across the bleachers.

After joining Nikki in the bleachers, we watched the game. The cool breeze brought a chill that made it difficult to pay attention to the game, so I was relieved when Luke gave his jacket to me. Nikki talked to me for most of the game, but Luke didn't seem to mind. Harrisburg High ended up winning by three, after scoring a field goal to break the tie with a few seconds left. Nikki went down to congratulate Greg, while Luke and I applauded Ben. The air seemed to be getting colder by the minute, so we decided to head home.

Luke held my hand all the way back to my car. I sighed when he let go to open my door for me. We talked idly about the game on the way to his house, and then I pulled to a stop in front of it.

"I had a lot of fun tonight." I said and leaned over to give him a hug.

Surprisingly, he didn't put his arms around me. Instead, he pulled his face back slightly to look into my eyes. I was about to pull back, thinking there was something wrong, when he grabbed my face with both hands and kissed me. My surprise quickly turned to excitement, and it was more than a few seconds before he slowly pulled away from me. I again thought my heart would pound right out of my chest. Just like the last time he had kissed me. It took a few seconds, but eventually I came back to reality.

"Sorry about that." He said sounding dazed.

"Don't be." I smiled at him. "I'm not."

A long moment passed while we just stared at each other smiling. I could have drowned in his eyes.

"Elizabeth Scott?" He eventually said.

"Yes?" I replied.

"What are you doing tomorrow?"

"Nothing…" *Hopefully seeing you again.* I thought to myself.

"Okay, then I need you to find an excuse to get away and meet me here at ten tomorrow morning."

"What?" I asked excitedly. Was he toying with me?

"I don't care what you tell your dad, but if you need to, we can park your Tahoe in my garage."

"Where are we going?"

"That's a secret. But you need to dress warm and be prepared not to get back until after sundown."

"Okay." Now I was really curious. "Do I need to bring anything?"

"Nope. Just your beautiful self." He leaned over and gave me one more kiss on the forehead, and then he opened the door and stepped out of the car. Turning back to me he added "If you can't come let me know, otherwise I'll see you at ten." The car door closed, and he disappeared through his front door a minute later.

I don't think the smile left my face until I got home and walked in the front door to my house. Even then I had to force it to go away. My father was surprisingly passed out on the couch with Alex sleeping on his lap. I slipped past them and decided to get ready for bed. I wanted to be up early so I could get ready for the day with Luke. I also needed to think of what I was going to tell my father.

***

Jeremy noticed the flashing red and blue lights in the rear-view mirror just before hearing the siren chirp. He glanced down at his speedometer and realized that he was going seventy-seven miles an hour. Thinking that the speed limit here was seventy-five, he was confused as to why he was being pulled over. He knew the Oregon border was still some thirty miles to the north, so it must be California Highway Patrol. *I hope this guy doesn't make me kill him.* He thought to himself as he slowly hit the brakes and began to pull to the right.

There were no other cars in sight, and he hadn't seen one in almost five minutes, but that was to be expected when driving on the interstate at two thirty in the morning. Jeremy liked driving at this time though. It was easier to think with less traffic.

It had been over a year since he had been changed. A night he would literally remember forever. At least if Jareth let him live that long. He had been driving home from the UCLA campus when it had all happened. Having just received his M-CAT scores from the month before, he found out that he got a thirty-four. Between that and his 3.91 GPA he was a shoe in for medical school. He had just started to merge onto the off ramp that night when someone had landed in front of his car. He hit them and his car flipped over landing in the ditch upside down after rolling once.

After getting out of the car he ran to check on the person he had run over. Instead of finding a body though, he found two people lying on the ground. The one on top was jerking around and flailing his arms loosely. The other man, who was much larger, was lying underneath the first and holding him in some kind of choke hold.

Jeremy had thought about running but felt too guilty. He had also thought about helping but was too afraid. So instead, he got out his cell phone and dialed 9-1-1. His phone was still ringing when the man on top stopped moving, and then a recording came on his phone saying that all dispatchers were assisting other callers.

Suddenly he had felt nauseous and dropped the phone. When he finally finished puking his guts out, the man had been standing over him. Jeremy felt too weak to fight, so the man had effortlessly placed the bracelet on him. It wasn't until later that he discovered his newfound abilities.

Since that fateful night he had been a servant. Sleeping by day and hunting by night, he was searching for the people with the sun tattoos. The ones who called themselves the bloodline.

It was the only way he could earn his freedom and have the curse lifted. Or at least that was what Jareth had claimed. He had no choice but to follow him anyway, so at least it gave Jeremy some hope to hold on to. Jareth had said that if Jeremy helped him to kill two of the tattoo people, he would be turned back to normal and could have his life back. It was that motivation that helped him to make every decision now.

He came to a complete stop on the side of the road and threw the car in park. While he hoped that this trooper would be weak enough to manipulate, he knew what had to be done if he wasn't. The trooper got out of his car and shined a spotlight in Jeremy's rearview mirror, obstructing his vision. Jeremy then heard the man approach as his boots crunched the gravel with each step.

"Good morning, sir. I'm going to need your license, registration and proof of insurance." The trooper said once he reached Jeremy's window and Jeremy noticed that he looked young. He couldn't have been a day older than twenty-five.

"Okay. Did I do something wrong officer?" Jeremy said reaching above the visor where his registration, license and insurance papers were.

"Well, you were doing seventy-eight in a sixty-five." The trooper answered. "Didn't you see those road work signs back there?"

"Honestly I didn't sir I'm sorry." Jeremy concentrated and attempted to pull at the trooper's mind. "Don't you just want to give me a warning though and let me go?"

"Sorry sir I don't do warnings." The trooper replied sternly, and Jeremy realized his compulsion wasn't affecting him. "Especially when people ask for them."

"Listen to me" Jeremy started concentrating more and pulled as hard as his mind would allow. "You are going to let me go because I just need a warning."

The trooper visibly relaxed and repeated Jeremy. "You're right; I am going to let you go. You just needed a warning." He said in a dazed tone before turning to walk back towards his car.

Jeremy relaxed when he realized that it had worked the second time. The trooper was almost to his car now, so he shifted his own back into drive when suddenly he heard the trooper shout.

"Hey, wait a minute!" he said as he almost ran back up to the car. "I never checked your license. I'm going to have to ask you to step out of the car sir.

So, this cop is stronger willed then I thought… too bad for him. Jeremy thought to himself. He stepped out of the car as the trooper backed up with his hand on his gun.

"Just keep your hands where I can see them sir, and don't make any sudden movements." The trooper barked. "I need you to step back in front of my vehicle."

Jeremy had had enough with being ordered, so he quickly lunged at the trooper, pulling his radio off his belt with one hand while he threw him off the side of the road with his other. The man screamed as he landed sideways on one leg, and Jeremy heard his leg bone snap. Turning to face the man, he saw that the trooper was pulling out his gun as Jeremy walked towards him. The trooper fired three shots at him, two striking him in the chest, and one hitting his forehead, but Jeremy barely noticed. His open palm caught the trooper in the temple, knocking him back and sideways a few feet. The trooper's body lay still. Jeremy walked quickly back to the man's car. It was unlocked, so he reached in and ripped the dashboard camera out of the front of the dash.

Walking back to his car he glanced around to make sure no one was watching. They weren't. He got in his car and drove away, this time not caring about the speed limit. His Mercedes could go over a hundred easily enough, so he would drive it that fast until he reached Oregon.

He would need to buy a new car somewhere and dump this old one, since within an hour everyone would likely be looking for him. Luckily for him they would only have a license plate since he had taken the camera. The plate hadn't even belonged to the car anyways. Everyone would be looking for a white Mercedes when his was black. It should buy him enough time to burn the car or get another plate.

After that he could go back to hunting. Northern California had taken him much longer than expected to sweep. It had been over a month since he first arrived in San Francisco, and he had only covered a few hundred miles. He hoped to be able to find these people soon. While he didn't like having to hurt people, he was determined to do anything he had to. As long as it meant getting his life back.

CHAPTER VIII

Selling my father on going with Luke to some unknown location would never fly. So, I decided to call Nikki. I told her my dilemma, and she said that she would cover for me. The story would be that I was going to her house to watch chick flicks, because her dad was out of town on a business meeting. I would give him her cell phone number in case he couldn't get in touch with me, and my Tahoe would have to hide in Luke's garage.

While I felt bad about lying to my father, I was too excited for my surprise date with Luke to let it bother me. Besides, I knew I could trust Luke. My dad was too paranoid to understand, so I was sheltering him from worrying about me. At least that's how I rationalized my guilt.

I woke up extra early to make breakfast for Alex and my father. One thing I had learned about men is that they frequently let their guard down, and are always nicer, when they are fed. I intended to exploit that weakness. We were finishing up the breakfast I had made for them when I popped the question. My dad looked at me for a long second while chewing a piece of bacon before answering.

"That sounds like a good idea. You've been hanging out with that Luke kid too much lately anyway. It would be nice for you to have some girl time."

He went back to eating his food, so I went upstairs and called Luke to tell him I would be coming. He sounded distracted on the phone, and it sounded like someone was arguing in the background, so I kept the conversation short and told him I would see him in a couple hours.

After cleaning up the kitchen and washing the dishes, I decided to hang out with Alex for a little while. I would be gone the rest of the day and didn't want him to feel neglected. He asked about Luke several times while we were playing a matching card game.

"Can Luke come over and play with me while you hang out with Nikki?" He had asked. It took some explaining before he realized that Luke would only be coming over to hang out when I was home too, but eventually he got it.

I took my time getting ready, donning a white long-sleeve shirt under my forest green sweater. After finishing my hair and mascara I grabbed my blue winter coat. It was much thicker than the one I had worn the night before. I also threw some gloves and a beanie in the coat pockets just in case I got cold again. The temptation was there to leave the gloves at home, because I thought it might be nice to have an excuse for holding Luke's hand. Then again, considering last night's kiss, I was hoping he wouldn't need excuses for things like that anymore.

After saying goodbye to my father and Alex, I drove to Luke's house. He walked out the front door right as I pulled to a stop. Wearing a plain white tee shirt and blue jeans, he must have been freezing. He jogged over to my Tahoe waving at me, so I rolled down the passenger window.

"Hey Liz. Just park it in the garage." He said pointing behind him down the driveway.

"Okay thanks. I was just about to ask you that, but you read my mind." I replied with a smile.

The garage door opened, and I saw Ben standing in the garage. He motioned to me as I backed into the garage where their hummer was normally parked. I didn't see their Hummer anywhere, and for a moment I wondered if maybe we were just staying at his house. The thought of meeting the entire family of superheroes was exciting, but also made me nervous.

I got out of the car and thanked Ben for backing me in. For some reason I had always hated backing into spaces while driving. Maybe it's because I was such a bad judge of distance.

"No problem, Liz. It's good to see you." He said smiling.

"You too Ben. By the way, congratulations on last night's game. That last interception you caught was incredible."

"Oh thanks. I was just lucky to be in the right place at the right time."

"Yeah right. I doubt luck had anything to do with it." I teased.

He chuckled lightly. "So, I've got a question for you."

"What's that?"

"What do you call a cow with no legs?" He asked smirking.

"I don't know, a midget cow?" I guessed.

"Ground beef."

He was smirking slightly while trying to keep a straight face, and I couldn't help but laugh. It was good to have the old Ben back and relieving that nothing was awkward between us. Hopefully he had come to his senses and realized that there wasn't anything special about me. Now I just had to hope that his brother never had the same realization.

As if on cue, I no sooner thought of Luke than he emerged from the door leading into the house. He had put on a blue sweater with white stripes over his tee shirt. I tried not to stare at him but failed miserably.

"I'm glad you dressed warm." He said as he walked up to me and gave me a quick hug. "It might be a little chilly where we are going. I brought an extra coat for you just in case though."

"That was thoughtful of you." I smiled at him. "And just where are we going, might I ask?"

"Well, I'm not supposed to tell you." He teased. "But something tells me you'll know where once we go out back. What's on the trailer is kind of a dead giveaway." He grabbed me by the hand and led me towards another door on the back side of the garage.

We passed through it onto the side of his house where a gravel path spanned past the length of the house. It was wide enough to drive a vehicle down, and I saw his Hummer parked at the back of the property. Attached to it was a black trailer with a canoe on top. At least I thought it was a canoe. The dark cherry wood had a glossy finish, and the boat looked big enough to hold three or four people. Hand carvings lined the side of the canoe, and it looked extraordinarily fancy. Like it belonged more on a display at a boat symposium than on the back of a trailer.

"Wow it's beautiful." I said while marveling at it.

"Well, you did say that you would go with me to Fern Ridge Lake, and I wanted to take you before it got too cold."

"Really?" I didn't bother trying to keep the excitement out of my voice. "Just the two of us?"

"Well… if that's okay with you?" He replied.

"Absolutely; it sounds perfect." I flashed him a big smile.

We walked over to the hummer, and I saw a man staring at me out the back window of the house. His hair was graying but his face looked young, possibly in his early forties. For some reason he looked vaguely familiar, and I thought that I had seen him before. Then I remembered the weekend before and it came to me. He was the man I had seen driving with Jazmine.

I smiled at him and waved, but he just stood there staring at us through the back window. His face looked stern and his expression unreadable. It was honestly a little unnerving. Not wanting to look at him anymore, I surveyed the rest of the back yard. A large swimming pool sat in the middle of the yard, with a rock cliff on one side. It looked like some kind of reddish sandstone, and a slide led from the cliff down into the water. A large grass area sat next to the pool, with pine trees lining the length of the back fence.

"That's a nice pool." I said to Luke, trying not to think about the strange look the man in the window was giving me.

"Oh yeah, thanks. Hopefully we'll be able to get some use out of it next summer."

He held the passenger door of the Hummer open for me and I climbed in. I glanced over at the window again as we were pulling out of the back yard, and the man was still staring at me.

"So… I'm guessing that's Isaac?" I asked Luke.

"Yeah." Luke replied glancing over at the man just before we pulled out of his view.

"Does he always look so happy?"

"Yeah well…let's just say Isaac doesn't like strangers." He gave me an apologetic look, and I thought it best to drop the subject.

We pulled out of Luke's yard and headed for the highway. Again, crossing the bridge to Junction City, we turned and headed in a Southwest direction. It occurred to me that I hadn't told Luke how to get to Fern Ridge Lake.

"I thought you said you had never been to Fern Ridge Lake before?" I asked.

"I haven't" he replied glancing over at me. "But I do have MapQuest, and the directions to get there are pretty simple."

"Oh… I didn't think about that."

We drove a while longer, mostly in silence, while I enjoyed the scenery. The further we got from the city the more beautiful the landscape became. Rolling green hills turned into lush forest, with occasional houses being replaced by frequent cabins off the side of the road. Eventually the lake came into view off to our right, but instead of turning towards it, he kept driving on the main highway.

"I think that was the turn off." I said, thinking perhaps he just hadn't seen it.

"I know." He glanced quickly at me. "But that's the turn off to the main dock, I know a better spot."

About two miles further down the road he suddenly slowed and turned down a small road on the right side of the highway. I hadn't even seen it until we were turning onto the path. Vegetation had grown in on both sides of the dirt path, and it was barely wide enough to fit his hummer and trailer. Tree branches just missed scraping the top of the hummer as we drove.

The lake soon came into view again, but it wasn't any part that I had seen before. A small cove roughly two hundred yards wide and twice as long lay before us. I could see where it connected to the rest of the lake at a small opening on the opposite end of the cove. That opening couldn't have been more than five feet wide. Unless you knew what you were looking for, this place was virtually hidden. Also adding to its seclusion was the line of tall trees that separated the cove from the rest of the lake on the shoreline between the two.

Luke backed up the Hummer so that the back of the trailer was only a few feet from the water. After he opened my door, we walked back to the trailer. I noticed that the symbols on the side of the canoe were all tiny carvings that were etched into the wood. Most of them were animals. There were several different kinds of birds, horses, tigers, as well as what appeared to be suns, moons and stars. What surprised me even more than the beauty and detail of the carvings was the fact that each one looked unique. These weren't some kind of premade molds that were carved by a machine. They all must have been engraved by hand.

"Wow, these are incredible." I thought aloud while running my fingers gently over the carvings. "Do you know who carved them?"

"Yes, I do actually." He paused momentarily before finishing. "It was Isaac."

"The same Isaac who was looking at me like I had some kind of disease earlier?" I asked surprised.

"Oh, I would hardly say he was looking at you like that. He's just suspicious of everyone until he gets to know them is all, but yes. He's the one who made the boat." He answered.

"Where did he learn how to do this?"

"Well, his father was a carpenter, and I think he taught Isaac a lot about it when he was younger. The fact that he's had almost two hundred years of practice probably helps also."

"Two hundred years?" I asked incredulously.

"Yeah well, I thought I mentioned it to you, but maybe I didn't. You see… we don't age as quickly as most people."

"What do you mean?"

"Well normal people age at the same rate their entire lives, but for us the aging process slows down in our late teens."

"Slows down how?"

"Well once our aging slows completely, we age at about one tenth the rate of a normal person."

"So… exactly how old does that make you then?" I asked intrigued.

"Liz, I already told you. I'm seventeen."

"Seventeen physically? Or really seventeen?"

"Both." He replied patiently. "I haven't noticed my aging beginning to slow yet. Don't worry; I was born January 1st, 1990. So, I'm only a few weeks older than you."

I did the math in my head, making sure it added up right. It did. So, his aging was going to slow down huh? Hopefully that wouldn't make him lose interest in me. Although it sounded like something that hadn't even started affecting him yet. Regardless, it didn't influence the way I felt about him, so I wasn't about to let it bother me.

"So… exactly how old is Isaac?" I asked, turning to look up at him.

"Well, he was born in Ireland in 1812, so I guess that would make him a hundred and ninety-five years old." He answered.

"A hundred and ninety-five!" I exclaimed wide eyed. "But he doesn't look a day older than forty."

"I know. He definitely doesn't look his age." He said before turning to untie the two ropes that were securing the boat to the trailer. I noticed that the back of the trailer had a drop tailgate that doubled as a ramp, but it looked steel, and I couldn't help but think that it would scratch up the boat if he tried sliding the canoe off the back of it.

"So… how did you plan on getting the boat off of the trailer without scratching the wood?" I asked.

"Oh, that's easy." He said as he finished untying the last rope. "Like this."

He grabbed the side of the canoe with one arm inside and his hand on the outside and lifted it straight up off of the trailer. Then he casually walked off the back of the trailer and set the canoe onto the edge of the water, with about half of the canoe still resting on the beach.

I stood with my mouth half open, dumbfounded. He had just made carrying that canoe, which easily weighed two hundred pounds, look like it was nothing. It might as well have been a beach ball for all the effort it took him to lift it.

"What?" He said when he caught me staring at him.

"Nothing." I managed to say after regaining my composure. "I just didn't realize exactly how strong you were. That's all."

"Oh please Liz, this boat's not even that heavy."

He motioned to me with his hand, so I walked over to him. One of his feet was on the edge of the boat, probably to hold it in place, while his other anchored him to the ground. Grabbing my hand as I reached him, he gently turned me before lifting me with both his arms. A second later he was setting me down on my feet inside the canoe. He stepped in, pushing off of the land with his other foot. We glided slowly out into the water.

I noticed that there were two small benches in the middle of the canoe, so I took a seat in the one closer to the front. Luke came and sat on the other one, so we were facing each other. Our knees were touching, which of course didn't bother me at all. I only wished that the benches had been a little closer.

Luke picked up one of two large paddles and placed an end into the water. His quick pull looked effortless, but we sped through the water momentarily after a single stroke. I smiled and looked around. There wasn't another soul in sight, unless you counted the flock of birds flying over head. They were too high up to distinguish what kind they were, but their dark feathers did more gliding then flapping as they soared through the air. The wind was virtually nonexistent, and it had definitely warmed a few degrees since yesterday. I could barely feel the cool air on the back of my neck as we cut through the water.

"Did you want me to help paddle?" I asked reaching for one of the oars.

"If you want to." He replied, pulling in his paddle and setting it on his lap.

I grabbed the paddle with both hands, sticking the wide end into the water. The pull of the water on the paddle as it entered the lake almost made me drop it. Barely holding on, the boat slowed quickly and turned sideways before I was able to pull the paddle out. I hadn't realized how fast we were going until my oar had touched the water.

"Okay, maybe I should let you do it." I said as he chuckled.

"Are you sure? I don't mind watching you paddle." He smirked.

I couldn't help but smile too. We sat there for a few seconds, just looking at one another as the boat slowly spun in the center of the cove. Then Luke leaned in slowly and kissed me. After a couple seconds he pulled back a little, and I could see he was smiling. I smiled back, then leaned closer to him and kissed him some more.

What seemed like seconds later, but was probably a few minutes, he pulled away and I reluctantly let him. His hands slid down to grab mine as he pulled back, and I squeezed his gently. He was smiling broadly again and shaking his head slightly as he looked at me.

"What?" I asked. Unsure what he found so amusing.

"Nothing it's just…" He looked like he was deciding if he should say something or not. "You really are incredible Elizabeth, you know that?"

"No, I'm not. But I'm glad you think so." I paused for a moment. "So, what were you really thinking just now that you didn't say?"

"What do you mean?" He tried to look innocent.

"Leuken Bennett. Just because I don't have any special powers doesn't mean I can't tell when you are trying to keep something from me."

"Well, it's really nothing importa" He began.

"Then tell me." I interrupted. He looked at me for a long while before answering.

"Okay, but it might sound a little crazy so try not to get weirded out."

"I won't." I reassured.

"What I was thinking was… that I couldn't believe that not only did I literally find the girl of my dreams, but I also couldn't believe that she actually liked me too."

"What makes you think I like you?" I teased smiling.

"Well, I just assumed…" He stammered.

"I'm just kidding. Of course I care about you. I don't see how I could be the girl of anyone's dreams, but as long as that means I get you; I'm not going to argue."

"No Liz, I don't think that you understand." He added with a pause. "When I say you are the girl of my dreams, I'm not just trying to give you a cheesy compliment. You literally were in my dreams before I ever even met you." I raised my eyebrow at him in confusion.

"I told you about how I could see the future sometimes right?" He added, and I nodded. "Well, I literally started seeing you… in my dreams… months before we even moved to Harrisburg. Unlike any other foretelling dream I had ever had, these ones were different."

"You mean you literally saw me? Or was it just someone who looked like me?"

"Oh, I am absolutely certain it was you. Do you remember that day when we first met, and I blatantly stared at you when I walked into class?"

"Yes, actually I do." I smiled broadly as I thought about it.

"Well, the reason I was staring is because I thought that maybe I was dreaming. Having seen you every night in my dreams for months, when I actually saw you in person it seemed surreal." He glanced off at the lake.

"Tell me more about these dreams. Exactly what was I doing in them?" I asked curiously.

"Well in all of them I would see you one second, and then you would disappear. But even after you left the dream your face was burned into my head. And it wasn't just because of how beautiful you are. For some reason I always had the impression that I needed to find you whenever I saw you. Then after every time you disappeared, I felt it again even stronger."

"Do you still have the dreams?"

"No. That's the funny thing. The dreams came consistently every night for months, but the night after I met you, they stopped suddenly." I looked at him, unsure what to say. "I'm sorry Liz, I know this sounds crazy. You probably think that I'm some kind of weirdo now, but it's the honest truth. I'm not trying to scare you."

"No…I definitely don't think you are a weirdo. Incredible yes, adorable yes, but a weirdo… never." I pulled his hands up to my lips and gently kissed the back of them. "To be perfectly honest Luke, the only scary thing about you is how I feel like I have already fallen completely for you." He looked surprised, so I elaborated.

"You see Luke, from a logical standpoint I should probably be scared of you. My father raised me to be paranoid and not to trust anyone but family. 'Don't ever believe anything that sounds too good to be true', he always told me. And then here you come along, doing supernatural things and in every way seeming too good to be true. Add in the fact that you're absolutely gorgeous and make me feel like I never want to be separated from you, and it makes you logically even more dangerous. Now here I am all alone with you out in the middle of a lake, and I've only known you two weeks. My father would kill me if he knew I was here with you."

"Sorry about th" He began.

"No… Luke… you're missing the point. Let me finish." I interrupted. "What I'm trying to say is that even though logically none of this makes any sense, and I shouldn't trust you; I do… Implicitly. Not only do I absolutely trust and adore you, but I feel like a part of me is missing whenever you're not around. There's honestly nothing you could say that would make me think anything less of you, and nothing that would scare me away."

"Really?"

"Really." I reassured.

He looked somewhat doubtful, so I kissed him again, and then put my arms around him with my face looking over his shoulder. He held me like that for a couple minutes. Hopefully I hadn't been too forward with him, but I was so content in his arms I didn't care. For some reason I couldn't explain, I just knew that we were supposed to be together. Everything about him just felt… right. Granted his very presence was intoxicating, but that wasn't the only reason.

We spent another hour or two together on the water. Some of the time we talked, but mostly we just held each other. When he eventually looked down at his watch and started paddling towards the trailer I sighed.

Beaching the canoe on the shore, he lifted me out before hefting it back onto the trailer. He tied it down rather quickly, and then opened my door for me. We made our way back towards the highway on the narrow road. I was surprised that there weren't more people who knew about this nearly hidden path.

After pulling back onto the main highway Luke took his hand off the gear shifter on the center console and placed it on my hand. I smiled without thinking and turned my hand over, interlocking our fingers. Again, I was grateful for how warm his hands were. He smiled back at me, and we drove in silence for a while.

"So…" he eventually broke the silence. "How would you feel about staying for dinner? Or would that be pushing it with your dad?"

"Well, considering he thinks I am spending the day with Nikki, it might actually look more suspicious if I come home too early." I smiled mischievously.

"So, you're open to meeting the rest of the family?"

"Of course. Hopefully the others like me more than Isaac though."

"Oh, I'm sure they will love you." He reassured. "Even Isaac doesn't dislike you. New people who he isn't positive he can trust make him nervous, that's all. Once he gets to know you, he will like you. He really is a good guy. After you become more acquainted, I'm sure you'll like him too."

"Well, I certainly hope you're right." I added.

Luke drove without speaking until we were crossing over the bridge back into Harrisburg. When he eventually did speak, his voice took on a more serious tone.

"Elizabeth, there is one more thing I forgot to mention."

"What is it?" I asked.

"I need you to make me another promise." He said solemnly.

"You sure have been asking for a lot of promises." I teased jovially.

"Well, this one is very important. You see, in order to keep my family safe. Especially my mom, you have to promise that you will never tell anyone what she looks like."

"Okay. That's not a big deal. But I don't understand how mentioning her would put her in danger. Aren't you the ones the Verdorben guys are looking for?"

"We are, but I'm almost positive that the one who killed my father is looking specifically for our family. He saw my mom the night my father died, so that's why she never really comes outside the house. The less people that know what she looks like the better."

"But if one of the tainted ones was around, wouldn't you know with that ring? I thought it heated up when they were close."

"It does, but it's not just the tainted ones I am worried about."

"Are there other monsters out there too?" I asked. The thought was unnerving.

"No, but the Verdorben have their way of getting answers out of people. You see they can actually compel people to do what they say."

"You mean like… by torturing them?"

"No… although that's a possibility too. But I am referring to their compulsion. Just like we can manipulate people's emotions somewhat, the Verdorben also have abilities. They can actually control people with their minds.

"Okay, that's creepy." I felt a chill as I thought about it.

"Not everyone though, only most people." He explained. "Some people seem to be immune to their compulsion for whatever reason. And they have to be in close proximity when they use it. Depending on how strong the person is, the compulsion even works over time.

"For example, a little while before my father was killed, he helped to kill one of the Verdorben. It had shown up in town with a couple of pictures and was showing them to people. Just before he and Isaac killed it, they overheard the creature asking people if they had seen any of the people in the pictures it had. It was also telling them to call a specific number and leave a message if they ever saw any of those people.

"After they killed the creature, Isaac looked at the pictures and recognized two of them as other members of the bloodline. This means the creatures were using ordinary people to help hunt us down. So that is why we try to hide my mom. If the creature was able to get pictures of her and ever ends up coming to town, no one would be able to tell it where she is, because no one in town has seen her."

"Oh… Now it makes sense. Well, you have my word that I will never tell anyone that I have seen your mother or what she looks like." I assured.

"Thanks Liz." He seemed to relax a little.

CHAPTER IX

We were a couple miles from the bridge into Harrisburg, and I was soaking up every second of holding Luke's hand. The highway junction that turned south towards Eugene was coming into view ahead of us. A white semi-truck was approaching on the other side of the freeway.

My heart leapt suddenly, as I noticed a red car speeding into our lane from around the truck. It must have been trying to pass the truck, but clearly the driver of the car hadn't seen us. The car was less than two hundred feet away, and even at its high rate of speed, there was no way it would have time to pass the truck before it hit us.

My body lurched forward as Luke hit the brakes, but there was no way we would stop in time. The red car was flashing towards us, and I knew I had only a fraction of a second left to live. Time seemed to slow, and I noticed Luke raise his free hand in front of me protectively. Just when I thought there was no way we could possibly survive the crash, the red car veered off the road to our right.

I heard a loud crunching sound from behind and turned to see the red car flipping end over end through the air. The side of the highway had an angled drop, which must have sent the car tumbling when its front end struck the dirt.

Luke continued braking until we were almost stopped, turning to look at me with concern. "Are you okay?" He asked.

"Yeah." I tried to sound calm, but my heart was still pounding in my chest.

Luke made a wide U-turn back towards where the car had crashed behind us. The vehicle had come to a rest upside down, with considerable damage to the front, rear and one side of it. It resembled a smashed soda can more than a car.

We stopped on the shoulder of the highway, and Luke unlatched his seat belt. "Wait here." He said calmly as he put the car in park and stepped out his door.

I decided to ignore him and quickly exited, running around the front of the car to follow him towards the wreckage. Luke was walking so quickly that I didn't catch up to him until he had nearly reached the crumpled car, about fifty yards from the highway.

A broken line of plowed earth and busted shrubbery led from the car diagonally back to the freeway. It must have traveled close to five hundred feet before coming to rest. The driver side of the car was facing us and appeared to be the part with the least amount of damage. The door frame was slightly bent in and the window broken, but the red paint was still mostly untouched on the door itself. The same could not be said for the rest of the car.

As we neared the car, I noticed the driver for the first time. He was pale, and looked to be in his early twenties, with an unshaven face and buzzed hair, but it was difficult to tell with him hanging suspended, unconscious, by the seatbelt.

"Are you okay?" Luke asked loudly as he approached the door of the car.

The man inside the car stirred slightly, while slowly opening his eyes. He turned to look at Luke and something about his expression was disturbing. His green eyes with dilated pupils looked almost rabid, as if he was ready to attack anyone who got close to him.

Luke reached to pull the door open, but then stopped suddenly when his hands reached the door handle. Instead of opening the door, he clenched his right fist. I was about to ask him what was wrong, but he turned to me and spoke before I had a chance to say anything.

"Here" he said as he held his cell phone out to me. "Call 9-1-1."

I grabbed the phone from his hand but didn't understand the need for calling. While the man's car was certainly in shambles, he had been wearing a seatbelt, and appeared unharmed. I glanced at the man again and saw that he had just removed his seatbelt and was trying to push the door open.

Luke reached down towards the door again, and I thought he was going to help the man open it. Instead, he grabbed the frame of the door on both sides of the broken window and bent the metal together with his hands. The window opening was now too small for the man to fit through, and he began to scream.

"You better let me out!" the man screamed angrily.

I grabbed Luke by the arm, looking at his clenched face. "What are you doing?" I asked confused. The unmasked anger Luke was displaying concerned me, and I thought it was disturbing that he had trapped the man so.

Luke relaxed a little and unclenched his jaw when he saw my worry. "Look at the ignition Liz." He explained. "And the back seat."

I had to bend down to see the ignition through the bent window frame. Several wires were hanging out of the base of the steering column and appeared to have been tied together. *Oh, now I get it.* I thought to myself, as I noticed that the ignition switch had been torn out.

"So that's why he was driving like a maniac." I thought out loud "It's a stolen car."

Luke grabbed the phone back out of my hand and pushed a few buttons on it. "It looks like he just robbed a jewelry store or something too." He added, pointing to the back seat of the car.

I looked where he was pointing, through the broken window of the back seat, and noticed a bag lying on the inside roof of the overturned car. It was a black duffle bag, tipped over, with several gold chains and necklaces spilling out of it. I looked back at the man, who was frantically trying to pull the door open while shouting obscenities. The ferocious look in his eyes made sense to me now, and I felt uncomfortable when they rested on me. As soon as we made eye contact, his shrill threats turned towards me. I had been cussed out a couple of times in my life, but the things this man said were disturbing.

"Come on Liz." Luke said as he took my hand and pulled me back towards the road. "Let's wait by the car. You shouldn't have to listen to…Hello. Yes, I would like to report an accident." He must have called 9-1-1, because he spent the next minute explaining exactly where we were and what the car that flipped over looked like. He even gave the license plate number to the person on the other side of the phone. We reached the Hummer, and Luke opened my door for me. He got back in the driver seat but was still talking to the dispatcher.

"We're not going to just leave him there, are we?" I asked quietly when Luke finally hung up the phone.

"Actually… yes. That's exactly what we are going to do."

"But what about" I began.

"Liz relax. The police are on the way. We'll wait here until they show up, just to make sure the car doesn't catch on fire or anything." He looked at me directly before continuing. "I might hate crooks like that, but I don't think the guy deserves to die or anything. Not just for stealing a car and some jewelry anyway."

After what the car thief had called Luke, I wasn't really too concerned about what happened to him. Leaving him stranded in the car had seemed somehow wrong at first, but not if the police were coming. They could deal with him.

It was reassuring that Luke was calming down. I hated to see him upset. Everything just seemed better when he was happy. Perhaps his short temper when it came to criminals should have bothered me, but considering his near perfection in every other way, I was willing to overlook it.

Two minutes later Luke put the truck in drive and flipped another U-turn back towards Harrisburg. I was going to ask Luke why we were already leaving, but he must have read my mind because he pointed ahead of us towards the highway leading to Eugene. A few seconds later I noticed lights flashing on the highway as a state trooper's vehicle came into view.

The trooper sped past us when we came to a stop at the junction, and we drove in silence over the bridge into Harrisburg. It would be interesting to see what happened when the troopers found that vile man trapped in his car. I couldn't help but smile when I thought about the look that would be on the man's face when he saw the police showing up.

"I'm sorry you had to go through that." Luke said softly as we were exiting the freeway.

"Why? It's not your fault that maniac almost hit us." I replied reassuringly.

"Well… that's not entirely true." Luke protested. "If it wasn't for me and my curse, you wouldn't have almost been killed three times in the last month."

"Actually… if it wasn't for you… I would probably be dead." I countered. "Two of those three times you saved my life. Remember?"

"I'm just glad you're safe Liz. That means more to me than anything." He grabbed my hand again and squeezed gently.

I noticed that we were already pulling onto the last street before his house. My mind turned back to the introduction I would soon be facing. It was then I noticed myself getting anxious. *What if his family doesn't like me?* Hopefully Isaac wouldn't be too harsh.

As we pulled into the driveway Luke stopped the car and jumped out to open the gate. We drove into the back and parked the hummer. I looked at Luke when he turned the engine off.

"What is it?" He asked. Obviously, I wasn't very good at hiding my emotions.

"Nothing, it's just… is there anything I need to know or be careful not to say around your family?"

"Elizabeth, you'll be fine. Just be yourself and they'll love you."

Considering what I thought of myself, that wasn't very reassuring. We walked back up the side of the house and closed the gate, then went back in the side door of the garage and into the house. Inside the door, it led into a short hallway that opened up into the kitchen. The pleasant smell of food filled the air, though I couldn't distinguish exactly what was cooking.

The kitchen was open and inviting. Dark granite countertops and hazelnut-colored cabinets contrasted beautifully with the large Spanish tiles on the floor. The kitchen was also open on one end which led into a large family room. It had the same beautiful tile floor and a black sectional against the wall. The stunning girl I had seen the day I was stabbed was sitting on the couch reading a book, but I only had time to glance at her because another woman was standing by the stove. She turned towards us as we came in.

"You must be Elizabeth." She said warmly as she wiped her hands on her apron and walked towards us. "My boys have told me so much about you."

She smiled broadly, and her blue eyes glistened. Blond hair came a little past her shoulders and her face looked far too young to be Luke's mother. Were it not for the small lines on the sides of her eyes she could have passed for late twenties.

"Liz this is my mom. Mom, this is Liz." Luke said gesturing to each of us as he spoke.

"It is so nice to meet you." I said, extending my hand to shake hers.

She ignored my outstretched hand and gave me a welcome embrace with both arms. "We don't shake hands around here honey. And you can call me Sara, welcome to the Bennett home. It is so wonderful to finally meet you." She pulled back but kept her hands holding my shoulders as she looked at me. "You are even more beautiful than I imagined. And here I was thinking that Luke and Ben were just exaggerating." She smiled and eyed Luke sideways as she finished.

I felt my cheeks flushing slightly but didn't know how to respond, so I just smiled graciously. The girl who had been reading on the couch walked over to join us.

"Liz this is Jazmine. Jazmine Liz." Luke said nodding at each of us in turn.

"So, you're the one he won't stop talking about huh?" She smirked. "It's nice to finally meet you."

"Nice to meet you too." I replied. "And thank you for the clothes the other day. I forgot to bring them with me, but I washed them already. I'll bring them back to you next time."

"Don't worry about it. It's my pleasure. I am just glad that Luke was able to get to you in time." She replied.

"Me too, I thought for sure I was a goner."

"So Elizabeth, I hope you like chicken." Luke's mother said cutting in. "Ben is outside barbequing for us, and I just finished the mashed potatoes and gravy. Do you like asparagus? I steamed some for us, but I can always make another vegetable if you don't like that."

"That sounds wonderful." I replied excitedly. "I love potatoes, and asparagus."

Luke led me into the dining room while Jazmine and his mother brought the food in. It faced the back of the house, with a sliding door on one end and windows on the other. Ben was outside pulling something off of the barbeque with tongs. He smiled at me and waved through the glass.

Ben brought in the chicken a minute later, and it smelled delicious. We were all about to sit down when Isaac walked in from the opening to the family room. He looked friendlier than he had this morning as he approached me and extended his hand.

"Hello Elizabeth. My name is Isaac." His grip was firm as he shook.

Were it not for the suspicious glint in his brown eyes, I would have said he seemed cordial. He didn't look at all as old as Luke claimed. While his hair was completely gray on the sides, there were still quite a few dirty blonde strands mixed in on top. His skin also looked exceptionally healthy.

"It's nice to meet you, Isaac." I said politely as I let go of his hand.

"Likewise. So, we didn't scare ya off then did we?" While his tone sounded like he was joking, his face looked completely serious. I also noticed that he had a faint accent, but I couldn't quite place it. Perhaps it was Irish or Scottish. I would have to ask Luke about it later.

"No. There's really not anything to be scared of. You all seem like great people." I replied with a smile while meeting his gaze. I wasn't sure if he was trying to test me or not. But I was determined to show him that I could be trusted, which should be easy considering I would never do anything to hurt Luke or his family. It was just getting him to see that which might prove difficult.

Isaac nodded slowly, and his eyes flickered away momentarily. It appeared that he had just decided something about me, but I doubted he would share his thoughts. He took a seat next to Sara, and we all sat down. Luke was sitting on my left, with Sara on the other side of him. Ben was next to me on the end, with Jazmine sitting across from me and next to Isaac.

Sara insisted on blessing the food before we ate, so I awkwardly bowed my head when I saw everyone else doing it. The prayer was short, or at least I thought so. But I had never really been religious. Growing up my mom had believed in God but said she didn't like organized religion. My dad had grown up a Catholic in New Jersey but hadn't been to church in years. I had never given the whole religion thing much thought. Up until recently, I hadn't believed in miracles. Now I wasn't sure what to believe.

We started eating and I was amazed by the size of the portions everyone at the table was getting. Everyone besides Sara and I anyway. Ben heaped a couple pounds of mashed potatoes and gravy onto his plate, along with a good portion of Asparagus and three whole barbecued chicken breasts. Jazmine had less potatoes and gravy, but also three pieces of chicken, and Luke had almost as much as Ben. Maybe their abilities stimulated their appetites? There was no other logical explanation for why three skinny people could eat so much food without gaining some serious weight.

It was mostly quiet while we ate. Sara asked Luke and I if we had a good time, and then she proceeded to ask me all about my life story. The strange thing about it was that while the questions seemed to be just for the sake of making polite conversation, the entire table seemed unbelievably interested in every word as I told them about my life.

I mentioned being born in Portland. What it was like growing up with a paranoid cop for a dad, and I think that everyone but Isaac was teary eyed by the time I finished the story about my mom's death. I told them about Alex and his love for food, and Ben mentioned that Alex would fit right in with his family.

Considering the apprehension, I had felt about meeting Luke's family, the entire mealtime had been a pleasant surprise. Other than Isaac, who was mostly quiet while he ate his food, the rest of them made me feel perfectly welcome. Although there was nothing that could make me like Luke more than I already did, the fact that I already loved his family, after less than an hour with them, was a nice bonus.

After dinner we all made our way into the living room, while Luke and Ben washed up in the kitchen. I had offered to help Luke, but he had insisted I sit down and that "guests shouldn't wash dishes". Isaac politely excused himself, which left me sitting on one end of the sectional, while Jazmine and Sara sat half facing me on the other.

"Elizabeth you are absolutely adorable." Sara said slowly while looking directly at me. "I have to ask though, what did you think when Luke first told you about our family?"

I flushed a little after her first comment but decided it best to ignore the awkward compliment. "Well, honestly… I wasn't sure what to think. I was so surprised by what he told me that it almost felt like I was dreaming at first."

"Were you afraid?" She added.

"No…" I hadn't even thought about being afraid. "I actually wasn't scared at all, now that I think about it. Somehow, I knew I could trust Luke, so fear never even crossed my mind."

"That's nice. You know I felt the same way when I first met Nathan. He was their father." She said as she gestured at her two sons. "Logically I probably should have been afraid, but I wasn't. Granted I had never seen him before he saved me, so my first impression of him was as my hero. And from there the more I got to know him the more I fell in love with him." She stared thoughtfully at the wall as she spoke.

"How did he save you?" I asked curiously.

"Well, to make a long story short, my house caught on fire. My sister and I were sleeping in our bedroom across the hall from our parents when the fire started. It spread quickly, and by the time I woke up it had already engulfed the hallway outside our door. My sister was afraid of heights, so I couldn't convince her to jump out the bedroom window. Just when the flames started into our bedroom and the smoke filled in, Nathan suddenly appeared through the window and grabbed my sister and I. He picked her up first and jumped out the window with her, then appeared again through the smoke and lifted me up. I can still remember thinking he was going to hurt me as we were falling from the high second story window, but when we landed, I barely felt a thing."

"Wow that's incredible." I said when she finished.

"Yeah… even after he saved me though it took two years before my father agreed to let us be engaged. Needless to say, we were married three weeks later." She smiled reminiscently as she spoke.

"Talk about a shotgun wedding huh?" Chipped in Jazmine with a mischievous smile. "Oh, I have been wanting to ask you Liz, what did you think about him after the shooting and the rapist? I mean before Luke explained everything."

"Honestly…" I thought about making something up, but decided to just spit the truth out. "It sounds a little crazy, but I actually thought that maybe Luke and Ben were part of some government experiment. Like maybe they had been given some chemicals or something that made them super humans. The only logical problem with that though was that it didn't explain the healing."

Jazmine smiled. "A government experiment huh? That's probably what I would have guessed too if I had grown up a normal person."

We talked for a few more minutes, until Luke and Ben came to join us on the couch. Ben told a couple of jokes and Jazmine teased him playfully about how corny they were. Seeing how well they interacted almost made me wish I had siblings that were close to my age. Almost being the key word.

I glanced at the clock on the wall and noticed that it was almost eight o'clock. Luke must have noticed my eyes wandering.

"We should probably get you home huh?" He said standing.

"Yeah, I don't want my dad worrying, so that's probably best." I rose also with the help of his outstretched hand.

Sara was even more gracious with her farewell than she had been at our meeting. She offered to send me home with the leftover food, but I politely declined. The last thing I needed was to show up at home with unexplained food. It's not like Nikki and I would take the time to prepare such a meal between watching movies.

Jazmine was also incredibly friendly, and she even gave me a big hug. "I think we could definitely be friends." She said smiling as she pulled away. "Or maybe even sisters someday." She smirked at Luke then gave me a quick wink.

Luke blushed, and he gave her an exasperated look. "Jazmine please." He managed to say between gritted teeth. His expression changed to embarrassment when he finally looked at me again.

I gave Ben a hug too, but Isaac was nowhere to be seen. That didn't bother me one bit. Luke walked into the garage with me and closed the door behind him. When he turned to face me he looked worried.

"Sorry about my family, I know they can be a little over the top. Especially Jazmine."

"Don't be, I love them. They are perfect." I reassured him. "And I don't think any of them are over the top. They are just genuinely good people with a good sense of humor."

I could tell Jazmine's statement had embarrassed him, but it hadn't fazed me at all. She was obviously joking anyway. Even if she hadn't been, it still wouldn't have bothered me. While I was far too young to think about marriage, the thought of wanting to live happily ever after with Leuken had already solidified itself in my mind. Luke was still quiet, so I decided to set his mind at ease.

"Luke don't worry. I wasn't offended by what Jazmine said. I know she was only kidding."

"Okay cool." His face visibly relaxed. "She just talks crazy sometimes, and I didn't want you getting the wrong idea. I never want to scare you away."

"Well, it would take quite a bit to scare me off Leuken Bennett." I stepped closer and threw my arms around him. "Right now, I am exactly where I want to be. And with exactly who I want to be with."

"Me too." He replied.

We held each other for a minute, which seemed to last about five seconds. Then he opened my car door for me. "Why thank you." I said before kissing him. About another minute later, I reluctantly pulled away and got into my Tahoe. He kissed me again, this time lasting only half as long, and then closed my door.

He hit the garage door opener, then smiled at me as he turned back to face me. Sparing him one last smile and a quick wave, I pulled out of the garage. Once I turned onto the street, I immediately felt the urge to turn around and go back. The thought of not seeing him until tomorrow was just too dismal. The thought of him thinking I was a psychopath for coming back was even less appealing though, so I decided to be patient. I couldn't help but smile all the way home. I was excited for tomorrow morning when I would get to see Leuken again.

CHAPTER X

"So, are you guys like official yet or what?" Nikki asked. She was eyeing me and Luke intermittently as he walked away from us.

He had just finished walking me to first period, where Nikki was dutifully waiting for me again. Her hair was mostly straightened besides a few crimped strands, and everything about her black clothing accentuated her beauty.

"I'm not really sure to be honest with you." I answered thoughtfully.

"Well, he's walking you to class, and you guys are like holding hands, not to mention when you two hugged it was like totally obvious you wanted to kiss each other."

"Was it really that obvious?" I asked innocently.

"Yeah… just a little bit. You two make me and Greg look like we barely even like each other." She said sarcastically.

"I didn't even think about how we must look to everyone. For some reason when I'm with him it's like no one else exists. Not literally, but… I just can't think about anything else."

"Girl, you are so whipped. I would say he had you wrapped around his little finger, except that I think he's even more infatuated with you."

"You really think so?"

"Liz please. He looks like a lost puppy whenever he's not with you, and from the first time he saw you it was obvious he's got the hots for you. Just because he hasn't officially made you his girlfriend doesn't really matter at this point. You guys like, belong together."

It was reassuring to hear Nikki talk about us in that fashion. Even though I knew I belonged to Luke and honestly wanted nothing else, it was nice to know that other people thought we looked good together as well. Sometimes being with Luke made me feel so happy that I worried he couldn't possibly care for me as much as I did for him.

"So…I'm guessing you had a good weekend." Nikki smiled and winked.

"Yeah, I did actually." I replied. "Thanks for being my alibi."

"No problem. It's not like it was hard. Your dad never even called. Anyways, you have to tell me all about it. Where did he end up taking you? What did you do? I want all the details."

We only had a couple minutes before class started, so I gave her the reader's digest version. She looked jealous when I told her about the ride on the canoe, then laughed when I told her about how I almost dropped the paddle when I tried rowing. We made our way into class where I finished telling her about meeting the family. I didn't bother mentioning Isaac. Something about the way he had looked at me that first time still bothered me.

"So, his sister is adopted? That's like, totally cool." Nikki commented when I had finished.

I thought about telling Nikki about the incident with Jazmine. About how I had embarrassed myself by getting jealous of her before

I knew she was Luke's sister but decided against it. The truth was there was a lot about my relationship and life with Luke that would always have to be kept secret. I could never risk endangering him or his family.

As the day went on, I noticed that, even in the classes without Luke, time seemed to be passing by quickly. It probably helped that I spent most of those periods either talking with Nikki or daydreaming about my future with Luke.

Life in general seemed to speed up. When I wasn't happily spending time with Luke, I was excitedly anticipating the next time I would get to see him. At lunch the two of us always sat with Ben, Greg and Nikki, and usually one of Ben's other teammates would join us. From the time we got out of Sassenburg's class until four o'clock each day we were inseparable. That was when he had to get home on weekdays. After a few days of this I finally decided to ask him why he always had to go home at that time.

"Because that is when we train." Had been his matter of fact reply. He then went on to explain that they trained from four to six every weekday. His excuse was that they had to be in good shape in case one of the tainted ones unexpectedly showed up. Exactly what they did for their training he didn't say.

Every night after I put Alex to bed, I called him. He had offered to call me, but I didn't want to hear it from my dad in case he answered the phone some of the times. Hence, I would shut myself in my room to "do homework" and subsequently talk to Luke until I couldn't keep my eyelids open.

We talked about everything. From the songs we liked to our favorite foods, to the way we slept. I had always been a stomach sleeper, while he preferred to sleep on his side. Most of the foods we liked were the same, and I was excited to learn that he also hated coffee. "If you have to put a cup of sugar in something just to make it tolerable, I think I'll pass." Had been his exact statement on the subject.

You would think with all the time we spent hanging out or talking on the phone, that we would get tired of each other or run out of things to talk about, but neither ever happened. Not only did we not get sick of each other, but the more time we spent together the more I affirmed the one thing I knew with absolute certainty. I wanted to spend the rest of my life with Leuken Bennett.

When Friday came Luke and I decided to take Alex for a walk by the river. I had found the key for the padlock on the back gate, so we decided to slip out that way. I locked the gate again once we were outside. Alex immediately ran towards the river, and I had to yell at him.

"You have to be careful by the water Alex." I scolded once I caught up with him.

"Why Izzie?" He looked up at me with the most innocent expression. His chubby cheeks were flushed from the cold and his winter coat was pulled up over his head to help him stay warm. It was only about forty-five degrees outside, so he probably didn't need the hood up, but I didn't want to chance him getting sick.

"Because if you fell in the water you could drown. And that's only if you didn't freeze to death first." I said, trying to frighten him away from the water's edge.

"I could freeze to death Izzie?" He asked concerned.

"Probably not Alex, it was just an expression, but the water is really cold."

Alex reached down and put a finger in the edge of the water. "Whoa it's cold!" he exclaimed loudly.

"I told you it was, silly boy." I said smiling as I glanced over at Luke. He was smirking also.

"Have you ever skipped rocks before Alex?" Luke said as he squatted down next to Alex by the water.

"Skipped rocks? No, what's that Luke?" Alex asked.

"Here I'll show you." Luke replied.

He reached down and grabbed a small stone that was smoothly rounded and flat. Standing up, he cocked his arm sideways and threw the rock at the river. It skipped off the water and flew another twenty feet before skipping one more time and landing on the other side of the river.

"Oops." Luke said looking around. "I guess that was a little too hard."

"You need to be more careful Leuken Bennett." I said as I walked up behind him and put my arms around his waist.

"Yeah… that was an accident, but thanks for keeping me in check." He replied as he half turned to smile down at me. I raised up on my tip toes and kissed him once.

"Eww. You guys are gross." Alex said scrunching his face at us.

"Oops." I said smiling at Luke. "I forgot we had little eyes watching."

"I didn't mind." He grinned back.

"Izzie why did you call him Leuken? That's not his name silly. His name is Luke." Alex said as he reached down and picked up a rock.

"Well, Leuken is his full name, but he goes by Luke for short. They are both his name." I explained.

"Oh." Alex looked up at me again. "So, his name is Luke and Leuken?"

"Yeah, pretty much. Just like my name is Liz and Izzie."

"No, your name is Izzie and Liz and Elizabef. Those are all your names." Alex corrected.

Luke chuckled softly. I just looked at Alex in surprise. Having not heard him use my full name ever, I didn't even think that he knew it. It was cute that he mispronounced it. Alex raised his arm over his head and threw the small rock as hard as he could at the water. It landed with a tiny splash about eight feet away.

"Oh no. That wasn't a good skip." Alex said.

"For a five-year-old that was amazing Alex. Skipping is hard when you're little." Luke encouraged.

"I'm not little Luke. I eat lots of food." Alex admonished, giving Luke a serious look.

"Oh, sorry. My mistake." Luke apologized with a shrug, and I laughed.

Alex started walking quickly down the side of the river. Every few steps he would pick up a rock and throw it, but none of them ever went more that about twelve feet. Luke and I walked slowly after him from a short distance holding hands. I could feel his large ring against my fingers.

"So how close do those things have to be before this thing heats up?" I asked while tracing the ring with my thumb and a finger.

"The tainted ones?" He asked, and I nodded. "Well Isaac thinks it's about a mile, maybe even a little less. But we aren't exactly sure."

"How many of those things has Isaac killed?" I asked curiously.

"Well, that he has told me about… four, but there could have been more that he never mentioned. He is one of those guys that only tells things when he thinks you need to know."

"And you said that when you kill one the demon part just travels to someone else?"

"That's correct. Usually, it travels to the nearest human besides the bloodline, but sometimes it can randomly jump to someone else far away. We don't know exactly why that happens though."

"So basically, every time you kill one it takes over another body? That means someone dies any time you fight them." The thought made me cringe.

"Which is one of the reasons why we don't fight them. Between that and the chance that there may be too many to handle, it's simply not worth the risk." He explained.

"So, then there is no way to kill any of them permanently? That's depressing."

"Yeah, it is." He replied, looking deep in thought. "Although we do hold on to hope."

"Hope of what?"

"Well, there is an ancient legend that Isaac told me about, and he seems to believe it. The legend says that one day the Tainted ones will be defeated... by themselves. Supposedly there is more to the original legend, but that is all that has been passed on to this day. How that could possibly happen when they are all immortal is beyond me, but Isaac and Jazmine fervently believe it will someday."

The more we talked about the evil creatures the more disheartening the subject became. At least there was some kind of hope. Hopefully Isaac was right about the legend. Ideally it would be fulfilled soon, so Luke and I could have the rest of our lives together in peace. Although so far it hadn't been too scary. Yeah, there were the guys with the guns and ski masks, and almost getting killed by some rapist, but... other than those minor incidents, everything was completely safe.

Despite my sarcastic thoughts, I really never had felt safer than I did with Luke. Knowing what he was capable of probably had a lot to do with it, but that wasn't all. For some reason every part of me just felt peaceful when he was near. I stopped and reached over, embracing him firmly.

"What's that for?" He asked while hugging me back.

"Nothing… and everything." I replied. "Mainly because you are so incredible. Thank you."

"Thank you for what? I didn't do anything Liz." He looked down at me confused.

"You're right, besides saving my life, and making me happier than I ever imagined possible, you haven't done much." I smirked.

"Well, I think you're just being generous." He leaned down and kissed me. "But you're welcome."

We walked a little further. With his arm around my shoulder and mine around his waist, I could have gone forever. When he lifted his watch to see what time it was, I noticed that it was already three forty. We caught up to Alex and threw a couple rocks with him, then turned around and went back to the house.

I walked Luke out front right at four o'clock, so Ben was already waiting patiently in their hummer. After a quick goodbye, because I didn't want to kiss him too much in front of Ben, I went inside and made dinner. My father was still sleeping when the food was done, and I couldn't stop thinking about Luke.

Then a great idea came to me. I decided to bake some chocolate cupcakes, because Luke had said he loved chocolate, to take to him. My excuse would be to wish Ben good luck with the State Championship Football game tomorrow. It at least gave me an excuse to see Luke again.

And so, I found myself beating the cupcake mix together in the kitchen. Alex sat in his chair at the table, sneaking bites of his dinner when he thought I wasn't looking. He hadn't liked the idea of waiting for our father to wake up before eating. I thought I had heard my father's footsteps above us, so he should be down any minute.

"Izzie." Alex said suddenly as I was pouring the batter into the cupcake pan. "Are you going to marry Luke?"

I was so surprised by his statement that I accidentally poured too much batter. It overflowed onto the counter. Setting the pan down, I thought about how best to respond to my five-year-old brother.

"Where did that question come from?" I asked.

"Well, my friend Ben said that his daddy is getting married, so I was just wondering if you were gonna marry Luke."

"Alex that's not something people do at our age. Luke and I are way too young to be married." I explained slowly.

"But don't you love him Izzie?"

I was again taken back by his bluntness. "Maybe I do, but that isn't the only reason why you marry someone. You have to be older and have a job before you can get married."

"But you are old Izzie."

"Thanks Alex." I said sarcastically.

"You're welcome." He responded.

Obviously, my humor was lost on him. I was beginning to notice that as Alex got older, I found myself increasingly being asked questions that should be reserved for actual parents. Hopefully I wasn't telling him too much, or not enough. Being a sister/parent was complicated.

My father came in right as I was putting the cupcake pan into the oven. His hair looked disheveled, and his clothes wrinkled. He must have been planning on changing after dinner.

"Hey Liz, what're ya making?" He asked as he gave Alex a hug from behind, gently kissing the top of his head.

"Cupcakes. But not all of them are for us. Half of the batch is going to be for Luke's brother Ben. They have the state football championship tomorrow up in Portland." I explained.

"Oh, that's nice. As long as some of those end up in my mouth, I'm good." He sat down and looked at his plate. "Dinner looks good, thanks."

"Some of those can end up in my mouth too." Alex added eyeing the oven.

"Oh, don't worry Alex; I'll save some for you too." I said, and he smiled appreciatively.

I ate quickly while the cupcakes were cooking. The timer rang just as I took my last bite of dinner. I pulled them out of the oven, and the smell of fresh baked chocolate cake filled my nostrils. Breathing in deeply through my nose, I sighed. There was nothing I loved more than chocolate. Another thing I had been excited to discover I shared in common with Luke.

Minutes later I had a large plate of cupcakes frosted, wrapped and ready to go. Just as I was putting my shoes on, Alex came running up to me.

"Izzie, can I go with you?" He asked excitedly. "I want to go to Luke and Ben's house with you."

"I don't know…" I paused, trying to think of a good excuse not to take him.

"I think that's a great idea. Why don't you take your brother with you?" My father said loudly from the other room. He didn't say it as a question.

Realizing I wasn't going to win this one, I decided not to try and fight the inevitable. "Okay Alex, hurry and get your shoes on."

Alex actually did get his shoes on quickly, and we walked out to the Tahoe. After making sure he was buckled in properly, I placed the plate of cupcakes on the front seat. Hopefully none of the cupcakes would fall over as I drove. Two minutes later I parked in front of Luke's house. It was two minutes to six, so hopefully he would be done with his training. I still wondered exactly what his "training" entailed.

I walked up to the door, holding Alex's hand in one of mine, and the plate of cupcakes in the other. He pushed the doorbell, and I heard a short chime from inside. A few seconds passed, and I had just raised my hand to knock when the door opened quickly.

Jazmine was standing in the doorway wearing black workout pants and a black tank top. Her hair was done up in a ponytail, and she appeared to be slightly out of breath. When she saw me she smiled broadly.

"Hey Liz. I would hug you, but I'm all sweaty right now." She looked down at Alex. "Oh, he's adorable! Is this your little brother?"

"Yeah, this is Alex. Alex this is Luke's sister Jazmine." I said gesturing to her.

"You're pretty." Alex said with a grin. "But you can't be Luke's sister, you look different."

I was immediately embarrassed, but Jazmine spoke again before I had a chance to think of what to say.

"That's because I was adopted." She explained patiently still grinning. "We had different parents when we were born, but now Luke is my brother."

"Adopted?" Alex said quizzically. "That's weird."

Hopefully he hadn't offended her. At least she didn't look upset. She smiled at Alex again, and then looked back up at me.

"I'm guessing you want Leuken?" She raised an eyebrow mischievously while smiling.

"Yes." I replied. "If he's not too busy."

"I'm never too busy for you Liz." Luke said as he walked up behind Jazmine. "Although you might not want to smell me right now."

He was wearing a blue sleeveless shirt and black sport pants. His shoulders and arms looked larger and even more defined when they weren't covered. The fact that he was glistening with sweat also made the lines from his muscles and veins stand out more. I realized that I was staring and quickly averted my gaze back to his face.

"Hi." Was all I managed to say as I felt my heartbeat rapidly accelerating. I took a deep breath to try and calm myself and noticed Jazmine smile broadly. Realizing I'd been caught, my cheeks flushed involuntarily. I wanted to hide. Hoping to take the attention off my blushing, I held the plate of cupcakes out to him.

"I made these for you." I stammered. "I mean… I made them for Ben, to wish him good luck… but I wanted to give them to you…to give to him… but they're for you too of course."

The desire to disappear was exponentially increasing with each jumbled phrase. *What an idiot.* I thought to myself, unsure why I suddenly wasn't able to speak right.

"Well thanks." He said smiling, as he took the plate. His eyes looked confused. Hopefully he didn't understand why I was flustered.

"Luke, you have big muscles." Alex said suddenly. I had forgotten he was even there.

"Hey Alex." Luke said with a smile as he squatted down. "I didn't even notice you at first." He stuck his hand out, and Alex gave him a high five.

"That's cause you were staring at Izzie." Alex said with a grin.

"You caught me, Alex. What can I say?" Luke shrugged, smiling at me.

"I'm gonna head back down before Isaac blows a gasket." Jazmine said. "It was good to see you again Liz, and so nice to meet you, Alex." She flashed him another smile and he blushed. "Don't be too long lover boy." She added to Luke as she disappeared around the corner.

"Thanks for the cupcakes, they look delicious." Luke said as he eyed them. "Did you want to come in for a minute?"

"No thanks, I just wanted to drop those off to you."

While the invitation was tempting, it sounded like Isaac didn't like when their training was interrupted. The last thing I needed was to give him another reason to dislike me. He already seemed to have enough of those.

"Okay, well can I walk you to your car?" He asked as he turned and set the plate on a chair by the door.

"Sure." I said excitedly, but then remembered what he was wearing. "But it's cold out here, so you don't have to."

"Don't be silly. It's not that bad." He stepped outside with us, and we all walked towards the Tahoe. The wind was starting to pick up slightly, and the cool air made me zip up my jacket. I opened the door for Alex. He climbed up into his booster seat.

"Luke, does Jazmine have a boyfriend?" Alex asked dreamy eyed.

I couldn't help but chuckle. Luke laughed too. "You know Alex I'm not sure. I'll have to ask her."

Closing Alex's door, I grabbed Luke's hand and pulled him to the back of the Tahoe. He raised an eyebrow at me as I tugged but didn't resist. Once I knew we were out of Alex's sight I grabbed the back of his head firmly with both hands and pulled his mouth down to mine. He didn't fight it, and at least a minute went by before he gently pulled away.

"Wow." He said smiling. "What was that for?"

"Sorry I just couldn't resist. You look… really good." I was so excited it was difficult to keep my voice even.

"In workout clothes when I'm all sweaty?" He asked skeptically.

"Yes." I answered, unable to keep my eyes off him. I leaned up and kissed him one more time. "But I probably better get going."

"Okay. Thanks for stopping by. This was a nice surprise."

"It's my pleasure." I gave him one more hug. "So, what kind of training were you guys doing, and what did Jazmine mean when she said she better get back down? Down where?"

"Oh, we have a big basement under the house where we train at. It's mostly just fighting and defense techniques." I raised an eyebrow at him. "You know, in case any of the tainted ones unexpectedly show up. We need to be ready for them."

"You mean you practice fighting two hours a day, every day?" I said incredulously.

"Well yeah. On the weekdays anyway. I thought I told you that already?"

"You said you were training. I didn't know you meant fighting. That's a lot of practice."

"Yeah, but if one of those creatures show up, we won't get second chances. Besides, now I need to train even harder, because there's more than just my family I need to protect." He smiled down at me.

"Okay. Well, you better get back to it before Isaac comes looking for you." I kissed him one last time then got in my Tahoe.

He waved at Alex, and then ran back inside. Even after he was back in his house and we were driving down the road, I couldn't get him out of my mind. Everything about him was just so perfect. I hadn't realized how nice his physique was.

"Izzie, I like Jazmine." Alex's voice brought me back to reality. "We should go play at Luke's house after school sometimes."

"I'm sure you would like that, but Luke's mom is really sick, so they don't like to have too many people over." I lied. Considering how upset Isaac had been with Luke for bringing me over, I wasn't about to risk bringing others with me. Even if Alex was only five.

After we got home Alex didn't stop talking about how pretty he thought Jazmine was. He asked me about what the word adoption meant and I had a fun time explaining that to him. My father also asked some questions about Luke's family, since he heard us talking about it. I told him how their dad was dead, and they were raised by a single mom. "It sounds like she's one tough lady" had been his last comment after I gave him the reader's digest version of their family's story. It was the reader's digest version, minus everything about the bloodline, their abilities and the tainted ones, of course.

The next day Nikki, Luke and I drove up to Portland to watch the State football championship. Having Nikki in the car with us meant less kissing, but it was good to spend some time with her outside of school. I hadn't been giving her enough attention lately. Hopefully she didn't see me as a bad friend. Although knowing Nikki, if she had thought that she would have let me know already.

Harrisburg High School ended up losing, but it was a close game. The final score was thirty-five to thirty-one. Considering that they had lost in regionals the year before, even making it to the State Championships was a good improvement. Ben ended up riding back with us, and he didn't seem to mind looking at Nikki the whole time. Greg was the team captain, so he had taken the bus back.

The next night we had one last bonfire, but it started to rain about an hour into it, so we had to cut it short. We went to Luke's house and played board games with Jazmine and Ben until it was time for me to go home. Not wanting my father to see us kiss, we got our fill in the car before he pulled into my driveway. That way when he walked me to the door all anyone inside would see is a hug. After I was back inside the house, I realized that hiding how serious Luke and I were, wasn't very realistic. Alex had already seen us kiss several times, and he wasn't exactly a pro at keeping his mouth shut.

From that point on we didn't worry as much about kissing in front of my family. Granted we never kissed when my father was watching, or even in the room, but we didn't let Alex bother us. He complained occasionally about it, usually while rolling his eyes, but he liked Luke, so he tolerated it.

The next weekend I spent quite a bit of time at Luke's house. His mother was even more gracious than she had been during our first meeting, always saying pleasant things to me. At times I would have thought her praises phony, had it not been for her sincere nature. I could see in her why Luke and Ben had both turned out to be such compassionate gentlemen.

I also grew to like Jazmine even more. She was not quite as affable as Benjamin, or at least she didn't joke as much, but her good natured wit was humorous in a different way. Not only did she rarely say anything negative, but her jovial attitude was always such that she made me feel at ease. Laughing came as easily with her as it did with Ben. Like Nikki, she seemed completely sincere. Except that she seemed more down to earth than Nikki. Not that I didn't love my Latina friend, but she did spend quite a bit of time talking about herself.

December had arrived the week after the State Football Championship, and it was Friday when I realized there was only one week of school left before Winter Break. The thought of having two weeks uninterrupted with Luke was exciting. Hopefully Alex wouldn't be too demanding during the break.

We had just finished eating dinner, and I opened the Freezer door to get out some ice cream for dessert. I was surprised when there was none in there.

"That's weird" I said aloud. "I thought we had more chocolate Ice Cream in the freezer."

"Oh, Alex and I killed the carton while you were talking to that kid on the phone last night." My father responded, pulling out his wallet. "Why don't you drive to Howie's and pick up some more."

He pulled out a twenty and held it out to me. "You fly, I'll buy. Just don't be stopping at your boyfriend's place on the way okay?"

"Okay." I grabbed the money from him and headed to the store.

As I drove to the corner market, I realized that was the first time my father had called Luke my boyfriend. To me he seemed so much more than that, even though he had never officially asked me to be his girlfriend. Perhaps I should have corrected him, but I didn't see a point. Surely Alex had mentioned our kissing. I just hoped that my father never wanted to have "the talk". My mom had done that once with me when I was fourteen before my first date, and it had been awkward enough even with her. Sex was not a word anyone ever wanted to hear out of their parent's mouth.

I pulled into the parking lot at Howie's Market and decided to park in one of the spots on the side of the store, away from the gas pumps. It was small for a supermarket, but far larger than most gas stations. Being the only food store in Harrisburg, it was more convenient than driving the twenty minutes to Eugene, especially if you only needed one thing. There were four gas pumps in front of the store, and most of the parking was on the side. Glass windows spanned across the front of the store and about ten feet onto either side as well.

Making my way inside, I headed straight for the freezer section. They only carried three flavors of Ice Cream, so I was hoping they had chocolate in stock. Luckily, they did, and I got in line behind the only other person in the store. She was a middle-aged woman and looked vaguely familiar. I couldn't recall where I knew her from though.

I saw a dark sporty looking sedan pull up in front of the store with its lights shining through the front window. A man got out, but it was difficult to see him through the glare on the glass. The woman in front of me got her change and headed for the front door.

"Will that be all for ya?" asked the tall, slender, balding cashier as he rang up the carton of ice cream.

"Yeah thanks." I replied pulling out my debit card.

While I was waiting for the card to be accepted, I noticed the woman who had been in front of me talking to the man who had exited the car. They were standing right in front of the store entrance and he was holding something up in front of her.

The cashier handed me my receipt with a faint smile, and I grabbed the bag containing my ice cream. As I turned towards the front entrance, I accidentally bumped into someone. The man from outside had entered the store without me noticing, and I had ran right into him.

"Sorry about that, I didn't see…" I cut off as I glanced up and met his eyes.

His face didn't look much older than mine, though he stood a good six inches over me. His dark brown hair looked normal and was combed neatly to one side, but it was his eyes that caught my attention. Something was unsettling about his dark eyes as they met mine, and I felt a sudden chill, even though it was warm in the store.

"That's okay." He said politely as he stepped to the side. His voice sounded normal enough, but something about him was seriously creeping me out. "Maybe you can help me out. You see I'm looking for some of my friends that got lost in Eugene. I think they might have passed through here."

His presence was so unsettling that I didn't know how to respond, so I just nodded.

"Have you seen any of these people?" He asked holding up a stack of pictures that were in his hand.

The first one was a picture of a Hispanic male who looked to be in his late twenties. In the picture the man looked like he was sitting in an old sixties model mustang, and the picture was faded. I shook my head, and he flipped to the next picture. This one was of a boy who looked about eleven or twelve years old. Not recognizing him either, I shook my head. The man then flipped to another picture, and I almost dropped my bag.

Staring directly at me was a faded picture of Sara Bennett. She looked much younger in the photograph than she did in real life, but I recognized her beautiful face clearly. Remembering what Luke had said about the tainted ones, I suddenly realized what he was. My apprehension and suspicion towards the man turned to stark terror and my first instinct was to run.

Instead, I frantically fought down my fear and shook my head slowly, trying to make the same motion that I had with the first two pictures. The man turned to glance at the Cashier, and I noticed a small black crescent moon tattoo on the back of his neck. When the man turned back to face me, I suddenly felt a strange feeling come over me.

"You will tell me if you have seen any of them." He said slowly, and I felt the overwhelming urge to admit I had been lying.

I resisted the urge to confess and instead managed to say, "I haven't seen them."

"Good." The man said. "If you ever see any of these three, you will call me and leave a message telling me where you saw them. Is that clear?" The man held out a business card, and I grabbed it without looking down. The desire to do what he said flooded over me as he spoke.

"Yes. I will call you if I see them." I said slowly back. Whatever kind of hypnosis or mind game he was playing on me was almost working, so I thought it best to pretend it had.

He eyed me suspiciously for another second, then turned and walked over to the cashier. I didn't wait to hear what the man said to him. No sooner had he turned away from me then I was walking out of the store. Trying not to look panicked, I walked to my Tahoe and pulled the keys from my purse. I opened the door and got in quickly, closing it as I sat down. My hand was shaking as I attempted to put the key in the ignition.

I started the car and backed out of my parking space, sparing one more glance towards the man inside the store. He was already walking out the front door and met my eyes as I looked his way. Hoping not to attract any additional attention, I pulled slowly out of the parking lot and onto the street. As soon as I turned the next corner, I sped up and drove home as fast as I could.

I practically ran to my front door and closed it quickly behind me. Alex and my father were watching television, so I put the ice cream in the freezer and hurried upstairs. Still feeling panicked, I called Luke on his cell phone.

"Hello." I recognized his voice as he answered.

"Luke he's here. A tainted one is here. I just saw him at the gas station." I couldn't conceal my alarm as I hurriedly spoke.

"Where are you now Liz?" He asked concerned, not sounding surprised by my news.

"I'm at home. I came straight home after I saw him at the store."

"Where is the tainted one? Did it follow you home?"

"No, I don't think so anyway."

"Are you sure?" He pried.

"Yes. I'm pretty sure. I looked behind me a lot on the way home, and I never saw him behind me."

"What did it look like?"

"Well, he was average height and skinny with dark hair and dark eyes. He had a moon tattoo on the back of his neck, and he was driving a black Mercedes."

"Was it alone?"

"I think so. It's hard to say because the car had dark tint on it. But I didn't see anyone else with him."

I heard voices talking in the background on his end of the phone. It was difficult to make out most of what they were saying though.

"So, it's here then. Well, I'm tired of running!" I heard what sounded like Isaac's voice in the background.

"Me too." Ben's voice was unmistakable.

"Luke it's looking for your mom. It had pictures." I added.

"How do you know? Did you see them?" He asked.

"Yeah, it showed them to me."

"You mean it talked to you? What did it say?" The alarm in his voice grew.

"Well, it asked me if I had seen any of the people in the pictures that it had. And then showed me three pictures. One was a Hispanic looking guy in his late twenties, another was a young boy, and the last one was your mom. The picture was old, and she looked younger, but I'm sure it was her."

I noticed all the background talking on his side of the phone had stopped after he asked me the last question.

"And what did you tell it?" Luke asked slowly.

"Nothing. I lied and said that I hadn't seen any of you. Then it tried controlling my mind somehow and told me to tell it if I had seen any of them. I again told it that I hadn't, and then it gave me a card with a phone number on it and said to call if I ever see any of those people." I pulled the white business card out of my pocket and noticed that it only had a ten-digit number on it with nothing else.

"What did you say to that?"

"Well, I could tell it was trying to manipulate me, so I said that I would call it if I saw any of them. After that it went towards the clerk, so I got back in my Tahoe and drove home."

"Okay Liz, stay inside your house and keep the phone on you okay? I will call you back in a few minutes once I know what's going on."

"Okay, bye." I replied just before hearing him hang up.

I sat on my bed shaking with anxiety. After a minute I glanced down and noticed that my fingers were turning blue from my death grip on the phone, so I set it down on my lap. My mind was racing again. Only this time it wasn't because I couldn't stop thinking about Luke. A tainted one was here, which from my understanding would lead to one of two things. Either it would pass on after it realized that it wasn't going to find Sara Bennett, or Luke and his family were going to have to leave. I silently prayed for the prior. The thought of Luke leaving was not something my mind was capable of entertaining.

Jeremy drove slowly through the town of Harrisburg, distracted. He had already contacted a dozen people in this small town, and the most likely sources of information had proved to be useless. The clerk at the gas station supermarket hadn't even blinked when looking at the pictures. Usually, they were the best people in small towns because they saw everyone. But this was to be expected. It had been the norm for the last several months as he searched for these people who held the keys to his freedom. What had him distracted at the moment was the girl from the gas station.

She had been a petite little thing, with a face any man would welcome as it burned itself into his memory. At least that had been his first impression, and he still couldn't get her face out of his mind.

Not only had she been beautiful, with flowing dark hair and piercing green eyes accenting a perfectly shaped face, but something about her reaction bothered him.

Initially he had been so distracted by her beauty that he hadn't noticed. As she was leaving though, the look on her face made him realize that her reaction to his questions hadn't been normal. The initial fear she demonstrated was something he had grown accustomed to, as was the standard response of not having seen any of the ones he was looking for. What had been different had been when he had used compulsion on her. He had pushed as hard as he could, and she had agreed to do what he said, but her expression hadn't changed. If anything, she had looked even more terrified as she answered him.

While he was no expert on how this ability worked, he had noticed one thing over the last several months. Normally when he used compulsion on someone, they seemed to go into an almost sedated state as they did or said what he told them. There had been a few people who had simply been immune to his compulsion, but they had all reacted like he was crazy for thinking he could tell them what to do. That girl had not done either. It was almost like she knew what he was doing… and simply played along.

And so he found himself driving back and forth, canvassing the town. Street by street he searched for the girl's Tahoe. He had started on the North edge of the town and was working his way south. He knew the girl had driven west from the store, but she was likely being evasive, so that could mean anything. Maybe she was trying to throw him off by driving in the opposite direction from where she really lived. Either way he would find her. Her green eyes kept flashing into his mind as he searched.

He didn't want to hurt the girl. The fact that she was gorgeous and made him feel almost human again had a lot to do with it, but the simple truth was he really didn't want to hurt anyone. All he wanted was his normal life back. If this girl had information that could help him find the ones Jareth wanted, he would be that much closer to freedom. The thought of being free instinctively brought his eyes back to the silver bracelet on his left wrist. The artifact that kept him enslaved to that monster.

He had tried in vain several times to remove it. His only hope now was to do what Jareth wanted and hope that the creature would honor his word. So, he would find the girl, and hope that she could lead him to someone else. If she did, he would call Jareth, and wait until he arrived. If the girl ended up having no useful information, then he would move on, but not before he was certain. The thought of the possibility of getting his life back brought a smile to Jeremy's lips.

CHAPTER XI

"Hello." I answered the phone and quickly put it to my ear.

"Okay, we have a plan, but we need you to find a way to leave your house and drive your car over here." Luke's voice explained through the telephone.

"Okay. I'll make something up, probably just use Nikki again."

"That's fine, but I don't know how long it will take so…"

"Got it, I'll make it a sleepover then." I explained.

"Okay, Jazmine and Isaac are already behind your house; just don't look out any of your windows."

"What are they doing here? And why can't I look out my windows?" I inquired.

"Because the tainted one you saw earlier is parked across the street from your house a few doors down. Jazmine and Isaac are there to stop him in case he decides he wants to interrogate your family."

My adrenaline kicked in again, and the sinking feeling I had felt in the store earlier returned. So, it had actually found me. Which meant it must have seen through my lying at the store. At least I had tried. I could feel my heart accelerating as I thought about the danger Alex and my father were now in.

"Oh no, do you think he's going to hurt my family? I don't want anything to" I began.

"Liz, relax. Your family is going to be just fine. They would have to get through us first and that's not going to happen, okay? We are pretty sure this tainted one is alone. At least for now." He reassured.

"Okay, I'll try to hurry."

"Just be careful Liz. Whatever you do, don't look around when you're outside. Especially don't look at its car. In order for our plan to work, it must not know that we are on to it. I'll see you in a few minutes."

I heard the phone disconnect and suddenly felt completely alone. Also feeling overwhelmingly afraid, I decided I had better hurry up so as not to put my family in any more danger. The longer I sat thinking about the horrible ways this scenario could end, the worse my anxiety got. I decided to call Nikki.

She was at first excited when she answered the phone, but I was a terrible liar, so she soon caught on that something was wrong. Luckily, I was able to think quickly, so I made up a story about Luke's mom being really sick. Once Nikki thought that his mom might die, she was supportive of the importance that I needed to be with Luke through his difficult time. I told her the plan quickly, and she agreed to cover for me… again. Normally I would have felt bad lying to her, but tonight was different.

The house phone started ringing right after I hung up with Nikki, and I waited until I heard my dad answer before I casually walked downstairs. At least I attempted to look casual. My heart hadn't slowed a beat since Luke had mentioned the tainted one being right outside my house.

"It's for you Liz." My father said as he noticed me walking into the kitchen. "It's your friend Nikki." He handed the cordless phone to me and started to walk into the other room.

"Hey Nikki, what's up?" I said loudly into the phone.

"You like, totally owe me big time for this." Her voice teased through the phone.

"What? When? Tonight?" I kept my voice elevated to make sure my dad would hear me. He paused in the doorway. "I thought your birthday wasn't till next week?"

"Oh, you're good." Nikki complimented softly.

"I don't know. I'm not sure if my dad would let me so last minute." My dad turned to look at me as I spoke and raised one eyebrow questioningly. He folded his arms across his chest and waited for my question.

"Nikki's dad is throwing her a surprise birthday party, and she wanted me to come over for a sleepover. I guess her dad was going to take us to breakfast in the morning at some fancy restaurant in Eugene. Would you care if I went?" I wore my best smile and tried to imitate Alex's puppy dog face.

"Sure Liz. Just make sure you keep your phone on you in case I need you. I've still got Nikki's number too if I need to get a hold of you."

"Really?" I was relieved that he had fallen for it. Crossing the kitchen, I gave him a quick hug. "Thanks dad. You're the best." I saw him grin as he turned and walked back into the living room. It sounded like he and Alex were still watching a movie.

"Okay, my dad actually said it's cool so… give me a few minutes to get ready, and I'll come over." I told Nikki.

"Whatever girl. Just don't like go getting pregnant on me, okay?" Nikki teased.

"Okay, see ya." I replied as I hung up the phone. Judging by Nikki's last comment, she obviously had no clue that this ruse wasn't about having a romantic night with Luke. My main goal was just to stay alive, and hope that somehow Luke and his family would not have to leave town permanently.

I grabbed a quick change of clothes and some pajamas. Having no idea what we would be doing, I also threw in my small travel kit containing a tiny tube of toothpaste and other necessities. It only took me about fifty seconds to get ready, but I stood in my doorway for another minute so as not to seem overly suspicious. Once a minute passed, I couldn't wait anymore, so I went downstairs.

Grabbing my coat off the rack on the wall, I turned to look at Alex and my father. They were sitting on the couch, with Alex leaning up against my father who had his arm around him. Hopefully they would be safe. Luke had said that Isaac and Jazmine would watch over them, but for how long I had no idea.

I opened the door quietly, hoping not to draw Alex's attention, and slipped out of the house. Making sure not to look around, I walked quickly to my Tahoe. I had the distinct impression that someone was watching me. As I put the key in the ignition, I noticed my hand was shaking again. I backed out of the driveway, threw it in drive and headed for Luke's house. The lights didn't appear in my rear-view mirror until I was almost to his house, and even then, they were quite a distance behind me.

As I approached Luke's house, I noticed that the garage was open. Luke was standing in the doorway leading into the house, and he motioned for me to park next to him in the garage. He was wearing a black jacket and black pants. Pulling in next to their hummer, I parked my car much quicker than normal. The fear of being killed by demonic creatures made my fear of parking in tight spaces seem inconsequential.

No sooner had I put my Tahoe in park, then Luke hit the button on the wall. The garage door rolled shut behind me. Luke pulled open my door and offered a hand to help me down. I gladly took it.

"Sorry to drag you into this." He said apologetically as he wrapped his arms around me. "I never wanted to put you in any sort of danger."

"It's okay. You're worth it." I said as I looked up and gave him a quick kiss. "Besides, you did warn me ahead of time what I was getting into by being with you. I just hope that Alex and my father are going to be all right."

"They'll be fine. Isaac is still watching them from your back yard, and Jazmine is on her way back as we speak. The tainted one followed you here; he's probably parking across the street right now. Come on let's get inside." He took my hand and we walked into the house, closing the garage door behind us.

With Luke's hand in mine, I was already starting to feel safer. Even though a part of me felt guilty for leading the tainted one to them. We entered the living room just as Jazmine came walking in from the back sliding door. She was wearing all black with her hair done up in a beanie. Pulling the beanie off, she walked over to me and gave me a quick hug.

"Liz I am so glad you're okay. When Luke told us about you talking to the tainted one, I was worried, but you must have said the right things because he didn't catch on to you until later." Jazmine praised.

"Thanks Jazmine, but I don't know what you're talking about. I must have said the wrong things because I led that monster right to you guys. I feel terrible… but I didn't know what else to do."

"Liz don't be silly. If you hadn't done a good job talking to him he probably would have tortured you instantly. Then he would have had you take him to your family before killing you and torturing them for information. As far as you leading it here that was all part of the plan. If you hadn't come here eventually it would have tried to kill you and your family, which we wouldn't have let happen, but it could have got messy. If we kill it too close to you guys we risk allowing it to jump into one of your bodies. That is why you needed to come here. It's safer for your family this way." She explained.

"So… exactly what is the plan then?" I asked.

"We lead it out of the city and kill it." Isaac's deep voice from behind startled me and I turned in surprise. "Don't worry Liz, your family is safe. The tainted one is sitting two houses down in the driveway of that empty house. Ben is watching it, so if it tries going back to your family we can intercept it, but we must hurry." He reached into his pocket and took out a small black watch and a small black object that I didn't recognize. "Luke, show her how to use these, we leave in one minute."

Isaac was also wearing all black, and I noticed he had a large silver handle sticking up over his left shoulder. As he turned away to go up the stairs, I could see that the handle was part of a large sword that was held in a black scabbard attached to a strap running over his shoulder and around his torso on the other side. It looked like it belonged in an ancient war movie or something, and the handle reminded me of the large dagger Luke had showed me a few weeks before.

"Okay Liz." Luke's voice brought my attention back to him and the two small objects Isaac had given him. I also noticed that he was wearing a watch that looked almost identical to the one he was holding. "I need you to put this on and make sure it fits tight." He handed me the watch, and I began strapping it onto my wrist.

"If you need to talk to us just hit this reset button and talk normal. The mike is extra sensitive, so you don't have to talk into your wrist, we will hear you." He held up the small black object, and

I noticed that it was shaped like a tiny hearing aid. Stepping to one side of me, I could feel him putting it in my left ear. It fit snuggly and seemed to mold perfectly to my ear. "This is the receiver. Try not to play with it too much, but if you need to adjust the volume use these two buttons here." He pointed to two buttons on the right side of the watch, and I nodded.

"Where did you guys get this stuff?" I asked, impressed by the collection of high-tech gadgets.

"Isaac has contacts in different militaries around the world. Add that to the money he's accumulated over the last hundred plus years, and he can pretty much buy anything." Luke explained. "Anyways, here is the plan. Ben and I are going to ride with you in your car. We will duck down in the back seats, so it doesn't know we are there. You will need to drive towards Eugene and draw the tainted after us. Isaac will leave a minute or so after the tainted one and catch up to us on the freeway. We will pull over near the old industrial center, and Isaac and I will ambush the tainted one. If there is more than one Ben will get out and help, but the most important thing is that as soon as we get out of the car you must leave. Drive as fast as you can towards Eugene, and we will tell you when it is safe to come back."

"What about Jazmine and your mom?" I asked.

"I will be taking mom down into the bunker." Jazmine answered. "Those walls are thick enough to keep anything from getting in before you all return. I should be able to communicate with you still in case we have to do an emergency evacuation. Although I don't see that happening. Once you finish off the creature, I imagine you'll be back before midnight." Jazmine sounded confident in the plan, which was reassuring.

"Okay everyone, its time." Isaac's voice rang in my ear, and I quickly turned the volume down on the watch piece. "Just remember the spot Luke, and if we see any couples or kids nearby, we'll use the backup location. I will let you know once I am in position behind you. Make sure you follow the speed limit to give me time to catch up."

Ben came around the corner from the stairs while Isaac was talking and flashed a quick smile at me. He was also wearing all black with a black beanie. Behind him was his mother Sara, who quickly crossed the room to embrace me.

"Liz it's good to see you. I know you've got to get going now, but I just want you to know how grateful we all are that you're safe. Everything is going to work out fine tonight. I just know it." She reassured.

"Thank you. You're too kind." I replied as Luke grabbed my hand again and gently pulled me towards the door. "I'll see you in a little while." I added to her and Jazmine before walking back towards the garage. Ben was already climbing into the back seat as Luke held the door open for me.

"Be careful." I said to Luke as I kissed him one last time. "I expect you back without a scratch."

"As you wish." He replied before closing my door. He climbed into the back seat, and I started the car. "Oh, you might want this." He added from behind, and I saw his hand appear next to me holding a garage door opener. I grabbed it from him and clipped it to the flip down visor.

"Is everyone ready?" I asked trying to sound calm. My heart was pounding again.

"Only if you are." Luke said.

"Good to go." Ben added from the back.

"Okay…. here goes nothing." I let out a long breath, and then pushed the button. The garage door began opening loudly behind me. Checking the rear-view mirror, there was no sign of Ben or Luke. I glanced back though and could see Luke's knee sticking up behind the center console. Backing out of the garage slowly, I hit the remote again to close the garage as soon as my front bumper was clear.

I looked both ways before backing onto the road but didn't notice any cars nearby. Once I had backed into the street, I noticed the creature's black Mercedes parked in the driveway a few doors down through my rear-view mirror. I put the car in drive and turned onto the road that led towards the highway. Two turns later I was getting on the freeway and approaching the bridge to Junction City.

"Are you guys okay back there?" I whispered quietly.

"Yeah." Luke replied in a soft but normal tone. "You don't have to whisper though Liz. It's far behind us on the freeway. Even if it had better hearing than ours there's no way it could hear you."

"Oh. Okay, I just wasn't sure." My cheeks flushed slightly with embarrassment. At least Luke couldn't see my face.

"What about you Liz. Are you doing okay?" I could hear the genuine concern in his voice.

"Yeah, I'm fine. I think those are its headlights a couple hundred yards back, but it's hard to say." I said as I glanced at the rear-view mirror.

"I'm leaving to catch up now." Isaac's voice sounded off in my ear again. I had just thought about asking him if the creature was following or not. "It was trailing you at a distance, and I am pretty sure it's alone. Unless someone was hiding in the trunk anyway."

"Okay. We just crossed over the bridge." I said as I pressed the button on the watch. "Did I do that right?" I asked Luke after letting go of it.

"You were perfect." Luke reassured. "Just like always."

"Oh come on guys. Can you tone down the mushy talk please? You can get a room after this is all over, okay? We've got demons to kill." Ben teased sarcastically from the back of the car.

I couldn't help but smile. My heart was still racing, but I could feel myself relaxing a little. Ben must have been working his magic, because my whole body seemed to feel calmer. Perhaps it should have bothered me that he was toying with my emotions, but it didn't. After all the adrenaline I'd had coursing through my veins for the last hour, it felt good to relax a little.

My mind began to wander, and I found myself thinking about all the possible outcomes from our current endeavor. After they killed this tainted one, would more come in its place? Would they be forced to leave town anyway? There were still so many unanswered questions.

The thought of Luke leaving was simply unconscionable. Considering that they always had to stay in hiding, there would probably be no way to keep in touch with him. Not to mention the fact that I wasn't sure if my family would even be safe once they left. I had an idea come to me and decided to throw it out there.

"Leuken?" I spoke softly, hoping Ben could not hear.

"Yes?" he whispered back.

"If more tainted ones come after this one, will you have to leave?"

"Well, that depends on how many come." He said hesitantly. "But there's a good probability that we will have to. For everyone's safety of course."

"If that happens… can I come with you?" I tried not to sound too desperate.

"Elizabeth I would love that more than anything… but what about your family? I think Alex needs you too much. I've never seen anyone love their sister as much as that kid loves you Liz." He replied.

"What if they came with us too?"

"Yeah right, like your dad would go for that. Excuse me Mr. Scott, my family is going to move suddenly in the middle of the night for reasons I can't explain to you. Would you mind relocating your whole family so that your daughter and I can be together?" Luke said sarcastically. "I'm sure he would love that idea."

"Well, if I explained the danger that we would be putting my family in by staying, and you showed him what you guys are capable of… I think he might go for it. He might be stubborn, but he's not unreasonable. The question is do you think your family would be okay with it?"

"I don't know. Ben and Jaz would be fine, I'm sure. So would my mom, but I think Isaac would take some convincing. Why don't we cross that bridge when we get there? For now, let's just focus on killing that monster and keeping you safe."

"Okay, sounds fair enough. How much further are we going?" I asked looking at the signs on the side of the road. One of them was a large green sign that read "Eugene Airport 10, Eugene 17".

"As long as Isaac is in place, the exit is about 2 miles up." Luke replied.

"All right," Isaac's voice sounded through my earpiece again "I've spotted the target's vehicle. I'll hold back a ways to make sure it doesn't get suspicious. Let me know if we have to switch locations last minute. And remember not to get out until I have its vehicle blocked in. The last thing we need is a vehicle chase. We don't want to draw any unnecessary attention to ourselves."

If I didn't know better, I would say Isaac must be psychic or something. That was the second time I had thought about him, and he had immediately talked on the radio. They must have pretty good range for how clear he had sounded, even when he had been over a mile away. Another minute went by before Luke broke the silence.

"Okay Liz, take this next exit and turn right into that old abandoned industrial park. You'll want to park in the first big parking lot on the right. That should force it to either park right by us, or in the next parking lot over where it can keep an eye on us from a distance. Either way Isaac should be able to box its car in. We'll attack from there. Whether Ben comes with us or stays with you, just make sure you drive as fast as you can south until we tell you to turn around, okay? You can't be anywhere nearby when we kill that thing."

"Sounds good to me." I replied.

I reached the turn off for the exit and got over. There was nothing but darkness off to my right, until I approached the end of the off ramp. Then I could see large shadows under the pale moonlight that must have been buildings. Just before I turned right, I saw headlights exiting a few hundred yards behind me. They flickered off a half second later. That must have been the creature.

I drove slowly for a few hundred yards until I saw an empty parking lot on the right. Large shadowy buildings lay on the other side of the lot. Most of them had square outlines against the night sky, but some were rounded. Exactly what kind of industrial park it had been I couldn't say, but I wasn't about to spend time guessing at it. There were more pressing things on my mind.

"Turn in there." Luke said quietly as he peeked his head up just high enough to see out the passenger window. "And park in those last spaces." He was pointing to the other end of the parking lot as I turned in.

The pavement was old, and my car shook as I drove through the degraded lot. Medium sized cracks in the ground had gone unattended and covered most of the parking lot. Approaching the other end of the lot, I parked in the second to last space from the westernmost building. I placed the car in park but kept the engine running. If they wanted me to take off in a hurry, I needed to be ready.

"We're in position." Luke's voice echoed in my ear a split second after I heard it from his lips.

"Okay, it looks like he parked on the opposite end of the lot in front of another building. As soon as I'm in place make your move. If there is another Verdorben in there, I won't last long two against one. Remember if there are two of them, I want you two to concentrate on one and work together like we practiced. I'll take care of the other. Thirty seconds."

Hearing him talk about fighting tactics made me suddenly fear for their safety. Especially Luke. I had been so worried about losing him from their moving away, I hadn't thought about the possibility of him being killed or injured. Suddenly my emotions got the best of me.

"Luke please be careful." I said turning to look at his face. He was crouched in the back seat, but I could see him as he glanced over at me.

"I will be, don't worry." He said reassuringly.

"Okay… and I also wanted to tell you something before you go."

"What is it?" he said hurriedly.

"I…I've never said this to anyone before but…if something happens, I just want you to know…" I paused, fighting with myself over if I should say it or not. But it might be my last chance. "I love you."

He turned to look at me again, with surprise registering on his face. I started to feel embarrassed, but then he smiled broadly as he gazed into my eyes. "I love you too Elizabeth Scott."

"Now!" I heard Isaac's voice say sharply across the radio less than a second after Luke reciprocated my declaration.

Suddenly I saw headlights turn on about two hundred feet away. Tires squealed as Isaac's truck skidded to a halt behind the black Mercedes. Luke opened the door and jumped from the back of the car at near lightning speed and began sprinting quickly across the parking lot towards the car. Ben jumped from the back into the middle seat and sat looking after Luke out the open door.

Just as I saw Isaac exiting his truck, a man jumped out of the car and looked to be holding something.

"It's got a sword." Ben growled from the back seat. I instantly panicked.

"Go help them!" I said without thinking, and Ben leapt from the car.

"Drive Liz, go now!" He shouted as he raced after his brother.

Every part of me wanted to watch what happened, but I followed Ben's command. Quickly backing up, I threw the car in drive and punched the gas, pulling out the exit nearest me back onto the main street. A few seconds later I drove past them on my left and headed for the freeway on ramp.

I had only seen one tainted one, so hopefully they would all be okay. I held on to that hope as I got back on the freeway and continued south towards Eugene. Realizing what Luke had said back there brought a smile to my lips, in spite of the anxiety I felt. My foot was on the gas pedal and my knuckles were white from holding tightly to the steering wheel, but only one thing was on my mind. Leuken Bennett had better stay alive, because I was absolutely, unequivocally in love with him.

Jeremy pulled into a parking space on the opposite end of the parking lot from the girl he was following. From here he could see her outline through the light tint of the front passenger window. Why she had chosen this spot he couldn't say, but his premonition was that she must be meeting up with one of the people he was searching for. Probably the girl based on what her reaction had been earlier in the store. Although at this point nothing would surprise him.

He glanced around and noticed that they were parked in front of some kind of abandoned industrial plant. There were half a dozen buildings spread out before him, and the newest one looked at least thirty or more years old. Judging by the cracked parking lot, no one had even attempted to use this facility in years. About thirty feet in front of him he could see a shopping cart filled to the top with clothes and other miscellaneous items. He guessed that it probably belonged to some homeless person squatting in the area.

Looking back over at the girl's Tahoe, he noticed that she appeared to be turned around looking backwards. He glanced behind her vehicle but couldn't see anything, which confused him. *What could the girl possibly be looking at?* He thought to himself. Could she have seen him? He had been careful to turn off his headlights before exiting the freeway after her and had been far enough back that it was inconceivable she had seen his dark car in the dismal moonlight.

He started to get a strange feeling that something might be wrong, when suddenly a bright light engulfed his car, and he heard tires screeching from behind. Turning to look, he saw headlights coming to a stop just a few feet behind his vehicle. At that instant he realized why she had driven to this secluded location with no lighting. While it may have been the perfect location to meet someone discreetly, it was also good for other reasons. It was the perfect place to quietly dispose of someone who was following you.

So, this whole thing had been a trap. For the first time in months Jeremy felt afraid, and it made him panic. Reaching for the floorboard behind his seat, he grabbed the sword that Jareth had spent countless hours training him to use. He instantly regretted not having trained more with it on his own as Jareth had suggested, but this was no time for regret. Pulling it free from the scabbard, he pushed open his door and jumped out. Taking a defensive stance with the sword in front of him, he prepared for an attack.

Now that he was out of the direct shine of the headlights, he could see that the light was coming from a pickup truck that had parked directly behind him, blocking his Mercedes in. Next to the vehicle stood a man. At first Jeremy thought that the man looked older, because his hair was mostly gray. But as he studied his face he saw a man who couldn't have been a day older than forty. The man just stood there looking at Jeremy, as if studying him. He was about the same build as Jeremy, and the expression on his face looked too relaxed for someone who was going to kill him. Had it not been for the silver sword that was glowing almost white in his right hand, the man would have looked harmless.

Jeremy waited for the man to attack, but a long second went by with the man just staring at him. It was almost as if he was waiting for something. Suddenly Jeremy heard a sound approaching fast off to his right and jumped backwards. As he did so another man charged right through where he had been standing holding another glowing blade. This weapon was smaller than the sword the older man held and looked more like a dagger or long knife. Jeremy lifted his own blade to strike at the second attacker, but the man was too quick, and jumped sideways onto the top of the car as Jeremy's blade swung through the air at where he had just been standing. This second man looked young, more like a teenager, but was obviously no ordinary teenager. He stood half a head taller than Jeremy and looked stockier as well. His blue eyes glared, and Jeremy could see the unmasked hatred in the young man's face.

Seeing movement off to his right, Jeremy turned and brought his sword up just in time to block the older man's blade as it swiped towards his right arm. He must have flanked him while distracted with the younger one. The old man was fast, and immediately flipped his sword around in a half circle as it bounced off of Jeremy's blade with a loud clang. That circular movement was aimed at Jeremy's other arm, and he tried to counter it but was taken off guard and wasn't able to move his blade fast enough to block the old man again.

Pain flashed through his left arm as the man's blade caught him just above the elbow, and Jeremy felt a sharp flash of pain in his upper arm. His left arm had been severed, and he saw it fall to the ground with the control bracelet still attached to his wrist. The man quickly flashed the blade again in another circular motion back towards Jeremy's remaining arm, but Jeremy was able to deflect that blow as he jumped backwards and screamed in agony.

"Aaagh!" Jeremy shouted as he jumped back. "Please! Stop!" The burning pain in his arm was unbearable, and he wanted to grab what was left of his arm but didn't dare drop the sword.

"Stay back Luke!" The older man barked.

Jeremy turned and noticed that the younger man was standing about ten feet away to his right behind him and looked poised to attack him with the dagger at a moment's notice. He was scowling at Jeremy but followed the older man's command. Jeremy quickly jumped onto his car so that he could keep an eye on both men, but most of his focus was on the older man with the sword.

"What do you want?" Jeremy asked, trying to keep his voice steady through the agonizing pain. He was surprised when he glanced at what was left of his arm and saw no blood coming from the severed limb. The white-hot blade must have cauterized the wound as it cut through the arm.

"That's what I was going to ask you." The older man replied firmly.

"I'm just looking for people; that's all. I wasn't planning on hurting anyone." Jeremy lied, hoping to buy himself time while he thought about what to do.

"I might have believed that." The man's voice was calm, but his eyes looked cold and callous. "At least before you swung at my nephew. When you jump out of your car with a drawn sword, that's not what I would consider a diplomatic move."

"You attacked me first. I was only defending myself." Jeremy eyed his surroundings, searching for an escape. Jareth had told him that if he ever faced members of the bloodline, his only hope was to fight. Supposedly they were faster than he was. After seeing how fast the younger one had moved, he believed Jareth. Considering that less than two seconds of fighting had resulted in him losing an arm however, he was willing to take the risk of running. The younger man was circling around behind Jeremy, as if he knew what Jeremy was planning.

"Who sent you?" The older man asked him.

"Jareth." Jeremy didn't see any point in lying. He thought maybe his answer would distract them.

Sure enough, the old man's expression changed, and he suddenly looked around cautiously. "Where is he?" He asked, still looking around.

Jeremy glanced over at the young one who was now also looking around, and decided it was now or never. He noticed what appeared to be an opening between two buildings behind him away from the two attackers and thought that would be his best chance of escape.

"He's in the car." Jeremy said as he turned and jumped from the car. He landed at a full sprint, running for the darkness between the buildings. Suddenly he saw movement in front of him to his left, and instinctively swung his sword as he ran.

Something collided with him, and he felt his sword catch something as he toppled forward. He landed on his back and felt a burning pain on his upper leg. He couldn't keep from groaning in pain. On top of him was another person, but as he looked at this one's face it was just a boy. The kid couldn't have been a day older than fifteen, with his blond hair and green eyes. Jeremy noticed that his sword was sticking through the kid's stomach.

The boy let out a guttural moan, then his teeth gritted in rage as he wrenched a dagger from Jeremy's leg and raised it overhead, preparing to strike. Jeremy let go of his sword and pushed the kid as hard as he could, flinging the body off of him before the dagger fell. He jumped up to run again but staggered as he realized his leg wouldn't function properly.

He heard footsteps approaching fast and turned just in time to see a glowing blade flash at him. Having no weapon, he raised his hand to block as he jumped back and instantly felt excruciating pain in his wrist as the blade struck. Jeremy tried to turn and run but fell down when he put his weight on the injured leg. Trying to catch himself with his right arm, he noticed his hand was missing as his wrist touched the ground. He fell forward on his face.

"Please" Jeremy moaned, barely able to speak through the agonizing pain. "Please...don't kill me."

"Aaaaaagghhh!" Jeremy heard a boy screaming and turned to see the dark-haired boy pulling Jeremy's sword from the blond boy's stomach. The young boy fell to his hands and knees and the older boy turned to look at Jeremy. His blue eyes and face were contorted with rage.

"Please… please don't… kill me… I don't want… to die."
Jeremy stammered between heavy breaths. The dark-haired boy
dropped the sword, and pulled the dagger from his waistband,
walking slowly towards Jeremy with pure hatred in his eyes.

The old man raised a hand towards the dark-haired boy, but he
didn't seem to notice. He just kept slowly walking towards Jeremy
with the look of death in his eyes. Jeremy had never been so certain
of death in his life. While he didn't want to die, the thought of his
excruciating pain ending didn't seem so bad. For all Jeremy knew, he
had died anyway the day Jareth turned him into whatever he now
was.

Suddenly the gray-haired man raised his sword over his head, as
if preparing to swing at Jeremy. The glow from the blade illuminated
the man's face and Jeremy was surprised by the man's expression.
Unlike the older boy, there was no rage or anger in his eyes. If
anything, he thought he saw… pity.

Realizing that his pleas were in vain, Jeremy gave up on them.
Closing his eyes, he noticed something he hadn't felt in a long time.
For the first time in over a year, he was free. With the bracelet lying
on the ground by the car, still attached to his left arm, Jareth no
longer controlled him. The beautiful green-eyed girl had been the
perfect trap. And he had fallen right for it. Her face was the last thing
he saw before the blade burned through his neck.

CHAPTER XII

I realized that I was driving too fast. The reading on the speedometer was ninety-five miles per hour, so I slowed back down to seventy. With a speed limit of sixty-five on the highway, the last thing I wanted was to get pulled over. It had been less than two minutes since I left the others, but I figured I had probably put enough distance between myself and them.

Seeing an exit coming up, I decided to get off so that I wouldn't have to drive for too long to get back. I hadn't heard anything through the earpiece yet, and I was getting anxious. Hoping that if something was wrong, they would have already said something, I drove slowly down the off ramp.

While I felt anxiety at not knowing what was happening, it was overshadowed by my excitement. I had guessed at Luke's feelings for me, and he had told me that he cared about me a lot. But for some reason actually hearing him profess his love had left me feeling complete. I couldn't wait to get back to him and throw my arms around him.

An unsettling feeling had come over me when I had watched him run away, but hopefully it was just me worrying for his safety. If Isaac had killed tainted ones before, and they outnumbered the creature three to one, losing wasn't likely. I just needed to stop thinking about it and be patient. In a few minutes I knew I would see Luke again.

As I came to the stop sign at the bottom of the off ramp I looked around. To my left was the underpass that went beneath the freeway. On the other side of that were some run down looking apartment buildings. The kind my father had constantly told me to stay away from because they were "ghetto". To my right were some shady looking old commercial buildings. They also looked run down, but were closed, and I couldn't see anyone in the parking lot.

I decided to take my chances with the old empty businesses rather than risk the apartments. Making a right turn, I pulled into the first parking lot. All of the dozen or so parking spaces were empty, so I parked facing the buildings. What at first had appeared to be a long strip mall was actually two separate buildings separated by a small alley. The building in front of me had two signs affixed to the front of it. One read "Tribal Ink Tattoo" and the other "L & L Liquor". Both businesses had glass fronts with roll down metal gates on the immediate inside to prevent intruders. None of the lights were on inside, which confirmed my premonition that the businesses were closed. From where I was parked, I couldn't read the signs in front of the other building.

Only a few seconds had passed since I had parked when I suddenly had a strange feeling come over me. At first, I had an overwhelmingly dark feeling wash through me, and I felt cold. My body shivered for a few seconds, and then I started to feel nauseous. The nausea worsened rapidly, and I had to open my door for fear of vomiting all over the interior of my Tahoe. I stepped down out of the

Tahoe and fell on the ground, realizing I was completely disoriented. My chills quickly turned into an intense fever, and I could feel my whole body beginning to burn.

Barely able to rise onto my hands and knees, I vomited uncontrollable for what seemed like minutes. The knotting pain in my stomach was intense. My vision was blurring, and everything around me seemed to be spinning. Once my stomach had emptied all of its contents and then some, I tried to sit back, but ended up falling sideways onto the ground. The cool black pavement felt good on my burning skin. I couldn't remember ever feeling a fever like this before, and it had come out of nowhere. My vision began to fade even more, and every part of my body ached tremendously. The thought came to me that I must be dying, and then I lost consciousness.

My eyes opened suddenly as I heard someone talking nearby. The first thing I took note of were the loud male voices. I also noticed that it didn't seem as dark as it had earlier. Was the sun already rising? I needed to get back to Luke and Ben. They were probably worried sick about me. Unless… the thought that something might have happened to them was chilling as it suddenly jumped into my mind.

The night air no longer felt cool, and my fever must have broken because physically I was completely comfortable. In fact, my entire body felt great, and my disorientation was gone. Were it not for the sinking feeling in my stomach as I worried about Luke, I would have said that I'd never felt better.

"You two can fight over the girl, but I get the truck." One of the male voices was saying. His voice caught my attention, and I turned my neck to look behind me over my shoulder.

Three men stood about a dozen feet away, and the one who had just spoken was looking longingly at my car. The other two stared at me, and the twisted expressions on their faces looked all too familiar. They both reminded me of the look my attacker had given me a few short weeks before. The same man who had stabbed, and eventually tried to kill me. Luckily Luke had been there to save me then. A new panic struck me as I remembered that he wasn't here now. I was completely alone.

I sat up slowly, hoping not to provoke any sudden movements from them, and quickly surveyed the three. The man closest to me was short and looked like he was in his late twenties. From less than ten feet away I could make out every detail of his face clearly. It was dirty and hadn't been shaved in a few days, but his brown jacket and blue jeans seemed fairly clean compared to his grungy face. His hair was covered by a dark blue beanie, and his brown eyes were still intently focused on my Tahoe.

The other two made the first one look like royalty. Whereas he had a few days of growth on his face, these two looked like they hadn't seen a razor in months. One of them was shorter with a dark complexion and looked to be of Hispanic origin, with black straight hair matted on top that hung down to his shoulder in dirty clumps. He wore clothing so blackened with dirt and grease that it was impossible to guess at its original color. The third man was tall with dirty blond hair that curled slightly past his ears and rabid blue eyes. His clothing matched the Hispanics in filthiness, and they were both staring at me like I was some kind of appetizer.

The blonde man's mouth was even hanging open as he glared and smiled. I noticed most of his teeth were missing.

I glanced over at my Tahoe, which was about ten feet away from me, but knew that I wouldn't be able to make it back inside it before they reached me. They were standing already, and I was still sitting. My mind was racing as I tried to think about possible actions, but my situation was dire. Nothing with a decent chance of success came to mind as I looked around me and tried to formulate a plan. There wasn't another sole in sight.

"That's a nice SUV. What year is it?" The younger of the three said, still staring at my Tahoe. He spared a quick glance at me, and then did a double take locking his eyes on my face. "Whoa… maybe I will take a turn with you after all." The sudden lust in his eyes made my skin crawl.

All three of the men were smiling now and had stepped closer to me while the one was talking. Even the younger one was missing half of his teeth. Their sinister expressions made me want to run, but I doubted I could outrun all three. Even had I been able to escape, they would get my car and I would still be trapped in this despicable slum.

"Listen guys please, I don't want any trouble. You can have my purse just please let me go." I said as I slowly stood.

They all took another step towards me as I was standing up and were uncomfortably close now. The tall one could have almost reached out and touched me. A putrid smell of urine and vomit flooded my nostrils now that they were so near. It was difficult not to gag. None of their expressions changed, and they didn't seem to acknowledge that I had even spoken.

While I knew I didn't stand a reasonable chance against three male attackers, there weren't really any other options. I had to fight. Even though I already knew what the outcome would be. There was no way I would become a victim without fighting back.

The younger one suddenly lunged at me, and without thinking I bladed off and threw the hardest kick I could right at his crotch. Surprisingly I heard a loud crack that sounded like bones breaking as my ankle connected with him. His body lifted a few feet off the ground from the impact, and he landed face first on the ground.

Before I even had time to register what had happened, the tall one was grabbing at my left arm. I turned throwing my right fist at his face as hard as I could. This time I could actually feel my fist crushing his jawbone as it connected. His entire body flipped sideways as I heard more bones cracking. He landed in a contorted heap, with his neck hanging sideways from his head. I could see that the left half of his neck was ripped open. The arm that had been holding me was twisted backwards at the shoulder, with the hand palm down facing straight out from his back.

The Hispanic man's expression changed from a grin to a look of pure terror. He stared wide eyed at the two bodies of his fallen companions, then glanced quickly at me as he stepped back slowly. The realization of what I had just done suddenly hit me, and I took a step back from the petrified man. Seeing me move, he screamed loudly and incoherently as he turned and ran. After two seconds he had disappeared around the corner between the two buildings. Surprisingly I could still hear his footsteps for a while longer.

I stood in shock, unable to move. My body should have been shaking from the adrenaline I felt, but it wasn't. *I must be dreaming.* I thought to myself as I replayed in my mind what had just occurred. There was no logical explanation for what had just happened, other than it being a dream. I looked down at the body of the one I had kicked.

The man was lying on his back with his eyes closed. I reached down to feel for a pulse on his neck. His skin still felt warm, but he wasn't breathing and definitely had no pulse. As I looked over the rest of his body, I could see a pool of blood forming on the ground around his waist. The gruesome image of the second body was still freshly burned in my mind, and I dared not look at it for fear my eyes would confirm what I had before seen.

I looked down at my own body and flinched in horror. Blood covered my right leg around the ankle that I had used to kick him, and there was also blood spattered on the right side of my clothes. My hands were free of blood, until I touched one to my face to see what the moisture was that I felt on my right cheek. The dark blood on my fingertips as I pulled my hand away was unmistakable.

My panic jumped into a state of absolute desperation as I closed my eyes. "Wake up Liz. You're dreaming." The sound of my own voice did nothing to calm my nerves. Suddenly I realized that the cars passing on the nearby freeway sounded louder than normal. Opening my eyes, I turned to look at the freeway and noticed a white compact car starting down the off ramp.

Without thinking, I ran and jumped back into my Tahoe. I closed the door and quickly drove out of the parking lot back towards the freeway underpass. The white car had just stopped at the stop sign as I drove past, and I was relieved when it turned left after me. At least they wouldn't be seeing the bodies, which gave me more time to escape the scene of the crime.

Was it a crime? I went over what had happened again in my mind. I had felt something dark, and then I got sick. I got out of the car and puked my guts out, then passed out. When I woke up three men were standing over me and talked openly about raping me and stealing my car. They started to attack me, and I defended myself. The only tricky part would be explaining to the police how a tiny girl like me killed two grown men with my bare hands. I hadn't intended to kill them, but how could I explain my sudden superhuman strength?

Part of me wanted to call the police, but I didn't know what I would say. My guilt wasn't strong enough to overcome the fear of what would happen to me if I did call. Something told me the old Hispanic would-be rapist wouldn't be calling the police any time soon either. He probably didn't even own a phone.

As I merged from the on ramp back onto the freeway the traffic was light. I could see taillights a few hundred feet ahead, and two pairs of headlights a way back in my rearview mirror. A passing semi truck flashed his brights at me from the other direction of travel, and I looked down thinking my brights must be on. To my surprise my headlights actually weren't on at all. The freeway had seemed so well lit that I hadn't noticed.

I turned on my headlights and looked at the road ahead. There actually weren't any road lights on this part of the freeway. Maybe my eyes had just been playing tricks on me. I had always had good vision, but it seemed especially clear tonight.

The industrial turnoff where the others were came into view about half a mile ahead, so I figured I should probably make sure the others were okay. Pushing the button on my wrist piece, I talked into the watch.

"Hey, are you guys okay? I'm on my way back now."

I waited for an answer, but several long seconds passed with nothing but silence in my ear. Finally, I heard Luke's voice come across the earpiece.

"Okay Liz, just meet us by the truck. We took care of the tainted one and we think we've captured its new host. How far away are you?"

"I'll be there in about two minutes." I responded. "Is everyone okay?"

"Yeah, we're all fine. Ben got a little cut, but he's already healed." Luke answered.

"I would hardly call a sword through the stomach a little cut." Ben's voice sounded sarcastic as it came through the earpiece.

"Well, I'm glad you're all safe." I added.

The relief I felt upon hearing about Luke's safety was incredible. While I was also glad to hear that Ben and Isaac were okay, he had been my primary concern. I was surprised when I looked at the clock for the first time to learn that less than ten minutes had passed since I left them. My unconsciousness must have only lasted a couple minutes after all.

I pulled down my sun visor and looked at myself in the mirror briefly. To my disgust, drops of blood spattered the right side of my face and neck, with a small smear on my cheek where I had touched earlier. Luke couldn't see me all bloody like this. I was already unsure how I would explain to him what happened. Something I didn't even understand myself.

Two men were dead because of me. And whether it was self defense or not didn't change the fact that I had killed them. The fact that it had been an accident also wouldn't bring them back. I started to feel guilt taking over my emotions, until I reminded myself that they had been vile rapists. If I hadn't killed them, they probably would have raped and killed me. And who knows how many other women they would have victimized. Or how many they had already assaulted for that matter.

I was grateful for all the times that my father had talked about how rapists deserved the death penalty, because it helped me feel a little less guilty about what I had just done. If he had seen what just happened, he probably would have given me a high five. That being said, if I could go back in time, I definitely wouldn't have killed them. All I really wanted was to get away unharmed.

I arrived at the industrial exit and reached over to grab some baby wipes out of the glove box. Usually, I just used them to wipe

Alex up when he spilled food, but they would come in handy now. As I wiped the dried blood from my face, I thought about what I would say to Luke.

While I wanted to believe that I was still dreaming, I had pretty much ruled that option out by this point. Everything seemed too real to be a dream. Plus, I never usually thought about the possibility that I was dreaming whenever I was actually in a dream. Dreaming never worked that way for me. It was always after I woke up that I realized it had just been a dream.

Since waking up wasn't going to be the magical solution to my problem, I thought about my current situation again. I wanted to understand what had transpired. The overwhelming dark feeling, the cold and fever, the disorientation, my passing out, my waking with superhuman strength and accidentally killing two rapists. None of it made any sense. Something in the back of my mind told me that I knew what had happened, but I couldn't quite put my finger on it.

I threw the now bloody wet wipes into the plastic grocery bag attached to the center console, before turning left to drive under the freeway. As I emerged from the tunnel, I was surprised by how much brighter the industrial complex seemed. Whereas before I had barely been able to make out the shadowy outlines against the star lit sky, I could now make out some of the details on the rooftops of the buildings. Maybe the moon had somehow gotten brighter. I drove towards the parking lot where Luke would be waiting for me.

Isaac's truck and the black Mercedes came into view before I even turned into the parking lot, and I could see Luke standing next to Isaac's truck waving one arm at me. He reached in and turned the trucks headlights on for a brief second as I turned into the parking lot. Perhaps he assumed that I couldn't see where they were.

I pulled up next to the Mercedes and noticed Ben and Isaac. They were both squatted down on either side of another man who was lying face down on the ground. This man was wearing layer upon layer of dirty looking old clothing and had a full beard. His filthy demeanor reminded me of the men I had just dealt with in front of the tattoo shop, and I felt a stab of guilt. As I opened my door, I could hear Isaac talking.

"I think he is finishing the transformation. My ring is heating up. Be ready." Isaac's voice carried loudly through the quiet night air.

I turned and saw Luke walking quickly towards me. His arms were spread wide, so I opened mine as well as he scooped me up off the ground.

"I am so glad you're okay." He said excitedly as he spun me several times through the air.

"Me too." I replied happily, relieved to be in his arms again. "But you are the one I was worried about. I'm just relieved that you weren't hurt. I don't know what I'd do if anything ever happened to you."

He set me down and kissed me, then looked at me as he pulled away. Seeing him unharmed was terrific, but suddenly the sadness over what I had just done came back in a torrent. Tears rolled down my cheeks as I saw Luke's innocent face, and I knew that I had to tell him what I'd done.

"Luke, something terrible happened…" I began and had to look down while I thought of what to say. Hopefully he would understand.

"What happened? Are you okay?" He sounded concerned and gently lifted my chin with one of his fingers.

"Honestly, I don't know what happened. One second, I was sitting in the Tahoe, and the next I felt cold and sick…and then… oh I don't want you to think less of me. Please promise you won't think less of me, it was an accident." The tears were flowing freely now. I could barely keep my voice steady.

"Liz nothing could make me think less of you." Luke said with compassion.

He put his hands to my head and kissed me again. I instantly smelled something burning as I felt intense heat on the side of my head. Without thinking I pushed Luke back as I cried out. "Oww!" I was surprised when he fell backwards to the ground.

Maybe I had pushed him a little too hard. Instinctively putting a hand to my head where his ring must have burned me, I offered Luke a hand and pulled him back up. "Sorry about that. I didn't mean to push you. I think your ring burned me."

"It's okay. Sorry about the ring, I forget that the stone is on the outside. Is your head okay?"

He stepped onto my side, and I pulled my hair away so that he could see the burn. The pain was coming from just behind my ear. Hopefully it wasn't burned too badly. The smell of burnt hair was overpowering.

"Oh, it's not bad, just a little red mark where it burned you. Usually, it's not so hot but it's because the tainted one is so close." He said gesturing at the vagrant Isaac and Ben were holding. "What's this on your neck?" Luke pushed the hair on the back of my neck away more and then froze.

I turned to look at him and was surprised to see a look of pure terror on his face. "What is it Luke?" I asked.

He stepped slowly back, with painful disbelief registering in his eyes as they moved to study my face. All of the sudden it came me. Like a tidal wave the truth struck, leaving me devastated. There was a logical explanation for what had happened to me, and now I understood it. Luke and Isaac had killed the tainted one. I had suddenly felt darkness coming over me, and then my whole body had reacted strangely resulting in my loss of consciousness. When I woke up my vision was sharper than ever, and I had extraordinary strength.

Luke's terralium ring had burned my skin. Now there was apparently something on the back of my neck. Questions began flooding through my head as I thought about the implications of my transformation.

"No…" Luke's voice was soft but firm as he struggled to accept the reality he had just discovered. "It's impossible… you were far away by the time we… that man was closer." His voice grew louder and more upset as he continued speaking.

"Luke I'm sorry… I didn't want this…" I began to say as tears flooded from my eyes. The pain in his eyes was unbearable.

"No!" his anguish filled voice was louder now, and both his fists were clenched at his sides. "Why her!? It shouldn't be this way!" Tears were streaming from his eyes, but all I could see was ice cold fury and pain as he shouted. "You cannot have her! I won't let you use her body!"

I suddenly realized that his right fist was no longer clenched. It was now clutching a glowing silver handled dagger and Luke was raising it over his head. He looked ready to strike, and I realized that I must be his intended target.

"Luke please… I'm still me." I pleaded hopelessly.

He must not have believed me, because his expression didn't change. I wasn't even sure if I believed myself. Nothing but fuming determination registered on his face. His body pivoted slightly as if he was about to strike.

How would he ever believe me? How could I make him see that I still loved him? Regardless of what creature inhabited my body I was still in control. Or then again… was I? I had killed two men without even thinking and felt little remorse. I had fled the scene like some kind of murderer. And now I had crushed the heart of the one person who was my universe.

As I looked into his devastated eyes, I realized that he no longer saw me. Whatever taint had possessed my body was all he could see. The demon inside had already killed me as far as he was concerned. The woman to whom he had professed his love just a short while ago was gone. Elizabeth Scott was a dead woman. I was a dead woman. I let my sobs come freely as I closed my eyes and prepared for death to finish taking me.

I had dreamed of growing old and dying with the one I loved. Little did I know my death would come by his hand.

CHAPTER XIII

"LUKE NO!" Ben shouted, and I opened my eyes. He was in front of me now, and both of his hands were holding Luke's wrist. Luke struggled with him over the dagger.

"Let go Ben! I won't let it have her!" Luke snarled through gritted teeth.

The two of them were circling each other as they wrestled over the weapon, so I stepped back from them and watched. What else could I do? If Luke wanted me dead, I could see no reason for living. Isaac walked slowly towards the fighting pair, keeping most of his attention on me.

Luke suddenly slipped sideways, letting go of the dagger as he threw Ben over his shoulder. As Ben was flipping Luke pulled another silver dagger from Ben's waist and turned quickly towards me, raising the blade.

He stopped suddenly when his turn landed him face to face with Isaac, who had stepped in front of me. "Put that away Luke and get a hold of yourself!" He barked.

Luke flashed a disdainful look in my direction, breathing heavily from his tussle with Ben. He stood like that for a couple of seconds, clutching the weapon with a death grip. Finally, he looked away from me and put the dagger back into his waistband. Ben stood up behind him.

"Obviously there is something of the girl you care for left in her, or else she never would have come back to us." Isaac turned to look me in the eyes while he spoke. I looked down, ashamed of what I had become. "It's evident by her reaction that she didn't know what she was until you mentioned the mark on her neck. We wanted to capture the new one alive and killing her would only curse another innocent soul to share her fate. I am sorry for your loss Luke, but you need to control your emotions."

"You're right Isaac; it's just hard to hear." Luke eventually replied, staring down at his feet. He glanced over at Ben who was now standing on his left side. "I'm sorry Ben."

Ben said nothing as he breathed out a sigh. Then he turned to look at me. His expression was strange. Part of me thought that he was analyzing me, but there was no suspicion in his face. Sympathy perhaps, but he seemed to see that I was still me. "Are you okay Liz?"

I nodded quickly, unable to find words. By any definition of the word okay I was not, but considering Ben had just saved my life, I owed him that.

"Don't talk to it." Luke said to Ben as he glared at me with a curled lip. Then he turned suddenly and walked back over to the homeless man who was still handcuffed, sitting on the ground in front of the Mercedes.

Seeing Luke's unadulterated hatred of what I had become made me wish for death. Except it was probably too late for that. As far as I knew I was already dead. If this wasn't hell, I don't know what could be. To see the one you love despise you. To be repulsive to him. Fire and brimstone sounded appealing compared to the wrenching anguish that was seeping through my body. I closed my eyes and looked down; hoping no one would see the tears that again began streaming down my face.

"Listen Billy, I have two questions for you." I recognized Isaac's voice coming from the front of the car but didn't look up. He must have been talking to the homeless man. "The first is… do you want to live?"

"Yes sir. I do… I do please." A high-pitched raspy voice replied.

"Then you had better answer the second right." Isaac continued. "Can you promise that you will not call the police, and that you will never tell anyone about what happened here tonight?"

"Yes sir, I promise." The raspy voice answered.

"Good, because if anyone finds out and I see any of our faces or sketches on the news, I will find you and kill you slowly. Do you understand? You have thirty seconds to be out of our sight." Isaac's voice was cold and callous as he spoke.

I looked up again and saw the vagrant man running towards the nearest building. Luke was standing next to Isaac, holding a large metal object. As I examined it closer, I realized that it was the same metal restraint that had been on the vagrant's wrists when I had first arrived. It looked similar to a pair of handcuffs my dad owned, except that the steel was at least three times as thick. They looked big enough to hold a five-hundred-pound gorilla.

"Face away from me." Luke spat as he walked towards me with the metal restraint.

I did what he said. He grabbed one of my arms, pulling it behind me. Feeling cool metal touching my wrist, I heard a clicking sound. He then bent my other arm back, and I could feel the restraint snap tight against that wrist also. The distinct feeling of being a criminal came over me as I thought about the large handcuffs I was wearing. Luke also reached in my right ear and pulled out the earpiece that he had placed in there earlier.

"Why don't you drive my truck Luke, and I will take her in the Tahoe with Ben." Isaac suggested.

"That's probably a good idea." Luke replied. I glanced at him again, but he seemed to be purposely ignoring me. "I'll follow you guys in case it tries anything."

"Good idea, Ben you can sit in the back with her." Isaac said glancing at Ben. Then he turned to look at me. "Liz I'm not sure how much control of yourself you still have but understand this. If you try to escape, we will be forced to kill you."

The emotionless finality to what he said should have bothered me, but it didn't. I couldn't blame any of them for the way they were treating me. With that demon inside of me it made sense that I couldn't be trusted. Had the situation been reversed I would have treated them the same way. Knowing that didn't take away the sting I felt at being reduced to a second-class monster. At least Isaac and Ben still addressed me as a person. To Luke I was nothing more than an "it".

"Come on Liz, let's get in the car." Ben said sympathetically as he gently rested a hand on my shoulder.

We walked around the back of the truck, and I noticed two large black trash bags in the bed. The smell of burnt flesh filled my nostrils as we passed. That must have been where they put what was left of the other tainted one. Would I end up in a bag if I tried to escape? Isaac did seem a man of his word. I didn't see the point in running anyway. Everything I wanted was right here with me. Unfortunately, that person no longer reciprocated my feelings.

Ben held the rear passenger door of my Tahoe open, and I climbed inside. He reached over and latched in my seatbelt. A few seconds later he came in the other door and sat beside me. Isaac opened the driver's door and sat down, moving the seat back a few inches.

Isaac started the car, and we drove through the old parking lot. The Tahoe shook slightly again as we drove over the cracks. Depression was consuming me, and I found myself paying little attention to what was going on around me. Thinking about what I'd become had many implications. The most important of all was the fact that the man I loved now despised me. Even more than that he wanted to kill me. Had it not been for Ben I would already be dead.

The second I had woken from my unconsciousness my life might as well have been over. I couldn't decide which haunted me more. The overwhelming pain I had seen in Luke's eyes when he realized what I had become, or the venomous hatred that quickly replaced it. Either one by itself would have been enough to break my heart. As it was the combination was devastating.

I would never be able to hold him again. The days of talking into the night on the phone were over. His lips would never touch mine. My hands would never feel the comfort of being entwined by his as we walked together. There wouldn't be any walking together, except perhaps with me as his prisoner. For all I knew they might only plan on keeping me alive long enough to discover how to kill the demon inside me permanently. I curled up the best I could with my arms restrained behind my back, and decided it wasn't worth fighting the tears. Trying not to be too loud, I cried harder than I ever imagined possible.

Minutes went by as I sobbed uncontrollably. Ben kept looking straight ahead of him. He probably felt awkward, but I didn't care. The pain was too sharp to care about anything. Minutes went by before I finally regained some control. When I finally stopped the sobs completely, I could see the Junction City Bridge just ahead. So, we were almost back to Harrisburg. Something came to me as I stared out the window, contemplating what my dismal future might hold.

Isaac had mentioned that there was some of me left, which must mean that the demon inside had most of the control. What didn't make sense to me was the fact that I didn't feel anything or anyone else inside me. Other than when I had killed the two men who attacked me, I had always been in complete control. As I thought about it, even with those two I had only killed them because I didn't realize my own strength. I had thought I was fighting for my life against three men who were stronger than me. Never had I been more wrong. If I'd actually known my new strength, I definitely would have reacted differently. And those men would still be alive.

"You really are still in there, aren't you Liz?" Ben's sudden speech brought my attention back to reality.

"I must be…" I answered cautiously.

His expression was perplexed as he looked over at me. "Can you feel it taking control?"

"Honestly no. The only thing I feel is sickened by what I've become and depressed by how I've hurt Luke."

"I'm sorry Liz." He sincerely added, before looking down at my pants again. "I do have to ask though. How did you get the blood on your ankle?"

"If you must know…" I began, thinking about how to tell the story. "When I woke up after the change, there were three men standing over me. They talked about trying to do horrible things to me. I had no idea that I had been changed, so I thought that they were going to rape and murder me. I tried to talk my way out of it, but they attacked me right as I stood up. The blood on my pants is from kicking one of them in the groin… And the other one I punched in the face… still before I knew about my new strength."

"What happened to the third guy?" He asked curiously.

"He hadn't physically attacked me yet, so when I finished off the other two, I just looked at him. He screamed and ran away… so I got in my Tahoe and left."

"So, the blood is from kicking a rapist in the nuts?" Ben smiled slightly. "That's kind of cool."

"Ben… I don't think you understand. I killed them… both of them. Just because it was an accident doesn't change that. There is nothing cool about it." I could feel my eyes beginning to water again.

"They were trying to attack you right?" He asked.

"Yes."

"So, you were defending yourself, right?"

"I suppose."

"And in the process of defending yourself against a bunch of rapists you accidentally killed two of them? That sounds like nothing but self defense to me."

"Except that self defense doesn't explain how a tiny girl like me kills two grown men with my bare hands in less than two seconds." I quickly retorted.

"No, it doesn't, but that doesn't change the motive. Did you want to kill those men?" Ben asked with an inquisitive look.

I had to think long before I answered. "No…hurt them yes, but not kill them."

"And was your primary motivation for striking them to hurt them or to get away?"

"It was mostly just to get away. I only tried hurting them so that I could escape." I felt like I was on an episode of Dr. Phil. Except Ben was not annoying.

"So, you were outnumbered and attacked by three men, alone in a dark neighborhood, and in trying to escape you accidentally killed someone. No jury in the world would convict you of murder. I stand with my prior decision. You acted only in self defense and should feel no guilt.”

I felt a strange tickling sensation in my head as he spoke. “If only it were that simple Ben.”

He looked like he was concentrating hard at something as he looked me in the eyes. Half a minute or so went by before he frowned slightly and dropped his concentration.

“What is it?” I asked.

“Oh nothing.” Ben looked disappointed as he glanced down. It seemed like something was bothering him, but I couldn’t say what. Finally, he looked back up at me. “Did you feel anything different about your emotions just now?”

“No, why?” He had me completely confused.

“Because I was trying to soothe you and I wanted to know how you would react… if you even reacted at all.” He explained.

I thought about the tickling on my mind. “Are you soothing now?” I asked him.

“No.” I wasn’t feeling the sensation anymore.

“Do it again.” I prodded. His brow furrowed and the tickling sensation returned.

“Well…did you feel anything?” He asked excitedly.

“Actually, I think I did. Except… it wasn’t like before. Before when you would do that, it made me feel good without even realizing you were doing anything. Now I don’t feel any different emotionally, but I do feel a strange sensation. Almost like someone is scratching softly on the outside of my brain, trying to get inside.”

“That’s interesting.” Ben mused thoughtfully.

He didn’t say anything else until we were pulling into the driveway at their house. Jazmine was standing in the garage waiting for us with Luke, who had just stepped out of Isaac’s truck. Ben turned again to look at me as he un-clicked my seatbelt.

"Okay Liz, make sure you tell us if you start to feel that creature taking control of you." He stated somberly.

"I'll try, but I really don't know what that would feel like. I don't feel any different right now besides physically." I explained.

Ben came around and opened my door, and I stepped out. Luke's eyes were watering as he finished whatever he had been saying to Jazmine. He gave me one sad glance before walking into the house. The heartbroken expression on his face reminded me of the pain I had been feeling for the last half hour. Except the difference was I still loved him, while he completely despised me. If only I could somehow prove to him that I was still me. Perhaps then he would soften up a little.

Jazmine's hand was covering her mouth as she shook her head slowly from side to side. Her eyes were watering as well. Judging by the shocked expression on her face, I guessed that she must have just heard the news. The news that I was now a tainted one. That I was now the enemy. The part she didn't know was that I still considered myself an ally. I would never do anything to hurt Luke, or his family. At least not as long as I still had control of myself.

Jazmine was speechless as Ben led me into the house, keeping one arm on my shoulder. Isaac walked behind me, but nobody said anything. We crossed through the kitchen and into the front room, before turning down a side hallway. Ben opened a closet door at the opening of the hallway. At first, I was confused, because all I saw in the closet were coats. Then Ben pushed a button on the smoke alarm inside the closet, and the coats slid to one side of the closet while the back wall suddenly opened outward. Behind where the wall had been was a small hallway.

Ben pulled me through the makeshift closet and into the dimly lit hallway. The floor was black stained concrete and the walls stainless steel. It was narrower than a normal hallway, and Ben had to let go of my arm as he walked slowly in front of me. The hallway was less than ten feet long, and at first, I thought that it dead ended. Then I noticed Ben stepping downward in front of me and saw the stairs. Ben hit a silver switch that blended into the wall, and a light appeared at the bottom of the stairs.

We walked down about fifteen steps to another door where the stairs ended. This door was black, and instead of a normal handle it looked like a safe. A keypad was underneath the three-pronged steel handle. Ben put his hand up to the keypad but stopped when Isaac grunted from behind.

Ben turned and looked at me with chagrin. "Umm…I need you to turn around Liz." He said politely.

I turned and noticed that Isaac was about five steps behind me. His distance wasn't alarming, but the look on his face was. While at first, I thought he looked completely composed, I could see the muscles in his jaw were tightened. His eyes seemed deadly, and I got the impression he was ready to kill me at any moment. You would have thought I was a psychotic mass murderer by the way he watched me. He also had one hand on the hilt of the sword on his back.

I thought about telling him that I was harmless but didn't see a point. Unlike Ben, I got the sense that Isaac trusted me like a starving dog in a butcher shop. Nothing I said would alter his mind even an inch. If I wanted them to trust me again, I would have to convince Ben first. He was my best chance of proving my loyalty. None of the others had shown even an ounce of trust in me.

Several beeping sounds came from behind me, and then I heard a loud click. I was about to turn around, when I heard more beeps followed by another loud creak. Isaac motioned for me to go after that, so I turned back to Ben. He was ducking down as he passed through two small doors.

I followed him but didn't have to duck as I passed through the doors. They must have been about five and a half feet tall because the top of my hair nicked them as I walked through. I noticed that each of the doors had large two-inch-thick bars sticking out of the ends of them. They reminded me of the large door on my father's safe at home, except that the bars on these were twice as thick.

Inside the room I was surprised by what I saw. It was a large open chamber, with ceilings about ten feet high. Four large metal support beams were equally spaced around the center of the room. On my left was a long wall with two doors, spaced about 10 feet apart towards the middle of the wall. In front of me was a large open area with a matt for flooring. It reminded me of the wrestling room at my last high school, minus the foul stench of male body odor. Behind the matt area was a large metal contraption with steel bars connected to create what appeared to be some kind of obstacle course. Next to the metal section was a silver-colored sports car. It was resting on a circular platform about two feet off the ground. On my right were rows and rows of shelves. The front ones contained mostly large cans, and the labels on the front suggested that they were all food items.

They had quite the little fortress set up down here. Although I had to admit I couldn't see the purpose of the sports car in an enclosed bunker. If I ever regained their trust, I would have to ask one of them about it. That is if the demon didn't take over me first.

I was surprised when Ben pulled out a long silver key and unhooked the restraints on my hands. It felt good to have my arms back in front of me, and to be able to bend my elbows and wrists. Ben grabbed my shoulder gently again and led me towards the first door on the left. It also had a keypad on it, so I turned around to look the other way.

"You read my mind." Ben said from behind, and I heard seven more beeps. "Okay, you're good."

I turned back around, and Ben was standing next to the open door, gesturing towards it. Without thinking I walked through the door. Inside was a steel cell, or at least that was my first impression. Every wall of the room, in addition to the ceiling and floor, was covered in stainless steel. A single bright light hung from a metal hook in the ceiling, but the room was void of anything else. The door suddenly slammed shut behind me, and I jumped in surprise.

What little hope I'd had of gaining Ben's trust had vanished when the door slammed shut. I wanted to scream, to beg for them to let me out, but what was the point? If I acted too crazy, they would assume the demon inside had taken control, and then I was guaranteed never to be let out. I glanced around the metallic cell, and the finality of my imprisonment sunk in.

I sat down, put my arms around my knees, and curled my legs in close. At first, I was too depressed to cry. I felt like everything was too terrible to be real. Like I was trapped in the middle of some eternal nightmare, from which I couldn't seem to wake. Pinching my arm again, I realized that my hope was futile. No matter how much I wanted it to be a dream, it wasn't. I was alone, in an empty metal cell. The man I loved hated me. A demon was inside of me somewhere, waiting to take control. And there was nothing I could do to change any of it. I would never see Alex or my father again.

The detached from reality feeling vanished when I thought about Alex, and the little restraint I had left in me vanished. I rolled onto my side in the fetal position and cried hysterically. The sound of my crying echoed through the small room, but I didn't care. Being completely alone had one advantage. No one would see me crying like a baby. So, I cried… and cried. Time seemed to stretch out as I heard only the echo of my own lamentations.

Quite some time passed before I eventually stopped crying. It wasn't because I felt better, but even the crying itself seemed pointless after a while. I was unsure how long I had cried for, but it felt like hours. The floor was cold and hard, so even had I been tired I probably couldn't have slept.

Opening my eyes, I studied my surroundings again. The same empty steel room as before greeted me. My eyes were drawn to the door. It was the only part of the room that looked slightly different from the rest.

I could see a small slit cut into it, but I wasn't sure what it was for because it looked like it went a few inches into the door before ending. It was only about an inch tall and a foot wide.

I had no sooner begun looking at the slit then it suddenly opened. Brown eyes gazed in at me. At first, I wasn't sure who it was, but then he spoke.

"Step back from the door." Isaac's voice called sternly through the slit.

I obeyed, walking to the opposite corner of the cell. The keypad beeped again, and I heard the door unlatch. Isaac walked quickly into the room, followed closely by Ben. Isaac's hand was still on the hilt of his sword, but his face seemed more relaxed. His expression almost seemed... sad as he looked at me. Perhaps the man was capable of some compassion.

"I can tell that you are still in there Elizabeth Scott but make no mistake. If you even give a hint of trying to escape, I will kill you. That being said... I am sorry for your current predicament. Despite our precautions to prevent you from being infected by one of those creatures, it somehow found a way to get to you. Usually, the Verdorben transfers to the nearest human. Obviously in your case it didn't. There is a legend that they can actually choose their new host before they die... so perhaps that is why it came to you. Why it would choose you however, I don't know." He stared off for a moment as if lost in thought.

"Anyhow" He continued after a few seconds. "To be perfectly honest we don't really know how much of a roll the curse of the Verdorben actually plays in controlling a person. I personally believe that the new host has no knowledge or memory of the prior host. I have fought the same Verdorben when it affected two different people at different times, and they each had their own personalities and different fighting styles. So, there is quite a bit about them that we simply don't know. This brings us to you. We need to study you. I am sorry that we have to lock you up like this, but we cannot afford to take any chances." He paused again as if thinking of how to word something.

"When I say study… I mean run some tests on you. Unfortunately, we haven't the luxury of time, for we know not when or if others may come looking for you. This means that we need to hurry. Are you willing to cooperate with us Elizabeth?"

While I was surprised by Isaac being so frank and open with me, I wasn't sure how to respond. They had tricked me into coming down into this room, and then locked me up like some kind of animal. And now they wanted me to cooperate with them and be their lab rat? I shook my head without thinking, and Isaac raised an eyebrow at me inquisitively.

"I will do whatever I can to help." I said.

"Excellent" Isaac said with relief.

The truth was while I had every reason to be upset with them; I still couldn't blame them for their behavior. They were treating me like a rabid animal, but was a newly made, tainted demon creature somehow better? While it pained me to think of Luke, I would still do anything for the boy. Even if it meant being a lab rat for a while.

Hopefully these "tests" wouldn't be too painful. I honestly had no idea what to expect.

"I am going to start with some questions, and I need you to be completely honest." He began and I nodded. "Can you feel the taint or the demon inside you?" he asked.

"No. When it first came into me, I felt darkness, but now I feel nothing." I replied.

"Do you feel emotionally any different?"

"You mean other than the fact that the man I love now hates me and wants me dead; his family is holding me captive in an underground cell and no longer trusts me; I will probably never see my own family again, and I just killed two people? Yeah, other than that I feel normal." I said sarcastically.

"Sorry, what I meant to say is: Do you have any desire or cravings to do bad things. Things you normally would never even consider?" He explained carefully.

"You mean like bad things to other people?" I asked, and he nodded. "No… not at all. Like I said, I still feel normal. Other than my newfound physical strength, I feel the same. Emotionally and psychologically, I feel unchanged. At least as far as the curse is concerned."

"Have you heard any voices or anything else in your head?"

"No."

"Do you want to hurt any of us?" He asked.

"No. Absolutely not." I answered with conviction.

"Well, that's good because you might think differently when we are through, depending on how some of these tests go." He smirked slightly.

"I promise I won't." I turned to look at Ben, who was looking down at his feet. He looked ashamed, as if he felt bad for the way I was being treated. "I care about you all too much."

Ben almost seemed to flinch when he heard me say that. I had to get in a little jab after the way he slammed the cell door on me earlier. If he had explained everything before like Isaac just did, I would have been saved the heartache of thinking that nobody cared. I even would have walked in the cell and closed the door on myself, had I known why it was necessary.

Isaac reached into his pocket and pulled out a small silver lighter, taking a step closer to me.

"Can you hold out your hand please?" He asked. I eyed him suspiciously. "If it hurts you can pull away immediately. We aren't going to cause you any more pain than is scientifically necessary."

I complied and held out my left hand, with my fingers outstretched. Isaac brought the lighter close to my hand before igniting it. I waved my hand slowly over the flame but felt nothing. Then I rested my fingers just above the flame. The only thing I felt was warmth. My fingers should have been sizzling, but they weren't.

"Whoa… that's crazy." I said in surprise.

"What is it?" Isaac asked.

"I can feel the warmth from the lighter, but it doesn't hurt at all." I explained.

"So normal heat doesn't affect you. That's interesting." Isaac said thoughtfully.

I turned my hand over to assess if my skin was burnt. To my surprise it looked perfectly normal. I rubbed my fingers together and still felt nothing. The warmth from the flame had left as soon as it stopped touching my fingers.

"Ben, will you fetch that black bag please?" Isaac put the lighter back in his pocket and turned back towards me. "Now Liz these next few tests are a little more intense. I am, however, fairly confident that you will be unharmed. They are things we need to know if we are ever to find a way to defeat our enemies. That is why we must conduct these tests. Originally… we were hoping to use the homeless drug addict from the industrial complex, but…"

His words hung in the air, as if he was going to say something else, but he didn't. He didn't need to either. I could guess at what he was going to say. *But somehow you got cursed instead, so now you get to be our guinea pig.* At least he had enough consideration not to finish the phrase.

"I understand Isaac. I'll do anything if it means helping Luke. Since there's no hope for me anyway, I at least want to try and help you guys out." I realized how depressing the statement sounded after it left my lips.

Ben had walked back in as I was speaking and handed a black duffle bag to Isaac. He glanced up at me, and then looked away quickly, but not before I noticed a small tear escape his eye and run down his cheek. Perhaps I had been wrong about his heartlessness.

This night had me getting more confused by the second. I had thought Isaac hated me, but he was treating me more like a person now than he had before I became a monster. Ben had gone from saving me from his brother and being friendly, to tricking me into my new cell and slamming the door on me. Now he was being compassionate and seemed to care about me again. I couldn't make sense of it all.

Isaac had set the bag down in front of him and pulled out a small black leather case. He opened the case on top of the bag and pulled out a needle. With the case open I could see what looked like several needles inside.

"As I said, I am almost certain this won't hurt you, but we must be sure. Can you give me your hand please?" He stretched his empty hand out to me as he spoke.

I had never liked needles, but they didn't scare me like they did Alex. Placing my hand in his, I left it limp so that he could easily manipulate it. He turned it facing palm up, and then slowly moved the needle towards my palm.

"Please tell me exactly what you feel." He said as he pushed the needle into the palm of my hand.

As the needle reached my hand I felt slight pressure, but no pain. I could see my skin pushing inwards ever so slightly, but the needle never broke through. He increased the pressure gradually, until the needle suddenly snapped. The tip of the needle made a faint sound as it struck the metal floor.

"As I suspected." Isaac murmured. "That needle was reinforced stainless steel. Did you feel anything?

"Just… light pressure when the needle was pushing against my skin." I replied.

He repeated the process with four more needles, but all of them had the same result. The only difference between the five was the amount of pressure applied before the needle snapped. One of them also bent slightly before breaking.

After the needles he pulled out a small crystal knife. I raised one eyebrow at him, hoping it was a joke. It wasn't. "Sorry, but it's impossible to get a diamond needle" Isaac explained.

"Make it quick." I said as I shook my head slowly and held out my hand.

He pressed the blade against my hand, slowly at first, and then harder. I felt more pressure than I had with the needles, but still no pain.

"I figured as much. It was worth a try anyhow." Isaac said softly before turning to Ben again. "We are going to need the cork barrel now."

Ben nodded and left the room. He reappeared a few seconds later carrying a large barrel. It looked like it could easily hold fifty gallons. Based on what Isaac had called it, I was guessing it was solid cork. Ben set the barrel down against the opposite wall from the door. *What in the world did he want a cork barrel for? I thought to myself.*

No sooner had I thought the question then Isaac pulled out a black handgun and racked the slide backwards. It looked like the Glock that my father carried, but easily could have been a different model. I had been shooting with my father a couple of times but hadn't paid much attention to the names of all the different types of guns. It was definitely a semi-automatic handgun. That much I could tell, because it didn't have the round cylinder part that revolvers do.

"This gun only shoots a twenty-two bullet, so even if it does affect you, it won't do any lasting damage." Isaac tried to sound reassuring, but the idea of being shot with any real handgun just wasn't appealing.

"Are you serious?" I asked incredulously. "Is that really necessary?"

"I have seen your kind shot before, and they appeared unaffected, but I wanted to try some different types of bullets to see if they have any effect." He explained.

I shook my head again slightly as I walked over to the barrel but couldn't find the right words to say. They were actually going to shoot me. I really hoped Isaac was right about this one. A needle poke in the hand wouldn't have been a big deal, even if he had been wrong. But a gunshot wound? I couldn't believe I was going along with this. Then again, did I really have a choice? Isaac had sounded like it was either I go along, or they hold me down. At least if I went along there was less chance of getting hurt. And besides… in spite of everything, I still wanted to help them.

I placed my hand on top of the barrel. Isaac walked over and stood next to me. He lifted the gun until the barrel was pointed at the fleshy part of my palm opposite the thumb. At least there wouldn't be any bone damage there if Isaac was wrong.

"Hold very still." Isaac said. A second later I heard a loud bang as the gun went off. It was piercingly noisy and echoed off the metal walls. I felt the pressure as something struck my hand, but there was no pain. A little bit of warmth, but no pain. There was also no sign of being struck at all as I examined my skin.

"That was loud." I said as I examined my unharmed hand.

"Indeed." Isaac added with a furrowed brow. He turned to me again. "I have three more bullets to try."

"Go ahead." I said calmly. Now that I knew there was no pain involved, being shot didn't bother me at all.

I was expecting Isaac to go back to the bag for another gun magazine, so when he suddenly fired another round at my hand it caught me off guard. The noise made me flinch in surprise. I noticed Ben take a step towards me with concern on his face.

"I'm fine. It just surprised me is all." I explained as they both looked at my hand in confusion. The hand was still fine, so I was sure they were just wondering about my flinch. "I didn't realize you already had the different bullets loaded into the gun. That's all."

"Oh... well did you feel anything different?" Isaac asked.

"No, just the pressure, and maybe a tiny bit of warmth. Still no pain though, so by all means, keep shooting." It sounded weird as the words left of my mouth. I had simply never imagined being a test subject for target practice with real bullets.

Isaac shot my hand two more times, and the result was virtually identical to the first two shots. I never felt any pain. Isaac seemed somewhat disappointed with the outcome. Hopefully it was only because he had been anticipating finding another weakness, and not because he wanted to see me suffer. I didn't feel like adding any physical pain to what I was already going through emotionally. Although a trade off would have been welcome.

Isaac put the gun back into the bag and began to close it.

"What you don't have any hand grenades or rocket launchers in there to test on me?" I asked sarcastically.

Isaac paused and looked at me. "I hadn't even thought of that. What a great idea." He said seriously.

"Isaac… I was kidding." I explained quickly.

"And so was I." He smiled back and gave me a small wink. "Thanks for your help, Liz, that is all for now. Why don't you try and get some rest."

Ben retrieved the barrel and walked out of the room, followed by Isaac. I glanced around the once again empty cell and thought to myself: *Yeah right, how am I going to sleep in this?* Moments later Ben reappeared in the doorway holding a rolled-up foam mattress and a pillow.

"Do you want a blanket too?" He asked as he set them on the ground inside the door.

"No… but thank you." I said politely.

"You're welcome…and…um… I'm sorry… for everything." His eyes were starting to water again and he quickly turned and walked out of the room, closing the door behind him. At least this time he didn't slam it shut.

I unrolled the mattress and laid down on it. With my head resting on the pillow, I was surprisingly comfortable. Unfortunately, I wasn't tired. With sleep came the possibility of at least a dream where I might be human again. My mind was still racing, and I couldn't seem to calm my own nerves enough to rest. It must have been well after midnight, but I couldn't sleep.

Predictably, I found my mind wandering back to Leuken. More than anything I just wanted to see him again. Not the current Luke, but the one from before. The one who had actually liked me. If only I could somehow find that Luke again. I knew it was only wishful thinking, but at least it gave me something to hold on to. My mind needed something to get me through this nightmare.

CHAPTER XIV

Luke sat at the dining room table, staring down at the ice cream sundae his mother had prepared for him. Chocolate ice cream smothered in chocolate syrup, was topped with almonds and peanut butter cups. For as long as he could remember it had always been his favorite dessert. He had left it untouched for the last ten minutes and could see that the ice cream was already melting. But he wasn't in the mood to eat.

He felt like his heart had been ripped out, shredded, and then glued together again before being shoved back into his chest. When his father had died, Luke had been too young to fully grasp the emotional pain he had gone through. He remembered crying a lot. Memories of his mother crying were even more prevalent from that dark period in his early life. Yet compared with what he now felt that grief seemed inconsequential.

Over the last couple months, he had fallen madly in love with Elizabeth Scott... but now she was gone. She had been killed, and her body infected by the vilest parasite. What was left of her physical body was now only a host for one of the tainted ones. One of the same creatures that had killed his father just fourteen years ago.

Luke could still remember the face of the tainted one responsible for his father's death. He had seen the creature in a dream just minutes before his father died, as well as in person from the back of their car as they were escaping that same night. Its long red beard and pale face atop its massive body wasn't something one could easily forget.

Luke still couldn't understand how the tainted one had taken over Liz's body. She had been miles away. There must have been dozens, if not hundreds of people between her and the creature when they had killed its last host. For it to jump that far and go directly into her body was inconceivable. As much as it pained him to think about it though, he knew it had happened.

He had seen the mark of the Verdorben on her neck and had felt her incredible strength when she pushed him. The darkness that emanated from her now was unmistakable.

He still couldn't decide if the demon inside her was simply using her memories in order to try and attack them later, or if perhaps it took some time for the demon to take full control of her body. He was inclined to believe the prior, but there was no real way of knowing. At this point it didn't really matter much. Either way she was dead the moment that demon entered her.

With that death sentence came an emotionally crushing blow to Luke. Elizabeth Scott was the girl of his dreams…literally. She was the one he had chosen for the telling. What his family and other members of the bloodline called it when someone from inside the bloodline divulged the truth about themselves to someone outside the bloodline. This was traditionally done when someone from the bloodline had found the one who they wanted to eventually marry and spend the rest of their lives with. For Luke, that someone had been Elizabeth Scott… but now she was gone.

"You still haven't touched your sundae." Luke was surprised when he heard his mother's voice from behind. He had been so lost in thought that he hadn't even heard her enter the room. "I even made your favorite."

"Yeah sorry. I don't have much of an appetite." He said somberly as he tried to fight back the tears he felt reforming in his eyes.

His mom was the one person from whom he knew it was impossible to hide his feelings. She walked around where he was sitting and took a seat across the table from him. He had gone back to staring at his bowl of melting ice cream but could feel her eyes on the top of his head.

"You know Luke… I think you might be wrong about Elizabeth being gone already." Luke glared up at her without thinking. "Before you get upset just hear me out, okay?" She finished.

"Go ahead." Luke tried to sound patient, but knew he wasn't fooling her.

"Well, I just came from the observation room, where I was watching Isaac conducting tests on her. Before he went into the room I saw her face, after she was done crying. The anguish in her eyes… reminded me of the same pain I now see in yours. That kind of heartbreak, from losing someone you care about more than anything, is tough to fake. I think Elizabeth is still herself, even if that demon is inside of her somewhere. And I think she's hurting just as bad as you are."

"And I think that demon is just trying to use her to get to us." Luke replied bitterly.

"I think you're wrong Leuken." Jazmine's voice sounded from behind him as she walked into the room. "That girl we have imprisoned down there is still Elizabeth Scott. I can feel the good in her. It's masked by the dark outer shell of the taint, but inside of that is the same sweet girl you fell in love with.

Honestly, I think we may have been wrong in our assumption that the demon controls the host. Perhaps over time it gains more influence, but Elizabeth is still very much in control of herself. Judging by the way she has been acting, I would say she's more heartbroken by how you treated her than by the fact that she's become Verdorben."

Luke could feel the anger boiling up in him again when she talked about how he had treated the creature. "Don't you try to make me feel sorry for how I treated that thing." He snapped. "We have lived our whole lives in hiding because of those monsters, and I even lost a father to their cruelty. So, I will not apologize for treating them like the despicable creatures that they are."

"Leuken relax, I wasn't passing judgment. All I am saying is that I think you should try and talk to her so that you can see for yourself. I think if you do, you'll realize that it's still her down there." Jazmine raised her voice slightly but was patiently trying to calm Luke down.

"Just because you want to fall for that creature's tricks doesn't mean I will. It took Liz from me already, and I won't stand by and let it weasel its way into a position where it can hurt us again." He realized he was standing with his fists clenched and decided it was probably best if he left the room. As angry as he was, he didn't want to take it out on the people he cared about. After all, his family was all he had left. He turned and quickly left the room.

"You aren't the only one who's lost loved ones to those monsters Leuken. That's no excuse to be irrational." He heard Jazmine call after him as he walked towards the stairs.

Luke almost turned around to shout back at her, but what she had said stung him. She was of course referring to the fact that both of her parents and her little brother had been killed by the Verdorben years ago. While Luke had been feeling sorry for himself over losing first his dad and now Elizabeth, Jazmine had lost everything. He felt a stab of guilt for speaking hastily.

As Luke reached his bedroom door at the top of the stairs, he thought about going back down to apologize to Jazmine but worried it may just turn into another argument about that creature. Instead, he went into his room, closed the door and laid down on his bed. He needed to clear his head, so he could think of how to keep that creature from manipulating the rest of his family. It was so obvious to him what it was trying to do, but for some reason they all seemed to believe that monster more than him.

It wasn't long before he eventually realized how exhausted he was. He hadn't paid any attention to the time but was sure it was well past midnight. *I better get up before I fall asleep*, he thought to himself. It was the last thought he had before his fatigue caught up with him, and he dozed off.

His dreams were of Liz, but not the nightmares one would expect. The first thing he saw was her face, just as it had appeared in the months of dreams before he met her. With the picture of her face came the same impression he'd received before that he needed to protect her.

Suddenly the scene changed, and she was standing in the middle of an open field. Green blades of grass spotted with pink flowers surrounded her. She wore a breathtaking smile as she looked at him and he couldn't help but smile back. Her long white dress flowed gently to the side with the mild breeze. Walking to her, everything felt perfect as he picked her up and spun her in his arms. When he set her down, she pulled her hair to one side and turned, exposing her neck. The tainted mark was there, like a black spot on a clean wedding dress, but for some reason he didn't feel repulsed by it.

Again, the impression came that he needed to protect her. He pulled back, so that he could see her eyes, and she smiled merrily up at him. Her face was as beautiful as it had ever been. The trust and happiness in her eyes made his heart melt. And then, for the third time, he got the feeling that he needed to protect her, only this time it was stronger than ever.

"Don't worry Luke." She said suddenly as she stared into his eyes. "I'm still me."

Luke sat up suddenly, jerked back into consciousness. Glancing around the room, nothing seemed to be out of place, but he had no idea how long he had been sleeping for. He looked at his watch and realized it was almost two o'clock in the morning. He could still feel the strong feeling that had repeated itself in his dream, though it was beginning to fade.

Staring at his wall for quite some time, he pondered the meaning of this latest dream. It didn't make sense why the light was telling him to keep Liz safe, when it was already too late for that. Despite all his efforts to shield her, he had failed. The Verdorben had already taken her, so why was the light sending this message?

Why was he being told to protect the enemy? Nothing came to him at first as he contemplated this question. And yet… he thought back on what his mother and Jazmine had said. That Liz was still herself. *Could it be true?* He mused. *Could the person who was cursed still control themselves?* The only evidence he had against this was the fact that every tainted one Isaac had encountered, no matter how newly changed they were, had tried to kill him.

Was it possible that perhaps the older tainted ones had influenced the others into wanting to kill people from the bloodline? Luke found himself thinking about things from a whole new perspective. Deep inside himself he felt a surge of excitement begin to emerge at the thought that Liz might still be herself. He fought it back though, not wanting to get excited until he knew for sure that she was still in there.

Never in his life had he completely ignored the feelings he received from the light, and he wasn't about to start now. Every time he had a foretelling dream or impression in the past, he had followed it. And every time something good had come from it.

Luke got out of bed and made his way downstairs. He could see his mother and Jazmine still sitting at the table in the kitchen but didn't bother stopping to talk to them. Instead, he headed straight down to the bunker. Once he got through the double doors, he went into the second room on the right. His family all called it the observation room because it was where they controlled all the cameras for both the interior and exterior of the house.

He opened the door and was surprised to find the room unoccupied. Three large monitors lined the left wall of the room, with a control panel underneath them. On the center monitor Luke could see Isaac and Ben standing in the containment room with Liz. Or at least with the tainted one who looked like Liz. Luke still wasn't completely sold on her being herself.

Isaac was standing on the side of the tainted one and was holding her wrist with his hand while looking at his watch. Ben was leaning casually against the wall by the door. Luke hoped that Ben didn't let his guard down too much. Although with Isaac in the room, he doubted the creature could escape. Luke could hear Isaac talking through the speaker to the left of the screen.

"There we are. Interesting…" his voice sounded more robotic through the audio recorder than it did in person. "It looks like your pulse is at about 10 beats per minute. At first, I thought I just couldn't feel it when I felt only one beat in the six second check. After checking for the full minute however, I am confident in that number. Do you feel at ease?"

"No… I'm actually a little nervous, why?" Liz's voice was unmistakable, even through the recorder.

"I just wondered because most people's pulses speed up when they get excited or anxious. That's all. It could be that yours stays constant regardless."

"Oh…" she replied, looking up thoughtfully.

"Now for my last test I want you to try and hold your breath. It may sound strange, but I want you to plug your nose tightly with your fingers as well." Isaac continued.

"Okay." She took one long breath in and pinched her nose with her right hand. Luke glanced at his watch so that he could keep track of her also. Nothing but silence came through the monitor for over a minute.

"Now I want you to put up a finger if you start to feel a desire or need to breathe. Other than that, please try to hold it for as long as you can." Isaac added, breaking the silence.

She nodded and it was silent again for a few more minutes. Luke checked his watch a couple more times. It wasn't until close to five minutes that she finally held one finger up. Ten more minutes passed before she added another finger. At eighteen minutes he noticed her head beginning to bob up and down slightly, as if she needed air. She put up a third finger at this point. Finally, she let out a small breath and sucked air in loudly.

"Twenty minutes and fourteen seconds!" Isaac exclaimed. "You know what this might mean Liz?" He asked her excitedly.

"What? That I can hold my breath for a really long time?" She still sounded out of breath with her reply.

"Well that too, but I was thinking about the fact that we may have found another weakness. Did you hold your breath for as long as you possibly could?" He was standing in front of her now about five feet away.

"I might have been able to go a little longer, but I was beyond miserable. When I put my first finger up it was to say I was starting to want air. When I put two fingers up it was because it was becoming more and more uncomfortable, and I really wanted to breathe. The third finger was to say I don't know how much longer I can last. Eventually I couldn't take it anymore, so I breathed." She explained.

"Were you starting to feel lightheaded at all, or like you were going to pass out?" Isaac asked.

"Lightheaded yes, but I think I could have gone another minute or so before passing out."

"Wonderful. Well thanks again for being cooperative. Do you need anything, like… maybe something to eat?"

"No thanks. I don't have much of an appetite." She responded. "Although I do have a question?"

"Go ahead."

"Is there any way to remove the curse without killing me?" She asked slowly.

Isaac paused for a long moment before answering. Luke was beginning to have his doubts about her being manipulative. Why would a tainted one ask something like that? That question definitely came from Liz. Maybe she really was there. The surge of excitement in his chest came back, and this time he was barely able to fight it back. Now he could understand what his mother and Jazmine had been talking about. The girl they were holding absolutely seemed to be Elizabeth Scott.

"I doubt it… but to be perfectly honest we really don't know." Isaac finally answered.

"Okay… well thanks anyway. I was just being hopeful I guess." The tone of her voice sounded anything but hopeful.

Isaac nodded in understanding and followed Ben out of the room. Luke heard the door close and a couple seconds later the observation room door opened. Isaac seemed surprised when he saw Luke sitting in front of the monitor.

"Hey Luke, I didn't expect to see you down here. How are you feeling?" He spoke cautiously.

"Honestly Isaac… confused." Luke took in a deep breath and let it out slowly. Isaac just looked at him inquisitively, so he continued. "Up until a few minutes ago I was almost certain that the tainted one had completely taken over her body, and that she was pretending to be Liz so that she could attack us with our guard down later. But now… I'm not so sure."

"Well… exactly what was it that made you question your original theory?"

"I had another dream. Just like the ones I told you about from before I met her." Isaac raised an eyebrow as Luke talked. "Except this one was different. I had the feeling that I needed to protect her come to me several times. It was even stronger than I had ever felt it before, which doesn't make any sense."

"Why doesn't it make sense?" Isaac asked.

"Because I already failed at protecting her. The taint has taken over her body. That's why it was confusing. So, I thought about it more, and the only thing I could come up with for why I need to protect her is that maybe she really is still Liz. Maybe the demon doesn't control the host.

"Now that I have seen the way she is acting, I am starting to lean more towards that train of thought. Granted I only watched you guys for the last half hour or so, but she still seems to be completely herself, and completely in control."

"I feel the same way. It's quite possible that I was wrong in my assumptions. Every tainted one I have ever fought has been hunting us down, even the newly made ones. But I have never had the opportunity to interact with one right after they were turned. Perhaps there is something the other tainted ones do to the new ones to make them more evil. Something that makes them want to hunt us down and kill us. Maybe the transformation isn't complete until another Verdorben finishes it." Isaac stared at the wall as if his mind was somewhere else.

Isaac's last sentence still rang in Luke's mind as he considered what Isaac said. *Maybe the transformation isn't complete until another Verdorben finishes it.* While Luke was repeating this in his mind, he suddenly had another impression come to him. It was the same feeling as in the dream, only fainter now. The impression that he needed to protect Liz. *Obviously, the light is trying to tell me something* he mused. *But what am I missing?*

"That's it." Luke blurted out excitedly. "Liz never finished transforming."

"You think so?" Isaac asked.

"It has to be. Why else would she still be acting like herself and offering to help us. If that demon had any control over her it wouldn't sit by while we run tests on her. It would fight us until we killed Liz and jump into another body where it could run away.

"I think what you said is right, they must not become evil until another Verdorben influences them somehow. Which means that Liz isn't completely gone yet." Luke turned to look at Liz through the monitor as he finished.

He could feel the excitement flooding through his body but didn't bother trying to fight it. So, the girl he fell in love with was alive after all. Even if Liz's body had been changed, she was still mostly human. Or at least Luke was fairly certain of it. He would still be cautious around her, in case his theory was wrong, but he had a good feeling about it now.

"I am inclined to agree with you." Isaac began.

"I need to talk to her to be certain." Luke interrupted. He turned the knob that controlled the volume on the audio transmitter all the way down as he stood up.

"Good idea." Isaac replied. "I'll go with you."

Luke paused in the doorway as he was walking from the room. He wasn't sure if Liz would open up to him like he wanted her to if Isaac was in the room with him. If he was going to hold on to hope again, he wanted to be absolutely certain.

"Okay Isaac, but would you mind waiting outside?" Luke asked. Isaac raised an eyebrow at him again. "I just think it will be easier to read her if she thinks we are alone. You can wait outside the open door, and Ben can watch on the monitor." He explained.

"That's fine but be careful Luke. We don't know for sure exactly who or what we may be dealing with." Isaac added.

Luke walked past Ben, who was standing in the doorway, without a word. Isaac began explaining the plan to Ben, as Luke stood staring at the door to the containment room. He was trying to think of what to say to Liz, to see if she was in actuality still herself.

Isaac emerged from the observation room and nodded at Luke. The keypad chirped with each number as Luke entered the code for the containment door. He heard the locks click and twisted the door handle to unlock the large internal bolts. Pulling open the door, he spotted Liz sitting in the corner with her arms around her legs. She looked up as he stepped into the room but seemed surprised to see him.

Her surprised expression quickly turned to one of embarrassment as she looked down at her knees. Her dark hair and beautiful face were breathtaking, even though she still looked the same as she always had. No matter how many times he saw her he could never grow accustomed to her stunning perfection. He had noticed before she looked down that there were dark spots underneath her eyes. They were probably from crying. *Probably from me*, he thought.

With that thought came the realization of just how terrible he had treated her. Not only had he been short with her and treated her like an animal, but he had also tried to kill her. Of course, it wasn't Elizabeth he had wanted to kill, but the creature he thought was already responsible for her death. Unfortunately, she probably didn't know that.

Liz glanced up at him briefly, only this time Luke noticed that her eyes were watering. She had a fresh tear rolling down one of her cheeks. Luke relaxed his mind to try and concentrate on her emotions, but he couldn't read any emotions from her. All he felt from her was a strange darkness, and even that was difficult to read. And yet... as he examined the dark and almost invisible aura that now contained her, he felt something else. Deep inside the slippery darkness, he could still feel light emanating. It was masked by the shadowy exterior, but he recognized the same goodness in her that he had felt from the first time he saw her in class.

In spite of the guilt he felt for how he had treated her, excitement overcame him. He couldn't help but smile. Without her even saying a word, he was convinced that Elizabeth Scott was still alive. Now he just needed to keep her that way. And hope she would forgive him for being an absolute jerk.

***

I wanted to look up at him but was too ashamed and heartbroken. I didn't know why Luke had come to visit me, especially alone. Hopefully it wasn't to finish what he had tried to do unsuccessfully earlier. Although if he still wanted me dead, then perhaps it would be for the best anyway. At least death might take away the pain that was consuming me.

It had been close to a minute since the cell door had opened, yet Luke still hadn't said a word to me. He was just standing there. Eventually I worked up the nerve to look at him again and saw that he was smiling now. The smile didn't seem directed at me, so much as at whatever was on his mind. *Oh great! Now I've turned him crazy*, I thought.

Seeing him so close and knowing that I would never be able to hold him again was painful. As I looked back down at my feet, I felt a tear running down my cheek, but didn't bother wiping it. If I did it would only draw Luke's attention, and I was embarrassed enough as it was. Embarrassed by what I had become and saddened that I didn't know of anything I had done wrong to deserve such a curse.

The silence was awkwardly depressing. I could still feel his eyes on me, but he hadn't said a word. Likely he was studying me to see how I would behave, but I didn't understand why he still hadn't spoken. Then he broke the silence.

"It really is you still… isn't it?" He said softly. I looked up in surprise.

His eyes were watering, but he must not have been sad because his smile stretched from ear to ear. I was completely taken aback by his comment. When he first walked in the room, I thought he was going to try and kill me. Now I wasn't sure if he was playing some kind of trick on me or not. My heart leapt inside me at the mere possibility that he was sincere.

"Yes…" was all I managed in response. There was so much that I wanted to say, but I wanted to wait to make sure he wasn't testing me.

"You know I thought that…that you were gone." He began slowly as tears crept from his eyes. "I thought that you were dead and that the tainted one was using you… if I had known you were still in there, I never would have…I never would have treated you like I did. Please understand how truly sorry I am." He was stepping slowly closer to me as he spoke.

"I'll understand if you don't want to be with me anymore after how I treated you…" He continued, "But I want you to know how terrible I feel about being so rude to you. I thought… I thought the whole time that you were dead, so I was treating you like the monster that killed my girlfriend… which I now know you are not. I'm so sorry. I will try to make it up to you if you'll let me."

His tears had stopped, and he was now standing directly over me. His eyes still glistened slightly from the moisture in them, amplifying his blue pupils. He had one hand outstretched to me, and it looked like he was offering to help me up. I hadn't stopped looking at him since he started talking. Actually, I hadn't moved an inch since he began, other than bending my neck to watch his face as he got closer.

My mind was in shock as I thought about the implications of what he was saying. *Leuken Bennett actually believes me!* I could see no underlying trickery in his eyes, and Luke had never been the deceptive type anyway. Which meant that he must be sincere. I hesitated on taking his hand. Part of me expected that I would wake up at any second, still lying on the cold metal floor.

Finally…I grabbed his hand cautiously, and he easily lifted me to my feet. Not knowing the right words to say, and too excited to contain my emotion, I threw my arms around him. He seemed surprised at first, but quickly put his arms around me and squeezed. I held him close, never wanting to let go.

"Liz…not so tight." He said with labored breath. I realized I was squeezing him too hard and loosened my hold.

"Sorry about that. I'm still getting used to this." I replied.

"That's okay."

"Oh Luke, I am so sorry about being changed. I didn't want it to happen, but I couldn't do anything to stop it. It just came out of nowhere… and it happened so fast."

"No Liz, don't be sorry. You didn't do anything wrong. We're still trying to figure out why the taint jumped to you, because it doesn't make sense to us, but it's not your fault. I am the one who is sorry for dragging you into this. If it wasn't for me, you would still be a normal, happy, beautiful teenage girl with her whole life ahead of her." He said somberly.

"Actually, if it wasn't for you, I would still be a depressed teenage girl who couldn't get over her mother's death. Besides, I still feel normal. I'm definitely happy as long as I have you, and I don't think my looks have changed too much. Although I have to admit I still think you're delusional for thinking I'm beautiful… but I'm glad that you do."

My head was against his chest, and I could hear his heart beating. The sound was surprisingly loud, but comforting nonetheless. We held each other for a while in silence. His natural scent filled my nose as I breathed him in. Finally, I pulled away slightly, so I could look up at him.

"So, what now?" I asked, smiling.

He didn't answer me, but instead leaned down and kissed me. All of the pain and misery I had felt for the last few hours seemed to wash away with that kiss. He put one hand on my face and the other on the small of my back as he pulled me closer to him. I couldn't remember ever feeling so ecstatic and relieved in my entire life.

When he finally pulled away, I noticed that he was blushing. I had no idea why, because we were certainly alone. The only other time he had blushed like that had been when we had kissed in front of Alex for the first time.

"Are you blushing Leuken Bennett?" I teased putting a finger to his cheek.

"Yeah sorry, I just remembered we're being watched." He replied.

"What are you talking about?" Giving him a confused look, I turned my head to scan the room, but didn't see anyone.

"The cameras." He said pointing to the light on the ceiling.

For the first time I actually examined the light and noticed that there was a small black hole on one side of it. My eyes seemed extra sensitive to light since the transformation, so I hadn't looked closely at it before.

"Have you been watching me all this time?" I asked in surprise.

"I haven't… but Isaac has been since they put you in here. Ben has been with him most of the time too."

"Why weren't you?" I thought out loud.

"Honestly… seeing you was just too painful until a few minutes ago. I thought that you were dead and didn't want to look at the monster that had possessed your body."

"So, what changed your mind?"

"Well… a number of things. I was firmly convinced that you were already dead and wallowing in my own pity. My mom and Jazmine thought differently. They watched you on the camera for a little bit and were insistent that you were still yourself.

"I didn't believe them at first, because I was too depressed and angry to even think straight. So, I went up to my room to be alone, and fell asleep. I had a dream, and you were in it. In this dream, I had the feeling that I needed to protect you, and it kept repeating itself. When I woke up, I was utterly confused. So, I figured I would come down and look at you, to see if perhaps I had been wrong all along. Once I saw you interacting with Isaac, I had a feeling that I had been wrong about you. But it wasn't until I came in here and felt the goodness still in you that I knew for certain." He smiled as he finished.

"So that's why you were quiet when you first walked in. And why you were smiling too." I laughed softly as I finished.

"What?" He asked.

"Oh nothing… it's just funny. When you first walked in, I actually thought you were here to kill me. Especially after you smiled… I thought maybe you had snapped and were smiling because you were about to get your revenge."

"Really?" He looked at me in disbelief.

"Yeah well… you did try to kill me a few hours ago… remember?" I retorted, and he winced.

"Ouch…I guess I did deserve that." He said thoughtfully. "Luckily Ben was there to keep me from making the worst mistake of my life. I owe him big for that."

“Yeah, me too.”

He hugged me again, and I thought more about my situation. Now that I knew Luke believed me, I felt like all of my problems were solved, but I knew that was only wishful thinking. I was now a tainted one, and as far as anyone else knew, the only way to cure that was to kill me. Even though I was still in control of myself for the time being, there’s no telling how long that would last.

“You know, you never answered my question.” Luke eyed me quizzically, so I explained. “Don’t get me wrong I enjoyed the kiss. It’s just I was wondering what’s going to happen to me now. Do I have to stay in this cell until we know it’s safe? Does everyone else know that I’m still me? Isaac seemed somewhat skeptical when I saw him last.”

“You know,” he replied, “Those are good questions. I just wish I had the answers.”

CHAPTER XV

I sat alone in the cold cell, impatiently waiting for Luke's return. He had left an hour before to persuade the others that I was harmless and that they should let me go. I was beginning to think he must have been unable to convince them.

The door finally beeped, and Luke swung it open. Stepping into the room, his expression was anything but optimistic. I felt my chances for freedom dwindle.

"So… how'd it go?" I was fairly certain his answer would be disappointing.

"Well… it could have been worse, but it's not good." He mostly looked down at his feet as he spoke; only glancing up occasionally.

"What do you mean?"

"They agreed to let you out of here, but the terms are terrible." He must have seen my confusion because he continued before I had a chance to speak. "They want a guarantee that you won't just run away right when you get out. I'll let Isaac explain the details, but please understand that I didn't want this."

He stepped up to me and put his arms around me. It felt good to rest my face against his chest, but his words were disheartening. What could he possibly be talking about? Why hadn't he looked me in the eye since coming back in here? I was about to ask when another voice interrupted.

"We will let you out of here on one condition." Isaac announced as he joined Luke and I in the cell.

"Okay… what is it?" I asked hesitantly.

"Please understand that what we require is not because of any lack of trust in you. It is the taint you have been cursed with that we do not understand or trust. If we are to let you roam freely, we need something in place to keep tabs on you in case the Verdorben side of you takes control. Because of that possibility, we need to place a tracker on you." Isaac reached into his right pocket as he finished speaking.

He pulled out a small round silver object that couldn't have been more than a centimeter in diameter. As he twisted it in his hand, I noticed that it was flat on both sides and didn't look any thicker than a penny. I turned to look at Luke in confusion.

"Okay…What's so bad about that? I could put that thing anywhere." I asked Luke.

"No Liz, what Isaac meant to say is that he wants to put the tracker in you, not on you." He glared at Isaac as he spoke.

"Just inside the skin, it doesn't have to be deep in your tissue or anything. I was thinking if we put it in the side of your foot it shouldn't interfere with normal functioning. Unless of course you had a preference for where we insert it?" Isaac explained.

"So, the only way you will let me out of here is if I put that little thing inside me somewhere. Can't I just tape it on or something? Why does it have to go inside me?" The device was small enough that I didn't imagine it would be too painful, but the idea of being cut open was never appealing.

"Because we need to be absolutely certain that we can find you if the creature inside takes control. A tracker is too easy to throw out, but if it's implanted it would be difficult even for you to remove. Plus, the tracker also has a heat sensor in it so we would know immediately if it was ever removed."

It sounded like it was the only way to get out of this metal cage, so I didn't feel like arguing anymore. I leaned down and started untying my left shoe.

"I guess we had better get started then. Does it matter which foot?" I asked before pulling my shoe off.

"No, whichever you prefer is fine." Isaac replied.

I took my sock off as well, hoping my foot didn't smell. After all, I had been wearing the same shoes for nearly twenty-four hours. Once the sock was off, I checked, but didn't smell anything. *Do I even sweat anymore?* I thought to myself. Both my sock and foot felt dry. Perhaps I was simply less sensitive to heat and cold.

Ben walked into the room and stood next to Isaac. He was holding one of the silver-handled terralium daggers. The metal blade was glowing with heat as he handed it to Isaac. Then he turned to look sheepishly at me.

"Sorry about this Liz." Ben almost mumbled his voice was so soft.

"Okay Elizabeth. This is going to be extremely painful so why don't you lie down." Isaac said to me before turning to Ben and Luke. "Ben, I want you to hold her leg so she doesn't move it too much. Luke, you need to hold her hands and keep her upper body on the floor. Can you manage that?"

"I think so. But no guarantees, she's pretty strong now." Luke smiled and winked at me as he answered.

I got down on the floor and stretched my left leg out straight, keeping my right leg bent at the knee. With how hot that dagger looked, I didn't want my other foot anywhere close.

"Now I know this is going to cause significant pain, but you need to hold absolutely still while I cut open the foot. Otherwise, you might get cut and burned a lot more than is necessary. Are we clear?" He looked me in the eye as he spoke.

"Crystal." I replied. "Don't worry I won't move. Just please try to make it quick." I focused my attention back on Luke, who was now squatting down next to my head. He wore a nervous grin, so I smiled back at him. "You know Luke that expression is hardly re-assuring."

"Sorry Liz." Luke glanced away quickly, and then looked back at me with a calmer, more serious face. "Is that better?"

"Actually, I liked the fake smile better." I replied, and he chuckled.

He grabbed my two hands in his and pulled them to his lips. At the same time Ben leaned down by my leg and grabbed it with one hand below my knee and the other above it. I also felt Isaac grab my foot and started to prepare for the pain. Or at least started to think about how bad it was probably going to hurt.

"Okay Isaac" I began "as soon as you're ready you can… Aaaaagh!" I screamed as I suddenly felt a flash of heat on one side of my foot and an intense pain in the middle of that same side.

My body flinched involuntarily, and I felt Ben and Luke's grip on me tighten. The heat lasted only a split second, but the stabbing pain remained. It felt like someone had sliced my foot open to the bone with a red-hot knife. Ironically, that's exactly what happened. I just hadn't been prepared for the excruciating pain.

"Almost done." Isaac mumbled from my feet and then I felt another intense pain. This time it felt like someone was trying to rip open the existing cut with a piece of cold metal. "There we are." Isaac let go of my foot and the pain began to subside a little.

I sat up to see how big of a hole he had cut and was instantly disappointed. On the outside part of my left foot, about midway between the heel and pinky toe was the cut. Having expected to see a deep laceration stretching half the length of my foot, it was a letdown when I noticed that the cut was at most half an inch in length. It also looked to be barely skin deep, although the skin was reddened and looked burned for half an inch around the cut as well.

"That's it?" I thought aloud. "I thought you sliced my foot halfway open with how bad it hurt. But that's barely even a cut."

"I tried to keep the incision small. All we needed was a big enough hole to put the tracker in." Isaac replied calmly as he began wrapping gauze around the middle of my foot. He wrapped medical tape outside the gauze to hold it in place, and then stood up. "Okay young lady, you're all set." He turned to Luke. "You see? I told you she'd be fine with it. You're blinded by your emotions boy."

Luke shrugged and blushed slightly as he turned back to me. "How are you feeling Liz?" He asked with obvious concern.

"Good. It was painful while he did it, but already it's starting to feel much better." Much was probably too strong of a word. I moved the foot from side to side and felt a sharp pain where the cut was. Even still, the twinge was nothing compared to the pain I'd felt when the blade had cut into me.

"I'm sorry you had to go through that." Luke began.

"Why?" I cut him off. "You shouldn't be. I understand completely why it was necessary. If this thing inside me did take control I want you guys to be able to find me so you can kill me fast. After how easily I killed those two thugs earlier, I wouldn't want anything with these abilities roaming around victimizing others."

"I know you're right it's just... I hate to see you in pain." He leaned over and kissed me briefly.

"Oh... well in that case... Oww... it hurts so bad." I said teasingly, hoping for another kiss. It worked.

"Okay you two." Ben interrupted our second kiss. "There are much better places to do that than in a metal cell in front of your little brother." He turned and exited the room.

"That's true." Luke replied as he stepped back, still holding one of my hands. "Shall we?" He gestured towards the door, and we walked out after Ben.

We stopped in front of the room, and I surveyed the basement again. It was exactly as I remembered; only now I knew what was behind door number one. I wondered if the other door was another cell. The door to this second room had a normal silver handle.

"So, is that other door a cell too?" I inquired, pointing to the second door.

"That one? No, it's the observation room. That is where we watched you from. Through the camera on the ceiling and the one in the door." Luke explained.

"You mean there was one in the door too? And here I was thinking my vision had improved. Maybe I just need to pay more attention to detail."

"Well, the one in the door is even more concealed than the one attached to the light. It's tucked back in the slot that opens to allow us to talk through the door. We can also put food through that slot, but you never ended up wanting or needing food anyway. Which reminds me, you still haven't eaten anything all night, are you hungry? I could make you something." Luke's thoughtfulness was touching.

"No thanks. I really just don't have much of an appetite." I replied.

It was nice to have my Leuken back. This night had been nothing but a rollercoaster so far. It went from just another normal dinner with the family, to absolute craziness in a matter of hours. And now my life would never be the same. At least for the time being I had Luke, until I either went crazy or died. Until then I would savor every moment I was given with him. Even being possessed by an evil, tainted demon didn't seem so bad with him by my side.

"Why don't we head upstairs?" Luke suggested, as he gently pulled me towards the stairway.

"Sounds good to me." I replied. "As much as I've enjoyed my stay down here…" I smiled at Luke, and he just looked down… ashamed. "I'm only kidding." I reassured.

Ben was already headed for the stairs, so we walked after him. The sleek car on the platform looked quite sporty, but I couldn't tell what kind it was. Its purpose for being down here struck me as odd.

"What's with the car on the pedestal?" I asked curiously just before we passed through the door.

"You mean the Shelby Series One?" Ben said excitedly, as he turned to look at me. "It's only the awesomest car every made."

"What's so awesome about it?"

"Other than the fact that it's supercharged, goes zero to sixty in three point two seconds, and was designed from tire to roof from scratch by Mr. Shelby himself? Nothing… but you can't deny it looks sick." His infatuation with the vehicle showed even more through his reverential tone than by his description of it.

"Wow… sounds like a nice car. How fast can it go?"

"They say one seventy… but Isaac got it up to one eighty four once on a gradual downhill. The handling on it is sick too." Ben explained.

After closing both doors behind us, we made our way up the stairs.

In the living room Jazmine, Sara and Isaac were waiting for us. Well… Jazmine was actually out cold, with her head tilted sideways on one of the couch cushions as she slept. Sara and Isaac were sitting on the longer part of the sectional. Luke's mom stood up when she saw me.

Crossing the room quickly, she threw her arms around me. "I am so sorry you got dragged into all this." She began. "Luckily you were able to help Luke see reason. He can be a little pig headed at times."

"Come on mom… seriously?" Luke mumbled.

"Well, I'm just saying… you have to admit you were being stubborn."

Luke shook his head slowly. "Well in my defense I did think the girl of my dreams had been killed by the tainted ones. Can't I get a little slack?"

"I forgive you Luke." I said as I turned and put my hand affectionately on his left cheek.

"And that's all that matters to me." He smiled back at me.

"Wow. I think you two are even worse than before. Haven't you ever heard the expression 'get a room'?" Ben said feigning disgust as he sat down next to his sleeping sister.

"Well, there won't be any room getting in this house. Not unless we have married guests anyway." Sara scolded. "I know I raised you boys more proper than that."

"Like I said mom, it's just an expression." Ben added defensively.

"So… Jazmine sure looks tired." I turned to Luke, hoping to end the awkward topic.

"Yeah." He yawned, obviously grateful for the subject change. "I think it's been a long night for all of us."

Luke offered to let me rest in his room, and then his mom offered Jazmine's bed. I declined both offers, still feeling surprisingly alert. The sun was already beginning to shine on the shutters of the east windows anyway, so I didn't see a point.

Ben and Isaac both mentioned being hungry, so Sara and Ben went into the kitchen to make something. Luke and I sat down on the end of the couch, with Luke next to Isaac. Isaac was staring thoughtfully at the window shutters and seemed oblivious to the rest of us.

"So, I don't know if part of it is because of the transformation or not, but these couches feel extra soft this morning." I said to Luke as we got situated.

"Or maybe it's because you spent the last few hours in a hard metal cell?" Luke replied.

"Yeah, you're probably right. Well, it feels good to be comfortable again. Although I have to admit the best part is being able to hold you." He squeezed my shoulder gently with the arm he had around me. Our eyes met, and we couldn't stop smiling.

After a minute Isaac suddenly turned towards us. "Elizabeth, there is one more thing I forgot to mention."

"What's that?" I asked.

"I'm not sure if Luke has mentioned it or not, but we have never encountered any of the Verdorben during the daytime. We really don't know why that is, but you might be able to help us. If you don't mind anyway?"

"Sure... so... are you saying that the sun may affect me now somehow?"

"Honestly, we don't know. There is a theory that the sunlight hurts you, but we can't be certain if it's true."

"You mean like a vampire or something? That would suck. I love the sun."

"It's just a theory." Luke interjected. "For all we know you could be completely unaffected by the sun."

The thought of never being in the sun again was disheartening. I glanced over at the windows where the bright sunlight was being held back by white plantation shutters. Then an idea came to me. I stood up and quickly walked over to the window. Luke jumped up after me and grabbed me from behind as I was reaching for the shutters.

"What are you doing Liz?" His voice was elevated.

"I'm seeing if the sun affects me." I replied calmly.

"But it might hurt you." Luke argued still holding my shoulders.

"And there's only one way to find out." I turned to look at him defensively. His jaw muscles were tight and his expression stubborn. "Okay how about this Luke? I'll put my pinky finger in the light and stand over here. I doubt the sun on my pinky will kill me." I sidestepped next to the window and held out my right pinky finger.

Luke just stared at me for a long moment, obviously worried about what I was trying to do. Finally, Isaac stepped around him and pulled the shutters open.

"Don't let love blind you Luke." He said under his breath as he opened them.

I saw the sun light up my exposed pinky but didn't feel anything. After a few seconds I put my whole arm in front of the light. Still nothing happened.

"See Luke, nothing happened." I said relieved.

Luke just stood there, but his face was now relaxed. Isaac was looking at my hand, still seeming deep in thought.

"Perhaps…" Isaac began. "Perhaps the direct sunlight has a different effect?" He was looking at me, so I shrugged.

"Let's go and see." I replied as I walked towards the back door. Luke and Isaac followed me.

"Just make sure you're careful." Luke said as he walked in front of me to open the sliding door.

I stepped out into the cool morning air. The backyard was still in the shadow of the house, so we walked to the east side. When I reached the edge of the houses shadow, I cautiously poked one finger into the direct sunlight. Just in case the sun did hurt me, I wasn't about to jump right into it and get roasted or anything. This time I could actually feel the warmth as the sun hit my finger, but it didn't hurt at all.

"Well… I didn't catch on fire." I said as I put my whole hand into the sun.

Still feeling no pain, I stepped out into the sunlight and instantly regretted it. The light from the sun was almost blinding, and I closed my eyes, putting my hands over them as I hunched down involuntarily. The light had been so bright it made my eyes burn and my headache. I could still see the yellow spot from the sun in my vision.

Luke picked me up and jumped back into the shade. "Are you okay Liz?" He asked with concern.

"Yeah, I'm fine." I replied, opening my eyes again. "The sun is just really bright. Painfully bright to be honest."

"Are you sure? Do you hurt anywhere? Can you see me okay?" Luke set me down gently, before leaning in close to me and waving his hand next to his face.

"Yes, I can see you perfectly. And no, I'm not hurt. I think my eyes are just ultra sensitive to the sun, that's all."

"Okay good. You had me worried when you grabbed your eyes like that." Luke sounded relieved again.

"Do you feel any different?" Isaac asked while eyeing me.

"What do you mean?" I asked, confused.

"I mean ability wise. Do you feel tired, weaker… anything at all?"

"I don't think so." I flexed my hands and looked down at myself, but nothing seemed different.

There was a small stack of two by fours sitting on the ground against the back of the house. I reached down and picked one up. It couldn't have been more than a foot and a half long and looked perfect for testing if my strength had been affected.

"Do you care if I break this?" I asked Isaac. He shook his head.

"Be my guest. Those are just remnants anyway." He explained.

Grabbing either end of the piece of wood, I tried to bend it and was surprised when it easily snapped in half. Small chips of wood were thrown into the air from the break. I hadn't even been trying hard when it broke. No wonder I had killed those two guys last night. If I could snap a two by four without even trying, and I had kicked and punched them as hard as I could, it no longer surprised me that the force had been lethal. It made me wonder what else I was capable of with my newfound strength.

"Well… I don't think the sun weakens me at all. Although I can understand why no one would want to move around in the daylight with the sun being so bright. My light sensitivity is definitely heightened."

"It was worth testing anyhow." Isaac sounded disappointed again.

He had probably been hoping that the sun would have some kind of negative effect on me. Not that he wanted me to suffer, but he seemed dead set on finding another weakness for the tainted ones. I was just relieved that I could still be in the sun, but I would definitely be wearing sunglasses outside from now on.

We were headed back inside, when Isaac told me and Luke that he wanted to test the tracker. We agreed. Luke drove his hummer up the street and back while I sat in the passenger's seat. When we returned, Isaac said the tracker was working perfectly. By this point

Ben and his mother must have finished breakfast, because the pleasant aroma of hot food greeted us when we came back into the house.

"Breakfast is ready." Sara confirmed as Luke and I entered the kitchen. "Sorry it's not much. We just whipped it up real quick like." She looked at me apologetically, but I couldn't tell why.

Spread in front of us on the kitchen counter was quite the assortment of hot foods, all of which smelled delicious. And I wasn't even hungry. There was bacon, sausage links, scrambled eggs with cheese and peppers mixed in, fresh pancakes, biscuits and country gravy.

"Are you kidding me? This looks incredible." I told Sara before turning to Luke. "I'm not even hungry, and I think I'm gonna have to help myself."

"Me too." Luke's stomach growled loudly as he spoke.

The smell of cooking food must have aroused Jazmine because she soon joined us at the table. She congratulated me on my still being myself and apologized for my transformation. I couldn't understand why they all felt so guilty for what had happened to me. None of it was in any way their fault. Or at least I didn't think so.

After we finished eating Luke and I offered to clean up. Sara insisted on helping as well, so it didn't take us long. I was surprised that there weren't any leftovers. There had easily been enough food to feed over a dozen people, and I hadn't eaten much. The Bennett's sure knew how to put food down. It must have been that the effects of the bloodline increased their appetite. I for one had felt satisfied after just a few bites.

After cleaning up the kitchen, I looked at my phone and realized that it was almost ten o'clock. The last thing I wanted was my father calling Nikki to check up on me, so I decided to head home. Luke offered to come with me, but he had dark circles under his eyes and looked like he was barely able to keep them open. I had insisted that he stay home and rest.

Before leaving I got the change of clothes I had brought from my Tahoe and switched outfits. I could only imagine how Alex or my father would react if I came home covered in blood. Even being creative it might have been difficult to come up with something my dad would believe. Alex was easy because of his gullibility, but my dad was another story.

Luke did walk me to my car, after I said goodbye to the rest of the family. It was nice to be alone for the first time all morning in the garage. We made use of the solitude. By the time we finally stopped kissing it was nearly eleven, so I reluctantly drove home.

When I came through the front door Alex was waiting for me. He was still in his pajamas and wore a wide grin when he saw me.

"Izzie!" he screamed as he ran up and threw his arms around me. I picked him up and spun him around, being careful not to squeeze him.

"Hey Alex. I sure missed ya. Did you have fun with dad?" I asked as I gently set him back on the ground.

"Yeah… we ate Ice Cream and watched movies all night." He answered excitedly flashing his chubby little dimples.

After thinking I would never see him again just a few hours before, it felt incredibly good to see Alex. I couldn't remember the last time I had been away from him for the night. It must have been before mom died. Now I was more excited about seeing Alex than I could ever remember. Maybe it had something to do with my near-death experience.

The sound of the television was blaring from the other room. I couldn't tell if my father had the volume turned up too high, or if I simply wasn't used to my heightened sense of hearing. Either way I could hear the announcers saying something about a first down. He must have been watching the football game.

"What's wrong Izzie?" Alex asked suddenly as he walked closer to me.

"What do you mean?" I squatted down to his level.

"You got tears. Why are you crying?" His voice sounded concerned.

I suddenly realized that there were tears running down my cheeks. Why I had tears was confusing because I actually felt incredibly happy. Wiping them away I looked Alex in the eye.

"Sorry Alex. I was just so happy to see you again. I really missed you last night."

"Why are you crying if you're happy? Tears are for sad people silly." Alex said matter of fact like.

"Well, these are happy tears. Cause I missed you so much." I explained smiling. "Now give me another hug." I gently squeezed him close to me again.

"I'm glad you're home Izzie." He said quietly in my ear.

"Me too."

"Cause now you can make me lunch." He pulled away and beamed at me.

"Oh… so that's why you missed me? Because of food?" I teased.

"Oh yes Izzie. I am so hungry." He rubbed his right hand over his stomach in circles as he spoke.

"Why, didn't you have any breakfast?"

"Well dad made eggs, but he cooked them too long. They did not taste like your eggs. And he put the cheese on too late, so it was cold. And he burnt the toast." His face was distraught as he explained his morning dilemma.

"Oh no that must have been terrible." I feigned sympathy just to humor him.

"It was Izzie. It was terrible." He added.

I couldn't help but smile. Considering the night I had just experienced, the juxtaposition was quite humorous. What I would have given to be in his shoes. Where the worst thing that happened all week was an overcooked meal. It's funny how easy it was to take simple things in life for granted… until you were faced with losing them.

After saying hi to my father, who didn't bother taking his eyes off the television as he quickly waved back at me, I went into the kitchen. Alex requested a grilled ham and cheese sandwich, so I obliged him. I made a couple for my father as well, since I knew they were also one of his favorite foods. Why I bothered throwing some fresh vegetables on the plate next to his sandwiches I didn't know, because I knew he wouldn't touch them.

At least Alex would eat all of his food. That was another thing I loved about him. He was the ultimate human garbage disposal. While he preferred junk food over everything else, he would always finish his entire plate. It was nice to make meals and have them genuinely appreciated.

I asked my father if he wanted to join us in the kitchen to eat, but of course he declined. Instead, he asked me to bring him his plate. Heaven forbid he actually had to get up to grab it himself and risk missing a commercial or something.

After lunch I read to Alex before playing some board games with him. He enjoyed the games more than the books, but I thought it was important to help him with his reading. I could still remember the countless hours my mom had spent reading to me when I was a child. Even after I had been old enough to read, I still preferred hearing the stories from her.

I wondered what she would think about me now, if my mom could see what I had become. She probably wouldn't have changed the way she treated me at all, but she definitely would have had some good advice. I could picture her telling me that all that mattered was the person I was on the inside.

For dinner we had some frozen pizza. My appetite was still lacking, so I only had one slice. After we finished eating my father started complaining about how there was no ice cream left.

"It's not my fault you and Alex polished off the whole half gallon in one sitting last night." I said sarcastically when he asked if I wanted to run to the store. He ended up taking Alex with him for another ice cream run, so I finally got to have the house to myself.

First, I took another shower. I had taken one after lunch, but for some reason I still felt dirty. Even though I knew the blood from my face and leg was gone, it felt like it was still there. Perhaps it was just the guilt I felt over what had happened. Either way it was nice to take another shower.

I heard Alex and my dad return as I was putting my pajamas on. It was only eight o'clock, but I planned on calling Luke. Hopefully I would be able to talk to him for a few hours before going to sleep. It felt awkward being at home doing normal things. Especially when I knew that part of me was a demon. That I was now a tainted one.

For weeks just thinking about the mystical creatures had given me chills. Only a day ago I had met one of the creatures and been petrified with fear by him. Now I was one. While this thought was strange, I found it even stranger that I didn't feel anything different. Emotionally and psychologically, I was the same, plain old Elizabeth Scott.

I studied myself in the mirror after I finished brushing my hair. Nothing seemed particularly different. Except for the fact that I could now clearly see every imperfection in my skin. Luckily, I was still young and didn't have many wrinkles or blemishes yet, otherwise I would have been disturbed by myself. As it was, I still just looked plain. Luke must have been crazy for thinking I was beautiful, but I didn't mind.

Thinking about him made me walk back into my bedroom and pick up the phone to call him. When he answered he said that they had just finished eating a late dinner. He had slept from the time I left until an hour ago. Even then he had only got up because his mom woke him for dinner. He said that Isaac was down in the observation room, keeping an eye on the neighborhood. For some reason Isaac was worried that other tainted ones might come looking for the one that was missing, and he didn't want to be caught off guard.

Luke and I talked for hours. A couple of times I thought about sneaking out my window so that I could go and be with him in person but decided against it. He said it was best if I stayed away during the night so that they would feel it if another tainted one showed up. From half a mile away, I barely warmed their terralium rings, so if another one came to town while I was at home, they would feel it. Luke said it was one of the reasons Isaac had picked the house they were in now, because it was right next to the freeway off ramp. No tainted ones would be driving into town without them knowing about it.

It was almost midnight by the time Luke said he had to go. It was his turn to take a shift in the observation room, and he didn't think Isaac would appreciate it much if he was distracted by the phone while performing his duties. I reluctantly said goodbye and hung up the phone.

I still wasn't feeling very tired, so I went downstairs to get a drink of water. It was no surprise when I found an empty carton of chocolate ice cream sitting on the coffee table in front of the television. At least my father had put Alex to bed before leaving for work. I had heard his heavy breathing when I walked by his open doorway prior to coming downstairs.

I got a drink of water, and then returned to my room. For over an hour I laid in my bed, trying to fall asleep. For some reason I had a strange feeling in the back of my mind. It was similar to the dark presence that I had felt when the taint had first entered me, except much smaller. This felt more distant and isolated. Almost like a small part of my brain could feel the taint, but it was far out of my reach.

A part of me wanted to call Luke, because I could feel the presence getting closer. I almost worried that it might be the taint inside of me taking control. It was still so small and distant though that I didn't bother. If it had gotten any worse by morning, I would tell Luke about it. Finally... after what seemed like hours... sleep arrived.

Jareth stood looking at the unoccupied Mercedes. He thought it strange that whoever had killed his latest apprentice would leave the body and the car in this abandoned industrial complex. Reaching down, he grabbed the lip at the bottom of the trunk with both hands. It made a loud wrenching noise as he quickly ripped the trunk from the car. Having expected the body to be inside, he was surprised to find it empty. Other than a small suitcase and a spare tire there was nothing.

This confused Jareth because he could feel the pull of the bracelet through his ring, and it was coming from the trunk. Or at least that's how it had seemed. He put his hand on the bottom of the trunk and felt the bracelet still pulling from below.

Stepping back from the Mercedes, he bent down and located what was left of Jeremy. Directly underneath the middle of the trunk was his bracelet. The artifact was still attached to what was left of Jeremy's arm. Jareth reached down and picked up the arm, tearing the bracelet free from the flesh.

He then examined the upper part of the arm, where it had been disconnected from Jeremy's body. It was no surprise that the end looked neatly sliced and cauterized. Only a terralium blade could cause that kind of wound to one of his kind. But Jareth had already known the cause of death before he saw the wound. When he had felt the bond between artifacts cut, it had been nighttime, so there was no way Jeremy could have been exposed to sunlight and killed naturally. The fact that the bracelet had been left behind ruled out the other Auserwalt as well.

All of this meant one thing. His late apprentice had been killed by someone from the bloodline. Jareth had also trained Jeremy extensively with the sword he had given him, which meant that whoever killed him had been skilled. The part that bothered him was how the bracelet and arm had been left behind. If he hadn't scanned the area before getting out of his car, he might have suspected a trap of some sort, but there was no one else around. Perhaps some drunken beggars sleeping somewhere in the abandoned factory, but no one who could threaten him.

Jareth sighed as he walked back towards his car. Light was beginning to brighten the eastern horizon, so he only had a few more minutes of twilight left. He would find a nearby hotel and wait for nightfall. Then he would go and meet his new apprentice. He had felt them about fifteen minutes north of here as he was driving but didn't see a point in confronting them yet. Just in case it was someone worthy of keeping, there wasn't any point in confronting them without the bracelet.

Now that he had what he'd come for, he was ready to go back for them. If the new apprentice wasn't worthy, he would kill them and find one that was. Either way it meant more months of training someone. He was beginning to tire of losing apprentices. Once he picked up his new assistant, he would have to search out the one who had done this. With only half a dozen terralium swords still unaccounted for, it would be nice to secure one more. Even more pleasant was the prospect of a worthy fight, and the chance to kill another member of the bloodline. Jareth glanced down at his right hand. Where the pinky and ring finger should have been were two half inch stubs. It had been over a decade since he had last fought someone with a terralium blade. That fight had cost him his two fingers and another apprentice. Hopefully this one would die easier when he was found.

CHAPTER XVI

I woke in a panic. I could feel the dark presence getting closer, and it was almost to me. It seemed to be tugging gently at the back of my mind. I felt like it was approaching from the north, which didn't make any sense. The first time, when I had been turned, it had seemed to appear inside of me without warning. This was definitely a similar feeling, except that I could feel the presence outside of me. It was still at a distance but closing in fast.

Not knowing what to do, I frantically tried to push back against the darkness that was growing inside my mind. I refused to allow the taint to take complete control of me. No matter what it took, I would not become the demon Luke despised. It may have changed me physically, but my mind was still mine, and I intended to keep it that way.

My anxiety grew as I realized my attempts to push against the curse were in vain. No matter how hard I concentrated, the darkness was still getting closer. It felt as though any second it would arrive and take complete control of me. And I was powerless to stop it. My mind flooded with emotion as I realized that Alex and my father might just be the monsters first victims once it took control. *Nooo!* I screamed inside my mind and tried again to keep my head straight, ignoring the looming darkness.

Suddenly I realized that the presence seemed to be passing by me. It then continued south. Just as I had felt the presence approaching me, I now noticed that it was going away. Perhaps the taint inside of me had tried taking control… but had been unsuccessful? I shook my head, unsure what to make of it all. The one thing I did know was that the dark presence seemed to be getting farther and farther away. While I could still feel the gentle pull in the back of my head, it was growing fainter. This was reassuring. I thought about calling Luke, but what would I tell him? That the darkness was trying to take over me? I didn't even know if that's what it was or not.

Glancing at my clock, I realized that it was almost dawn. For how little sleep I must have had, I felt surprisingly refreshed. My alarm would be going off in a few more minutes anyway, so I didn't bother trying to go back to sleep. Instead, I tried, unsuccessfully, to understand what had just happened to me. I decided not to tell Luke about it unless it happened again. The last thing I wanted was to scare him away. And besides, I still felt completely in control of myself, so why create unnecessary worry?

Once my alarm finally went off, I hopped out of bed and got ready for the day. It wasn't long before the sun began peeking through my bathroom window. I had to close the shutters to keep my eyes from hurting, because it was so bright.

So far that was the only noticeable drawback to my transformation. While a little light sensitivity wasn't a huge deal, it seemed exponentially worse with sunlight. It was another mystery that didn't make any sense, but at least the sun didn't hurt me in any other way. So far the extra strength and energy more than made up for those negative side effects.

I had just brushed my hair back into a ponytail for school when I saw the edge of the Verdorben mark on my neck in the mirror. Ponytails would be out of the question from now on as well. With the mark it looked like I had a tattoo. I had never been a big fan of tattoos myself, but my father would kill me if he thought I had gotten one.

I grabbed my small makeup mirror from the counter so that I could see the whole mark. As I did so I was intrigued by the darkness of it. It was remarkably crisp and distinct as it contrasted with my skin. Like a freshly inked tattoo, minus the redness. The moon was a half crescent with a circle around it. Looking closer, I noticed that the circle was actually small characters curving around the moon, similar to the ones I had seen on Luke and Ben's terralium daggers. The symbols and characters were so small I could barely see them, even with my enhanced vision.

Alex would be awake soon, if he wasn't already, so I decided to get breakfast started. I heard him breathing heavily as I passed by his room on my way downstairs. Still having no appetite myself, I decided to make him chocolate chip pancakes. He always loved those, and my father would eat them as well.

When I finished the pancakes, I put six of them on a plate for my father and three on another for Alex. I still hadn't heard Alex moving around at all. His late night must have left him exhausted because he usually woke up at about the same time as I did. I thought about waking him up but decided against it. I was anxious to see Luke again, and my father should be getting home any minute.

I heard his car before I saw it pulling up and into the driveway. Grabbing my backpack from the living room, I headed for the front door. When I opened the door, the sunlight was overpowering. I shut it quickly and went back inside for a pair of sunglasses. There was a pair in my Tahoe, but I wasn't sure if I would make it that far without keeping my eyes closed.

"Hey." My father said tiredly as I was walking out the door.

"Hi dad. Breakfast is on the table for you, but Alex is still sleeping so… you might want to eat yours before it gets cold."

"Okay thanks." He almost mumbled as he turned and walked into the house.

With my sunglasses on the sun was tolerable, but just barely. I kept my sunshade down the whole way to school. Something about the drive seemed different than it had every other day, but I couldn't quite put my finger on it. Then Harrisburg High School came into view, and I realized what it was.

I must have been a good three hundred yards from the part of the parking lot where I normally parked, and from here I could actually make out the faces of the dozen or so students in the parking lot. Prior to my transformation, their entire bodies would have been just blurs, but not now. Only one of them really mattered to me, and I spotted him standing next to his silver hummer.

A minute later I was pulling into the parking spot next to Luke's hummer. He had been standing in the middle of the empty space, probably to save it for me, and only moved once I was pulling in. As I put the Tahoe in park he was already opening my door for me.

"Good morning beautiful." He said as he helped me out of the car. Once my feet were on the ground he leaned down for a kiss, which I was more than happy to oblige him on.

"It is a good morning now." I said as he pulled away.

"So I can't tell if you look like a hot celebrity, or just a beautiful girl with a hangover, but either way I like the sunglasses." He teased with a smile.

"Thanks… the sun's unbearable without them."

He closed my door for me and grabbed my hand. We started walking towards the school, and I realized that the whole sky was spotted with scattered clouds. Even with the sun currently behind one, it still seemed bright outside. And that was with the sunglasses on. Now I understood why he had teased me about wearing them. Once we came inside the school courtyard, the light was more tolerable.

"Liz!" Nikki's voice was exceptionally loud this morning. And I'm pretty sure it wasn't just because of my newfound hearing abilities. She was wearing all red today and looked every inch the Latina fashion model. As we approached her, she practically ran up to us and gave me a big hug. She added a quick hug for Luke as well.

"Hey you two love birds, I hope your weekend went well." She winked at us, and then took on a more considerate tone. "I'm so sorry to hear about your mom Luke. Is she like, going to be all right?"

His confused glance in my direction only lasted a split second, so I was hoping Nikki didn't notice. I realized that I had forgotten to tell Luke about my other lie to Nikki. Hopefully he wouldn't think any less of me for it. Considering the life and death situation I had been in at the time, I doubted it would ever become an issue.

"Oh, she actually started doing better again last night, so we're optimistic. At least for the time being. Thanks for asking. And thanks for covering for Liz too. We both owe you." Luckily, he was smoother than I gave him credit for, because even having created the lie myself, I almost believed him. He handled that surprise question like a seasoned politician.

"Okay Liz, so I like have to ask..." Nikki turned back to me "What's up with the sunglasses? It's cloudy and we're standing in the shade. Were you drinking last night?" She put her hands on her hips and looked at me disapprovingly.

"No, of course not." I reluctantly took off the sunglasses. Even with the small amount of indirect sunlight coming through the courtyard, it was difficult not to squint. "You know I don't drink Nikki. I just have a bad headache that's all. The sun was making it worse." I lied.

"Oh…" She replied.

"Well, I'd better get to class." Luke said as he gave me a quick hug. "See ya Nikki." He nodded at her before turning to leave.

We both watched him walk away in silence. I knew once he was out of earshot Nikki would want every gritty detail from the whole weekend. I scrambled to come up with a story that would both appease her and be believable at the same time. How could I have forgotten about the curiosity of my best friend?

Sure enough, the second Luke was out of earshot Nikki turned to me excitedly. "I want all the details, and it better be good." She was practically hopping in place as she spoke.

"Well… there really isn't much to tell…" I trailed off, still concocting the story in my mind.

"Oh please Liz, you owe me big time. I practically lied for you." She feigned indignation.

"What? You practically lied for me huh? So, does that mean my dad actually called you then? Why didn't you tell me?"

"Well, no… he didn't call. But I was ready to lie for you if he did." She said defensively. "That's pretty much the same thing."

"Oh, so… then you didn't actually have to lie?" I smiled as I rested my case.

She stuck her tongue out at me before continuing. "Same difference. But now you're dodging the question."

"I'm not dodging anything. I'll tell you whatever you want to…"

"Oh my gosh Liz! I can't believe it." She exclaimed suddenly, interrupting me. A group of girls standing twenty or so feet away turned to look at us as she shouted.

"Can't believe what?" I asked looking around the courtyard. By the way she screamed I thought she must have seen something, but her eyes were fastened on me.

"The night spent with Luke. And then you didn't call me the next morning… and now you're having morning sickness and trying to hide something…"

"It's not morning sickness Nikki, I just have a head…"

"You're pregnant." She interrupted in a loud whisper.

"What are you talking about Nikki? I'm not pregnant." I began.

"Liz, you don't have to hide it from me. I can keep a secret."

"Nikki listen." I put both my arms on her shoulders. "I can't be pregnant because I'm a virgin. Not only have I never had sex with Luke, but I've never had sex with anyone. I haven't even been past first base. A couple guys tried back in Portland, but that's beside the point. Luke and I haven't done anything more than kiss. That's all. And I really do just have a headache." I tried to sound patient but stern as I explained.

"Really?" She sounded disappointed as her shoulders slumped.

Where did she come up with this stuff? I thought to myself. Maybe she had caught on to the fact that Luke and I weren't being completely forthright, but pregnant? That was just ridiculous. I suppose it was better than her knowing the truth. Even still, I wasn't about to let my best and only girlfriend think that I was some kind of hussy.

"And besides Nikki, even if Luke and I had done it, which we didn't, there is no way I would already have morning sickness."

"Why not?" She asked.

"Because you don't get morning sickness until later. Didn't you ever pay attention in health class?"

"No… not really. I just thought that it happened when you got pregnant." I could tell she felt stupid, so I decided to change the subject without embarrassing her any further. Having finished the story in my mind, I recited it to her.

I told her that I had gone over to Luke's house after I got off the phone Friday night. His mom had been really sick, and they had a doctor over to look at her. The doctor had just left when I arrived, and Luke and I spent most of the night just cuddling, besides talking to his family. I did include that we had made out in the garage for almost an hour (the only part of my story that was actually true), but that was the most excitement that had happened.

Nikki then told me about her weekend. I was surprised when she mentioned that she had actually gone to church with Greg on Sunday. She had never struck me as the religious type. The next ten minutes she spent explaining to me that she actually wasn't religious but wanted to support Greg. His parents were ultra conservative and went to church every Sunday, so she had been dragged along for the ride.

We walked into first period just before the bell rang. Mr. Anderson gave a boring lecture for most of the period, but I was too distracted to pay attention to anything he said.

Several of the other kids in the class were whispering loudly. Or at least at first, I thought it was loudly, until I noticed that no one else in the class seemed to notice them. Then I realized it was just my own advanced hearing. Another something that was definitely going to take some getting used to.

Another thing keeping me distracted was the dark feeling in the back of my mind. It wasn't any stronger than it had been after the incident this morning, but it was still there. I felt like I could feel the taint, or whatever it was, just waiting off in the distance. Perhaps it was waiting for another chance to strike, so that it could take control of me. If that same thing from this morning happened again, I was definitely going to tell Luke.

As the day progressed, I began to grow accustomed to the loudness of others, or should I say to my own sensitivity. The distant dark presence in the back of my mind also became more familiar to me. I felt like I was beginning to learn how to ignore the part of my brain that sensed the darkness.

At lunch we sat at our usual table. Ignoring the flood of noise was much more difficult in a crowded room. Ben wasn't there, so it was just Greg, Nikki, Luke, and I. Nikki asked Luke about where Ben was at. He said that Ben was at home, helping to look after their mother. Luke had explained to me the real reason why Ben didn't come to school the night before. He had said that Isaac wanted to have three of them at home in case another tainted one showed up during the day. Jazmine had also stayed home from college, even though she usually drove back into Eugene early Monday morning for her classes.

After lunch Luke walked me to Sassenburg's class, and I was relieved that there were no side conversations going on in his class. My eardrums felt like they needed a break, or maybe it was just my sanity that craved a little peace and quiet.

It wasn't until we were sitting in English class that I noticed Luke was wearing an earpiece. His black watch was also the tactical kind that matched the earpiece, as opposed to the watch that he normally wore. When we left class, I confronted him about it.

"I didn't know that you were wearing an earpiece." I mentioned once we were out of hearing range from Sassenburg's door.

"Oh sorry, I guess I didn't say anything about it." He explained. "Isaac wanted me to wear it in case one of the other tainted ones showed up. It makes it easier to communicate in an emergency."

I suppose it made sense, but it seemed as though he hadn't mentioned it to me on purpose. Although it might have been because they wanted Luke to have one in case I suddenly lost control as well. After the strange feelings and the dark tug in the back of my mind, it probably was a good idea. At that moment I thought again about telling Luke what had happened earlier but decided against it.

"Those clouds sure look dark." Luke said casually as he looked towards the western horizon.

While the rest of the sky was spotted with light colored clouds, the ones in that part of the sky were ominously dark. I didn't doubt that it would be pouring on us tonight. At least the clouds would block the sun. Even with my sunglasses on and the clouds overhead it seemed brighter than usual.

When we got to my Tahoe, I realized that Luke's Hummer would need someone to drive it. With Ben gone there was no excuse to drive Luke in my car. I was about to say something about this, but Luke beat me to it.

"So, I was thinking I would just follow you to pick up Alex, since I have my Hummer." Luke stated as he opened my door for me.

"Okay, that sounds good to me." I replied, leaning up to kiss him.

"After you arrive home safely though, I need to get home myself." He said as he pulled away.

"Why?"

"Well, I suppose I should probably tell you instead of just showing up later." He began and I looked at him curiously. "I guess the first thing I should ask is how good of a sleeper is Alex?"

"What do you mean?" I was utterly confused.

"Does he sleep light, or can he sleep through an earthquake?" Luke rephrased the question.

"Oh… he usually sleeps like a rock. Why?"

"Because… I was planning on taking the night shift, after your dad goes to work."

"What night shift?"

"Well, we talked about it this morning, because I worried about you all night. And we decided that while the tainted ones will most likely come after us, there is a chance that they might come after you too. Either way we want to be prepared, so we are going to take shifts at your house, to help keep an eye on you."

"Really?" I was pleasantly surprised.

"We will stay in your back yard of course, so that your dad doesn't get suspicious. Jazmine will come by first, probably from six to ten, and then I will take from ten to two. After that Isaac is going to take until sunrise, which should cover the whole night." He explained.

"So, you're going to come tonight?" I said eyeing the storm on the horizon again. "But it's probably going to be raining. Not to mention cold and windy. I couldn't possibly let you stand out in that."

"That's why I was asking if Alex is a light sleeper. If he's not I was hoping you could unlock the back door after your dad leaves. You said he goes to work at ten, right?"

"Yeah, he usually leaves at about ten till."

"That's perfect. Would you mind letting me in then? I promise I won't bother you. I could just chill on the couch while you guys sleep."

"No, of course I wouldn't mind." I tried not to let my excitement show too much. "That would actually be perfect. I have had trouble sleeping the last couple of nights anyway." As if he could ever bother me. That was impossible… or at least impossible in a bad way.

"Okay great." He sounded excited also. "I mean… not great that you can't sleep, but great that I can come in tonight." He smiled and gave me another quick kiss.

The thought of him staying in my house tonight was thrilling. So, I grabbed him by the back of his head as he was pulling away and pulled his lips back to mine. A minute or so later I remembered that we were in a school parking lot and reluctantly pulled away. My whole body felt intoxicated.

"Wow..." Luke said as he caught his breath. "You really are incredible Liz. Did you know that?"

"I think you must be high on something if you think that." I replied. "But I'm glad you do."

"High on you maybe…" He whispered, and then froze and looked down at me. "Oops… did I just say that out loud? I'm sorry."

"Don't be…" I kissed him again. "I liked it."

"Well in that case I'll have to be vocal with my thoughts more often… although that might get me in trouble." He smiled. "Okay… you need to go pick up Alex before you're late. And I need to go home and get some sleep if I'm going to be alert tonight."

"Okay." I hugged him one more time before stepping up into my Tahoe.

"I'll see you tonight." He said grinning as he closed my door.

"I can't wait." I smiled back.

I couldn't tell if my heart was racing faster or my mind as I drove towards Alex's school. Leuken Bennett would be spending the night with me. Except this time, we would be alone in my house, instead of in front of a camera in a cold hard cell. Definitely a more romantic setting. My mind began to wander, and I couldn't stop smiling.

I pulled to a stop in front of Alex's school and glanced in my rear-view mirror. Luke had parked behind me and through the mirror I could see him smiling at me. There was no way he could know what I was thinking, but I blushed in spite of myself. He must have seen me smiling.

Alex's bell rang a few seconds later, and he came out to the Tahoe. "Where's Luke?" he asked as he sat in his car seat and looked around.

"He's in the silver hummer behind us." I said casually as I flipped a U-turn. Through the rear-view mirror, I could see Alex turn and wave at Luke. Luke waved back with a smile.

"Hey, what's he doing back there Izzie? Why's he not in here with us?" Alex asked curiously.

"Because he has to help his mom with something, so he can't come over and play today. He's just following us to make sure we get home safely, that's all." I explained.

"Awww… that's a bummer." Alex grumbled from the back. "Oh… I have an idea Izzie." He suddenly sounded excited.

"What's that?"

"We can play at his house. That way Jazmine can play too." He smiled proudly as if he had just solved world hunger with his idea.

"Well as fun as that sounds Alex, I don't think they want anyone over at their house today. Luke's mom is really sick."

"Okay Izzie. I don't care if Jazmine can play at our house then. That would be okay." I couldn't help but smile at his attempts to see Jazmine again. He must have quite the little crush.

"I don't think Jazmine can play either. She has school Monday through Thursday down in Eugene, so she only visits Friday through Monday."

Alex didn't say anything, but I saw him fold his arms and pout through the rear-view mirror. It was hard not to laugh. I pulled into the driveway at our house and got out of the car. Luke waved from where he was sitting in the hummer, so I waved back. Alex didn't wave; instead, he just stomped up to the house and in the front door. He must have been more upset than I thought.

I took the opportunity to walk over to Luke's hummer. He rolled down the window as I walked around the front to his side.

"What's his problem?" He asked as I stood up on the running boards and leaned in the window to kiss him again.

"His problem is that he has a major little boy crush on your sister."

"He's quite taken with her huh? Poor little guy." He said compassionately.

"He'll get over it. Anyways, I'll let you go, just wanted one more of these." I kissed him one last time then hopped back off the running boards.

"Wasn't that two?" He teased with a smile.

"There'll be plenty more tonight." I smiled mischievously. "Just don't be late."

"Well in that case I'll be early."

"Okay but not too early. Remember my dad doesn't leave till like nine fifty." I warned.

"Don't worry. I'll be careful." He put the hummer back in drive.

"You'd better." I added as he started pulling away.

I couldn't help but get excited as I watched him go. If only there was a way to fast forward the next few hours. All I wanted was to see him again. I could already tell that the rest of the day was going to drag by.

Alex refused to talk to me for almost half an hour because he was still upset. It wasn't until I made him some lunch that he finally opened up. By the time he was done with dessert he was his normal cheerful self again. I put in a movie, hoping that it would help to pass the time. Instead, I spent the entire movie trying not to be anxious or think about Luke, but I failed miserably.

Eventually it was time for dinner, so I went into the kitchen to prepare it. I made us a casserole because I didn't feel like doing anything fancy. My appetite was still virtually nonexistent, in spite of only eating half of a sandwich at lunch and having no breakfast.

As I set the timer on the oven, I heard thunder in the distance. Looking out the window, I could see the tree's swaying in the heavy wind. The rain was starting to come down in heavy scattered drops, but for now they were few and far between. This weather seemed uncharacteristically strange for the time of year.

My father joined us in the kitchen as I was dishing the casserole onto their plates. He asked Alex about school, and I set their plates on the table in front of them. As I sat down to start eating I noticed the taint in the back of my mind starting to intensify once more. I ignored it at first, but it was gradually getting stronger and stronger, as if the taint was about to try and take over me again.

We didn't talk much while we ate. This was one of Alex and my father's favorite meals, so they were too busy stuffing their faces to worry about conversation. Considering the inner turmoil, I was trying to make sense of in my mind, I was grateful for the silence. My father volunteered to wash up after we finished eating, but I declined his offer. The darkness seemed closer and closer now, and I wanted to stay busy to keep my mind off of it.

Alex and my father went into the other room to watch television, while I washed their plates. The darkness seemed to be almost to me again, but instead of passing by it slowed down as it approached. The closer it got, the slower it came. Eventually the darkness became so intense in my mind that I started to panic. I grabbed the phone to call Luke, fearing I was about to lose control, when suddenly I heard a loud knock at the door.

I walked towards the front room to see who it was. My father was just opening the door, when suddenly he slammed it back shut. Or should I say he tried. As he tried to close the door, I saw a hand grab the door from the outside. Then the door instantly slammed inwards, flying off the hinges as it knocked my father off his feet and back into the living room about twenty feet.

Standing in the shattered doorway was an absolute barbarian. The man stood almost to the top of the doorframe and was nearly as wide. More notable than his stature though were his features. His reddish-brown hair was jaggedly cut above the neck, and a curly red beard hung several inches from his chin. His large coat looked antique, like something I would expect to see in an ancient war movie.

My alarm turned to terror as I looked in the giant's eyes and realized exactly what he was. The dark tainted feeling in the back of my brain had not been the taint inside trying to take over me after all. It was the creature standing before me that I had been sensing all along, and now that he had arrived, I could feel that he was right in front of me.

I was surprised when the man turned to look at me because he actually grinned. Or at least that's what I thought the expression was under all that facial hair. My first thought was for Alex's safety, but I couldn't see him so he must have already been hiding. I looked over at my father, who was lying unconscious on the floor, with wood chips and splinters scattered around him.

As much as I wanted to run, I couldn't leave Alex or my father behind. Not when I knew they wouldn't stand a chance against this monster. Lightening flashed directly in front of our house, and the echoing thunder followed instantly. The man standing in the doorway took a few steps inside the house.

"Hello. You probably don't understand what's going on so let me explain." The man was slowly walking closer to me as he spoke. "If you cooperate with me, your father will live. If you do not, I will kill both him and your little brother."

"What do you want?" I asked through gritted teeth. Thinking about what this man had just done to my father, and what he was threatening to do to Alex, made my blood feel like it was going to boil. Never before had I instantly hated someone like I did this man. Everything about him was pure evil.

"Take my hand, and I'll show you." The man said calmly, as he stopped about six feet from me. He was holding out his left hand.

I looked at his outstretched hand for a long second but didn't even consider grabbing it. There was no way I was going to comply with this man in any way. He probably knew how to dispatch of me fairly easily, but I wouldn't go down without a fight.

The man must have seen the angry determination on my face, because he suddenly lunged at me. Without thinking I kicked him in the stomach as hard as I could, just hoping to keep him away from me. To my surprise I didn't hear any bones crack as my foot connected, and it also didn't rip into his body as it had with the rapist the night I was changed. Instead, his body folded slightly forward as he flew backwards through the air and crashed into the wall.

His body broke a human sized hole in the drywall as it struck, and he landed slumped against the exposed framing. He appeared to be unconscious, so I quickly went to my father to check on him. His pulse was strong, and he was breathing fine. I gently slapped him on the cheek. That creature might have been knocked unconscious, but I doubted it would stay out for very long.

"Dad wake up. Come on dad… wake up!" I said urgently as I tried to shake him.

Hearing a noise from behind, I turned quickly, but it was too late. The man was lunging at me and caught me with one massive arm around my waist as I tried to jump out of his way. I twisted, preparing to throw him with his own leverage, but he let go of my waist and grabbed my right wrist with his left hand. I could feel him trying to pull me closer to him, so I turned back towards him and jumped. Kicking at him with both feet, his now two-handed grip on my wrist was broken as I again sent him flying through the air. This time he hit the fireplace not far from my father, cracking the rock decoration.

The man slowly stood back up, and then started to laugh. He laughed heartily for a few seconds, while I stood waiting for him to come at me again. I was hoping to draw his attention from my father, who was now starting to sit up just a few feet from him.

"What's so funny?" I asked. If the man wanted to talk, that was fine with me. Anything to buy me more time until Jazmine showed up. I glanced at my watch and saw that it was only five forty-seven. *Could I stall this monster for thirteen minutes?* I had to try anyway.

Suddenly I noticed that there was a silver bracelet on my wrist next to my watch. It was thick and had the same symbols etched onto it that I had seen on Luke's dagger. He must have slipped it on my wrist when he was holding that arm.

"Your pitiful attempts at freedom." The monster replied. "I must admit I like the fight in you. You must have the gift of strength as well, judging by how hard you hit me. Once I have broken you in, I think you might actually be worth keeping." His sinister smile was disconcerting.

"What are you talking about?" I tried to pull the bracelet off my wrist, but it seemed tight against the skin and wouldn't budge.

"You belong to me now girl." The man pointed at me with his right hand, and I noticed that two of his fingers were missing.

"Not if I can help it." Luke's voice suddenly sounded off from behind me, and I turned to see him walking quickly through the doorway. He stopped in front of me, placing himself between me and the creature.

"And just what are you going to do boy?" The giant said still smiling.

Before Luke had a chance to answer the room erupted with gunfire. My father had pulled his Glock handgun from his waistband and was unloading on the intruder. Shot after shot ricocheted off of his body until my father's gun ran out of bullets. The intruder had turned to look at my father and seemed somewhat annoyed.

The man grabbed the coffee table from the ground next to him, and threw the wooden table at my father, striking him in the head and knocking him back to the floor. As he did so I lunged forward to stop him, but I was too far away. I reached him and kicked at his kneecap a split second after he threw the table. I heard a crack as his knee bent inwards slightly, but at the same instant he turned and hit me in the chest with an open palm, throwing me backwards into the wall.

Simultaneously as he struck me, he turned to strike Luke with his other hand, which sent Luke flying into the wall next to me, but not before Luke's terralium blade stabbed through his left thigh. It was the same leg I had kicked him in and he dropped to the ground with a scream.

Luke and I were back on our feet in an instant. The man pulled a massive axe from his back as he turned towards us and hobbled up on one leg. The blade on the axe had to have been over a foot long, with the handle at least four feet in length.

Luke started to advance towards the man, so I followed him closely. There was no way I was going to allow Luke to be hurt by this monster.

"Grab him." The man suddenly shouted at me.

I felt a warm tingling sensation from the silver bracelet as I helplessly obeyed. My body moved but seemed disconnected from my mind. I could feel it but had no control as I jumped forward and grabbed Luke's arms from behind, pulling him backwards onto me.

As we fell back the man swung at one of Luke's legs, slicing through his right shin and calf. If it hadn't been for the blade bouncing off of my leg, it probably would have severed his entire leg below the knee.

"Liz let go!" Luke screamed in anguish. "Don't do this."

"It's not me Luke." I tried to explain. "He's controlling me somehow with this bracelet. I can't control my own body."

The man was standing over us now and grabbed Luke's right arm at the wrist. He suddenly wrenched on Luke's wrist, and I heard bones snap as his wrist bent backwards. Luke's terralium dagger clanged to the floor as he shouted again.

"Elizabeth! Please!" He cried in agony. I tried with every fiber of my being to regain control of myself and release Luke, but I was utterly powerless.

"You know boy… I recognize you now." The man said as Luke struggled to break free of me. "You're that boy from a few years back… yeah… I remember your face. You were just a baby then." The man chuckled sadistically. "I killed your daddy you know. He screamed like a stock pig when I cut him to pieces. And to think he gave his life to save you from me. How ironic, that I'm now going to kill you anyway." He snarled as he finished speaking, raising the axe over his head.

"No!" I shouted as I felt Luke struggle even harder, but it was all in vain. My body wasn't under my control, and the monster's axe was about to end Luke's life. I had never felt so powerless in all my life.

"Aaagggh!" The creature grunted as it paused suddenly. At first, I was confused, until I saw a glowing terralium blade emerging from the center of the man's chest. I no sooner saw it, then it was pulled free. The man fell sideways with a little help from behind, and as he fell, I saw Isaac standing behind where the monster had just been. He was breathing heavily and still held the terralium sword in his right hand as he examined us.

I let go of Luke immediately and was relieved to see that I again had control of my own body. Squatting next to Luke, I gently grabbed his arm to look at it. The bones looked like they were snapped about ninety degrees back from where they belonged and were sticking out of his skin on the under part of his arm where it had been broken from.

"Oh, Luke I'm so sorry. He was controlling me with this thing." I said as I pulled the bracelet from my arm. Surprisingly it was no longer tight and came off easily. "When Isaac killed him, it must have stopped working." I turned to Isaac again. "Thanks for showing up when you did Isaac. That monster was going to…"

I stopped suddenly when I realized that Isaac was still holding his terralium sword tightly. In fact, it was raised over his head with one arm, and he looked like he was ready to cut me open. His jaw was tight and his knuckles white from clenching the blade so tightly.

"Don't move another inch… or I will kill you." Isaac said coldly, and I froze. He turned to Luke. "What happened?"

Luke locked eyes with me for a long second before answering. I felt like he was somehow gazing into my soul. "It's like she said, that creature was controlling her with this." He said as he picked up the silver bracelet from the tile floor. "Now can you put that away and reset my arm please? It kind of hurts." I could hear the pain in his voice as he spoke.

Isaac studied me for a few more seconds, and then sheathed the sword back into its scabbard on his back. He bent down and grabbed Luke's arm, examining the break. I also looked at Luke's leg, but it must have healed already because the skin looked intact underneath the torn, bloodstained clothes.

"Okay Liz, I need you to hold here as hard as you can." Isaac said pointing to Luke's arm just above the elbow. I grabbed his arm and squeezed it tightly, then heard two snaps as Isaac bent the bones back to where they were supposed to be.

"Now make sure you hold still for a few seconds while they heal." Isaac instructed him.

Just then Ben and Jazmine came running into the living room through the front door. Ben had his terralium dagger out, and they both looked dissatisfied when they saw that the action was over.

"Oh great, we missed all the fun." Ben said disappointedly.

"What is that?" Jazmine sounded disgusted as she pointed to the ground next to where Isaac had just killed the tainted one.

Looking over, I noticed for the first time that there was a pile of old decayed bones. You could tell the skeleton belonged to a human, but the bones looked like they had been rotting for hundreds of years.

"That must be Jareth." Isaac said calmly. "Or at least what's left of him."

"Jazmine is that you?" I was startled when I heard Alex's voice coming from behind one of the couches.

"Alex?" I asked as I walked over to where he was hiding. "What are you doing?"

"I'm hiding like daddy taught me." He explained, still covering his eyes as he sat behind the couch. "Can I come out now though Izzie? I'm scared."

"Sure Alex. Everything is going to be just fine." I consoled him as I picked him up. "But for now, I need you to keep your eyes closed while I carry you up to your room."

The only thing that could possibly make this night any worse would be Alex seeing an old human skeleton, and his dad lying on the floor unconscious. I ran him up to his room and told him to close the door and wait for me. When I got back downstairs, Ben and Luke were already sweeping the old bones into a large trash bag.

"Just in case someone called the Sheriff." Luke explained when I looked at him quizzically.

Isaac was sitting next to my father, who still looked unconscious on the tile floor. I hurried to his side. Looking down at my father I grabbed him by the head to straighten his neck and felt wetness. I pulled my hand away to reveal fingers covered in blood. There was very little blood on the ground, so I was hoping the blood only came from outside his skull.

"It looks like at the very least he has a concussion, his pupils are dilated substantially. His pulse seems weak as well; I can barely even feel it." Isaac explained.

I put my hand to his neck to confirm my father's pulse and was surprised by how feverish he felt. "Oh my gosh! He's burning up. You've got to help him please." I said as my father's body started to convulse. Throw up began oozing from his mouth as his body went into full seizure.

Isaac put both of his hands gently on my father's head. I sat impatiently, waiting for my father to be healed, but he kept convulsing. Finally, the convulsions stopped, and Isaac looked up at me confused.

"Did you heal him?" I asked.

"No… I couldn't. I tried to but… it felt like my abilities hit a wall when I tried to heal him. All I felt was… darkness." He glanced down at my father's body.

Luke came over to stand by my side and put his arm around me. I welcomed his embrace. "Do you think he's gonna be okay?" He asked Isaac.

"I don't know it's hard to say. For some reason I can't seem to heal him. I don't know if it's something the tainted one did to him or what…" Isaac explained, obviously confused.

At that moment I realized why my father couldn't be healed. Isaac had killed the tainted one… and my father had been the closest non-bloodline human in proximity. His body had just gone through chills, fever and nausea. Now Isaac's abilities no longer affected him. These facts alone were enough to tell me what was happening to my father, but then the confirmation came.

When Isaac had killed the other tainted one, I had felt the taint and draw to him in the back of my mind vanish. Suddenly it reappeared, only now I actually knew what it meant. As I looked down at the man lying on the ground with my eyes I saw my father, but what I felt through my mind was unmistakably a tainted one.

Acknowledgements

I would like to thank all of the friends and family who helped to make this dream a reality: Michael, Kaatia, Betty, Jacque, Brett, Jonathan, Aaron, Belle, Greg, Alisha, Amber, Kelli, Matt and Elin. Without their feedback, this story would not have been the same.

A special thanks to Kimball Larsen, whose editing and advice helped to take this project from dream to reality. You think you can write well, until a former BYU English Professor takes a red pen to your work. I am truly grateful for all of his time and support.

And last but certainly not least, to my beautiful wife Jessica: Thank you. For being supportive even before you knew about the hundreds and hundreds of hours that you would have to sacrifice me to the computer to make this dream a reality. For believing in me, even when I wasn't sure about myself, and for tending to our four little angels while I was immersed in this story.

About the Author

Lee Larsen currently possesses a B.A. from the University of Nevada, Las Vegas, and lives in Las Vegas with his wife and four children. He enjoys reading, running, swimming, basketball and doing just about anything with his family.